# Teapots
## and
# Tequila
## Shots

*Also by Kathleen Kole*

Breaking Even

Dollars to Donuts

Favorable Conditions

Tales from the Laundry Pile

# Teapots and Tequila Shots

### Kathleen Kole

Sublime
Coyote Media

This is a work of fiction. Names, characters, places and incidents are either the product of the author's imagination or are used fictitiously, and any resemblance to actual persons, living or dead, business establishments, events or locales is entirely coincidental.

TEAPOTS AND TEQUILA SHOTS

Copyright © 2015 by Kathleen Kole

ISBN-13: 978-1927791-02-8
ISBN-10: 1-927791-02-2

This book is published by Sublime Coyote Media. For more information please visit www.sublimecoyote.com.

As always, for Peter.

Thank you for being the living, breathing, loving inspiration for every good man I've ever written.

# Chapter One

Ginny sorted through a pile of returned books stacked at one end of the library's horseshoe-shaped front desk. "Fiction, cooking, children," she muttered to herself while systematically scanning each book then placing it into its designated category.

"He's *baaaack*."

Ginny smoothed her thumb across the well-worn cover on a copy of *The Lion, the Witch and the Wardrobe* and remembered when she'd read it to her daughter, years ago.

"Hello? Gin? Did you hear me?"

Ginny put the book down then looked at her co-worker, Tamara, standing on the opposite side of the desk. "Sorry, dear. What did you say?"

Tamara cocked one of her manicured eyebrows. She was pretty certain Ginny had heard her the first time. However, instead of calling her out, she indicated with a jerk of her head toward one of the three revolving book stacks at the opposite side of the library. "I *said*, he's *baaaack*."

Ginny grinned at Tamara's facial theatrics. Subtle, she wasn't.

"And, it needs to be said," Tamara added, her green eyes dancing merrily, "I don't think it's an accident he's back *again. I* think he's got his eye on *someone.*"

Ginny pulled her turquoise reading glasses from her face and placed them on top of *The Lion, the Witch and the Wardrobe*. She turned to her right to look past the six computer workstations situated in the center of the library; beyond the comfortable, red leather couches and chairs arranged around a sturdy, wooden coffee table in their seating area and, finally, regarded the patron to whom Tamara was referring.

He was an older gentleman - say mid-sixties - and he'd been frequenting the library regularly for the past couple of weeks. Always well dressed, Ginny had no doubt he was monetarily affluent; she'd checked out his shoes the last time he'd been in and could tell they hadn't been purchased from the local shoe barn. If there was one thing she'd learned from her late husband, it was to check out a man's shoes.

"He's a bit of a hottie, has a sort of James Brolin charm wouldn't you say?" Tamara tucked her hands into the front pockets of her denim skirt and leaned up against the desk to study him further.

Ginny looked at her, blankly.

"What?" Tamara asked, confused by Ginny's expression.

"*James Brolin?*"

"Yeah, absolutely," Tamara agreed, nodding. "He's an actor, married to Barbra Streisand—"

"I *know* who he is," Ginny interrupted. "I'm just wondering how, or when, *you* came to know who he is? Isn't he a bit past your generation?"

"Oh, okay." Tamara grinned, as she grasped the confusion. "My Mom's a huge Streisand fan. I grew up listening to her and hearing all the celeb gossip—"

"And she's married to James Brolin," Ginny finished, picking up the thread.

"Exactly."

"Right. Well, now that we've sorted that out," Ginny said, straightening the hem on her beige cardigan sweater then gesturing to the piles of books on the desk. "We can get back to work sorting the rest of these out."

"*I* think," Tamara offered, ignoring her and backtracking to their original conversation, "mystery man is trying to get up the nerve to talk to *someone*."

Ginny smirked and reached for her reading glasses.

"What?"

"*Mystery man*," Ginny said, still smirking.

Tamara grinned. "Have you got a better name for him? *Hottie* man, perhaps? I think he'd need some sort of cape for that one."

Ginny chuckled, but refused to be baited.

"*Anyway*," Tamara said, determined to finish her thought. "As I was saying, mystery man seems to be trying to talk to *someone*."

Ginny waited a beat.

Tamara remained silent.

"Okay, fine," Ginny said. "I'll bite. Who?"

Tamara rolled her eyes at the utter cluelessness. "Take a wild guess," she said, before turning around to reach into a crystal candy bowl on the desktop and pick out a *Hershey's Kiss*.

Ginny shrugged her slim shoulders. "I don't know. You?"

Tamara released a bark of laughter then peeled the silver foil from her chocolate and popped it into her mouth. "Me?" she said, talking around the candy. "*Please.*"

Ginny's blue eyes widened. "Why is that such a stretch? Have you looked at yourself in the mirror lately? Young, curvy, gorgeous, shiny dark hair—"

"Not *that* young," Tamara interrupted, rolling the wrapper from her *Kiss* into a small ball and handing it across the desk.

It was Ginny's turn to laugh. Tamara was in her late thirties. "*Believe me,*" she said, taking the wrapper and tossing it into the garbage, "you're young. And mystery man would have to be blind not to notice you."

"No way!" Tamara wrinkled her nose and shook her head. "He's gotta be sixty, easily. Old enough to be my Dad."

"Oh, goodness," Ginny bantered, a wry grin curling her lip as she tucked her greying, shoulder length hair behind her ears. "*That* old."

Tamara, realizing she'd accidentally stepped in it, quickly back-pedaled. "Not that being older is bad, *obviously!*"

Ginny pressed her lips together to keep from snickering. A flush was climbing Tamara's neck beneath her purple top as she tried to undo her blunder.

"*Anyway*, as you well know, he's not exactly my type." Tamara cleared her throat and fidgeted with the silver charm bracelet around her left wrist. "Regardless of whether or not he's… uhh… well… out of my age group."

"Oh, please, stop," Ginny said, taking pity on her. "I'm just teasing."

Tamara visibly exhaled at being let off the hook.

"However," Ginny said, folding her arms across her chest, "I'm sure it hasn't escaped your attention that men in *my* age group have a strong tendency to seek out women a couple decades their junior. Makes them feel like they're recapturing their youth, or some such foolish thing."

Tamara ran her fingers through her thick hair, sweeping it off of her face, and continued her original pitch. "While that might be so, I don't think that's the case here. I've seen mystery man watching *you*."

Ginny snorted and waved her words away.

"No, seriously," she insisted. "I've actually witnessed him looking and—"

"I'm sure you're imagining things, my dear," Ginny stated, cutting her off at the pass. "Like it or not, men - whatever their age - do not acknowledge pension age women."

"You are not pension age," Tamara challenged.

Ginny chuckled. "Close enough."

"No," Tamara argued. "You're only sixty two, not sixty five."

"Semantics," Ginny stated. "The rest is still dead on accurate."

"Come on. You don't really believe that's true."

"I'm afraid so," Ginny told her, lifting her hands, palms facing up, in a whatchya-gonna-do gesture. "With every passing year over the hump of fifty, we become as appealing as day old - no, make that *week* old - bread. Nothing to do but sit on the shelf, growing stale and watching the show go on around us."

Tamara couldn't help herself and snickered at the dramatic commentary. "Sounds like a Greek tragedy," she teased, making Ginny return her giggles. "However," she continued, preparing to offer another counter argument, before being cut short by a patron approaching the desk with an inquiry about a newly released bestseller.

Ginny, still grinning, waved her off.

"Don't think I'm finished," she said, over her shoulder, before leading the way to find the book in question. "I'll be back."

Ginny inhaled the lingering sweet scent of Tamara's vanilla body spray and sighed. She was such a character, always offering up sensational ideas, not to mention had an intriguing imagination, wit, and kind heart. Combined with the obvious fact she was stunning, it was a wonder she was still single.

"These are the mysteries of life," Ginny muttered, to herself, as she slipped her glasses back on her face.

"Pardon me?"

"Oh!" Ginny said, by way of reply. She hadn't realized a patron was standing almost directly behind her, within earshot. "Nothing, sorry. Just talking to myself. A bit of an occupational hazard, I'm afraid."

The woman to whom she was speaking smiled tentatively, making Ginny feel like a babbling fool. She squared her shoulders and did her best to plaster a professional expression on her face. "Is there something in particular I can help you find?"

The woman shook her head of short, dark hair as she began to shuffle away. "No, thanks. Just going to browse until something catches my eye."

Ginny waved her off, in a much more subdued manner than she had Tamara, then inwardly groaned. On a positive note, she imagined the tale of the elderly library lady chatting away to herself would make for an amusing story at dinnertime. She gave herself a mental shake. She needed to harness her wandering thoughts and get back to work.

"Alright, done," Tamara said, returning to the desk.

"Good," Ginny replied, all business as she moved *The Lion, the Witch and the Wardrobe* into the stack she was creating for the young adult section of the library.

"What happened?"

Ginny looked into her inquisitive face. "What?"

"You're all pulled in," she said, gesturing to Ginny's hunched shoulders. "Did something happen while I was gone?" She spun around, looking for clues, then snapped her fingers. "Oooh! Was there some mystery man contact? Did I miss it?" She stamped her foot. "Dang it! I missed it!"

Ginny relaxed her shoulders. "No," she said, dismissing the idea with a shake of her head. "You didn't miss anything. I just got caught talking to myself, *again*, by a patron."

"Oh, well, whatchya gonna do," Tamara said, before parroting Ginny's earlier remark. "Occupational hazard."

Ginny resumed scanning and separating the returned books into their respective categories. "That's exactly what I said to the woman, but I don't think she found it funny. More like she was worried for my mental stability."

Tamara grinned appreciatively then pointed at a stack of children's books. "These ones ready to go?"

"Uh-huh," Ginny said, transferring the pile to the returns cart. "I should be finished with the rest by the time you're done putting these ones back."

Tamara got behind the cart. "Back in a sec," she said, before pushing it in the direction of the children's section.

Ginny watched her go then, not being able to help herself, shifted her gaze to the right and tilted her head forward, allowing herself a furtive glance at mystery man over the turquoise rim of her frames.

Head cocked at a slight angle as he read the dust jacket on a Jeffrey Archer novel, Ginny found herself admiring the thickness and color of his short hair; chocolate brown, sprinkled with a smattering of steel grey. She let her eyes travel downward to admire the hunter green, tailored shirt stretched across his broad shoulders... then smartly stopped herself when she was about to dip her gaze further to check out his charcoal grey trousers.

Enough, she silently counselled. The man just liked books. Nothing more.

She peeked again.

Alright *fine*, if pressed she'd possibly admit to herself he was slightly intriguing. But that was a completely justifiable thought, based on the fact that he *had* become a steady patron seemingly out of the blue - at last count, in the past two weeks, he'd visited the library at least five times. Not that she was counting.

And, for the record, it certainly didn't mean it had anything to do with her. In fact, the very idea was preposterous. She was a *grandmother*, for goodness sake. And a widow. Not that *he* knew any of that, of course, but *still*. Tamara was just being silly. She'd read too many of the romance novels that decorated the library's shelves and was making up stories where there were none.

Ginny pulled her gaze away and smoothed the collar of her pale pink blouse beneath her cardigan. She needed to get a grip. Enough of Tamara's fantasies, even if they were much more fun than reality.

Her cellphone vibrated in the pocket of her black slacks and Ginny was glad of the distraction. She fished out the phone and read the reminder message she'd set for herself.

*Dinner at Fran's. 7pm.*

Ahh, right. Reality. She slipped the phone back into her pocket, plucked a *Hershey's Kiss* from the candy dish and sighed.

****

Ginny darted through the door to her kitchen, shutting it firmly against the elements trying to sweep into the house behind her. "Whew!" she exhaled, giving herself a shake and sending droplets of rain water scattering across the tiles. "Almost made it."

She pushed back the soaked strands of her hair falling across her face as thunder rumbled noisily overhead, vibrating the walls of the house, and slipped out of her loafers. Her calico cat, Martini, poked his head around the doorway, assessing the situation.

"Hey there, gorgeous," Ginny said, while peeling her sodden cardigan from her shoulders and giving an involuntary shiver. "I don't recommend you going out there anytime soon. It's raining cats and dogs."

Martini sauntered across the floor for a closer inspection and tentatively touched his nose to her sopping shoes while Ginny snickered at her play on words.

"Anyway," she continued, padding on stocking feet out of the kitchen, "other than the weather report, it turned out to be quite a busy day at the library."

Martini looked up from her shoes. He abandoned his inspection to follow her down the hallway toward her bedroom. It had become their routine since he'd settled into the house, after being given to Ginny by her son and daughter-in-law, that she told him about her day when she returned home. Sure, it probably qualified her for membership into the crazy cat lady club, but such was life.

"We had a group of parents and kids turn up," she went on, "I'd guess they were around five or six years old, and no matter how we tried we couldn't impress upon them the need to keep it down."

While Martini slunk past and sprang effortlessly onto the bed, Ginny dropped the cardigan into the laundry basket, followed by the rest of her soggy clothes. Standing in her delicates, a white cotton bra and matching underpants, she reached into the bureau for her peach colored velour pants.

"There was this one boy," she elaborated, shaking out the pants. "He tried so hard to be quiet and the only way he knew how was to effectively stage-whisper everything."

She stepped into the pants, sliding them smoothly over her hips, and chuckled at the memory of the little boy while pulling a matching crew-neck sweater from the drawer. He'd been such a dear and once she'd assured his fretting mother there were far worse problems to be had than an enthused child being a little loud in a library, everything had moved along smoothly.

Martini settled himself onto the bed's thick pink comforter, sighed and closed his eyes.

Ginny slipped the soft cotton sweater over her head. She ran her fingers through her still-damp hair and had to resist the sudden, overwhelming urge to climb into the bed beside him. Nothing sounded better at that moment than a hot cup of tea, her pillow, cat and a good book.

The telephone rang in the kitchen, interrupting her yearning, and Ginny's face lit up. "Hey! Hear that? Maybe the universe heard my thoughts and that's Fran calling to cancel."

She turned smartly on her heel and strode from the room while Martini, still curled up on the comforter, yawned and flexed his black-tipped toes.

****

Ginny moved swiftly across her kitchen, the hem of her velour pant legs brushing soundlessly against the pale tile floor. She scooted around the island then reached across the peninsula adjacent to the sink for the phone.

"Hello?"

"Hey, doll!"

Ginny smiled at the sound of her best friend's cheerful voice on the line. "Jan, I was just thinking of you."

"Oh?" She said. "All good, I hope."

"More like wishful, truth be told."

"Even better. What sort of genie magic are we talking?"

"None powerful enough for these wishes, I'm afraid," Ginny said, while thunder rumbled powerfully overhead. She tucked the phone into the crook of her neck and picked up the kettle, turning on the tap over the sink. "I have a dinner party at Fran's tonight and no amount of wishful thinking is going to magically change that into you and me having a girl's night with pizza and a chick flick."

"You could use the weather as an excuse," Jan replied. "And it would be justified; it's really coming down out there."

Ginny filled the kettle and placed it on its base to boil. "Don't I know it," she said, turning off the tap then reaching into a drawer for a spoon to measure out Earl Grey Tea. "I got drenched just running from the garage to the house."

"There you go," Jan said, cheerily. "Just tell Fran you don't feel comfortable driving in the storm."

"And she'd send Todd to pick me up," Ginny stated, referring to Fran's husband.

"You think so?"

"Absolutely." She dug the spoon into a canister beside the teapot. "She's very determined about this dinner."

"Is it a special occasion?"

Ginny stopped measuring tea into the pot and lifted her gaze to the large bay window above the sink. Instead of taking in the view of her backyard, the dark pane of glass offered nothing more than her rain smattered reflection staring back.

"Hello? Gin?"

Ginny blinked. "Sorry, distracted. What was the question?"

"Is the dinner party for a special occasion?" Jan repeated.

"Oh, no, I don't think so. I'm pretty sure I've been invited to even up the numbers with some man I've never met."

"Maybe he'll be really nice," Jan offered, trying to help.

"Oh, I don't doubt it."

"She said with zero enthusiasm," Jan commented, wryly. "What if he turns out to be a *dream come true...*"

"Ha," Ginny said, as the kettle clicked off. She reached for the pot.

"What?" she asked, her voice full of mirth. "We're ruling that out? There's no chance he could be a dream come true?"

Ginny poured the freshly boiled water over the leaves in the teapot then inhaled with pleasure as the spicy, citrus smell of oil of bergamot began permeating the kitchen. Finally, she replied, "I think it's irrelevant either way, quite honestly."

Jan dropped the teasing tone. "Not feeling up to it?"

"And then some." Ginny opened a white, bead board cupboard door and retrieved her favorite mug - white with delicate, hand painted pink, orange and yellow flowers, given to her by her kids for Mother's Day five years past.

"Are you sick?"

Ginny shook her head at the concern lacing the question. "No, no. Nothing like that. I feel fine. It's just that I'm just *sooo* not interested. In any of it. Truth be told, he could be the nicest person I've met in a long time, but the whole idea of dating and getting to know someone, telling of histories... Ugg." She grimaced and poured her tea, the fragrant steam rising mistily from her cup.

"Is it George?"

"No, no. Not at all."

"Honestly?" Jan pressed. "You'd tell me, right?"

"Honestly." Ginny placed a hand lightly over her heart as though she was taking an oath. "We're coming up on the two year anniversary of his death and something's really shifted in me. It's like a weight has been lifted. I feel lighter. My grief counsellor told me it would probably happen and she was right."

"My goodness," Jan breathed. "I know I've said it before, but it's hard to believe it's been nearly two years now. The time has just gone…"

"I know," Ginny agreed, gazing at her reflection in the window. "It's rather a miracle, for me. If you would have told me at the time, there's no way I would have believed there was a chance I could make it to where I am now."

Jan went quiet, listening. She'd had the same fear, at the time, and the memories could still make her uncomfortable.

Ginny continued, her voice thoughtful. "I thought I would just go to my bed and eventually fade away. I figured, if I laid there long enough, it could happen."

Jan nodded, even though Ginny couldn't see her. She remembered it all with a clarity she sometimes worried would never leave her.

She'd been making dinner, lazily stirring a meat sauce simmering on the stove, and in the next instant the phone had rung and on the other end of the line had been Eric, Ginny's son, telling her the news of his father and the horrific car accident that had taken his life.

She'd barely managed to put down the wooden spoon before her knees had buckled and she'd slid down the cabinetry to sit on the tile floor, mouth opening and closing like a fish out of water, trying to make sense of the words. Her husband, Darryl, had entered the room and swiftly wrapped his arms around her as grief had welled up; seeming to squeeze her heart as she'd listen to Eric trying to explain, the tremor in his voice so audible she thought she'd crumble into unrecognizable pieces in the face of his pain.

And then there'd been Ginny. Jan had been so scared for her friend.

She'd watched, helpless, as Ginny transformed from a vivacious woman into something resembling a zombie. She'd lost her appetite, consuming only enough calories to barely keep her alive, and lost weight at an alarming rate. Her normally intelligent, vibrant eyes had taken on a glassy stare; as though the lights had been dimmed and she was running on autopilot. She'd stopped caring whatsoever about leaving her house, spending hour after hour sitting in her dressing gown or lying prone in bed. Conversation all but dried up, the only time she seemed to speak was when directly addressed. It had been terrifying and Jan had spent many nights crying in her husband's arms, at her wits end as to what to do to help her broken friend.

"Thank goodness for the anger," Ginny said, shaking off her stillness and interrupting Jan's train of thought. "Do you remember?" she asked, leaving her tea to cool and reaching into the refrigerator for a container of chopped salmon. "I think I scared myself with the intensity of it."

Jan laughed. "I don't think any of us will even forget."

It had come on suddenly. Or at least felt that way at the time. Jan had left Ginny's house on a Monday - she'd been making daily visits for weeks on end, fearful if she missed a day it might be the very one Ginny chose to give up the last shred of will she had to keep on breathing - and when she'd returned on the Tuesday it was to a whole different animal.

Sometime between the hours she'd been absent and then returned, a new emotion had taken up residence in Ginny's body. Rage. The silent, tomb-like house had been transformed and Jan had nearly been knocked sideways by the volume of the television, radio and Ginny's voice when she'd opened the front door and stepped across the threshold.

Jan had been frightened in a whole new manner.

Whereas previously she'd been concerned Ginny would sink into a depression from which she'd never find the strength to climb out, she'd suddenly found herself shifting to alarm that her friend might do something to cause herself harm.

And the profanity. Wow.

Jan was no shrinking violet, not to mention she'd raised two teenagers, but the language that had spewed from between Ginny's lips had been like an assault. Jan had physically winced while she'd frantically called Darryl for backup.

Ginny chuckled and scooped the salmon into a blue bowl with a black paw print embossed on the side, on the countertop. "I know I was like a demon, but boy-oh-boy did it ever feel great to have so much energy after feeling so dead inside for all of those weeks."

"Thank goodness that demon didn't stick around," Jan said, grinning. "Otherwise, I think Boxwood Hills might never have been the same."

Ginny grimaced, remembering how vile she'd been to more than a few people unfortunate to cross her path during that time. Thank goodness Jan had been there to apologize on her behalf.

"Have I told you how much I appreciate you, lately?" she asked, genuinely grateful.

"Hey, it goes both ways," Jan said, matter of fact.

"Seriously, you really did save me," Ginny insisted, while placing the blue bowl on the floor. "I'll always be in your debt for dragging me to my therapist."

"It wasn't just me," Jan reminded her.

Ginny smiled softly. That was true. Jennifer, her amazing daughter, had put aside her own grief over

George's death and worked with Jan to get her mother the help she'd so desperately needed.

"Hold that thought," she said, before calling out, "supper time!"

A moment later, Martini streaked around the doorway as though he was being chased. He came to a sharp halt near Ginny's feet and promptly stuck his face into the waiting bowl.

Ginny grinned, watching him. Perhaps she should have called him Garfield.

"Did I ever tell you," she said, while returning the rest of the salmon to the fridge, "shortly after I started therapy, I actually began trying to talk myself into the idea I was sort of lucky George had worked away from home so much?"

Jan's eyebrows lifted. This was news. "No."

"I realize it sounds delusional, possibly even morbid, but I got stuck on the idea that him being away so much would mean I'd adapt better to his absence than other women whose husbands came home at the end of the work day, every day; because I was already used to him not being here all the time."

"Ahh," Jan said, nodding. "I get that. It makes sense you'd think that way. Trying to find some sort of positive amidst the horror of it all."

"That's what the therapist said, when I admitted my thoughts to her."

Jan wished she was there to hug her.

Ginny shifted the phone to her other ear and picked up her teacup. "She also assured me it was perfectly normal reasoning - not the workings of a morbid mind - and said it showed I have a strong coping mechanism."

"I like that," Jan said. "Do you think she was right?"

Ginny could hear the hope in her voice and adored her for it. "Yes. I can honestly say time has done exactly what we're told it will do."

"Time heals all wounds," Jan said, giving voice to the old adage.

"Exactly," Ginny agreed, sipping her tea. "My wounds feel healed now and, miracles of miracles, I've even gotten used to living in the house on my own. It's a huge relief."

"I can imagine," Jan said, wishing she could offer more, but was still - after all that time - slightly overwhelmed by the emotional journey her friend had taken.

"Even the sting of George's absence when I step into the house has shifted now. It's softened, more like an occasional whisper as compared to a shout, you know?"

"I totally agree. In fact, now that you've said it, I'm just realizing I don't feel odd anymore when I visit."

"Odd?"

"For the first while, after George passed," Jan admitted, "it felt really strange to come over and not have him stroll into the room at one point."

Ginny smiled and drank her tea. She understood.

"Not that I don't still think of him," Jan added, suddenly awkward about what she'd said. "I do. It's just that now I feel okay when —"

"No, no, you don't have to explain. I get it, I really do. I finally don't feel that yucky void, like someone is glaringly missing, either." Ginny winced at the sound of her words then asked, "God that sounded a bit cold, didn't it?"

"No. It sounds healthy and balanced."

"It's just that I'm at the point of accepting things as they are," she explained, walking over to the kitchen table and placing her cup on its well-worn surface. "I've learned that in every dark corner there's light, if you're willing to look for it. And, if you're patient enough, that light will eventually seem so bright you'll forget the darkness was there at all."

"Wow, Gin, that's..." Jan said, lost for words. What did a person say in the face of such obvious strength of character?

"Simply put," Ginny finished, saving her. "I'm okay now and I'm content living by my own agenda. I'm finally at peace with moving on."

"Just not into another man's arms," Jan said, returning them to their initial conversation.

"You've got that right," Ginny agreed, glancing at Martini sitting regally on his haunches and licking the salmon from his lips with broad strokes of his pink tongue. "I'm happy being the crazy cat lady."

Jan laughed. "I'm just glad you didn't name him George when the kids brought him over, like you threatened."

Ginny snickered and sat down.

It had been on the one year anniversary of George's passing that her son, Eric, and daughter-in-law, Kimberly, had surprised her with the cat, hoping he would help soften the blow. She'd later told Jan she was considering calling it George, believing he would have appreciated the humor.

"God, can you imagine it?" Jan continued.

"I still say *George* would have found it funny." Ginny leaned her elbows on the table and traced her finger around the knots in the smooth pine.

"So, tell me," Jan said, shifting gears. "What are you bringing to Fran's soiree?"

Ginny chuckled at her choice of words. "Orange pound cake."

"Oooh, the one with the freshly grated orange peel?"

"Yup."

"Mmm," Jan murmured, approvingly. "I'm sure it'll be a hit."

"I have a second one made for us," Ginny said, reading her mind.

She snorted. "Am I that transparent?"

"Yup."

"So, what are you wearing? Something come-hither?"

"Not quite. I think I'll play it safe and wear my black dress."

"Ahh, good call. It'll remind them that, even though it's been two years now since George has passed, you still morn him."

Ginny smirked and reached for her mug. Her best friend knew her too well. "Tease all you want, but it could end up being my get-out-of-jail-free card if he turns out to be a horror."

"But what if he's not?" Jan posed, playing devil's advocate. "What if he's the complete opposite of a horror? A delight. What then?"

"Your youth and optimism impress me."

Jan made a wet, raspberry sound down the line. "Oh, stop! I'm only six years younger than you. Quit trying to deflect and answer the question. What if he's a complete delight and there you are, in your funeral garb?"

Ginny chortled at her choice of words. "Then I'll claim my daughter-in-law forced me to wear something nondescript and swiftly turn on the charm so he forgets all about my dress."

Jan laughed out loud. "Excellent. As long as you have a reasonable plan, you should be good to go."

****

"These crab cakes are divine, Fran. Just to die for!"
Fran dimpled in delight.

"And the crust!" Bruce gushed. "Out. Of. This. World!"

Fran squirmed and giggled like a little girl in her seat and Ginny, sitting opposite her across the dining room table, felt her jaw go slack. The sound came as a complete surprise. In all her time knowing Fran - and it had been a few years - she had never once heard the woman giggle.

Ginny pulled her gaze from her friend and planted it on Todd, Fran's portly husband, gauging his reaction. Nothing. He appeared indifferent to the conversation, his balding head tilted forward as he focused upon transferring the food from his plate into his mouth with gusto.

Ginny picked up her fork and returned her attention to the crab cake duo, her head going back and forth as they bantered.

"Both rich and light at the same time," Bruce elucidated.

"Exactly at it should be," Fran agreed.

"And I'm guessing old-school butter and lard frying wasn't used to create these heavenly delights," Bruce said. "Am I right?"

"You are!" Fran confirmed, positively glowing from all of the attention. "Just a bit of vegetable oil and… some other things." She mimed locking her lips, before adding, "It's a secret family recipe."

"I knew it!" Bruce's eyes sparkled as he wagged a finger at her. "Well, fair warning, I may just have to wheedle it out of you. I know these would be a complete hit amongst my seafood loving friends."

Fran giggled, again, displaying a smudge of pink lipstick across her front teeth. "Charm away!"

Ginny chewed methodically while repressing the desire to roll her eyes. Not as a silent commentary on the merits of the crab cakes, let it be clarified. Not at all. On that point she agreed with Bruce; they were delicious. No, the thing troubling Ginny was how obvious the mismatch was between her and Bruce, her so-called date. It had become crystal clear during the hour they'd spent visiting before sitting down to dinner, they weren't looking for the same thing; or to put a finer point on it, they *were* looking for the *same thing*.

Not that Ginny had any issue with that part of things. *Please*. Absolutely not.

She was as open-minded and accepting at they came.

No, it wasn't anything about Bruce that was the cause for her annoyance; it was Fran and Todd. Apparently, they were so self-absorbed they'd been willing to dupe both she and Bruce just to have dinner guests. Or, at least it felt that way. More likely the truth was they were blithely unaware, which was even more bothersome as it made her seem childish for her snit. Phooey.

"Everything okay?" Fran asked, her round face creased with concern when she heard Ginny sigh.

Ginny met her big brown eyes across the elaborately laid, eight-seater table and debated on how to respond. There was no possible way she could express her feelings on the matter, not without creating serious misunderstandings and upset. However, there was still the irrepressible fact that she wanted nothing more than to be back at home - in her comfy fleece pants - with this whole evening behind her.

It appeared she had no choice. She'd have to play the headache card to cut things short in a polite manner.

The question was *when*? Before dessert? After?

Ginny let her gaze trail through the dining room in her search for an answer, but the white wainscoted walls, overstocked china cabinet, glittering chandelier and imposing grandfather clock gave nothing back.

"Did you need more wine?" Todd lifted a crystal carafe of red from the middle of the tabletop and swayed it back and forth invitingly.

"No, thanks," Ginny replied, a small smile curving her lips as she put down her fork then smoothed the white linen napkin laying across her lap. He'd inadvertently helped her case along and she was grateful. "I'm fine. Just a touch of a headache. I should know better than to drink red, but it's so delicious I forget to stop myself."

"Oh, I hear that!" Bruce reached out, the sleeves of his burgundy dinner jacket slipping back to allow his gold cufflinks to flash in the light from the chandelier, and patted her wrist companionably. "Those darn tannins. I often go for white if I'm feeling a touch headachey."

"Me, too," Fran effused, her cheeks flushed beneath her helmet of generously sprayed, tightly wound auburn curls. She leaned forward on the floral patterned seat of her chair and held out her glass for a refill.

Todd extended his pudgy arm, reaching past the girth of his straining waistband, to connect the carafe with the top of her silver rimmed goblet.

"Don't worry about me," Ginny said, picking up her water glass. "If it gets worse, I'll be sure to let you know."

"That's a lovely watch," Bruce said, admiring the wrist he'd just patted.

Ginny looked at the watch. Its delicate pearl face displayed the time in black roman numerals and was surrounded by ornately woven silver, inlayed with tiny, sparkling diamonds.

"Is it Swiss? It looks Swiss."

Ginny sipped her water, smiled benignly, then took the offer to divulge as it was being given. "It's antique. My late husband, George, gave it to me as an anniversary gift a few years ago."

Bruce brushed his blonde fringe from his forehead and looked at her with sympathetic eyes.

"Oh, *Geoooorge!*"

Ginny went rigid in her seat, reflexively tightening her grip on the glass in her hand. Fran's wail stopped them all in their tracks.

"What a dear man. A dear, dear, man. Gone so soon. *Too* soon." Fran fixed glistening eyes on Bruce, her mouth starting to tremble. "You would have adored him, Bruce."

Bruce smiled, congenially.

Ginny put down her water goblet and peered at her friend. Were those unshed tears in Fran's eyes? Clearly she had hit her wine limit.

"How long has it been now, Ginny? More than a year? Surely, more than a year? It feels like ages and ages."

"Umm," Ginny said, blinking and trying not to make direct eye contact with Fran's penetrating stare.

"He was the nicest person you could've ever hoped to know," Fran expounded, waving her hand in the air, not waiting for an answer. "Kind and considerate, willing to help. A fabulous sense of humor. Fabulous! Oh, the stories he told. So many laughs we had!"

Ginny observed the show, both fascinated and horrified. What was happening? Was Fran really blathering on about George's virtues to *Bruce*? Seriously? Wasn't he supposed to be her date? Not to mention, when all was said and done, wasn't *she* supposed to be the grieving widow?

"It was such a shame," Fran sighed, dropping her hand onto the solid oak table with a thud. "Such a terrible shame…."

Ginny squirmed in her seat. If Fran continued, things were going to start feeling macabre. She wished she could slip out of the room unnoticed.

"He was a solid friend," Todd said, attempting to pat things down. "A good egg."

Ginny watched him wipe his brow with the back of his hand and wished she could think of something to help him move things along. Unfortunately, it was all so unexpected she was at a loss for words.

Thankfully, Bruce wasn't.

"Did you set this glorious table yourself, Fran?"

Fran raised her downcast eyes to peer at her guest. "Pardon?"

Ginny blinked and exchanged a look with Todd. His obvious bewilderment made it plain she wasn't the only one brought up short by the non-segued question.

"The *table*," Bruce said, again, while sweeping his arm back and forth in a wide, all-encompassing arc. "Did you put this all together?"

Fran, although visibly taken aback by the sudden change of topic, cleared her throat, rallying. "Yes. Yes, I did."

"Well, you went above and beyond the call of duty, my dear." He sparkled at her then reached over to clasp her hand. "I mean, really, look at these silver fish forks!"

Ginny regarded Fran as her face made the transformation from distraught to glowing, and was happy for her. And, admittedly, Bruce's blatant disregard of her friend's momentary despondence was, at the very least, odd, but after all was said and done she was pleased *someone* was enjoying her blind date.

"And this fabric," Bruce carried on, practically purring as he released Fran's hand to gently rub his fingers across the intricately patterned, white lace tablecloth. "It's *ahh-mazing*. Is it antique, like Ginny's watch?"

Oh, lord, *again* with the watch. Ginny stiffened. She was afraid to meet Fran's eye, lest she be set off for a second time.

"As a matter of fact, yes, it is. *You* have a great eye, green eyes," Fran bantered, her voice flirty as she fully embraced the spirit of the conversational shift.

Ginny relaxed her tensed shoulders and released the breath she hadn't realized she was holding. Apparently, George's impromptu eulogy was fully behind them.

"Where on Earth did you find it?" Bruce's expression was one of pure admiration as he regarded both Fran and the cloth.

Ginny looked at Todd, again, hoping to gauge his reaction, but he'd gone back to his crab cakes.

Fran smoothed the fringe on the sleeve of her navy, frilled dress then reached out to pat Todd's forearm while she spoke. "Todd's grandmother gave it to us as a wedding present. Oh dear, that certainly dates me, doesn't it? Sounds like it's not the *only* antique in the family!"

Bruce chortled, making Ginny want to grab a fistful of the much revered white cloth and wave it in defeat. Why-oh-why hadn't she trusted her instincts and told Fran she had to cancel when she'd had the chance? Why hadn't she listened to Jan's suggestions? She was done with the whole fix-up scene. This one would make eight in total since the one year anniversary of George's death. Eight! It was as though the moment the first year had passed, it was open season on fixing up the widow. Well, enough was enough. It was too much like work.

Todd chuckled heartily at Fran's comment and Ginny grinned robotically from her end of the table. *When in Rome,* as the saying goes.

"Anyway, I think we're about done with our first course, wouldn't you say?" Fran beamed winningly at Ginny. "I'll start clearing and we can get cozy in the family room with some port until the next course is ready."

Ginny blanched. *Next* course? Fran hadn't mentioned there would be courses when she'd extended her dinner invitation.

"That sounds brilliant, but you must let me help." Bruce was up from his chair in a flash. He smoothed the creases from his tan slacks then began gathering up the china.

"Well, aren't you just a peach!" Fran waggled her eyebrows up and down at Ginny.

Ginny resisted the urge to childishly stick out her tongue in return.

"My mother raised me right," Bruce said, catching Todd's eye. "Besides, you ladies are too beautifully turned out to do the work, isn't that right Todd?"

Todd, on the spot with nowhere to turn, nodded briskly. "Absolutely."

"You see?" Bruce grabbed the reply and swiftly built on it. "We wouldn't want a hint of anything to mar the elegance of Ginny's classic black dress, nor the cheerful pattern on your navy frock."

Fran lifted her glass and tipped the last of the wine into her mouth then rose unsteadily to her feet. "Todd's going to have to hang around you more often."

Bruce tittered as he swept past Ginny, carrying the first set of dishes toward the neighboring kitchen. She swallowed against a cough when the full force of his sharp cologne hit her nostrils.

"Better hurry," Fran urged Todd, as Bruce disappeared around the corner. "He'll have it all done before you've lifted a finger."

Todd pushed back his chair and with a grunt slowly eased himself upright. He took his time adjusting his leather belt across the width of his brown slacks, his belly suspended above his waistline as though by some magical force. Ginny watched the show and thought it was glaringly evident by the disgruntled expression on his face, Todd was a man unused to being pressed into service at the end of his meal.

"Your pants are fine," Fran tutted, now using her empty glass as a makeshift pointer; swinging it back and forth between Todd and the kitchen. "Go. Go."

Ginny, feeling caught in some sort of silent marital game of chicken, sighed and stretched her neck. Yup, no question about it. Her headache was definitely getting worse.

****

## Ginny's Delectable Orange Pound Cake

### Ingredients

1    cup butter (at room temperature)
2    cups brown sugar
4    large, free-range eggs
⅓    cup grated orange zest (approx. 4-6 oranges, depending on size)
3    cups whole wheat flour
½    teaspoon baking powder
½    teaspoon baking soda
1    teaspoon salt
¼    cup freshly squeezed orange juice
¾    cup buttermilk
1    teaspoon pure vanilla extract

### Directions

Preheat oven to 350 degrees F.

o   Grease and flour two 8½ x 4½ x 2½ -inch loaf pans, line the bottom of the pans with parchment paper.

o   Cream butter and brown sugar in a large bowl, until light and fluffy. Beat in the eggs, one at a time, then add the orange zest.

o   In a separate bowl, sift together the flour, baking powder, baking soda and salt.

o   In a third bowl, combine the orange juice, buttermilk and vanilla.

o   Add the flour mixture and orange juice/buttermilk mixture alternately to the butter/brown sugar batter, beginning and ending with the flour.

o   Divide the batter evenly between the pans, smooth the tops and bake for 40-50 minutes, (depending upon how hot your oven bakes) until a cake tester comes out clean. (If needed, feel free to cover tops of pans with foil at the 30 minute mark.)

o While the cakes bake, combine ½ cup of brown sugar with ½ cup orange juice in a small saucepan over low heat until the sugar dissolves.

o When the cakes are done, let them cool for 5 minutes then turn them out of the pans onto a baking rack. Place the rack over a baking tray and gently spoon the orange syrup over the cakes. Allow the cakes to cool completely.

o If saving the cakes for a later date, wrap well and store in the refrigerator.

# Chapter Two

"So, correct me if I'm wrong," Jan said, her words laced heavily with mirth as she reclined on the sunflower yellow sofa in Ginny's sunroom. "But, I'm getting the strong impression this Bruce fellow turned out *not* to be your cup of tea?"

Ginny, seated on the adjacent matching armchair, snorted. She and Jan were engaging in their usual Sunday morning ritual - one they'd been doing for more years than either of them could remember - catching each other up on the week's events. Needless to say, she'd been expounding on her experience at Fran and Todd's dinner and, go figure, Jan had put two and two together.

"Not going to be the love affair to remember?" Jan teased, as she shifted her hourglass figure, hidden by baggy sweatpants and a white, loose-fitting tunic, to better see Ginny's face.

"That's the understatement of the year," Ginny replied, leaning forward to pick a fresh-from-the-oven banana chocolate chip muffin from a plate on the coffee table. "He was more interested in Fran's tablecloth than me."

"Pardon?"

Ginny took a bite of the muffin and spoke around it. "You heard me right. The tablecloth. And the table settings. And the crab cakes. God, he even wanted her recipe."

"Huh," Jan said, flatly.

"I know." Ginny nodded. "Not exactly riveting conversation. There was discussion about the damn cakes at the table and then they came up *again* before we moved onto the next course."

"Figuratively, I hope."

Ginny chuckled. "Yes, thank goodness. Although, that being said, Todd was being so generous with the booze they had a very real possibility of making another appearance. Who knows, perhaps they did after I left."

"Ewww." Jan grimaced. "So, that lovely picture aside, how many courses did you actually get through before you managed to bail out?"

"Three. The crab cakes, a soup course and a pasta course."

Jan shook her head of short, tousled brown hair. "Wow."

"Tell me about it," Ginny said, taking another bite of muffin. "I'm pretty sure Fran had two more planned, never mind serving the cake I brought."

"Good god," Jan said, feeling slightly queasy at the thought of all that food and alcohol mixing together. Urgg.

Ginny held up a finger, swallowed and said, "As an amusing aside, by the time I managed to squeeze out the door, Fran had had so much to drink it looked like she was ready to trade Todd in for Bruce."

Jan laughed and adjusted an orange throw pillow under her head. "It sounds like he was a charming and kind hearted guy."

"Absolutely," Ginny immediately agreed, before popping the last of the muffin into her mouth. She chewed then added, "Regardless of our glaring disconnect, he was a gentleman through and through."

"How did Fran and Todd meet him, anyway?"

"Through friends of friends, or some such thing." Ginny picked up a napkin from the walnut coffee table and wiped her fingers. "I have to confess, I pretty much tuned out when he and Fran began rhapsodizing about the china pattern on her cups."

"No way," Jan said, incredulous. "Not really?"

"Honest to God." Ginny placed her hand over her heart then crumpled the napkin and tossed it onto the table top.

Jan blinked, digesting the information.

Ginny tucked her sock-clad feet beneath her on the chair. "Yup, I was as gob smacked as you are. And by then, poor Todd looked like he was ready for a nap and their chatter was his sleepy-time story."

"Well, then," Jan finally said, "since I have nothing to say about *that*, I'll tell you instead that Darryl thinks you're brave. He told me to tell you."

It was Ginny's turn to blink and stare. "Brave?"

"Uh-huh, it's true," Jan said, referring to her husband's claim. "He told me point-blank he thinks you're brave and, I gotta say, I agree with him."

"Brave?" Ginny repeated. "Why on Earth would Darryl think me brave?"

"Because you've been so kind and understanding when these women try and set you up. He's very much aware of how hard you've worked to get to where you are since George's passing and he said he admires your fortitude."

"*Fortitude?*"

"Yes, *fortitude*." Jan reached for a blue cotton blanket draped across the top of the sofa. "Your strength. Your resilience. Your mettle—"

"I *know* what it means," Ginny interrupted, laughing.

"Good." Jan grinned. "Because he admires you for it."

"They really do mean well," Ginny offered, generously. "It's hard not to go along with it, they seem so eager to save me from my aloneness."

"Or, maybe they're just worried you being on your own could mean you'll steal their husbands."

Ginny released a bark of laughter. "Right. And the best way to distract me from their *irresistible* mates would be to set me up with men who have no interest in me whatsoever. Ingenious."

Jan fussed with the blanket, arranging it over her legs and torso. "Can you imagine how the last two courses went? In her condition, it sounds like a food poisoning nightmare waiting to happen."

Ginny considered it and wrinkled her nose at the thought. Not pretty.

"Are you going to call and find out?"

"Actually, I did call to thank her for inviting me."

"And?"

"I got the machine, thank goodness."

Jan settled back onto the sofa.

"Anyway," Ginny gave a dismissive wave of her hand. "The facts are, Fran and I have always been more couples-friends than friend-friends. And since George passed, I can count on one hand how many times I've seen them."

Jan nodded. She and Darryl had the same relationship with them.

"Oh, and I forgot to mention," Ginny said, snapping her fingers. "To add insult to injury, I wouldn't have put Bruce at a day over fifty."

"So?"

Ginny shot her a sardonic look.

"What? What's with the look?" Jan insisted.

"Please. Like I'm going to be interested in a man easily ten years my junior."

"Ten years isn't that much."

"We're at least a *decade* apart."

"Oh, please."

"Oh, please, nothing," Ginny said. "When you can give the age difference a name, we have an issue."

Jan chuckled. "Semantics. Things have changed. Women can date men younger than them and no one cares."

Ginny grimaced then ran her fingers through her hair, pushing the salt and pepper waves back from her face. "Ugg. No thanks. Sounds like work."

"What's this outfit you're wearing, by the way?"

Ginny looked down at her velour sweater and matching, elastic waistband pants. "What about it?"

Jan propped herself up on her elbow, her brow furrowed as she gestured at Ginny's clothes. "Well, for starters, I *know* I've never seen it before. I'm sure I'd remember."

Ginny couldn't help herself and laughed at the obviously wry tone. "Because you find it so fetching?"

"Or *something*," Jan replied. "What color is that, anyway? Baby vomit?"

Ginny laughed harder at her frankness.

"And what's all over it? It looks like you were accosted by a Bedazzler."

Ginny snorted in mirth then caught her breath. "How do you really feel?"

Jan echoed her snort.

"It was a gift," Ginny said.

"From who?"

"Kimberly," Ginny said, referring to her daughter-in-law.

"Kimberly!" Jan shook her head. "Why? Did you make her angry, or something?"

Ginny bit her lip to keep from laughing and, instead, shook her finger. "Stop it. You're being terrible."

Jan sat forward, the blue blanket pooling around her hips, and held her hands up in mock surrender. "Okay, fine. But, I still don't understand how she could have seen this and had even the fleeting thought it would suit you. Or *anyone*, for that matter."

Ginny raised her eyebrows.

"Come *on*," Jan said. "You have to give me that. I honestly cannot imagine that would be flattering on anyone."

"Thanks a *lot*," Ginny said, attempting to sound indignant.

Jan reached for her tumbler of orange juice on the coffee table. "Oh, please. You *know* what I mean."

"Yes, unfortunately, I do," Ginny conceded, not genuinely offended. It was nothing she hadn't thought when she'd opened the box it came in. She, too, had been taken off guard by the outfit's lack of form, style, flair, taste; well, the list could go on.

Jan drank from her glass then set it back down on the table. "So, what was the motivation behind this so-called gift?"

"She claimed she wanted to get both of the mothers in her life a token of her appreciation."

"You mean she bought this same get-up for her mother as well?"

"Apparently." Ginny tipped her head back against the chair's soft cushions, enjoying the sunshine warming her through the window, and closed her eyes.

"Wow."

"Maybe I'll wear it out and test it on these younger men I can supposedly date without ridicule," Ginny offered, keeping her eyes shut as she spoke. "Maybe old lady velour is a head turner to the younger set."

Jan chuckled and settled herself back under the blue blanket. "Tut-tut. Chin up and all that. You win some, you lose some."

"Ugg."

Jan waited.

"I'm so sick of fix-ups." Ginny opened her eyes and watched Martini slink into the room, looking for company. "I mean, I appreciate the intent behind them, but eight so-called dates in the last year and I'm done."

"Eight? Really?" Jan raised her eyebrows. "It's been that many?"

"Yes."

"Wow. No wonder you said you were done with exchanging histories and all that."

"When did I say that?"

"Before you went to Fran and Todd's."

"Right." Ginny nodded. "Well, I meant it then and I mean it now. When the one year anniversary of George's death passed, it was like open season." She shook her head. "And, before you say it, I know many widows get left behind and forgotten, so I realize I'm one of the fortunate few who has people who care. *But*, that being said...."

"Time to move onto *other* things, I think."

Ginny straightened up in her chair. "Intriguing. Any ideas?"

"Something fun." Jan threw off the blue blanket and sat up. "Something new. Something you and George never did, so we can feel you've really started taking steps into a new life."

Ginny nodded, thoughtful.

Jan saw the expression on her face and added, "I hope that sounds okay? I don't mean we're forgetting about George, just—"

"No, no." Ginny waved away her explanation while Martini jumped deftly onto the arm of her chair and stretched out to catch the rays of sunshine warming the fabric. "I get it. And that can't happen, anyway. We were married for nearly forty years. He's always going to be a part of me and my history. The therapist really helped me with that, too. She helped me come to terms with the fact that I can't stop time and I can't shut down and stop living. It doesn't work that way. The only way to move forward is to acknowledge and celebrate my past while living fully in the present, until it's my time to go. I sincerely think that's the way George would have wanted it, too."

Jan looked at her with admiration and affection. "Have I told you recently how proud I am of you?"

Ginny matched Jan's grin with her own and reached out to stroke the cat. "So, what new things do you have in mind?"

**\*\*\*\***

# Ginny's Lazy Sunday Morning Banana Chocolate Chip Muffins

## Ingredients

⅔ cup mashed bananas
⅔ cup brown sugar
⅔ cup Miracle Whip dressing
1⅓ teaspoons vanilla
1⅓ cups whole wheat flour
Dash of cinnamon
1⅓ teaspoons baking soda
⅓ teaspoon salt
½ cup chocolate chips

## Directions

Preheat oven to 375 degrees F.

o   Grease a 12 cup muffin tin.
o   Mix together mashed bananas, sugar, Miracle Whip and vanilla.
o   In a separate bowl, combine dry ingredients.
o   Blend dry ingredients and chocolate chips into banana mixture.
o   Distribute the batter evenly between the 12 muffin cups.
o   Bake for approximately 9 minutes, or until the tops turn golden brown and the tester in the center of the muffins comes out clean.
o   Turn out onto cooling rack.

# Chapter Three

Ginny sat on the smooth cobblestone path that meandered around her house - her backside cushioned by a green, foam pad - deadheading the gold, fuchsia and orange zinnias growing in one of her many flower gardens. It was a welcoming afternoon, the sky a soft powder blue, the valley breeze warm and sweet smelling; perfect for puttering in the backyard and visiting with family.

Ginny examined the fragrant blooms, picking and choosing which to leave and which to prune, while the murmured conversation of her adult children and sing-song voices of her young grandchildren playing across the yard blended together to wash over her in a gentle, harmonious cascade. Heavenly.

"I don't know how you do it," Kimberly remarked, shaking her head.

"Do what, dear?" Ginny shifted her gaze from her flowers to her daughter-in-law perched on a wicker lounge chair on the patio, a few feet to her right.

Kimberly gestured with a manicured hand toward the prolific plants decorating the backyard. "Keep all of these plants alive."

Ginny looked out at her self-created oasis and smiled with pleasure.

"It's like you have your own nursery out here," she elaborated, while keeping one eye on her busy, tow-headed two year old, Layla. "I don't know how you keep up with it all."

"Oh, well..." Ginny shrugged and dropped flower clippings into a yellow bucket at her side.

Layla, oblivious of her mother's close scrutiny, looked up from her brightly colored toys and fastened her gaze upon the yellow bucket.

"What's that one?" Kimberly asked, tucking a strand of her long blonde hair behind one ear.

Ginny paused, pruning shears held aloft, and looked at the plant she was pointing to with a slim finger; its delicate pink-red blooms bright and cheerful against its green stems.

"Red-Flowering Currant," she said, smiling.

Layla dropped a green stacking ring clutched in her chubby fist and it bounced once on the patio stones before going still beside her feet. She took a step toward the bucket.

"And those?" Kimberly nodded toward a set of pale blue lilies, their anthers a bright yellow, growing between slabs of limestone in a flowerbed a few feet away.

"Wild Hyacinth. Aren't they beautiful?"

"And those?" She kept going, while sitting forward and readying herself for her daughter's next move.

"Those!" Layla parroted, taking another step toward the bucket.

Ginny laughed affectionately at her blue-eyed granddaughter then asked, "Which ones? The Pink Fawn Lilies next to the pond? Or the Snow-in-summer around the hedges?"

"Either of them," Kimberly replied, before the jarring metallic screech of a blue jay rang sharply from one of the yard's thickly leafed maple trees.

Layla stopped in her tracks, her tiny toes peeking from the top edges of her white sandals, and turned her head back and forth, eager to discover the sound's source. Kimberly took swift advantage of the diversion and picked up a red-haired rag doll from the adjacent lounge chair and shook it invitingly. Layla grinned and executed an about-face, her hands outstretched as she retreated from the bucket toward the doll.

Kimberly, silently grateful to the blue jay for its inadvertent assistance, placed the soft toy into her daughter's embrace then continued her inquiry by pointing to an expanse of ground cover nestled around two large clay pots a few feet away. "How about those ones over there?"

Ginny's face lit up. "Oh, those are just wonderful. Look at their colors. The reddish-brown and the pale yellow; gorgeous. They're called Monkey Face Orchids."

"Monkey Face Orchids?" Kimberly repeated, disbelievingly. "Come on. Are you making that up?"

Ginny laughed and slipped her shears into a pocket on the canvass gardening bag sitting next to the bucket. "Well, okay, that's not their official name, but they've been coined that because their blooms actually look like little monkey faces. Have a look for yourself, if you want."

Grace, Ginny's granddaughter from her own daughter, Jennifer, overheard the comment and piped up, "Monkey faces? Where, Gramma?"

Ginny looked across the yard and smiled at her adoringly. At just eight years old, Grace was so inquisitive and eager to learn. It seemed no matter what information was offered, she took it all in. Ginny had started teaching her to bake - and not just performing the small stuff of mixing, but the actual tasks of measuring and egg cracking - and she'd taken to it like a natural.

"In the flowerbed," Ginny told her, delighted when she ran across the lush, green lawn, her long dark hair flying behind her like a cape, to see for herself. Perhaps, Ginny thought, she'd have to introduce her to the real stuff of gardening soon, too.

"Where?" Grace asked, her brown eyes alert and curious.

Ginny pointed at the lilies. "Right there. Have a look."

Layla, having watched Grace streak across the yard, stood up. "Me look!" she said, excitedly, her blonde hair flashing in the sunlight in the same manner as her mother's.

Grace walked over to her and crouched down. "Do you want to see the flowers, too, Layla?"

"See flowers," Layla repeated, before gently patting Grace's shoulder.

Ginny felt her heart might just melt right there, they were so sweet. It seemed like only yesterday Grace was that tiny.

"Is it okay, Auntie Kim?" Grace asked.

Kimberly smiled at her niece then nodded. "Just make sure she doesn't try to grab them, she's quick."

Grace took Layla's hand and slowly walked her over to the flowerbed.

"Well?" Ginny asked, when they'd had a look.

Grace turned around, her young face lit up. "They DO look like monkey faces, Gramma!"

"Mommy face!" Layla announced, proudly, making Grace immediately dissolve into giggles.

"*Monkey*, Layla," she said, around her giggles. "Not Mommy."

"Mommy," Layla repeated, not understanding, but thoroughly enjoying her cousin's merriment.

Grace continued to snigger while Kimberly asked, "Do they really look like monkeys?"

"Really, Auntie Kim," Grace insisted, catching her breath. "You should look, too."

Layla clapped her hands rhythmically and chanted, "Mommy, mommy, mommy," under her breath.

"Do you want to show Mason?" Ginny asked, referring to Grace's brother, younger by three years.

Grace didn't need any more encouragement. She kissed Layla's soft cheek then tore back across the grass in her bare feet to share the news with Mason; swinging happily on the sturdy wooden swing-set under the tall maple tree.

Ginny cherished both the swing-set and the neighboring strawberry-red playhouse with its cobalt blue trim and white, shingled roof. The memory of George building them when Grace had been just four and Mason a year old was one she held close to her heart. Every detail and lick of paint had been a labor of love. And with the reality being the children would only ever remember their Grandfather by the stories they heard - maybe Grace had been old enough to hold a small memory or two - it gave her rich pleasure that something tangible of George lived on after him.

"Come to Mama," Kimberly called to Layla, before shifting in her seat and squinting into the bright sunlight.

Layla looked torn between returning to her mother or beetling across the yard after Grace.

"I have snacks," Kimberly bribed.

The bribe worked. Layla toddled back over to the patio.

"What about those white flowers with the yellow centers?" Kimberly picked up the thread of her inquiry, while retrieving a bag of animal crackers from the small table next to the lounger. "They're really pretty."

Ginny pulled her gaze from the kids and looked at the blooms she was indicating. "Evening Primrose. They smell so sweet at night and, fun fact, they can be used medicinally."

"Really?"

"Uh-huh. Great for women hitting menopause." Ginny grinned and added, teasingly, "Not that you need to know that quite yet."

Kimberly, barely thirty one, returned the smile and shook her head. "No. But I'll have to remember to ask you again when that time comes around."

"Cookie," Layla said, taking the animal cracker Kimberly offered her from the bag.

"That's a tiger," she said, referring to the shape of the cracker her daughter was stuffing into her mouth. "Tiger, tiger, tiger."

Layla chewed and tried to mimic the sound. "Grrrr-grrrr."

Kimberly grimaced when cookie crumbs sprayed from Layla's mouth.

"You're actually lucky to see the Primrose," Ginny offered, as Grace returned with Mason to check out the charm of the Orchids. "They bloom and wither in just one day and those ones are on their way out."

"Honestly?" Kimberly's face was incredulous. "So that means they won't be here tomorrow?"

"No, not *those* ones anyway. More will bloom, but those will be shot."

"Wow." Kimberly shook her head and regarded Ginny, respect visible in her eyes. "You must really like them to watch them come and go so fast. And I can't believe you know the name of every single plant out here."

"It's all a labor of love," she said, adjusting the ruched, beige Tilley hat she'd grabbed from a hook at her backdoor to protect her head from the afternoon sunshine.

"Seriously, though. I still don't know how you manage to keep up with it all."

"Well, they're all native to Boxwood Hills, which helps immensely."

"Cool flowers, Gramma," Mason announced, before grabbing Grace's hand and the two of them skipped back across the lush lawn to resume swinging.

Ginny watched them go, tickled by their sweetness. Jennifer and her husband, Chris, were doing an admiral job with their children.

Kimberly exhaled a small sigh, before handing Layla another cracker.

"And, more importantly," Ginny added, hoping to gently quell the mounting discontent rounding her daughter-in-law's shoulders. "I'm not a young parent anymore running around after little kids. *That* can have a tendency to put a dent in the spare time available in a person's day, go figure."

Eric overheard his mother's remark and chuckled as he crossed the flagstone patio to join them. "I don't know, Mom. I think you might be stretching. I recall a lot of flowers being around when we were kids, you didn't miss a beat."

Ginny caught the glare Kimberly shot at him and quickly mediated. "Well, thank you, dear. And, I suppose you're right, I always had flowers. *But*," she quickly clarified, when Kimberly looked even more offended, "you must also remember the weeds kept up their assault just as well."

"Oh, I remember." His mouth twisted into a smirk. "You used to pay us to pull them."

Ginny grinned, recalling the bribes she'd offered her three offspring to elicit their help.

"A dollar went a lot farther in those days," he added, his face wistful.

"Anyway, the simple fact is, keeping an orderly garden is something for us older gals to do. You young things have so much on your plates these days, you make my generation look lazy. The chauffeuring alone is amazing! In my day, you recall, the kids walked or rode their bikes to get around. I find it a wonder you can get it all done and still have any energy left at all."

"Yeah, my bike got a lot of mileage, that's for sure," Eric agreed, leaning down to tickle Layla's leg. She shot him a cookie laced grin as he flopped into the matching wicker lounger adjacent to Kimberly's. He gazed out at the green mountain landscape that surrounded the valley, his expression nostalgic. "Do you remember it? Green and black, I thought it was so slick. And Brian was always stating his case for why I should give it to him and buy a new one, which made it even more valuable of course."

Kimberly's face softened as he reminisced about his brother and his childhood, and Ginny exhaled in relief. Clearly the correct cord had been struck to put an end to any possible hurt feelings.

Kimberly pointed at a purple and pink diaper bag leaning against the end of the lounger. "Hon, can you get Layla's red sippy-cup for me?"

Eric sat up and reached into the bag, fishing around.

"Side pocket," she coached, before adding, "it *is* time consuming, taking care of a family singlehandedly. More so than I ever would have imagined." She kept silent about her other observation. The tedium. Performing the same tasks over and over again, day in and day out, was a challenge to her sanity she hadn't anticipated at all.

Eric pulled the red, plastic cup from the side pocket as instructed and reserved comment. He wasn't touching her statement with a ten foot pole. Kimberly often *remarked* about the stresses of taking care of their home life and he'd discovered, from first-hand experience, there was no response that would do anything but get him in hot water. Forget positive encouragement, or helpful solutions; silence was the best defense.

Ginny nodded. "I remember. Some days were so busy it felt as though I'd barely gotten out of bed and then, bam, it was time to prepare dinner."

"Exactly!" Kimberly shot Eric a smug look before holding out her arms in invitation to Layla.

Eric watched his daughter climb into her lap and continued to keep his mouth shut, refusing to be baited.

Poor Kimberly, Ginny thought. Instead of relaxing and enjoying her time with her daughter - which would fly by so fast she'd be flabbergasted - she often seemed compelled by the driving need to prove she was doing an actual job. She tried to help some more.

"I even remember a few times where I was tempted to just pour cereal into bowls for dinner."

"But, you didn't?" Kimberly handed Layla her sippy-cup.

"No. But, pretty close. Instead, I cut myself some slack and found a happy medium by making pancakes and bacon."

"Breakfast for dinner," Eric remembered, nodding. "We loved that."

Kimberly grinned and smoothed the skirt on Layla's purple sundress. "Smart. I'll have to remember that tip."

"So, I've heard a rumor," Eric offered, amusement lacing his words.

"Rumor?" Kimberly repeated, while Ginny raised an eyebrow. "About what?"

"About Mom," he clarified, as he leaned back and stretched his long, muscular legs along the length of the lounger.

"Me?" Ginny said, wide-eyed. "What about me?"

"Word around the yard is you had a hot date last Friday."

"Around the yard?" Kimberly echoed.

"Oh, for pity's sake," Ginny said, waving his words away and returning to her pruning. "Ignore him."

"Date," Layla mimicked, holding her cup upside down and shaking it.

Kimberly, forgetting the cup was spill proof, reflexively braced herself for water to rain down from the spout.

"Of course, I'm not at liberty to reveal my source," he teased, tapping the side of his nose.

"I don't understand," Kimberly said, while miming at Layla to turn her cup back to an upright position.

Ginny glanced at her son over her pruning shears. With his black hair and dark eyes, strong jaw and broad shoulders, he was the spitting image of his father at that age. "Well, you can tell your *source* to stop pulling your leg."

"Seriously," Kimberly said, her jaw tightening. "What are you guys talking about?"

"I don't know, Mom," Eric offered, a cheeky grin curving his lips as he bypassed Kimberly's questions. "She, or rather, my *source* seemed *pretty certain*—"

"Jennifer!" Ginny interrupted him to admonish her daughter. "Quit telling tales to your brother!"

Eric cracked up, slapping his thigh in his amusement.

Kimberly looked at him, her face twisted in annoyance, and said, "What tales? What haven't you told me?"

Jennifer, situated by the barbecue in the shade of the wooden pergola, turned around and echoed Kimberly. "What tales?"

Ginny pointed an accusing finger across the patio. "Hot date, indeed!"

"Date!" Layla said, a second time, then dropped her cup into her lap and turned her focus to her shoes.

Comprehension dawned on Jennifer's face and her laughter blended with Eric's.

Chris, Jennifer's husband, chuckled under his breath as he continued to flip the burgers on the grill. She'd told him all about Ginny's fiasco at Fran's house.

Ginny rolled her eyes at the pair of them then gave in and snickered as well.

"What's a hot date?" Mason asked. He was a mini version of Chris; hazel-eyed with sandy blonde hair and a smile to light up a room.

"It means they like each other." Grace, standing behind him and pushing him on the swing, offered her knowledge in a voice much more worldly than her eight years. She not only looked like Jennifer at that age, but sounded like her as well.

Jennifer laughed harder.

"That's right, isn't it, Daddy?" Grace queried, while the sweet, lilac scented breeze lifted the ends of her hair, making them dance.

"You bet, sunshine," Chris replied, doing his best to keep a straight face for Ginny's sake.

"Do you like someone, Grandma?" Mason asked, his voice thoughtful as he swung forward and back on the green seat suspended securely by thick, plastic covered chains.

"Only as a friend," Jennifer said, on Ginny's behalf.

Ginny raised her hands in mock surrender and went back to her flowers. The conversation was out of her control.

Mason's brow furrowed, making him look momentarily like his former three year old self as compared to his now five year old self, and he muttered under his breath, "What other way *is* there?"

"I don't know what's so funny," Kimberly remarked, by-passing her nephew's comment in much the same manner Eric had her questions.

"We're just teasing." Eric ran his fingers through his wavy hair, his bicep flexing beneath the cloth of his black t-shirt.

"Because you find it so amusing?" She plopped a pink sunhat on Layla's head then released her from her grasp.

Layla slide down from the chair, expertly flipped her white sandals from her feet and charged toward her older cousins, her bare soles slapping against the flagstones with each step.

"It was a fix-up that went south," Eric elaborated, noting the confrontation in her tone. "And Mom knows we're just teasing."

Kimberly rose from the lounger, picked up Layla's sandals in one hand, then smoothed her tan shorts over her slim hips and straightened her copper colored, empire-waist top. "Well, I have to be honest. I find the whole thing off-putting. It's all in *very* bad taste."

Not pleased with her sister-in-law's judgmental tone, Jen's face twisted in irritation. She adjusted the green scrunchie holding her dark hair at the base of her neck and asked, "Bad taste? What does *that* mean?"

"I just think," Kimberly told her, "in light of the *circumstances*, your Mom's so-called friends might have some consideration for her condition."

Ginny's eyebrows lifted in surprise. She had a condition?

"Condition?" Jennifer repeated, her eyebrows mirroring Ginny's. "Mom has a *condition*?"

"What's a condition?" Mason asked, trying to catch the eye of one of the grown-ups.

"Well, of *course*," Kimberly replied, talking over him, her voice scornful as she placed Layla's tiny white shoes next to the diaper bag.

Uh-oh, Ginny thought, unsettled by the mounting tension permeating the air.

Jennifer left Chris' side and walked across the patio to the lawn, jaw set in a firm line. "Do you care to enlighten us as to what that condition is, exactly?"

Ginny, despite her immediate desire to pat things down, had to admit she too was curious as to what Kimberly believed.

Kimberly strode across the flagstones to stand a couple of feet from Jennifer. "Oh, come *on*, I can't be the only one who knows it, surely," she said, watching Mason jump off the swing to join Grace and Layla in the shade of the maple tree.

"Apparently, you are," Jennifer stated, folding her arms tightly across her chest as she faced her sister-in-law.

Ginny stood up and brushed the knees of her jeans. She walked over to the lounger Kimberly had vacated and sat down, the floral patterned cushion releasing a soft whooshing sound beneath her bottom.

Eric turned and grinned at her.

"It was the *cushion*, you goofball," she said, before jerking her chin toward Jennifer and Kimberly and adding, quietly, "You may need to run interference there."

He nodded. "I'm ready."

Kimberly put her hands on her hips, her face incredulous as she looked at Jennifer. "Oh, for goodness sake. Well, it's *obvious,* isn't it? She's still in mourning. And she's going to be for a long, long, while. It's only natural."

"What's Grandma doing in the morning?" Mason asked, as he settled back into the soft, freshly mowed grass and moved his legs and arms as though making lawn angels.

"I'll explain it all to you later," Chris told him.

Mason nodded, recognizing the keep-out-of-it undercurrent in his father's tone.

Jennifer frowned. "Mourning? Get real. It's been almost two years since Dad passed—"

"*I'd* say it's *not even been* two years," Kimberly interrupted, her face flushing and her voice accusing. "And, does that mean you're saying you'd be ready to just forget about Chris less than two years after he passed away? Easy come, easy go?"

Chris looked up from the barbecue. "Keep me out of it."

Ginny caught her breath. She'd had no idea Kimberly held such strong opinions about any of this. In all the time that had passed since George's death, she'd never once voiced them - granted, no one had ever mentioned hot dates before, either - and the information was coming out of left field. Ginny might have expected such feelings from her three offspring, but *this*, well she was frantically trying to get her bearings before things got really out of hand.

Kimberly turned on Chris. "So, does that mean *you're* telling me it wouldn't bother you to know that Jen was out canoodling with strange men less than two years after your death?"

"*Canoodling?*" Jennifer repeated, pulling the focus away from her husband. He shot her a grateful look.

"That's what I said," Kimberly stated, folding her arms tightly across her chest.

"It was a blind date for *dinner*, for goodness sake, and they weren't even alone. And who said anything about canoodling? Except maybe one of *The Golden Girls* in the eighties. Mom's not exactly Blanche Devereaux."

While Chris flipped burgers and chuckled at his wife's remark, Ginny reached over and nudged Eric. Hard.

He understood and quickly got to his feet. "Hey, hey," he said, raising his hands in surrender while nearly sprinting across the patio. "Come on now, Kim. There's no way Jen is saying Mom would, or should, forget about Dad."

"Of course not!" Jennifer's nostrils flared.

Kimberly shrugged and gave her sister-in-law the up-down. "Sounded like it," she said, her eyes tripping over Jennifer's red t-shirt then resting on her ripped, jean shorts.

Jennifer's eyebrows shot up.

"*Kim*," Eric said, grimacing at his wife's confrontational tone. He was starting to feel like a man trying to bail a large sinking ship with only a small bucket.

She visibly stiffened. "*What?*"

"Wait," Ginny called out, as she stood up and crossed the patio as swiftly as she could, saving Eric from his clumsy attempt to redirect the situation.

His face was almost comical, he was so visibly relieved she'd spoken up.

Ginny eased her body forward, to stand between the two women. She placed a hand on Kimberly's shoulder and looked directly into her eyes, hoping she'd see her sincerity. "Before we have any further misunderstanding, you need to know that Jenny is one hundred percent aware her father will always be a part of my heart. Always."

"Clearly," Jennifer said, her jaw stiff.

Kimberly shot her a skeptical look, but kept quiet.

Ginny placed her other hand on Jennifer's shoulder and squeezed it gently. "She cares more than you know that I'm happy and not lonely."

"Well, there's no fear of *that*, obviously," Kimberly said, her usually pretty face muted by smugness. "*We* gave you Martini and he's the perfect housemate and companion."

Ginny blinked. Good lord. How was she going to redirect that comment?

Jennifer rolled her brown eyes, refusing to take the bait. Instead, she patted her mother's hand affectionately then turned toward Chris, still tending the barbecue, and said, "It's starting to smell like charred meat. Are those burgers and dogs about ready?"

He grinned, pushed his glasses up on his face and nodded. "You bet. Grab your plates and let's eat."

\*\*\*\*

"Out like a light," Eric announced of his daughter, while strolling past the kitchen into the adjacent family room.

Kimberly, putting away the last of the supper dishes, sighed with pleasure; it was one of her favorite times of the day.

"She sure loves that book," Eric commented, settling himself on the tan sofa across from the big screen TV.

"The one about the little bear?"

"Yeah," he said, a smile curving his lips. "I read it to her three times before she finally fell asleep."

"Mmm," Kimberly murmured, while observing with satisfaction her freshly cleaned kitchen.

"And she gets so excited, even though she knows what's coming next."

Kimberly nodded, distracted by the wave of contentment washing over her as she reveled in the gleaming stainless steel appliances, spotless beige and black-flecked quartz countertop and the crumb-free, blonde hardwood floor.

After a day of barely controlled chaos, everything was back in its place; it was times like this that made her wistful for the days she'd spent managing the art gallery before Layla was born. There, she'd had complete control and ran the place like a Swiss timepiece. Not an item out of place nor a work of art askew. Not one smudge or speck of dust found that wasn't swiftly eradicated. She exhaled as the tension lifted from her shoulders; precision a sweet relief.

Eric yawned, picked up the remote and settled back into the plump sofa cushions.

"I have to say, I still don't get your sister," Kimberly commented, reaching into a small wicker basket on the counter for a pink scrunchie to match her yoga pants and tank top.

Eric paused, remote control pointed at the TV. It has been a long day, Layla was in bed and all he really wanted was to watch the sports wrap-up, *but*.... He put down the remote. He knew she was waiting for a response. "Meaning?"

"*Meaning*," she explained, nearly tripping over his reply, "the fact that she didn't seem to think your Mom being set up on dates by her so-called friends was any sort of big deal, is totally odd."

Eric shrugged.

"That's it? That's all you've got? A shrug?"

Eric took a breath, released it, and ran his fingers through his dark hair. "Didn't Mom talk to you afterward about things? I saw you two talking and I assumed she was explaining she's fine and there's nothing to worry about."

Kimberly waved a hand dismissively before pulling her hair back from her face and securing it with the scrunchie.

"Oh, sure, she said all sorts of placating things to smooth things over. But, in light of the situation, what else could she do? Tell me that I was right and her clueless daughter was out to lunch? Not likely."

Eric swallowed against a groan. He should have gone straight from Layla's bedroom to theirs. He could have watched the wrap-up on his iPad.

"So, tell me then," she went on, turning off the overhead light in the kitchen then walking around the island to join him in the family room. "You honestly have no thoughts about it? No feelings, at all?"

He wanted to say 'no' and end things right then and there. However, he was well aware his wants and the reality of things were at complete odds. A 'no' would just turn the conversation on him, creating critique about his supposed lack of concern. As the saying went, it wasn't his first rodeo.

Kimberly tucked herself into the opposite end of the sofa near his feet and stared at him expectantly; waiting.

Eric cleared his throat then took a breath and said, "I don't know. I guess, if I think about it, I sort of expected it was bound to start happening."

Kimberly frowned. "*Bound* to start happening?"

He nodded.

"I don't follow. *What* was bound to start happening, exactly? You need to elaborate."

"It's like we were saying this afternoon. It's been two years since Dad died—"

"Not quite."

"Close enough," he countered, ignoring her grimace. "And you have to admit, that's a long time for her to be alone."

Kimberly's face softened. "We *did* offer to move to a new house with a granny suite."

"Well, yeah," Eric agreed. "But, it wasn't a realistic idea."

"Why not?"

He looked at her steadily, until she finally shrugged her shoulders. They'd had the discussion over and over again for nearly a half year after his Dad had passed and, at the end of the day, had agreed Ginny was nowhere near being granny suite material.

"Anyway," Eric quickly pressed his point home. "It seems to me, her going out on dates is the next logical step."

Kimberly shook her head. "Okay, *that* I don't agree with."

Eric rubbed a hand across the dark stubble on his chin and sighed. He was ready to wave a white flag if it meant an end to the conversation. "Yeah, you made that very clear."

"And I meant what I said about it being in bad taste," she went on, ignoring him. "I mean, what kinds of friends are these, setting her up with no regard to how it might make her feel?"

"Maybe they've done the same two-years-is-a-long-time-to-be-alone math as we have."

"No." She shook her head, her face twisted as though she'd smelled something putrid. "I think it's more along the lines that they've conveniently forgotten she's a *widow*, not some young chippy in desperate need of dates."

Eric pulled himself upright, adjusted his blue and black checkered flannel pants, and challenged, "I doubt they've forgotten, Kim."

She refused to make eye contact.

"And," he added, building on his premise, "maybe their actions come from caring about her enough to remember she's only sixty two. Not exactly ready for the senior's home."

"Well, maybe—"

"Not to mention, she and my Dad were happy and—"

"Exactly!" she interrupted, her face smug as she grabbed the conversation back. "And that's another reason why I pointed out she's still in mourning."

"*And,*" Eric repeated, determined to finish his point. "*Because* they were happy, Mom knows from personal experience what it's like to be in a good relationship."

"So?" Kimberly shook her head, not following, her ponytail swinging back and forth with the movement.

"*So* - while I don't know for sure about the whole being in mourning idea - I think it makes sense that now she's feeling better she'd want to at least entertain the idea of having that sort of thing in her life again, if she can."

Kimberly folded her arms across her chest and shot him a skeptical look. "Do you think your Dad would agree with you?"

Eric stretched his neck back and forth, buying time to consider her question.

"Not to mention," she pressed, "how would *you* feel about it? The idea of your Mom with another man who's not your Dad. That's gotta make your insides turn over."

Eric sidestepped. "Why are you bringing this up? Why now?"

"Because of your sister!" She shifted sharply on the sofa cushions to face him. "I'm not the bad guy here, you know. And why won't *you* answer the question?"

"Which one?"

"The *first* one. Do you think your Dad would agree with her dating?"

Eric was ready this time and nodded. "I do."

Kimberly exhaled loudly.

"Hear me out," he said, lifting his hand like a traffic cop. "No matter how much I'd like to make it otherwise, my Dad is gone. Nothing is going to bring him back and—"

"So, you're honestly telling me," she cut in, "you think your Dad would be fine with your Mom dating another man? Holding hands with another man?"

Eric opened his mouth to respond, but she kept going.

"*Hugging* another man. *Kissing* another man...." She visibly shuddered. "I'm not going to even *think* about anything else. Gross."

Eric gritted his teeth and ran his fingers through his hair again, making the muscles in his bare chest flex. "Are you done? Do you even want me to finish answering the question *you* asked?"

She nodded, having the decency to look contrite.

"Okay," he said, taking a breath. "I honestly think, if he had the choice, Dad would want Mom to be happy. He loved her. And if that means she eventually finds a new... uhhh, *relationship*, so be it."

Kimberly shot him a knowing look when he stumbled over *relationship* then leaned forward and grabbed the purple fleece blanket lying across the leather ottoman. She draped it across her body and tucked the edge up under her chin.

"Okay, fine. You obviously knew him better than me, so I can't argue, but *I* still think it's gross. And, for the record, if it were *my* Mom I wouldn't be encouraging her to get friendly with strange men at her age. There are a lot of odd-balls out there."

Eric thought of Kim's mother, seventy one years old and, no offence, acting as though she was ninety one and ready for the rocking chair. She and Ginny were polar opposites.

"No, if she was widowed now, the last thing I'd be doing is encouraging her to add another man into the mix to take care of when she'd done that her whole life already with my Dad. I mean, don't get me wrong, I love my Dad, but I'd be supporting her in her hobbies and such things. Things for her."

Eric desperately didn't want to continue the conversation. She had her opinions set. There was nothing left to be said. All he wanted was a moment to relax and watch TV.

Kimberly's laptop pinged and she reached to pick it up from the wooden side-table. "It's probably Kris. She said she'd get in touch when the boys were in bed."

Eric wasn't sure why their preferred method of communication was typing on Facebook, but he wasn't about to ask now. Instead, he silently cheered his sister-in-law for the perfectly timed interruption, picked up the remote and turned his focus to the TV. Much to his relief, the conversation was over.

*****

Jennifer gave a last stroke to her thick hair with a paddle brush then placed the brush on the bathroom countertop. She stretched her neck back and forth, left then right, and sighed. The kids were in bed and the house was finally still. She turned off the overhead light and padded on slippered feet into the adjacent master bedroom.

Chris, stretched across their king-sized bed in blue boxer shorts and a white t-shirt, looked up from his iPad screen. "Hey, cutie, nice jammies," he said, referring to her yellow flowered, pajama shorts and matching tank top.

"What did you think of Kimberly's comments about Mom dating?"

Chris' eyebrows lifted at the bluntness of the question. "I don't know. Which part?"

"All of it." Jennifer shrugged the pink bunny slippers from her feet - a gift from Grace last Mother's Day - then reached for an elastic band on her bedside table. "Because it really bugged me how opinionated she was."

"Kim's never been one to shy away from offering her opinion."

"Oh, believe me, I'm well aware," she huffed, snapping the elastic band around her dark hair, creating a slapdash bun on the top of her head. "But, this time, I thought she was really out of line."

He turned off his iPad, giving her his full attention.

"I mean, seriously, did it not cross her mind to think that Mom might be a bit embarrassed by her holier-than-thou attitude?" She put her hands on her hips and frowned. "Acting as though Mom was doing something illicit and then basically implying I'm an accomplice."

"She did seem pretty put-off about the idea," Chris acknowledged, pulling his glasses from his face and setting them on the nightstand.

"And even that right there," Jennifer said, starting to pace across the beige carpet. "That she would think she has any right to have an opinion about it one way or another."

"True."

"Because, in the end, if Mom feels okay about it, who are we to stick our noses in? It's really none of our business."

"I agree."

Jennifer stopped pacing. "And then, after all that fuss, she barely looked me in the eye for the rest of the afternoon—"

"Your Mom?" Chris interrupted.

"No, Kim."

"Oh." He nodded and moved his iPad to the nightstand beside his glasses. *That* made sense.

Jennifer's brown furrowed. "It was so bloody obvious what she was doing, not to mention just plain childish.

What did she think, that if she gave me the silent treatment I would capitulate and agree I was the bad guy for supporting Mom?"

"If so, she really doesn't know you."

Jennifer smirked. He wasn't wrong.

"I think it just comes down to the fact of her holding some rigid ideas—"

"That's an understatement." A puff of exasperated breath blew sharply from between Jennifer's lips while she shoved back the white comforter on her side of the bed and climbed in.

"And you rocked the boat by speaking out in favor of your Mom's choices."

Jennifer shook her head. "As though she has any idea whatsoever of what it would be like to suddenly be faced with being all alone, the slate wiped clean, and having to create an entirely new future. As though any of us do."

Chris nodded, thoughtful. He'd considered it, on Ginny's behalf, a number of times. And each time he came up with heaps of respect for her strength. His mother-in-law was one strong woman.

"I mean, does she not remember how bad things got with Mom? How far down she went before she came back up?" Jennifer grimaced at the memory and rubbed her eyes. "'Cause *I* do."

Chris nodded, again. He did remember. It had been a rough time, a walking-on-egg-shells sort of time, and wasn't a set of memories he particularly wanted to revisit.

Jennifer adjusted the covers around her torso and leaned back into her pillow. "Anyway, what I really wanted to do was give Kim a firm shake and tell her to be supportive, for God's sake, instead of all high and mighty. I just hope Eric had the balls to tune her in and remind her. Although, knowing my brother, I'm guessing not."

Chris reserved comment. He knew it made Jen crazy, how unwilling Eric was to stand up to Kim for... well, almost everything. He also knew sibling relationships could be tricky, so just supported his wife and did his best to stay out of it. He pulled back his side of the plush, cotton duvet and slid between the smooth, freshly laundered sheets.

The sound of Grace and Mason giggling drifted through their bedroom door from across the hallway.

"To bed!" Jennifer called out, sharply, as she reached over to pick up a bottle of body lotion from her side table.

"We *are*," Grace replied.

"Sure doesn't *sound* like it," Chris remarked, trying to keep the amusement from his voice.

"They had too much of Mom's chocolate cake," Jennifer commented, squeezing lotion from the bottle and rubbing it into her elbows and forearms, the fresh peach scent permeating the air.

"I don't blame them, it was fantastic," Chris said, almost salivating at the memory of the luxuriously rich and fudgy cake melting on his tongue. "We should definitely have the left-overs for breakfast, tomorrow."

"Gracey is just saying goodnight to me, Daddy," Mason offered, from his bedroom.

Chris smiled and called back, "I thought she already said goodnight."

"*And*," Jennifer added, while catching his eye and sharing his wry grin. "*One* goodnight is enough. Grace Virginia, get back to your room please."

"Ooh, both names," Chris said, chuckling softly.

The sound of their daughter's footsteps thumping across the hardwood in the hallway met their ears and they waited.

"Goodnight, family!" Her little girl voice rang out, before she sped into her bedroom.

"Goodnight, Gracey," Mason called back, happily.

"Goodnight *both* of you," Chris replied, laughter threatening to bubble over.

Jennifer whispered, "Who are we, *The Waltons*?"

Chris turned his head and laughed into his pillow.

Once silence returned, Jennifer snuggled into the covers and resumed their conversation. "Mom told me Jan suggested they start doing some fun things. Things she never did with Dad. Shake things up a bit and sort-of do the whole step outside your comfort zone thing."

Chris pulled his face out of his pillow and caught his breath. "That sounds like a great idea."

"I thought so, too," she said, smiling. "She's only sixty two, after all. Plenty of life ahead. She should be finding new things that interest her."

Chris reached out and pulled her toward him, his warm hands sliding beneath her clothes.

Jennifer met his eye and her pulse quickened.

"*I* have an idea of something *we* could do *inside* our comfort zones," he said, an inviting grin on his face.

She started to giggle. "Get the door and the lights," she said, before slipping her tank top over her head.

\*\*\*\*

## *Ginny's Delectable Chocolate Miracle Whip Cake*

### Ingredients
1   cup Miracle Whip
1   cup brown sugar
1   teaspoon vanilla
2   cups whole wheat flour
¼   teaspoon salt
½   cup cocoa powder
1   teaspoon baking soda
1   cup water

### Directions
Preheat oven to 350 degrees F.

o   In a large bowl combine the Miracle Whip and brown sugar, stirring until smooth. Mix in the vanilla.

o   In a separate bowl, mix together the whole wheat flour, salt, cocoa powder and baking soda.

o   Add the flour mixture alternately with the water into the Miracle Whip mixture, beginning and ending with the dry ingredients. (After each addition, blend until smooth.)

o   Bake in a greased 9 x 13 pan, or 9½ inch (10 cup) Bundt pan for 20 to 30 minutes (until tester comes out clean.)

o   If desired, once cake is completely cooled, glaze with vanilla icing sugar glaze.

# Chapter Four

"I'm so glad you enjoyed it," Ginny said, smiling encouragingly at the dark-haired little girl holding her mother's hand in the children's section of the library.

She'd just finished reading *Higgenbloom and the Dancing Grandmas* to a group of young children and Ginny never tired of the sight of their rapt faces as they leaned in to find out how the story would end.

The girl's eyes sparkled in her cherubic face as she said, "I liked the part where we danced with the little bee."

Ginny nodded and tucked her reading glasses into the pocket of her grey cardigan sweater. "Me, too. That's one of my very favorite parts. My grandchildren love it, too."

The book was wonderful and encouraged the kids to get involved in the story. Every time they got up off the carpet and wiggled their small bodies along with *Higgenbloom*, Ginny watched in delight. Of course, she had to dance as well which was another fun perk. A perfect combination of interaction and learning.

"My Granny reads to me, too," the girl informed Ginny, all the while swaying back and forth and making the hem of her yellow cotton dress brush across her knees. "She has hair just like you."

"Isn't that something," Ginny said, amused by the offering.

"Except that *hers* is red colored, not brown and white."

"Jayda!" her mother said, visibly wincing at the comment.

Ginny chuckled to indicate she'd taken no offence. "Your Granny sounds nice, Jayda. You can bring her to story-time anytime you want."

Jayda's mother bent down and placed a hand on her small shoulder as she asked, "Would you like to come again, honey? Maybe next week?"

"With Granny?" Jayda asked, before wiggling from beneath her mother's grasp.

Ginny pressed her lips together to hold back further giggles; the little girl reminded her of days gone by with Jennifer. Inquisitive, independent and never staying still for more than a moment. It was inspiring and, if she remembered correctly, often tiring.

"Maybe," Jayda's mother said, putting into play the tried and true platitude of motherhood.

"Granny is very busy these days," Jayda offered, sagely, her small face grave as she explained to Ginny her mother's reply.

Ginny nodded and continued to try and keep her own face straight. "Right. Of course. That's understandable."

"Yes, she is," her mother agreed, her tone stiff. "But that's quite enough talk about Granny, okay?"

Jayda assessed Ginny's black slacks and oxford shoes and added, "*She* likes to wear pretty skirts and shoes in all different colors."

"Jayda, *please*," her mother said, her face flushing as pink as her t-shirt. "Enough about Granny."

Ginny had to take a slow, steadying breath to keep her laughter from bubbling over. She understood Jayda wasn't being rude, just observing out loud as children so often do.

"I like the stories with puppies, too," Jayda said, heeding her mother's request.

She exhaled in audible relief and Ginny resisted reaching out to pat her arm comfortingly.

"And kittens," Jayda remarked. "I like kittens, too."

"Well, that's just perfect," Ginny told her. "I think next week's story has a puppy *and* a kitten in it."

"Can we borrow the book we read today?"

Ginny's heart warmed at the question. It was always her hope that reading to the children would spark their interest to take it further. "Actually, the book I read today was a digital book."

"That's why it was on your iPad?"

Ginny nodded, impressed. While clearly less than five years old - it was a weekday and if she'd been any older she would have been in school - Jayda was very well spoken.

Jayda turned to her mother. "Can we get that book on your iPad?"

"It's okay if Mommy only wants to borrow paper books," Ginny swiftly interjected. "I just keep that one special, for story-time. You and Mommy can look over there on those shelves and see what else there is to borrow."

Jayda's mother smiled at Ginny, her blue eyes kind, before telling her daughter, "We'll check for it when we get home, Sweetie."

"Sorry about that," Ginny began to apologize as Jayda, satisfied with the reply, wandered over to the rows of books pointed out.

The woman shook her head of blonde curls. "No, no, don't worry. It is a great book. Besides, I'm the one who should be apologizing to you. She's not usually so, umm…"

"No, no," Ginny echoed her and waved her words away. "Don't give it another thought. I have grandchildren, so nothing fazes me; besides children at that age are delightfully frank. It's something I treasure."

"That's very kind," she said, before holding out her hand. "I'm Charlotte, by the way."

Ginny shook the hand she offered and replied, "Ginny. Nice to meet you, Charlotte."

"Jayda is in awe of her grandmother, my husband's Mom," Charlotte began to expound, taking Ginny off guard. "She's in her mid-fifties and wildly inappropriate, so naturally Jayda finds her enthralling."

"Right," Ginny said, at a loss. She wasn't sure what sort of feedback Charlotte was seeking, if at all. It was entirely possible she was just looking for a willing ear.

"She wears clothes that are way too revealing - never-mind how loudly she laughs - it's like she's trying to create a party everywhere she goes." Charlotte rolled her eyes. "Honest to God, she just can't seem to bloody tone it down."

Ginny nodded and thought the woman actually sounded like quite a bit of fun. Watching Charlotte huffing and wringing her hands; however, inspired Ginny to keep her musings to herself. Instead she glanced down at her own clothes, understanding why Jayda had felt compelled to note their glaring *oppositeness* to what she knew from her grandmother.

"Anyway, I won't bore you with the intimate details, but thanks again for being so forgiving of Jayda's frankness. My mother-in-law could use some lessons from someone wiser like you."

Ginny smiled and gave in to the impulse to lightly pat Charlotte's arm, suddenly grateful for her relationship with Kimberly. She knew the in-law relationship could be fraught with difficulties and she felt fortunate she and her daughter-in-law were on pleasant terms.

"Before we go," Charlotte said, adjusting the large, brown handbag across her shoulder. "What was the title of that book again?"

But wait, Ginny thought, suddenly hearing Charlotte's words as though they'd returned in an echo. Did she say 'someone wiser like you'? What did that mean? Was it an indication Charlotte was of the mind that she, Ginny, was much older than Jayda's mid-fifties grandmother? If so, that was unsettling. Not that Ginny cared all that much about age, but still, it was a bit startling to think she might be giving the impression she was a good half-decade older that she was.

"Ginny?"

"Hmm?" Ginny replied, blinking a bit as she registered Charlotte saying her name.

"The book you read to the kids?" Charlotte repeated. "What was the name of it, again?"

"Right. Sorry. Mind was somewhere else. It was *Higgenbloom and the Dancing Grandmas.*"

"I'll have to write it down before we leave, or I'll never remember. My mind is a bit of a sieve these days."

Ginny laughed. "I'll do it for you and leave it at the desk."

"Thank you. And thanks again for listening." She gave a small wave as she went to join her daughter.

Ginny returned the wave just as Tamara strolled into the children's section pushing the returns cart. Instead of rolling the cart past Ginny, she paused beside her and leaned over to whisper in her ear, "He's here, *again*. In the cooking section this time. Did you notice?"

Ginny busied herself with retrieving her iPad from where she'd placed it on one of the yellow, child-sized round tables.

"Don't even try to pretend you didn't hear me," Tamara said, laughter lacing her words as she tucked her hair behind her ears then grabbed a set of DVDs from the cart. "Did you see him, yes or no?"

Ginny frowned. "Who now?" she asked, while pretending to scan the library.

"Oh, get off it," Tamara said, snickering.

"Okay, *fine*," she relented and straightened her cardigan over her white blouse. "I may have noticed. But, in my defense, we don't get a lot of well-dressed men coming in in the middle of the afternoon to look at cookbooks."

"Uh-huh, thought so." Tamara lined the DVDs side by side in a neat row on the shelf.

"Hey," Ginny said, suddenly. "Here's a thought. Maybe he's married."

Tamara turned away from the shelf and stared into Ginny's eyes. "Pardon me?"

"What?" Ginny shrugged and fiddled with the cover on her iPad. "Why the shocked face? It *is* possible, you know."

"Uh-huh," Tamara said, her expression becoming quizzical as she attempted to put the puzzle pieces together as to why Ginny was offering this train of thought into the conversation.

"Maybe he's just on holiday and needed something to occupy his time while his wife is busy."

Tamara folded her arms across her chest. Ahh, now things made sense *and* they confirmed what she'd suspected all along; Ginny *was* curious about the mystery man. Tamara watched her try to straighten an already even row of books and contemplated the importance of the revelation. It was big. Very big. Since George's death, men had been off the table. And now, for the first time since her husband's passing... well, it made sense she'd prefer to believe mystery man could be married instead of just not interested in her.

"Look, Gin," she began, trying to find the right words.

"And, besides, who cares if he is?" Ginny blustered. "Certainly not me. It's not like I have any sort of investment in him. He's a stranger, for goodness sake. And, as I've said, I'm done with dating. Not that he would want to date me! I'm just saying—"

"*Gin*," Tamara said, hoping to halt the stream of consciousness.

"What? It's true." Ginny stopped fake straightening and tried to affect a nonchalant shrug. It came off as more of a twitch. "He *is* a complete stranger."

Tamara sighed. "I feel like we're going in circles. You want to explain to me what's really happening here?"

Ginny took a slightly shaky breath and shook her head. "The truth is, I don't know, exactly."

"Well, then let's move on, shall we?"

Ginny nodded.

"Good." Tamara checked the cart for any other items that belonged in the children's section. She picked up one more DVD before asking, "So, do you think he'll check anything out this time? Or, better yet, be brave enough to approach the desk when you're there?"

"I don't think he's doing it on purpose," Ginny said, referring to the mystery man's previous visits to the library. It was starting to appear as though he timed his checkouts for when she was away from the desk; or at least Tamara thought so.

Tamara gave her a level stare and hiked her red chinos further up her curvy hips.

"*And*," Ginny went on, sliding her focus away to wipe a smudge of dust from her trousers. "Did it ever occur to you to consider the idea *I* was right and he's taken with *you;* thus, waits until I'm out of the picture? He probably just thinks I'm a pleasant old woman who's getting in the way of the gorgeous young thing."

"*Please*." Tamara grabbed hold of the cart handles.

"What? It's very possible he thinks I'm an old woman."

Tamara put her hands on her hips. "Where on Earth is all this coming from?"

Ginny bit her lip. She didn't want to reveal what Charlotte had said.

When Ginny didn't offer a reply, Tamara pressed on. "Anyway, whatever *that's* about is obviously not true as he's clearly he's smitten with you—"

"Smitten?"

Tamara narrowed her eyes. She knew the deflection game. "Nice try."

"What?"

Tamara smirked at the expression of wide-eyed innocence Ginny was attempting to affect and said, "Don't even try to distract me, lady."

"Distract you?"

"We both know you intimidate him so much he's had no choice but to wait until you're busy elsewhere to check out his books. Poor guy."

Ginny laughed; until her chuckles got lodged in her throat when the *poor guy* in question stepped fully into view: still tall, still impeccably dressed and still powerfully masculine. She shook her head. He seemed the least likely example of a *poor guy* intimidated by... anything.

Tamara watched her track his movements and grinned knowingly. "Mark my words," she said, pushing the cart ahead of her as she left the children's section.

****

Jan wrote swiftly with her pen across her yellow notepad, completely focused upon her thoughts to the exclusion of everything else. Thus, when her husband walked into the kitchen and said "Whatchya got there?" she nearly jumped out of her skin.

"Whoa," Darryl said, laying a steadying hand on Jan's shoulder. "Sorry, I thought you heard me come in."

She placed her pen down on the table beside the notepad and shook her head while starting to laugh. "No," she said, between giggles. "I was so absorbed, I heard nothing."

He leaned across her shoulder and began reading the list she'd been creating. "Pottery. Pine needle basket making. Irish cooking. Line dancing. Sushi making. Rock climbing."

Jan watched his face as he tried to put the items on the list together. She knew how logical his mind was - her list would offer him no rhyme or reason - so instead of explaining she let her gaze trail across his features, enjoying the puzzlement that furrowed his brow over his sparkling blue eyes. Regardless of their thirty years of marriage and the laugh lines that had shown up along the way, she always saw the twenty-five year old young man he'd been alongside the amazing man he'd become. Heady stuff.

Darryl stopped reading and scratched his beard. "Okay, I give up. I'm stumped."

Jan laughed. She'd called it. "I'm brainstorming ideas for an outing with Ginny."

"Ahh," he said, a wry grin playing at his lips as he pointed to the next item on the list. "That explains 'drink fruity cocktails'."

She leaned back in her chair and flashed him a cheeky smile. "Gotta have a backup plan in case the others fall through."

He kissed the top of her head then crossed the room to the stainless steel fridge. "What's this all in aid of, anyway?"

"I told Gin it was time we did some different things."

"Different from what?"

"The usual stuff," she said, then made air quotes with her fingers as she added, "Doing the whole 'step outside your comfort zone' kind of thing that seems to be all the rage."

He opened the fridge door and reached inside for a bottle of beer. "Okay, I'll take your word for it. And, for the record, I'd say rock climbing definitely fits the bill."

"Did you know that it's been nearly two years now since George passed away?"

Darryl twisted the cap off his beer bottle, his face growing thoughtful. Had it really been that long? It didn't feel that way.

Jan watched him and nodded. "I know, hard to believe."

He sighed and said, "Time sure flies."

Jan stood up from her seat and walked over to the kitchen's two-tiered island. She reached into a ceramic bowl sitting on the top tier and chose a cornmeal biscuit for herself then held another out to Darryl. "Want one?"

He placed the bottle cap on the countertop, took the pastry she offered and asked, "New recipe?"

"Not mine, Ginny's," she said, before retrieving plates and butter from the cupboard and a knife from the cutlery drawer.

Darryl took a bite and nodded. "The perfect complement to beer."

Jan grinned and placed the plates, butter and knives on the table. "I'll be sure to tell her."

Darryl took a long swallow from the bottle in his hand then said, "Speaking of new stuff, it looks like things are going to go through with the new investor."

"Seriously?" Jan's face lit up as she spread butter on her biscuit.

"Yeah, we'll be signing the papers at the end of the week. The guys are pretty excited. This opens a whole new chapter for us."

"What was his name, again?" she asked, referring to the man who was about to change the work lives of Darryl and his partners.

"Rhodes," he said, placing his beer on the tabletop then pulling out a chair to sit down. "Max Rhodes."

"Right," she said, nodding. "And he likes your ideas for the new development?"

"Loves 'em. There was no haggling over details, just praise for the plans we've made." He popped the last bite of the biscuit into his mouth and added, "It's practically a miracle in the property game."

"Well, clearly he's a smart man and knows a good thing and a great design when he sees it." She snapped her fingers. "Hey, we should celebrate with a special dinner!"

"Absolutely. What are you thinking? Potatoes? Corned beef and cabbage? Steak and kidney pie?"

Jan looked at him in bewilderment.

He grinned and pointed at her list, more directly at option number three: Irish cooking.

Jan smirked then took a large bite out of her biscuit. "Smart ass," she said, around her mouthful.

Darryl, his blue eyes flashing with mirth, lifted his bottle in a small salute. "Sláinte."

\*\*\*\*

Eric grinned as he tapped at the screen on his phone. *Fantastic! Congrats!* he wrote, before sending the text off to his sister.

"Who's that?" Kimberly asked, striding into the kitchen, ponytail swinging back and forth and cleaning paraphernalia clutched in her hands.

Eric looked up from his phone, still smiling. "Jen. She got the promotion! She's now officially the front office manager!"

"Wow," Kimberly said, blinking rapidly and turning away to return the cleaning products to the pantry. She opened the glass-front door and stepped directly inside the small space, focusing on her breathing and working to quell the sudden anger that had risen up inside of her at the mention of Jennifer's success.

Not that she wasn't happy for her sister-in-law. She was. She knew Jennifer had worked hard for the promotion at the hotel, had put in the hours - often having to work night shifts which took her away from the family - and truly deserved the good fortune coming her way. It was just...

"Kim?"

Kimberly arranged the bottles back on the top shelf, smoothed the front of her yellow t-shirt, then plastered a smile across her face as she stepped out of the pantry back into the kitchen.

"Everything okay?"

"That's great news!" she said, sidestepping his inquiry. "She must be so thrilled! I'll text her as well and congratulate her. We'll have to do something to celebrate."

Eric watched as she bustled around the sink, straightening already straight towels and wiping at imaginary spots with a dishcloth, before spinning on her heel to charge out of the room; her eyes slightly wild.

"Okaaay," he said, to the empty kitchen.

****

Tamara picked up the books placed in front of her on the checkout desk of the library and began scanning them one by one. "Did you find everything you were looking for?" she asked, trying to keep the innuendo from her voice as she smiled into the clear green eyes of *mystery man*.

"Yes, thank you." He returned her smile before letting his gaze drift past her, his eyes perusing behind the desk and beyond.

I *knew* it, Tamara thought while she finished scanning. He wasn't interested in her, whatsoever. It was all Ginny, all the time. If only he'd arrived at the desk ten minutes earlier, he would have caught her at the end of her shift and then who knew what might have transpired? She wished she could chastise him, but that was the sort of thing that only happened in movies or novels, not real life.

"Not fair at all," she said, under her breath.

"Pardon?" Mystery man leaned in, questioning.

"Oh, umm, nothing," Tamara stammered, a soft flush rising in her cheeks. "Or, rather, do you have your library card?"

Mystery man smiled kindly and gestured toward where his card lay, beside the books, patiently awaiting her attention.

"Right, of course." Tamara snatched up the card, all business in the face of her embarrassment, and gave it a quick scan before handing it back. "Excellent. All done."

"Thanks," he said, picking up the books.

"Come again!" Tamara blurted, before inwardly cringing at her overly-bright, restaurant hostess tone. What was wrong with her?

He paused a moment, his face puzzled, then gave a small wave while exiting the library. Tamara dropped the hand she held aloft and massaged the bridge of her nose as the echo of her words ricocheted in her head. *Come again.* Really? Had she actually uttered those words to a patron taking books out of the library? Sure, if he'd been *returning* books maybe she could have gotten away with it, but this way her words implied she could be questioning his intentions to return the books he'd just borrowed.

"Excuse me," a patron said, walking up to the desk. "Can you help me a moment? I'm trying to find a few books to take with me when I babysit my grandchildren and am hopelessly out of touch as to what they might like."

"Absolutely," Tamara said, eagerly, grateful to have an excuse to put her buffoonery behind her.

She stepped out from behind the desk and followed the woman toward the Junior Fiction section, all the while going back and forth on whether or not she would share her blundering with Ginny at her next shift.

Probably.

It would give them both a laugh.

\*\*\*\*

## *Ginny's Drop Cornmeal Biscuits*

### Ingredients

1¾ cups whole wheat flour
⅔ cup cornmeal
2 tablespoons brown sugar
1 tablespoon baking powder
½ teaspoon sea salt
½ cup cold butter
1 cup buttermilk

### Directions

Preheat oven to 450 degrees F.

o In a large bowl, combine whole wheat flour, cornmeal, brown sugar, baking powder and salt.

o Cut butter into dry ingredients with a pastry blender or fork until the mixture resembles a course crumble.

o Add buttermilk to mixture and stir until just combined.

o Drop batter by ¼ cupfuls - approx. 1 inch apart - onto a greased baking sheet.

o Bake for 12 to 14 minutes, or until golden brown.

# Chapter Five

"Layla, Layla, bo-bayla, banana-fanna fo-fayla, fee-fi mo-malya, Layla!"

Layla, seated on her multi-colored play mat on the kitchen hardwood floor, chortled as Ginny sang. Her little face was a picture of delight and she clapped her hands while trying to join in. "Banana, nana, nana!"

"Very good!" Ginny, beside her on the mat, cheered and giggled while clapping her hands, too.

She was babysitting for Eric and Kimberly while they went grocery shopping and she was having a great time entertaining her granddaughter. It was the best of all worlds as far as she was concerned; playtime and snacks without having to worry about the mess or cleanup. She got to be the good guy the entire time. It was the same with Jennifer's kids, of course, except for the fact that Grace and Mason were older than Layla now. Instead of simple word games and preschool toys, they were now up for day-trips to museums and sleepovers and camping out in the backyard. She gazed affectionately at her still-tiny granddaughter, happy there were so many more fun things awaiting them on the horizon.

"Gamma, banana-nana!" Layla enthused, practically vibrating in her pink and green, polka-dotted sundress.

Ginny tucked her hair behind her ears and asked, "You want to try Gramma?"

"Now Gamma!"

Ginny grinned. "Okay, here we go. Gramma, Gramma, bo-bamma, banana-fanna fo famma—"

"Fee-fi mo-mamma, GRAMMAAA!" Eric chanted exuberantly, arms spread wide, the grocery bags clutched in his hands swinging back and forth as he and Kimberly walked around the corner and into the kitchen.

Ginny burst out laughing and Layla screeched happily, "Daddy, banana-nana sing!"

"You're all a bunch of crazies," Kimberly teased, grinning as she moved around Eric and lifted the green cloth bags she was carrying, onto the worktop.

"Mmm, that sounds good, actually," Eric commented, adding his four bags to those she had set down.

"What?" Ginny asked, while leaning over to kiss Layla on her soft cheek.

"A banana."

"There are some in the basket," Kimberly said, gesturing to the metal hanging basket next to the kitchen window.

"I think *you* need some juice, after all that singing," Ginny told Layla.

"Juice!" she enthused, springing to her feet.

"Oh, to be so young and move so freely," Ginny commented, as she unfolded her crossed legs and eased herself up from the red and blue mat.

Eric extended a hand. "Need some help there, Mom?"

Ginny took the hand he offered and let him help her up. When she saw the concern flit across his face, she said, "I'm fine. No worries. Just a little stiff from sitting on that foam."

"You can play with her in the family room on the carpet," Eric gently chastised.

"I know," she said, smoothing her jeans and straightening her blouse. "But we get so caught up here with her toys, I forget. It's my own fault."

"Even I feel that way after sitting on it for a while, Ginny," Kimberly commiserated, while pulling items from bags. "So don't feel too badly."

Ginny walked over to the fridge, Layla trailing her. "Those are cute shorts, Kim. They make your legs look sensational."

Kimberly paused, a box of tissues grasped in her hand, and looked down at her toned legs beneath her hunter green shorts. "Thank you," she said, smiling with pleasure.

Ginny opened the fridge door. "Believe me, if I could get away with it, I'd wear the same sort of thing in a heartbeat. Enjoy your youth."

"I don't know, Mom," Eric said, choosing a banana from the bunch in the basket. "I'm pretty sure I recall a number of short skirts you had when I was a kid."

"Oh, I don't think they were *that* short," Ginny said, cheekily, as she reached inside the fridge for Layla's sippy-cup of apple juice.

"That's because the skirts you wore when you and Dad first got together made the skirts you wore when we were kids look long."

"Pishaw!" Ginny said, closing the fridge door. "It was the seventies, everyone wore clothes like that."

"Nana!" Layla said, when she saw Eric peeling the yellow skin from his fruit.

"*Anyway*," Ginny said, closing the fridge door. "That's all in the past now. Only sensible length skirts for this gal, from now on."

Eric chuckled and handed a piece of the banana to Layla. "Right. So, what length constitutes as *sensible*?"

"Eric," Kimberly interrupted, taking the banana peel from him and dropping it into the trash can. "Quit badgering your poor mother."

"I wasn't badgering," Eric defended, before cramming the remainder of the banana into his mouth. "Ribbing, maybe…"

She grimaced at the thickness of his voice around the fruit. "Ugg. And if you're going to stuff, please do us all a favor and finish swallowing before talking."

Ginny handed Layla the sippy-cup. "Here you go, mademoiselle."

"Thank you, Gamma," she replied, grinning up at her.

"Good girl," Kimberly praised, before shooting a look of gratitude at Ginny. "Gramma is so wonderful, encouraging your good manners."

Ginny waved her hand dismissively. "It's nothing. She's so good, she makes it easy."

"It's *not* nothing and I really do appreciate it," Kimberly told her, earnestly. "Every little bit helps and she's so lucky to have *one* of her Grandmother's close by in her life."

Ginny paused, watching Layla put her cup on the floor then toddle off to her toys. "How are your Mom and Dad doing?"

Kimberly stiffened and Ginny's eyes widened. Uh-oh. Wrong question?

"It's been a little while since we've talked to Mike and Judy," Eric stepped in, giving Kimberly a moment to gather herself.

"But, the last time we did, they seemed okay," she added, squaring her shoulders beneath her blue tank-top.

"Busy, as *usual*. Maybe not spending as much time together as one would expect at their age, but that happens when life stuff is demanding."

Ginny kept quiet about the 'their age' comment. Kimberly's mother and father, respectively, were seventy-one and seventy-five years old. They'd had Kimberly and her sister, Kris, later in the game than most and, as such, had doted on the girls during their youth. Now, however, since she and Eric lived in Boxwood Hills and not the city, it had become a thorn in Kimberly's side that they rarely made time to visit. This, of course, Ginny knew via Eric; shared in private confidence during the time when Layla was first born and Kim was feeling completely ignored and overlooked.

"Mom puts so much of herself into her charity work and Dad seems to be out of the house more than he's in it these days. Anyway, they're *fine*."

"Good," Ginny said, still feeling awkward and wrong-footed.

"So," Eric piped up, deftly moving things along, "other than being a singing machine, how was our girl?"

"Perfect, as always," Ginny replied, smoothing her white blouse.

Kimberly dimpled and continued unloading groceries. It was the exact thing she loved to hear.

Eric kicked off his sandals and walked over to Layla; picking her up and swinging her gently through the air.

"Eeeee!" she cheered, her blonde hair standing out from her head from the motion.

"I'm amazed at how fast her speech is coming along," Ginny further complimented.

"I know," Kimberly agreed, opening the fridge. "It seems like every day she adds new words."

Eric began flying Layla around the room, making 'vroom, vroom' noises as they went. She giggled and waggled her bare, pudgy feet.

"Were you an early talker?" Ginny asked, while bending to pick up the sippy-cup from the floor and place it on a plastic, child-sized table tucked in the corner.

"To hear my parents tell it, you'd think so," she replied, rolling her eyes. "They love to tease me that I was giving orders before I could walk without assistance. Apparently, they weren't surprised in the least when I landed my first management position in the art gallery back home."

Ginny chuckled. "Aww, they must have been so proud of you, top of your class and getting hired right out of school."

Kimberly loaded fresh produce into the fridge drawers with military efficiency then closed the door. "They seemed to be, but I'm not doing that anymore, am I?"

"Umm," Ginny mumbled, taken aback by the briskness in her daughter-in-law's tone.

"No, ma'am," Eric said, his tone teasing as he flew Layla past one more time. "Now you manage us with military-like precision."

"Ha, ha," she replied, rolling her eyes. "Yes, that will look great on my resume. Keeps husband's sock sorted and cleans bathrooms like nobody's business."

Ginny swallowed. What was happening? Had she said something wrong? Suddenly she felt as though she was walking through a minefield, unsure of what to say next.

"Anyway," Kimberly said, while Eric gently placed Layla back on the floor to resume playing with her toys. "Life moves on and things change. How about Eric?"

"Yeah, Mom," he said, leaning up against the countertop. "Was I a smarty-pants like Layla, or did Jen talk so much I didn't bother trying to a get a word in edgewise?"

Ginny's mouth twisted into a wry grin and she shook her head. "*Please.* For one, your sister could never *out talk* you. Trust me, you held up your end quite well. And, two, I'd say you talked within the normal time frame expected of children."

"So, that's code for what? I was slow?"

"No!" Ginny chortled. Her son, the funny man. From the time he was little, he couldn't let an opportunity for a laugh get away.

Kimberly chuckled and pointed at the bags. "Come over and put these groceries away. You can say the names of the items out loud if you want to get in some speaking practice."

"Oh, I just remembered," Ginny said, snapping her fingers. "I won't be available on the fifteenth for any babysitting."

Kimberly stopped sorting and raised her eyebrows.

"No problem," Eric said, lifting a box of granola from a bag. "I doubt we have anything planned, anyway, right Kim?"

Kimberly did a quick mental calculation. "That's a Saturday?"

"Uh-huh," Ginny replied. "Jan asked that I keep that day free to have a girl's get together."

Eric walked over to the pantry, asking over his shoulder, "How's Darryl doing?"

"He's good," Ginny replied, while he stepped inside and stacked items on the shelves. "Busy with work."

"Well, that sounds lovely." Kimberly nodded, her face unreadable as she followed behind Eric. "Best friends having some tea time. Very *appropriate*."

Ginny kept quiet. She had a feeling from the heavy hints being dropped, Jan had more in mind than tea.

"As a matter of fact," Kimberly went on, while reaching around Eric for a box of organic animal crackers for Layla. "It makes me think I should call Becca and invite her over. We really should plan some best friend time just for ourselves."

Ginny could hear the tightness in her daughter-in-law's voice and wasn't sure how to read it. Was she miffed about the babysitting, or lack thereof, and hiding it? Or, maybe, she was suspicious there were other, less *appropriate* plans being made and didn't approve? It was a crap shoot and, unless she dug deeper, there was no way to know for certain. She decided to take the easy route, toss away the proverbial shovel and deflect.

"Well, I just wanted to give you notice, in case something came up and you needed a sitter."

"Don't worry about it, Mom," Eric said, gathering up a stack of low fat, high fiber snack foods and tucking them into the pantry as well. They may have been healthier - aka: like eating cardboard - than he preferred, but beggars couldn't be choosers. Kimberly controlled the food that came into the house. End of story.

Kimberly stayed silent while shaking animal crackers from the box into a small, pink plastic bowl.

That's my cue, Ginny thought, checking her watch then picking up her purse from the table.

"You heading out?" Eric asked, before stealing a cracker from the pink bowl.

Kimberly shot him an annoyed look - which he ignored - before smiling politely at Ginny. "Thank you, again, for watching her," she said, before turning her back and carrying the snack over to where Layla was playing. "Every little bit helps."

Ginny kept right on deflecting. "My pleasure, dear," she said, while waving to Layla. "Bye, bye, sweetie. See you soon."

Layla waved then clapped her hands as Kimberly sat down next to her, bowl in hand.

"I'll walk you out," Eric said, following behind her as she made her way from the kitchen toward the front door.

When they'd stepped outside, Ginny turned to him and asked, "Is everything okay?"

"What do you mean?"

Ginny watched his face, saw the surprise flit across his features, and said, "Kim seems a little off."

Eric cleared his throat and Ginny knew she'd hit the mark. She knew his tells and throat clearing was the one that showed up when he was trying to figure out an answer to a tough question.

"Let me rephrase that," she said, trying to help him along. "Is she upset with me, still, about the whole blind date thing?"

Eric sighed and shrugged his shoulders. "To be honest, I'm not sure."

"Seriously?" Now Ginny was the one to look surprised. She hadn't actually expected that to be the case, that had been almost two weeks ago. She was just trying to open the door to conversation if Eric needed to talk.

"No, no," he said, immediately. "I doubt that's it. I mean, admittedly she did bring it up again after the barbecue, but hasn't mentioned it since then."

"So, what then?" Ginny cocked her head.

He shrugged a second time. "I'm not sure, exactly. She's keeping her hand close to her chest. It could be a few things, or just one thing, I don't know for sure. She's not always an easy read."

Ginny reached out and patted his arm. She wished she could fix it, but knew she couldn't.

He smiled, appreciatively. "Don't worry, it'll work itself out. She'll stew for a bit and then she'll come clean. She always does."

"And in the meantime you'll do what? Lay low? Maybe repaint the fence to keep out of sight?"

Eric laughed. He knew she was trying to lighten the mood. "Hey, good idea. I'll be out of the way *and* gain some good husband points."

Ginny grinned. He was a strong man, she knew he's be okay. She leaned over and kissed his cheek before walking down the front path to her car.

"Love you," she called out.

Eric raised his hand in a wave. "Love you, too."

****

Kimberly carried the empty cracker bowl to the sink and rinsed it out, all the while taking deep breaths to calm her inner fuming. She needed to get a grip, quickly. Or, at the very least, figure out why it bugged her so much that Ginny had made plans without consulting them first.

Layla tapped a wooden hammer on a toy xylophone she'd retrieved from her toy box, the tinny notes echoing around the kitchen, and Kimberly sighed. The truth of the matter, if she was to be completely honest, wasn't that Ginny had made plans without so much as a nod toward them - it was *because* she could do so. She had so much freedom and maybe, just maybe, Kimberly felt slightly… envious.

"No," she said, out loud, turning off the tap she suddenly realized she'd left running.

Layla looked up, the wooden hammer held aloft, her eyebrows lifted in surprise. "No?"

Kimberly smoothed her t-shirt and plastered a grin on her face. "No, no, no," she said, softening her voice. "Mommy isn't envious, no, no, no. She's just *concerned* for Gramma."

"Gamma!" Layla sang then waved the hammer through the air.

"Mommy's life is much too busy for envy, right baby-girl?" Kimberly blathered, picking up a dishcloth. "No, it's just that Gramma needs to calm down a bit and act her age and everything will be fine."

Layla dropped the hammer and turned her focus to her sippy-cup of juice, still on the kid's table. She drank from the cup and watched her mother wipe down the already clean countertops. Back and forth, back and forth, as though she was stuck on auto-pilot.

****

"Wait a sec," Chris said, raising a finger to interrupt the conversation he was having with his brother-in-law. "I think they just pulled in."

Brian paused what he'd been saying and picked up his mug from his desk. He took a swallow of coffee then smiled when he could hear Jennifer's and the kid's voices filtering through the mic on his computer.

Chris turned away from the computer sitting on the kitchen table and called out, "Jen, your brother's on Skype."

Jennifer rushed into the room, her face breaking into a large grin when she saw Brian's face on the screen. "Hey!"

"Jenny Bean!" he said, affection lacing his words.

Jennifer laughed, dropped the shopping bags she was carrying onto the floor and sat down in the chair next to Chris. "Three-B," she replied, pulling out his childhood nickname.

Chris chuckled and shook his head at the pair of them. Brian's nickname came from childhood when both Jennifer and Eric had referred to him as baby brother Brian. Naturally, the title was shortened to Three-B and, as things go with siblings, stuck.

Grace and Mason came barreling into the kitchen, ice cream cones in hand.

"Aaah!" Brian bellowed, when he saw them on the screen. "Who are those large, grownup looking children? What has happened to my niece and nephew?"

Jennifer and Chris shared a grin while Grace giggled and licked her cherry ice cream. She was used to her uncle's teasing.

Brian leaned closer to the screen, his face still aghast. "Gracey? Mason? Is that really you?"

Mason, his five year old face earnest, stepped closer to the camera and said, "It's me, Uncle Brian. Honest."

Jennifer bit her lip to keep from chuckling. He was so sincere, it was adorable.

Brian pretended to peer at the camera. "Hmm, it does *sound* like you, Mason, but…"

"It really is!" he said, quickly licking his cone to prevent the chocolate ice cream from dripping onto his hand.

"Okay, prove it. What's my favorite ice cream flavor?" Brian demanded.

Grace whispered to Jennifer and Chris, "That's an easy one."

They nodded.

Mason's face cheered up fast as he replied, "Oreo!"

"Got it in one," Brian said, pretending to high five the camera. "Guess it really is you, buddy."

"Told you," Mason said, shrugging.

"Okay, you two," Jennifer said. "Now that you've said hello, finish those up and go wash your hands and faces. Daddy and I want to talk to Uncle Brian for a moment."

Both children knew their cue. They waved at Brian on the screen and made their way out of the kitchen into the neighboring family room.

"Man," Brian said, shaking his head. "They are seriously getting bigger and bigger every time I see them."

"Then you should get your butt out here and see them *in person* more often," Jennifer said. "The guest room is available anytime."

"I will, soon," he said, placatingly. He knew it had been too long since his last visit home.

"It's been way too long since you've been home," she chastised, as though reading his thoughts.

He ran his fingers through his brown hair, slicking the waves back from his face. "I know, I know."

"So, what's different about you?" Jennifer said, leaning closer to the screen. "You look so sharp."

Chris immediately said, "The beard."

"That's it!" Jennifer exclaimed, pointing. "What happened to the facial scruff?"

Brian rubbed a hand across his clean shaven chin and grinned. "Had to lose it."

Jennifer raised an eyebrow. "Because?"

Brian sighed. He knew his sister. She'd never let up until she had her answer. It had been that way his whole life, so he knew there was no fighting it.

"Well?" Jennifer pressed.

"It wasn't working," he said, shrugging.

Jennifer shared a look with Chris then said, "For *who*?"

Brian was loathe to say it, he knew the reaction he'd get.

"Is it a girl?" Jennifer said, her eyes bright. "Is it? Has a *woman* dared to dictate to mister anti-commitment?"

Brian laughed. God, she was so annoying, yet...

"*Ohmygod*, It IS!" Jennifer clapped her hands and whooped.

Grace and Mason came charging back into the kitchen.

"What's happening, Mom?" Grace asked, while Mason pushed past her to get closer to the table.

"Nothing. Nothing is happening," Brian said, raising his hands like a person trying to control traffic. "Your Mom just needs to calm down."

Jennifer was practically vibrating in her chair. "I will not! This is a very big deal."

"What's a big deal?" Mason asked, putting his face so close to the camera that Brian's view on his screen was all forehead and hair.

Grace pulled her brother back and said, "Mason! We can't see Uncle Brian when you do that."

"Chris," Brian said, pleadingly. "Help a brother out, man."

Chris, sitting on the sidelines, laughed and wrapped his arm around Jennifer's shoulder in mock restraint. "I'll do my best, but I can't guarantee anything."

Jennifer giggled when he tickled her, but still managed to ask, "It is serious? What's her name?"

"Who's name?" Mason asked, looking from one adult to the next.

"I think Uncle Brian has a girlfriend," Grace said, sagely. "Is that right, Mom?"

Jennifer looked at Brian on the screen. "Is that right, Uncle Brian?"

Brian grinned. He was actually glad his secret was out. "Yes. Her name is Paige and it's still early enough that I'm not saying too much so I don't jinx it."

Jennifer stopped squirming in Chris' embrace and, as only couples can do, met his eye to share a *look*. If Brian was saying things like that, it was a very big deal.

"I saw that," Brian said, matter of fact.

"You saw nothing," Jennifer retorted, smiling.

Mason, thoroughly bored, said to Grace, "I'm going back to the game."

"You can go, too," Jennifer said, to her daughter. "If there's any more news, I'll call you."

Grace's face lit up. As much as she was trying to play grownup, she was happy to be released without admitting she, too, was bored by the conversation. "Bye, Uncle Brian," she said, giving a small wave then swiftly following Mason's footsteps out of the room.

"See you soon, Sweetie," he replied.

"So, *Paige*," Jennifer said, leaning her elbows on the tabletop.

"*Never mind*," Brian countered, moving things along. "I want to go back to what I was talking about with Chris before you came in."

"Which was?"

"What's up with Eric?"

Jennifer straightened up in her chair. "What do you mean?"

Brian stroked his naked chin. "I talked to him yesterday and he seemed so…"

"Spineless?"

Brian let out a bark of laughter. "Jeez, Bean, don't pull any punches."

Chris laughed, too.

"What?" she said, wide-eyed. "Admit it, didn't I say what you were thinking?"

"Not quite," Brian clarified, still chuckling. "But, close enough."

"See," Jennifer said, giving Chris a knowing look.

"Hey," he said, raising his hands in surrender then taking a cupcake from a plate on the table. "Keep me out of it."

"So, what happened?" Jennifer asked Brian, turning back to the computer.

Brian ignored her question to stare at Chris. "What are you eating?"

Chris, his mouth full of cream cheese icing, grinned and waved the convection near the camera.

"Forget that," Jennifer said, trying to resume their conversation.

"Oh, man," Brian groaned. "That's one of Mom's cupcakes, isn't it?"

Jennifer sighed and nodded. "Yes. Lemon coconut."

"Awww," Brian whined and slumped back in his chair. "God, if there's one thing I miss, living here, it's her baking."

Chris finished the last of the cupcake in his hand and sighed loudly with satisfaction.

"Yeah, yeah, way to rub it in," Brian accused, smirking.

Chris chuckled and reached for a paper napkin on the table to wipe his hands.

"*Anyway*," Jennifer interrupted, trying again. "You said you spoke to Eric yesterday and…?"

"Right," Brian agreed, then cleared his throat. "It wasn't anything I could directly put my finger on, more like he was sorta off and couldn't have a real conversation."

"How do you mean?"

"Kim kept coming in and interrupting, going on about Mom—"

"What?" Jennifer's brow furrowed. "Mom? What about Mom?"

Chris stood up and left the table to check on the kids.

"Something to do with her being busy, maybe dating," he said, rocking back and forth on the rear legs of his chair. "I don't know all the details, but she seemed pretty bent out of shape about it and he seemed pretty eager to shut the conversation down."

"Oh, for goodness sake!" Jennifer huffed. "Is she still on that?"

"Okay, so there's actually something to it?"

"No. It's nothing. Mom was set up on a blind date a while back—"

"Another one?"

"I know, right?" she said. "Anyway, I don't know if Eric has actually told Kim it's been happening for a while or not, but whatever the case when she found out about it she got all... *Kim* about it."

"What does it have to do with her?"

"Exactly. That's the point, exactly. It has nothing to do with her, whatsoever," Jennifer affirmed.

"Well, whatever her shit is, I don't really care," he said, dismissively. "All I care about is Eric. He acts like he's walking some sort of tight rope around her and can't get a handle on anything. Seriously, it could turn a guy off commitment altogether."

Jennifer's eyes narrowed and she pointed at the screen. "Don't you dare!"

Brian affected the same wide-eyed look of innocence he'd used when they were children. "What?"

"You know *what*. Her name is Paige, you adore her enough to *shave* and we want to meet her. No excuses."

"*Fine*." He laughed and stopped rocking in his chair. "When I think the time is right, I'll bring her out."

"Promise?"

"Promise."

Jennifer nodded, satisfied.

\*\*\*\*

## Ginny's Lemon Coconut Cupcakes

### Ingredients

½ cup butter, softened
1 cup brown sugar
2 free-range eggs
1½ cups whole wheat flour
½ cup shredded, sweetened coconut
4 teaspoons grated lemon rind
1 teaspoon baking powder
¼ teaspoon salt
½ cup milk

### Directions

Preheat oven to 350 degrees F.

o Beat butter and brown sugar in large bowl until fluffy.
o Beat in eggs, one at a time.
o In a separate bowl, mix flour, shredded coconut, lemon rind, baking powder and salt.
o Blend dry ingredients into butter mixture, alternating with milk.
o Divide into 12, greased and floured, muffin cups (or use paper-liners, if desired.)
o Bake for 20 minutes or until tester inserted in the center of cupcakes comes out clean.
o Remove from pan, let cool completely on wire rack.

# *Lemon Cream Cheese Icing*

## Ingredients

2    tablespoons cream cheese, softened
1    tablespoon butter, softened
½    teaspoon grated lemon rind
1½ teaspoons lemon juice
1    cup icing sugar
½    cup shredded, sweetened coconut

## Directions

o   Beat together cream cheese and butter until fluffy.
o   Beat in lemon rind and lemon juice then add icing sugar and whisk until fluffy.
o   Spread icing over each cupcake then dip each into coconut.

Enjoy!

# Chapter Six

Ginny closed and locked her car door then slipped the key fob into the side pocket of her purse. It was a soothing evening - the setting sun still warm and sweetly scented lavender coating the breeze - and she meandered slowly across the parking lot toward the conservatory, allowing herself time to soak it in.

"Lovely," she sighed, gazing at the conservatory with adoring eyes.

Ginny loved the building, plain and simple. A solid piece of architecture constructed from grey granite and adorned with expansive windows and skylights, it was a structure she often imagined would fit seamlessly into an English countryside. It was a treat her gardening club met there once a month, saving her from having to make special trips to visit.

"Gin blossom!"

Ginny paused at the threshold of the conservatory and turned at the sound of her name being shouted across the parking lot.

Dixie, her friend and fellow gardening enthusiast, waved as she strode purposefully across the concrete.

Ginny grinned. Dixie had been there, alongside Jan, during the good, bad and ugly after George's death. While Jan had been her emotional rock when she'd needed a place to rage or cry, or both, Dixie had been the irrepressible spirit who resolutely brought in light and sunshine - not to mention tons of food - and pulled her from her near stupor whether she'd wanted it or not. Ginny held a deep well of gratitude for her vivacious friend and simply adored her.

Dixie charged up the path and enveloped Ginny a hug; her floral perfume gently cloaking them. "I'm not late, am I?"

Ginny squeezed her back. "No, we still have about fifteen minutes."

"Oh, good," she said, hiking her red leather purse up on her shoulder. "The day was crazy and I just finished showing my last house before I hightailed it over."

"Well, you make me feel positively lazy," Ginny teased, as she pulled on the steel handle of the large wood and glass entrance door to the conservatory. "*I* spent the afternoon doing far too much lounging in the shade and not nearly enough weeding in the garden."

Dixie grinned and followed her inside. "Good for you. I would have done the same, if I could have. Although, that being said, the heat worked in my favor. The house I was showing this afternoon made a big impression on my clients because it has central air. Might be a sale there!"

"Wonderful," Ginny said, genuinely pleased. Dixie was fabulous at her job and worked hard for her clients. She deserved every sale. "Say, how's your Mom doing?"

"Great. It turned out her back issue was a sciatica flare up, so I got her over to my chiropractor and now she's back in top form making *me* look lazy."

"Honestly, you'd never guess the woman was seventy eight years old," Ginny commented, shaking her head. "She's an inspiration."

"Don't I know it." Dixie smiled then added, "When I ask her how she's done it, she says, 'Dixie, sweetie, tek whey yuh get tell yu get whey yu want.'"

Ginny started to laugh. Dixie's imitation of her mother's Jamaican accent was spot on. She caught her breath and asked, "Pardon me?"

Dixie chuckled and translated. "'Take what you get until you get what you want.' In a nutshell it means that every opportunity, if used well, can be a stepping stone to manifesting your dreams. It's kept her moving forward with enthusiasm her whole life."

"I love that," Ginny said, grinning. It sounded exactly like something Rose would say.

"I've told her she should write a book," Dixie began, before her breath caught and she pointed across the white marble foyer at a large, nearly overflowing basket of stunning flowers sitting proudly on a round pine table. "Oh-my-god, look at *that*."

"Wow," Ginny exhaled, while her beige, leather ballet flats padding soundlessly alongside the sharp click of Dixie's purple stilettos on the hard floor.

Dixie stopped next to the table and leaned closer to read the card adjacent to the white, wicker basket. "Ahh, of course. Cami put this together."

Ginny nodded. It was obvious, once it was said. Cami, another member of the gardening club, was hugely talented when it came to flower arrangements.

"Look at the shade of purple on those gladiolas," Dixie enthused, slipping her bag from her shoulder and resting it at her feet.

"And the sunflowers are amazing," Ginny agreed. "I didn't know she grew both yellow and red."

"What do you mean? Are you saying these are all from her garden?" Dixie asked, her eyes wide with surprise as she admired the blue tulips and yellow buttercups tucked between the powdery pale lilacs.

Ginny nodded. "I think so."

Dixie exhaled and raised her hands in mock surrender. "Well, she has my respect. I can barely arrange *where* I'm going to plant, let alone put them together to create art."

"I hear that," Ginny said, before gesturing to the open doors of the conference room on their left. "We should get inside, they'll be starting in a few minutes."

Dixie picked up her bag and walked alongside Ginny, her stilettos resuming their sharp tap dance across the hard floors. "I can't believe we have just one more meeting left before summer break," she commented, while waving at a woman across the room.

Club policy stated the summer months and the holiday month of December were filled with too many other activities to make attendance feasible; thus, the break.

"I know, the time seems to be flying by," Ginny agreed, making her way around the rows of folding chairs toward a banquet table at the side of the room offering coffee, tea and pastries.

"Hang on," Dixie said, before striding over to one of the chairs and dropping her purse solidly onto it.

Ginny reached for a packet of Earl Grey tea from a tin on the tabletop while Dixie walked back to join her, her heels announcing her arrival. When she stopped, the silence was startling.

"I think I'm starting to develop a hunch from that thing," she said, picking up a green paper plate and serving herself two large crullers from a pink bakery box.

Ginny opened the tea packet and asked, "Was that Stacey you were waving at when we came in?"

"Yes!" Dixie's eyes grew round. "Can you believe how amazing she looks? It's like the moment she divorced Paul, boom! Gone with the frump!"

Ginny chuckled and kept her voice low. "You're terrible."

Dixie grinned and took a large bite of her pastry. She placed a hand across her mouth so she could speak around it. "I'm only saying what we're both thinking and you know it."

Ginny dropped her teabag into a white takeaway cup then poured hot water over it from a dispenser on the table. "Terrible," she repeated, trying not to laugh.

Dixie swallowed then extended her plate. "Want one? They're really good."

Ginny shook her head. "No thanks. I'm a cake donut gal."

"Right." Dixie nodded, remembering. She'd stumbled across Ginny's affection for chocolate cake donuts after George had passed and they were desperately trying to find something, *anything*, that would tempt her to eat. Turned out cake donuts were a good start.

"So, any plans for the summer besides selling a record number of houses?"

"Nothing set in stone. You?"

Ginny pulled her teabag from her cup and tossed it into a trash can beside the table. "Jan's been adamant we need to start doing a few things out of the ordinary."

"Oooh, that sounds like fun."

Dixie took another large bite out of her cruller and Ginny watched her chew, amused at how trim and fit she was in her dark wash jeans and low-cut, emerald colored top; despite the number of pastries she consumed at every meeting. She defied all calorie counting logic, it was fantastic. Granted, Ginny knew there were many who might find it annoying, but she wasn't one of them. Dixie's joie de vivre was a treat in an often serious, tow-the-line world.

"Hey," she said, suddenly inspired by the obvious question staring her right in the face. "Are you free a week from Saturday?"

Dixie's eyebrows lifted as she considered the question. She swallowed her mouthful of pastry, put her plate down on the table and reached into her pocket for her phone. "Hang on, let me check my calendar."

Ginny lifted her cup and sipped her tea while she waited.

Dixie did some fast tapping on the screen then grinned. "Free as a bird. What's the plan?"

\*\*\*\*

"Thanks so much for watching her," Kimberly said, hitching Layla up on her hip.

Jennifer waved her words away with a flick of her hand and said, "No problem at all. She's so good and the kids love entertaining her. Grace treats her like a living doll."

The truth was, Jennifer had been surprised to receive the phone call from Kimberly, asking if it she could babysit Layla for a few hours while she went to lunch with her best friend. After their last interaction, she wasn't sure where things stood. She was relieved the past was being left in the past and they could move on.

Kimberly's smile was wistful as she shifted Layla from her left to her right side. "I remember being just that way with my little cousins. Little did I know how much work it really is to be the mom."

"I hear that," Jennifer agreed, while picking up a cloth to wipe down the countertop. "I gave her the same snacks as the kids, if that's okay?"

"Oh," Kimberly said, thinking of the carefully prepared snack she'd arranged, still in Layla's bag.

"I was going to give her what you'd packed," Jennifer quickly clarified. "But she looked so forlorn when Grace and Mason had their cookies and juice, I couldn't stand it."

Kimberly's face softened and she nodded understandingly. "Of course, it's fine. You couldn't have had her feeling left out."

Jennifer took a deep breath and released it. Crisis averted.

"Did she like the cookies?" Kimberly asked, before finally giving up on carrying Layla a moment longer and placing her back on the kitchen floor. She'd recently become so squirmy that, unless they were on the move, it was exhausting trying to keep a hold on her.

"She loved them. They were Mom's peanut butter raisin recipe."

"Oh."

Jennifer wasn't sure how to read that '*oh*', so she kept things moving forward. "So, when did she start the disrobing phase?"

Kimberly's eyes widened then she began to splutter, "Oh, god, what did she do?"

"Do, do, do," Layla chattered and spun herself in slow circles, her arms outstretched.

Jennifer couldn't help herself and began to laugh. "It was nothing, really." Kimberly looked anything but convinced, so she added, "Seriously, she only pulled off her shirt..." She sped up when Kimberly's face scrunched up like a used paper bag. "Don't you remember when Mason went through that phase? We could hardly get him out of the house he was so quick at stripping down?"

Kimberly's face became slightly less scrunched and she shrugged her shoulders. "Yeah, sort of..."

"He didn't care where he was," Jennifer further reminded. "And there was that one time - he had to have been around Layla's age - when he managed to pull off his shirt when we were in the grocery store and I had to search through nearly every aisle to find it? You remember me telling that story, right?"

Kimberly, finally appeased, had to giggle at the remembered tale.

Layla stopped spinning and sat down on the tiled floor.

"So, anyway," Jennifer said, "don't worry about it. She'll outgrow it just like he did."

"The sooner the better," Kimberly stated, shaking her head. "And hopefully long before she starts disrobing in public."

Jennifer grinned and crossed her fingers. "Here's hoping."

Grace rounded the corner and interrupted them with a high-pitched squeal of delight. "You're still here!"

Layla clapped her hands at her cousin. "Gray-see!"

"I thought you'd already left. Can we play some more until you go, Auntie Kim?" Grace asked, her brown eyes large and imploring.

Kimberly nodded. "Sure. I'll be just a few minutes."

Grace held out her hand to Layla and she sprang to her feet.

Jennifer paused in her wiping to grin affectionately at the pair of them. "I'm telling you," she said, as they left the room. "Gracey might just want to keep her, so watch out."

"A future babysitter in the making," Kimberly agreed.

Jennifer cocked her head. Kim sounded almost melancholy. "Everything okay?"

Kimberly blinked then gave her blonde hair a shake. "Oh, it's nothing, nothing. It's just sometimes it bugs me that Layla has so little interaction with the rest of her family. At this rate, it feels like my sister's boys aren't even going to remember she's their cousin."

Jennifer tossed the cloth into the sink and nodded, understanding. Kimberly's sister, brother-in-law and their three sons all lived in the city and it was rare for them to visit Boxwood Hills. In fact, wracking her brain, she couldn't remember the last time they'd made the trip.

"Yeah, that's rough. I sometimes feel like that about Brian; that he's missing out on really knowing Grace and Mason. Do you think your sister and family might come out for a visit this summer?"

"Doubtful," Kimberly replied. "Both Kris and Grayson are so busy with work and the boys already have a slew of activities scheduled, so…."

Jennifer could hear the resentment in her words.

"Not that I don't understand, of course," she added, tightly, while bending to check the side pocket on Layla's diaper bag.

"And your parents?" Jennifer asked, hoping for a better response.

"Pfft," Kimberly said, pulling a pink sippy-cup from the pocket. "I'm not sure what's going on there. Dad's been acting out of character, at least according to what Kris has been telling me, which could be something or nothing. Either way, they're barely around to talk on the phone, let alone plan anything."

Jennifer groaned inwardly. Two for two.

"Speaking of which, can I ask you a question?"

"Sure." Jennifer opened the fridge and pulled out a pitcher of iced tea. "Want some?"

"No, thanks," she said, removing the sippy-cup's lid and taking it over to the sink to fill it with water for the drive home. "I'm still stuffed from the restaurant."

"Remind me again where you guys went?"

"Hippie Chicks."

"Right. I've heard good things about that place." Jennifer poured herself a glass of iced tea then returned the jug to the fridge. "How was it?"

"Surprisingly good, actually."

Jennifer took a long swallow of her tea.

"So, anyway, back to my question," Kimberly said, as she placed the cup back in the diaper bag pocket.

"Right." Jennifer placed her glass on the counter and folded her arms across her chest. "What's up? You sound serious."

She nodded and bit her lip, choosing her words.

Jennifer waited, her curiosity piqued.

"It's about your Mom," Kimberly said, finally. "Have you noticed she's been, umm, different lately?"

Jennifer scratched her cheek as she considered the question. "Different how?"

"Nothing bad, per se. Just not her usual self."

"Give me an example."

Kimberly shrugged. "I don't know, maybe I'm reading things that aren't there, but doesn't it seem she's been doing stuff lately that's out of character?"

Jennifer cocked her head, trying to listen with an open mind. "Out of character, how?"

"Well, like the cookies, for instance."

"The cookies?"

"Uh-huh," Kimberly said. "You said you used her recipe, instead of actually *having* cookies she's made and shared."

Jennifer stared at her, stumped. "I don't follow."

"Think about it," Kimberly insisted, hands on her hips. "When is the last time you remember not having some sort of baking on hand that came directly from your Mom's kitchen? Can you remember? 'Cause I can't. She bakes all the time and now, suddenly, you're having to use her recipe to *make* cookies because she hasn't dropped any off? What's that all about?"

"I *do* bake, from time to time," Jennifer told her, levelly.

"Well, I *know that*," Kimberly quickly interjected, "but, I still think it's out of character."

Jennifer shrugged. She didn't want to argue over baking.

"And then, on top of that, there's today. I originally asked her to watch Layla and she just brushed me off." Kimberly's eyes widened as she added, "She's *never* brushed me off. *Ever.*"

Jennifer bit the inside of her cheek to keep from laughing at the expression on her face. She looked so intense it was comical.

"And, before you ask, yes, I'm sure it was a brush-off."

"How do you know?"

"Because, when I asked her *why* she couldn't babysit, she didn't give me anything specific. Just some vague stuff about prior engagements."

"Huh," Jennifer said, trying to wrap her mind around her sister-in-law's comments and subsequent belief she had the right to full disclosure. Wow.

"Has she been doing that to you, too?" Kimberly asked, her face swiftly transforming from intense to fierce as she misinterpreted the lack of an answer to mean agreement.

Jennifer blinked, taken aback by the sudden change of expression and knife-like sharpness of her words. It was slightly terrifying how swiftly Kim could be inspired into no-nonsense rigidity. Had she always been that way? Jennifer wondered. Or was it a more recent development?

"Because if she has," Kimberly went on, gritting her teeth, "I'm definitely sticking it but-good to Eric when we get home."

Jennifer felt a surge of pity for her brother.

"He was so darn insistent I was making a big deal of out nothing," she continued, jabbing her finger in the air. "Acting like I was overreacting when, I now realize from your information, *he* was the one under reacting."

"Oh, well, I don't think… I mean…" Jennifer wracked her brain, trying to find the words to stem the flow of her train of thought.

"Auntie Kim," Grace said, as she and Layla returned to the kitchen.

Kimberly braced herself before slowly turning around. "Oh, thank goodness," she exhaled, relieved to see Layla still fully clothed.

"Layla is thirsty."

Kimberly smiled at her niece. "Thanks, sweetie," she said, reaching into the diaper bag for the cup she'd filled with water.

"You know," Jennifer began, attempting again to offer some calming words about her mother while Kimberly was momentarily distracted from her righteous stance. "I don't think—"

"Goodness is that the time?" Kimberly interrupted, before hiking the diaper bag onto her shoulder. "We should get going."

"Oh, but—"

Kimberly kept on talking, as though Jennifer hadn't uttered a word. "Thank you for being such fun for Layla, Gracey."

"You're welcome." Grace dimpled, then waved to her cousin. "Bye-bye, Layla."

Layla waved her little hand. "Bye, bye."

"And I'm really glad we had this chance to talk, Jen, you've been a big help," Kimberly added, lifting Layla up into her arms. "Eric should be home now. I look forward to cluing him in."

"Oh," Jennifer said, pathetically.

What else was she to say? The train had clearly left the station. All she could do was watch it go, child on one hip and diaper bag flapping alongside.

She swallowed uncomfortably.

Poor Eric.

\*\*\*\*

Jan hung up the phone, a grin decorating her face, as Darryl walked into the bedroom.

"Hey there, smiley, nice legs," he said, enjoying the sight of her sprawled across their red-orange brocade bedspread. "Good news?"

"Great news," she replied, letting the handset she was holding slip from her fingertips onto the adjacent pillow. "Dixie's going to join us on our girl's night."

Darryl laughed and shook his head.

Jan lifted herself onto one elbow. "What? What's with the laugh?"

He shot her an 'are you kidding me' look and she snickered. He was right. Adding Dixie into the mix meant a whole different girl's night out.

"Should I make sure I have bail money handy?" he joked. Sort of.

"I'm telling that you said that," she threatened, leaning back to grab a pillow and throw it at him; narrowly missing him as he ducked behind the closet door.

"Maybe just my bank card," he mused, loudly, remaining hidden from another attack.

Jan laughed and picked up the TV remote from the bedside table. Things were shaping up.

\*\*\*\*

## Ginny's Grandchild Approved Peanut Butter Raisin Cookies

### Ingredients
⅔   cup creamy peanut butter
½   cup butter
1⅔ cups brown sugar
2   eggs
⅔   cup milk
1   teaspoon vanilla
1⅔ cups whole wheat flour
2   teaspoons baking soda
1   cup raisins
⅔   cup chopped peanuts

### Directions
Preheat oven to 350 degrees F.

o   Cream together peanut butter, brown sugar, eggs, milk and vanilla until smooth.
o   In separate bowl, mix whole wheat flour and baking soda.
o   Add dry ingredients to creamed mixture, mix well then add in raisins and peanuts.
o   Drop dough by spoonfuls onto either parchment lined or lightly greased baking sheets.
o   Bake for 12-15 minutes.
o   Transfer baked cookies to rack to cool.

# Chapter Seven

"So, any big plans for tonight?" Eric asked, leaning back in his chair and propping his feet on the desk.

He was in his home office Skyping with Brian and hoped to live vicariously.

Brian grinned from his side of the camera. "Of course. It's Saturday night."

Eric felt a twinge of envy at his brother's blithe attitude. It had been a long time since he'd taken the promise of a night out, no cares to consider except for where to go next, for granted. "You and Paige going out?"

"Yeah, she got us tickets to some sort of interactive play," he said, chuckling.

"Interactive? What does that mean?"

Brian shrugged his shoulders. "Guess I'll find out when we get there."

Eric laughed and shook his head. "Good luck."

Brian leaned forward, his face filling up most of the screen. "How about you and Kim? Is she still stuck on Mom, or has she moved on and you guys are hittin' it old school tonight?"

Eric chuckled at the amusement in his voice. "Yeah, that's *exactly* what we're going to do. We'll be tossing some animal crackers and a bottle in Layla's crib and then we're going to show Boxwood Hills who the real party people are."

Brian snorted. "So, I'd take it that's a solid no?"

"Copy that," Eric said, before yawning widely and stretching his arms above his head. "We've got movie night on tap, after the munchkin goes to bed."

Brian rolled his eyes. "Man, you two better watch out or Mom's going to be stepping out more than you guys."

"Mom doesn't have a toddler."

"Oh, yeah, *that's* a great excuse why a sixty-two year old woman has a better social life than you."

"Fuck off," Eric said, pleasantly.

Brian laughed so hard he started to cough.

"Laugh all you want, party boy," Eric said, before yawning a second time. "But the clock's ticking for you, too."

"Please," Brian replied, dismissing his brother's comments. "I'd say *I* still have a while to go before I start turning into Dad."

"Hey!" Eric protested, nearly falling backward in his chair in his vehemence.

Brian held up his hands in surrender. "Alright, alright, sorry. Low blow. It's just that all the yawning was reminding me of days gone by."

Eric smiled wryly and conceded, "Fair enough."

"But, seriously, Mom's not available to babysit tonight? Isn't she your usual go-to for Layla?"

Eric ran his fingers through his hair and cleared his throat. What to say? Did he reveal Ginny had long informed them she was busy and he was, in fact, correct that Kimberly was *still* put out by her *daring* to have plans of her own? It was bad enough Brian had witnessed her complaining the last time they'd talked, divulging her dog-with-a-bone tendencies wouldn't shine any favorable light her way.

"What?" Brian said, his brow furrowing. "Is there something you haven't told me? Is something wrong with Mom?"

"No, no," Eric assured him, shifting his feet from the desktop back to the floor. "Nothing like that. She's fine."

"Okay, so what then? Does she have another hot date on the agenda or something? Is she someone's sugar-mama?"

Eric laughed then caught his breath when he thought he heard Kimberly coming down the hallway. She often seemed to want to monitor his conversations with Brian. As though she didn't trust them on their own. He leaned over to gently push the door closed.

Brian raised an eyebrow. Eric hadn't been very successful in hiding his flinch.

"No, I haven't heard any sugar-mama rumors. But she does have plans with Jan and Dixie."

"Ahh, *Dixie*," Brian repeated, nodding his approval.

"God, still?" Eric grimaced, referring to his brother's crush. "You know that sounds creepy when you say her name like that, right?"

Brian shot him a cheeky grin. "Hey, say whatever you want, but I'm not blind. She's a serious glass of dark—"

"Stop!" Eric blurted, loudly, before wincing and glancing at the doorway.

"What?" Brian said, his eyes wide on the screen. "It's a compliment. She has a butt you could bounce a quarter off and get change back."

"Seriously, *stop*," Eric interrupted, with a groan.

"*Again*," Brian insisted, "a compliment."

"Yeah, whatever." Eric exhaled then massaged the bridge of his nose.

"Are you telling me you haven't noticed?"

"I'm not *telling you* anything at all," Eric said, making Brian chuckle. Eric ignored him and added, "Seriously, don't let Kim ever hear you say stuff like that, or you'll get an earful."

Brian laughed loudly. He wasn't afraid of his brother's wife.

Eric stole another glance at the doorway, hoping their voices weren't carrying. "Listen, all I can say about their girl's night thing is that Kim's sure it's more of a girly, tea party sort of deal."

Brian smiled wryly and shook his head. "Doubt it."

Eric gave in and chuckled. It was true Dixie was more a grab-life-by-the-reins woman, as opposed to one you'd associate with tea parties and crumpets. It was actually a bit of a wonder to him how she and their Mom had become such solid friends. Sure, they had the gardening club thing in common, but what else? It was a mystery.

"You know, it occurs to me, if Kim's right about what they're doing," Brian offered, his voice teasing, "maybe you guys should have tagged along. You could have brought the animal crackers."

"Oh, sorry, did you not hear me the first time?" Eric returned, with a cheeky grin, and leaned into the camera. "Fuck. Off."

Brian nearly fell off his chair laughing.

\*\*\*\*

"What a fantastic idea this was! Great call!"

Ginny shared a delighted smile with Jan as Dixie and her friend, Gwen, climbed into the back of the black limo. Dixie's exuberance was exactly what was needed to shift the evening into high gear. Truth be told, when she'd asked if she'd be game to join her and Jan on a night out on the town, she wasn't sure how she'd respond. It would have been entirely feasible that, close friends or not, the idea of going out carousing with a sixty-two year old and fifty-six year old respectively, was not her idea of a good time. Apparently; however, at the tender age of forty eight, Dixie not only didn't think them too old for her, but figured Gwen would also be keen.

"I mean, *look* at all of this!" Dixie expounded, as the limo pulled away from the curb.

Gwen pulled a swooning face while she rubbed her hand along the limo's wrap-around seats. "*Ohmygod*, I could sleep here," she said, relishing the soft, buttery feel of the pale leather beneath her fingertips.

Jan laughed appreciatively while Ginny gazed at the interior of the car. They were right, it was something to behold. In addition to the seats, the floor was a dark rosewood so shiny it looked wet. The ceiling was not only mirrored, but lit with deep purple fiber optic lighting. Finally, not to be ignored, there were three TVs set into the walls and a teak, granite-topped, fully stocked bar that ran the length of one side of the car. Pure indulgence.

Dixie's dark eyes flashed with excitement as she bounced up and down on the seats like an enthused child. In the next moment, she lunged forward to start opening and closing doors on the bar console.

Ginny giggled under her breath. It was like watching Grace or Mason with a new toy.

Gwen leaned back with an audible "Ahhh", slipped her cocoa colored mules from her feet and gazed through the privacy glass, relishing the feeling of being cocooned from the night outside.

"Ah-ha!" Dixie declared, pulling a small remote control from a drawer and brandishing it above her head like a prize for them to see.

"Thank you so much for letting me come along," Gwen said, earnestly, looking back and forth between Ginny and Jan. "This is beyond what I expected, clearly there were no expenses spared."

"Jan is the mastermind behind all of it. She gets all the credit," Ginny stated, grinning at Jan.

Dixie placed the remote beside her on the seat and smoothed her short, crimson skirt over her long, shapely legs. She leaned forward, her face curious, and asked, "Do I dare even broach the subject of how much this set you back?"

Jan shrugged her shoulders beneath her raspberry, cowl-neck blouse and shook her head. "You don't want to know. And, besides, when I told Darryl what I wanted to do for Ginny, he was the one who pulled out our credit card and insisted we *'go big or go home'*."

A lump formed in Ginny's throat. The thought of Darryl caring so much was humbling. He was such a good person and he and Jan together were kindness personified. She took quiet, steady breaths to regain her composure. The last thing they needed to deal with was her blubbering.

"Well, you make sure to tell your gorgeous man we appreciate it!" Dixie stated, leaning across Ginny to pat Jan's knee. "You've taken this from a girl's night out, to a woman's night out."

Ginny grinned. She liked that. She settled back into her seat with a sigh and said, "You know, George and I talked about renting a limo, but we never did. He would have been completely wowed by this."

"Well, then we should have a toast to George," Jan said, shifting forward in her seat to open the door of a cooler tucked beneath the bar and pull out a chilled bottle of wine.

"I'll second that," Dixie said, as she picked up the remote and peered at it in the semi-darkness. Gwen gazed over her shoulder while she tentatively pushed buttons on its black surface.

"Need some help?" she asked.

"Hang on, I think…" Dixie began, before she was interrupted by a loud, four-four, bass beat.

Ginny's eyes widened while Jan visibly jumped at the suddenness of the music flooding from the car's hidden speakers.

"Whoa," Gwen said, laughing as Dixie began jabbing frantically at the remote's buttons in an attempt to find the volume control.

Ginny giggled, too, then exhaled with relief when the intensity of the music dropped.

"Whew," Dixie said, slumping back in her seat. "It's too damned dark in here, I couldn't see which buttons did what!"

Jan started laughing. "Welcome to the club."

Dixie wagged a finger at her. "No. No way. It was the darkness and that's that."

"Okay," Jan agreed, biting her lip to keep from laughing.

"And even if it wasn't," Dixie expounded, "which I'm *not* saying, there'll be no glasses for this chick. No way. Laser eye surgery, here I come."

Gwen chortled, fluffed her long blonde curls and said nothing.

"I said the exact same thing when I started needing reading glasses," Ginny commented, while the car hummed along so smoothly they could barely perceive they were moving. "But, you'll note, I still haven't done it."

Jan chose four, ornately cut crystal goblets from the bar and settled them into carved, plushly lined pockets on the granite countertop.

"Yeah, but on you they work," Dixie stated, before adding, "your dress is gorgeous, by the way."

Ginny fingered the black and purple patterned shift dress she'd purchased for their night out. "Are you sure? It's not *too....*"

Dixie cocked her head, her short, auburn hair enhanced by the sapphire blue halter top she was wearing. "Too what?"

"Desperately trying to look young?" Ginny finished, patting at her twisted chignon - which she'd chosen because she thought it would add some youth and lift to her face - embarrassed to voice her thoughts.

"No way!" Gwen said, immediately.

"Hardly!" Dixie agreed. "You're fit and look fresh and ready for fun. Perfect for tonight."

"Told you," Jan said, while she cracked open the wine and began pouring.

Ginny flushed and tried not to fidget. "Okay, okay. Thanks. I needed that."

"Spirits, ladies?" Jan gestured to the waiting glasses.

"Yes, please." Dixie took a glass and lifted it upward to sparkle in the optic lighting.

"These are gorgeous," Gwen breathed, taking the goblet Jan offered.

Ginny watched the colors play off the thick crystal. When Jan had suggested they start doing some fun things, she'd never once thought she'd find herself in a backseat of a luxuriously appointed, chauffeured car. The moment she'd laid eyes on it sitting curb-side in front of her house; however, she'd adopted an *if-you-can't-beat-'em, join-'em* attitude. Adding to the good vibes had been her neighbor, Donna. She'd come flying out of her house when the vehicle had rolled up and began expounding loudly on the impressiveness of the car. She'd even dragged her husband, Douglas, with her and the two of them had made such a fuss it had started the evening off in exactly the right spirits. Ginny sighed, happily. She was lucky she had such good neighbors.

"Gin?" Jan asked, holding out the bottle of wine.

"Hit me," she said, extending her glass. "The night's young."

"And so are we!" Dixie cheered, clinking glasses with Gwen.

\*\*\*\*

Eric stretched and shifted from his back to his side before opening his eyes and realizing he wasn't in bed. He was on the couch in his family room. He blinked a few times in the semi-darkness, noted Kim's absence and sighed.

They'd done it again. Or, rather, *he'd* done it again. Instead of staying awake until the end of the movie and then taking his wife to bed to remind her of the passion they'd shared before Layla had been born, he'd eaten too many ginger snaps and passed out long before the credits had rolled. He'd probably even snored. Some date night.

"Way to go, Casanova," he muttered, throwing off the blanket Kim had left behind and padding into the kitchen for a glass of water.

He drank his water then reached for his mobile on the countertop. One o'clock in the morning, he read on the screen, a grimace twisting his lips. Do you know where your love life is?

He placed his empty glass in the sink, turned on his heel and just as he was reaching to turn out the light over the stove, reconsidered. A vision of Kim's irritated face had appeared in his mind, inspiring him to backtrack, lift the glass out of the sink and gently open the dishwasher to place it in the top rack.

God, when had that happened? Before Layla? After? He wracked his brain, trying to remember when his wife's militant desire for order had become so... obvious. When had it become such a sticking point that the dishes made it to the dishwasher immediately?

He shook his head, too tired to give it much consideration. It didn't really matter, after all, *when* it had started. All that was relevant was he remembered to put his glass in the dishwasher before it became a catalyst for friction.

Padding back into the family room, Eric contemplated his next move. Did he stay on the couch, or try to climb into bed without disturbing Kim? He yawned and decided to risk it; bed it was.

He turned off the one light Kim had left on and in the ensuing darkness his mother flitted across his thoughts. He wondered how her evening had gone. Had she had a good time with Jan and Dixie? What had they done? He smiled at the thought of them having some fun, maybe going to dinner and a movie or some such thing. It was good.

The grin on his face remained as he crept down the hallway to the bedroom. Brian was right, it was rather comical that their mother was starting to have a better social life than him.

\*\*\*\*

"Do you know how much I love you?"

Jan's slurred statement made Ginny's eyes prickle with unshed tears. There they were - standing shoulder to shoulder in an overcrowded country bar at some unknown time of the morning - all because her best friend had decided her happiness was top priority. She was so lucky.

"Now, you may *think* that's the alcohol talking," Jan went on as she swayed unsteadily on her heels.

"No, no," Ginny protested, waving Jan's words away with such vehemence she slapped the broad shouldered young man standing next to her.

He turned toward her, his face intrigued, and Ginny felt a flush of heat rise into her cheeks as Jan nearly fell over giggling.

"I'm sorry!" Ginny blurted, reaching out to rub the shoulder she'd just slapped.

The young man grinned and glanced at her hand on his shoulder and Ginny quickly yanked it back, suddenly aware that what she was doing might be mistaken for of a come-on as opposed to an apology.

"Oh, and I'm sorry for that as well," she rambled, feeling she'd well and truly made a fool of herself.

The young man reached for her hand and looked directly into her eyes. "No need to apologize. It's late and I wouldn't be surprised if I've probably done something tonight to earn a slap."

"You've got that right," the young man's friend agreed, before lifting his bottle of beer in salute to Ginny.

Jan burst out laughing and Ginny couldn't help but join her. When had young men become so confident and charming? Were her own sons this way, too, or at least was Brian?

"Can I buy you ladies a drink as a thank you?" the young man's friend asked, while the young man released Ginny's hand and laughed out loud at his friend's cheek.

"No, no, we're fine," Ginny said, shaking her head and still blushing. "But, thank *you* both so much for being so gracious."

He nodded and winked at her then said, "Have a good night, girls", before he and the young man moved toward the bartender to refresh their beers.

Ginny linked her arm through Jan's and Jan patted her hand, the same one the young man had held while he'd been so sweet.

"Well, that was unexpected," Jan said, chuckling and swaying to the beat of the music thumping through the club.

"And then some. I'm just glad it's so dark in here so, maybe, he couldn't see how embarrassed I was."

"Awe," Jan said, leaning into her. "The flush on your face just brought out your youth and gorgeousness."

Ginny snickered and gave her a gentle nudge with her hip. "Right. Let's go with that."

"Do you remember," Jan asked, "what we were talking about before our encounter with the young, charming brigade?"

Ginny's brow furrowed as she tried to remember. "Oh!" she said, snapping her fingers and turning toward her. "You were saying something about the alcohol not talking."

"Really?" Jan said, puzzled. "Why on Earth would I be talking about alcohol not talking?"

Ginny shrugged her shoulders and thought, now that they were talking about it, maybe they should have taken those young men up on their drink offer.

"Oh!" Jan said, sounding like an echo of Ginny. "No, no, I wasn't talking about *alcohol* talking."

"No?"

"No. I was starting to say I wanted to tell you something and it wasn't because I'd been drinking alcohol, but because I wanted to share it with you."

"Right." Ginny nodded. "It was you, not the alcohol, talking."

"Yes."

"That's what I said."

"I know you did," Jan agreed. "And here's the thing, *I* was going to tell you that when George died it was like a... a...." Jan screwed up her face and leaned against the u-shaped bar as she searched for the words.

"A wakeup call!" Ginny shouted, above the thumping base beat. She could feel it in her chest, like a heavy heartbeat.

"Yes!" Jan pointed her index finger, jabbing the air for emphasis. "Exactly. And that's why I want you to know I value you and love you, booze or no booze."

Ginny reached out and enveloped Jan in a hug. "I know you do and I love you, too!" she bellowed in return.

"I can't believe how much I've danced tonight," Jan said, as they untangled themselves.

"I know!" Ginny agreed, her blue eyes wide with amazement. "I thought for sure I was going to be a wallflower all night, but—"

"Whooo-hooo!" Dixie, weaving her way toward them through the throng of people both young and not-so-young, cheered herself on. In her short skirt, tight top and impossibly high heels, she received more than a few appreciative glances from the patrons around the bar - the broad shouldered young men included.

"*There* you are!" Ginny leaned forward, the room shifting slightly under her feet. She grabbed Jan's shoulder to steady herself. Whew, maybe she'd gone past her limit and had consumed one cocktail too many.

"We were starting to wonder if you'd ever make it off the dance floor," Jan added.

"The music is so good and the guys are smokin' hot!" Dixie moved her hips back and forth to the beat. "I had one guy dance me around the floor so well I thought we might win an award."

"I saw you! You were like a whirling dervish, zipping by!" Jan cracked up, grabbing the edge of the bar for support.

Ginny raised her eyebrows. Maybe her best friend had had a few too many as well and it was actually a good thing she'd turned down the offer of more drinks.

"Where's Gwen?" Dixie squinted as she tried to scan the room.

"There." Ginny pointed to their right where Gwen was dancing a lively two-step, her flirty red skirt swinging around her thighs, with a man easily ten years her junior.

Dixie grinned and nodded appreciatively before asking, "Are you girls having fun?"

Jan, still struck by a fit of the giggles, managed to nod; her head bobbing up and down in unison with Ginny's.

"Wonderful! Thank goodness for line-dancing and real men!" Dixie waved a manicured hand at the young, handsome bartender. "Hey, Slim! A round of tequila shots for me and my girls!"

*Slim* grinned and tapped the rim of his brown felt Stetson before lining up the shot glasses along the bar.

Dixie reached into her push-up bra and pulled out a sizeable wad of cash, making Ginny's eyes widen. "Make 'em doubles, cowboy," she said, winking.

"Whoa." Ginny nudged Jan's shoulder with her own. "Someone came to play."

Jan regarded the money in Dixie's hands while a bottle of tequila was produced and the shot glasses were filled. "Oh, boy," she said, swallowing nervously.

"I second that," Ginny said. "I think the game's about to change."

"Might want to stay put there," Dixie commented, batting her eyes flirtatiously at "Slim" as she started peeling off notes. "We'll probably be having more than just the one."

The bartender's smile turned up a notch. "Whatever you need, Darlin'," he said, his voice deep and inviting.

"Oh, boy," Jan repeated, before accepting the first shot.

\*\*\*\*

Jennifer yawned widely and climbed back into bed beside Chris. She pulled the covers over her shoulders, settled her head back into her pillow and sighed. God, she was tired. If she would have known she'd be on the receiving end of a two AM wakeup call she might have gone to bed earlier. Hindsight really could be a bitch.

"Everything okay?" Chris asked, his voice seeming to float in the darkness of the bedroom.

Jennifer nodded, before realizing he couldn't see her. "Uh-huh. He just had a dream and thought it was real."

"Flying car, again?" Chris said, referring to Mason's latest trend of dreams.

Jennifer giggled. "Nailed it. He had to tell me all about how the backseat was actually a trampoline and then asked if we could do the same thing in our car."

Chris chuckled. That would be something.

"Don't even think about it," Jennifer said, snuggling further into her pillow.

"What? What am I thinking about?"

She turned over to face him and, even though she knew he couldn't see her, shot him a knowing look. "We are not buying a trampoline. No way. They're dangerous and I'm not taking a chance on either of our kids, or one of their friends, getting hurt on my time."

He grinned. She knew him too well. "Party pooper."

Jennifer snickered then said, "Hey, speaking of which, I wonder how my Mom's evening went. Do you think she and the girls had fun?"

Chris yawned loudly.

"Okay, fine," she said, nudging his calf with her foot before turning over. "We'll talk in the morning."

He reached out and pulled her close, spooning her up against his chest.

Jennifer settled into his embrace with a sigh.

\*\*\*\*

"Nah, nah, honey I'm good," Jan sang as she lurched through the limo door, nearly tripping over her own feet as she scuttled toward one of the soft leather seats.

Ginny ducked her head and followed, grabbing for anything solid. She'd definitely gone over her alcohol limit and felt as though she was on a drifting boat, instead of inside a parked car.

"Beep, beep," Dixie said, as she clamored in behind Ginny, giving her backside a push.

"Ack, careful," she said, giggling. "I lost my sea legs a while ago."

Gwen, standing curb-side with the driver, took a deep breath then let him ease her into the car. "Thank you," she said, as he gently closed the door behind her.

Jan - still singing quietly to herself - flopped bonelessly into the yielding cushions and let her head tip backward to meet the seat. She closed her eyes.

Ginny wobbled over to the seat next to her and lowered herself into it with an audible sigh.

"You said it," Gwen said, commenting on Ginny's exhalation while she crawled clumsily across both her and Jan's laps. "It's like an oasis in here, after the noise of that club."

"Yikes!" Ginny blurted, when Gwen's backside nearly bumped her in the face as she passed by.

"Watch out for low flying hinny," Dixie teased, before chortling merrily at her own joke.

Gwen settled herself on the other side of Jan. "Sorry," she said, giggling.

"I love that song, Jan," Dixie offered, while the car moved seamlessly away from the curb and carried them back onto the darkened streets. "Did you get a chance to dance to it?"

"Which one?" Jan asked, opening her eyes and squinting in the subdued lighting.

"The one you were just singing," Dixie said, stretching her legs along a bank of vacant seats.

"Oh," Jan said, before screwing up her face in concentration. "Was I singing out loud?"

Ginny repressed a grin. Apparently, Jan had gone past her drink limit as well. She tried to help things along and said, "The 'honey, I'm good' song."

"*Oh*, right!" Jan attempted to snap her fingers. "*That* song. That's a good one."

"Uh-huh," Gwen agreed.

"But, listen, whatever you do, DO NOT tell Darryl."

Gwen furrowed her eyebrows together then leaned forward to look questioningly at Ginny. Had she missed something?

Ginny, also confused, shrugged and asked, "Don't tell him *what*, Sweetie?"

"You *know*," Jan said, nodding her head lazily up and down.

They stared.

"What?" Jan asked, before yawning loudly. "Why are you just staring at me?"

"Because we have no idea what you're talking about," Gwen stated.

Jan, realizing she'd completely skipped a thought, started to snicker. It was so funny!

Ginny turned to meet Dixie's eye and share a grin. It seemed tequila was a potent drink for Jan.

"Okay, okay," Jan said, catching her breath. "Here is it. Don't tell Darryl that the guy I was dancing with to that song was the best lead I've ever had."

"Pardon me?" Dixie asked, loudly. "The best lay? Seriously? Where the hell was I?"

Gwen snorted, while Jan shrieked and flapped her hands wildly in the air. "Ahh! No! I said *Lead*! Best *lead* I've ever had. Best *dance partner*."

Dixie, still reclined, slapped her palms across her face to hide her amusement.

Ginny did the opposite and openly chortled at her best friend's vehemence.

"Why can't we tell your husband?" Gwen asked, entertaining them further by playing devil's advocate. "Will he be nervous you'll run off to find out if the best *lead* you've ever had is as talented in *other* activities as well?"

"Gwen!" Jan slapped her on the knee. "That's exactly what he'd think!"

"Then he'd be a very foolish man," Ginny said, before easing her shoes from her feet and flexing her toes with pleasure.

"And, *you*," Jan said, leaning around Ginny to point her finger at Dixie.

"*Me*?" Dixie's eyes widened.

"Buying drink, after drink, after drink," Jan said, wagging her index finger as the car turned around a corner.

"Whoops!" Gwen said, nearly tumbling off of her seat from the sudden motion.

"Worth every penny," Dixie breathed, lost in memory as she fanned the air in front of herself. "And, my god, that bartender..."

"Who had to be half your age," Gwen cut in, before regaining her balance and slipping off her shoes and groaning, "Oh, that feels good."

"That's what *she* almost said," Jan muttered, before letting her head tip back a second time against the soft leather of her seat.

Ginny snorted loudly and pressed her hand across her mouth.

"Uh-huh," Dixie agreed. "And that was his biggest charm, even though he was *not* half my age."

"Pretty close," Gwen countered.

"Maybe a decade," Dixie offered, then amended, "and a half."

"Which would make him…" Gwen started counting on her fingers.

"Anyway," Dixie cut her off. "Whatever the actual number, he was younger, firmer and had more stamina. I'll take it."

Ginny grimaced.

Dixie caught the look. "What? Are you telling me *you* wouldn't, if it was on offer?"

"Truthfully? No. He looked younger than Eric. Ick."

"Possibly even younger than Brian," Jan chimed in, referring to Ginny's youngest.

Ginny shuddered. "Double ick, then."

Dixie shrugged and grinned cheekily. "To each their own."

"This car really is amazing." Jan looked around at the interior appreciatively.

"I think I'm having deja vu," Ginny announced.

"Why's that?" Jan asked.

"Didn't someone say that, already? Oh, boy, was it me?" Ginny widened her eyes. "Am I having a senior moment before I'm officially a senior?"

Jan furrowed her brow, trying to remember.

Dixie laughed and shook her head at the pair of them. "No, you're not. *I* said it."

"I think I may have said something like it, too," Gwen commented, waving her hand in the air.

"Right. Then *I* said George would have loved it," Ginny added, before shaking her finger at Dixie. "You're a bad, bad woman. Those shooters have short-circuited all of our brains."

"A person shouldn't wait to share things, you know," Jan said, thoughtfully.

Ginny rubbed her face. It felt slightly numb from all the alcohol she'd consumed.

"I *said*, a person should share their feelings when they have them," Jan repeated, more forcefully.

"Something bugging you?" Gwen asked.

"A little." Jan sat up and reached into the minibar. "I was just thinking about Ginny's comments about George and it occurs to me we shouldn't wait to tell people we care."

Ginny nodded her head, her face thoughtful.

"Okay," Dixie said, extending her arms outward. "I love you ladies."

"Any water in there?" Gwen asked. "I'm parched."

Dixie laughed and shook her head. "And this is the reason we forgo sharing our feelings."

Gwen laughed, too, and blew a kiss at Dixie. "Sorry, Hon. You know I love you, too."

"Right, good, we all love each other," Ginny said, before pointing at her purse. "But, that aside, is anyone hungry? Because I have homemade granola bars if anyone's hungry."

"Only you would be packing homemade baking, Gin," Dixie said, giggling. "If I'm ever stranded on a desert island, I want you with me. You and your purse full of baking."

Ginny sniggered while Jan offered a counter suggestion, "Anyone up for a cocktail?"

"We probably shouldn't," Dixie cautioned, as she ran her fingers through her hair and massaged her scalp. "Ginny was right, we had a lot of tequila."

"Oh, *sure*," Jan teased, as she began pulling out bottles and examining their labels. "You're all casual about practically bagging a man half your age, but mention another drink and...." She paused, whiskey bottle held aloft, and looked at Ginny fumbling with her handbag. "What are you doing, Gin?"

"It's in here, somewhere," Ginny mumbled, as she fished inside her leather purse.

"No granola for me," Gwen said, pulling a face.

"No, no," Ginny said, still searching. "Not that."

Dixie picked up her small, square bag. "What do you need? A pain pill? I've got loads."

"No..."

"Cigarettes?"

Jan raised her eyebrows. "You have cigarettes? YOU?"

Dixie shrugged her shoulders and pulled a pack out of her bag. "What can I say? I like to have a smoke when I drink."

"Ahh-haa!" Ginny brandished her phone into the air with a flourish. "Jackpot!"

Jan leaned back to avoid being hit by her flailing arm. "It's after three in the morning and we're all here. Who on Earth are you calling?"

Ginny hiccupped and grinned. "You said it and you were right."

"About what?" Jan questioned, her brain fuzzy as she tried to recall what she'd said.

"Hold that thought," Ginny said, swiping her finger across the phone.

Jan looked at Dixie. "Do you remember what I said?"

Dixie shook her head and pulled a square, solid silver Zippo lighter from her purse.

"Do *you*?" Jan threw the question over to Gwen.

Gwen shook her head. "Nope. You said a lot of things, honey."

Ginny moved the phone back and forth in front of herself until she found the point where it finally came into focus. She tapped at the screen, her face set in determination.

Gwen watched Dixie light a cigarette then take a drag and say "Ahhhh" on her exhale. "Give me a drag of that, will you," she said, holding out her hand.

"Seriously, Gin," Jan tried, again, while waving away the smoke filling the interior of the car. "It really *is* late, practically morning. Are you sure you should be phoning anyone—"

Ginny held up her hand to cut Jan off, before practically shouting into the phone, "Eric!"

Jan's eyes widened and she began alternately laughing and then coughing at the smoke in the air.

Ginny, realizing her voice was much too loud, began snorting with mirth as she slapped a hand across her mouth.

Gwen handed the cigarette back to Dixie then tapped Jan's shoulder and asked, "Eric? Is that her son?"

Jan, giggling helplessly now at the image in her head of Eric's face, could only nod her agreement.

"Yes, yes," Ginny said, her voice slurring slightly, making her sound vaguely French. "Of *course* I know what time it is, honey. It's, ummm…"

"Please, for the love of god," Jan said, trying to regain her composure. "Crack a window already! It's like we're sitting inside a rolling chimney."

Dixie pressed the button to open the moon roof then turned back toward Ginny in time to see her still hemming into her phone and frantically pointing at her wrist. "Oh!" she said, shoving her cigarette between her lips and reaching into her bag for her phone. "Three ten," she announced, peering at its screen, the cigarette bobbing wildly up and down and scattering ash down the front of her top. "It's ten minutes past three in the morning."

"It's three o'clock in the morning," Ginny repeated, triumphantly, while Jan whooped and nearly fell off her seat laughing at the site of Dixie and her ash-covered clothing. "Ten minutes past three o'clock in the morning to be precise, but that doesn't matter! What *does* matter is that some things need to be shared and just can't wait until... umm..." She shot a questioning look at Jan.

"Later in the day!" Jan declared, pointing her finger definitively at the ceiling of the car.

"Right!" Ginny agreed. "Later sometimes never comes. *At all.*"

"Ooh," Dixie said, putting her phone on the seat beside her then blowing smoke upward toward the opened ceiling. "Cryptic."

Gwen began peeling off her stockings, muttering, "Darned things are just too hot. Why don't I ever remember that..."

"What's that, honey? Say again?" Ginny asked Eric, shifting the phone from her left to her right ear. "We opened the top of the car to let the smoke out, so it's a bit loud in here. Listen."

Jan raised an eyebrow at Dixie while Ginny pulled the phone away from her ear and directed it toward the limo's moon roof. They could hear the murmur of Eric's voice within the phone and he sounded a bit... put off.

Ginny pressed the phone back against her head. "Well, yes. Of *course* I'm here with Jan," she said, rolling her eyes in exasperation at the question. "I *told* you I was going out with her tonight. Why? Do you need to talk to her?"

"And Dixie," Jan said.

"Yes," Ginny said, nodding. "And Dixie's here, too."

"Can't forget the lady who almost went home with the bartender!" Jan announced.

"Almost, what a sad, sad word," Dixie said, while lifting her phone from the seat to snap photos of Gwen tossing aside her stockings.

Gwen stuck out a bar leg, mock pin-up girl style.

"Get in here, girls," Dixie said, still taking pictures. "Photo time!"

Gwen and Jan shuffled closer across the soft leather.

"You, too, Gin!" Dixie said.

"Hang on a sec, Honey," Ginny said, into the phone, leaning in with the girls.

Jan and Gwen struck goofy poses while Ginny put her phone in her lap and Dixie held her phone out to snap selfies of the four of them.

"Perfect!" Dixie said, as Jan and Gwen fell about laughing at their silliness.

"You have to send us those," Jan said, catching her breath.

Gwen nodded in agreement. "And the ones in the bar."

"Okay, I'm back," Ginny said, putting the phone back to her ear. "Well, my goodness, there's no need to be so *snippy*. I was barely gone more than a second."

"Ooh. I think someone's in trouble," Gwen whispered.

Jan covered her mouth with her hand and yawned. "Maybe he's just tired. Most people get cranky when they're tired."

"Okay, well, lesson learned," Ginny said. "Next time, I'll wait until after we've hung up."

Dixie took a last drag on her cigarette and rubbed it out in the ashtray on the sidebar. She lurched forward toward the fridge and yanked open the door. "Water?"

Ginny nodded along with the other two.

"Hey," Gwen said, "is there anything to eat in there that's not a homemade granola bar?"

Dixie began handing out bottles of sparking water and said, "Gimme a sec and I'll check."

"Yes, I *am* calling for a reason besides waking you up," Ginny insisted, sighing down the line. "And, even though it's late right now—"

"Or, early, depending on how you look at it," Dixie threw in, as she closed the fridge then started rummaging in the neighboring cupboard.

"Right. Or early. Doesn't matter which way you look at it." Ginny burped delicately, sending Jan into fits of giggles. "What does matter is I need to tell you, right now, you are my son and I love you. You, your sister and your brother are my three greatest blessings."

Jan stopped giggling and began to tear up. "Oh, that's so nice. You're a good Mom, Ginny."

"Thank you, dear," Ginny said, into the phone, while trying to smooth her hair from her face. What had started as carefully crafted curls had turned into unruly, tangled waves.

"Jackpot!" Dixie crowed triumphantly, pulling bags of potato chips from the cupboard.

Gwen clapped and bounced in her seat. "What flavors?"

"And the children!" Ginny further expounded. "Both yours and Jennifer's lovely, lovely children! Layla, and Grace and Mason are more of my blessings."

"Salt and vinegar, and barbecue," Dixie announced, peering at the bags in her hands.

"What's that?" Ginny said, stifling a yawn.

"Salt and vinegar, and barbecue," Dixie repeated, louder.

Ginny grinned then shook the phone. "No, no, not you. Eric."

"Salt and vinegar, please," Gwen said, holding out her hand.

"You should go and get some sleep now, Eric," Ginny said, as though he was the one keeping them on the line. "Layla will be up soon, I'm sure, and I have water and chips waiting for me." She pressed the button on her phone, disconnecting the call. "I'll talk to you tomorrow. Bye-bye. Love you."

Jan sniggered and said, "Gin, I think you just hung up on him."

"No. Did I?" Ginny frowned and peered her phone. "Are you sure?"

"Well, after you said we have water and chips, it looked like you hung up *then* said goodbye," Jan offered, while Ginny pressed the phone back against her ear to check it was off.

"Huh," she mused, dropping the phone into her lap then twisting the white plastic cap from her bottle. "You know, you might be right."

"He probably didn't even notice," Dixie commented.

"That's highly possible," Gwen agreed, philosophically, before stuffing a handful of chips into her mouth.

Ginny tipped her head back and took a large swig of water, swallowed and declared, "I'm not done."

"You're not?" Jan asked, clasping her bottle between her hands like a child.

Ginny wiped her mouth with the back of her hand. "Hold this, please," she said, handing her water over to Dixie.

Dixie took the bottle and put it on the bar while Ginny picked up her phone and began tapping at the screen. She leaned back in her seat, waiting to see what was going to happen next.

"Jennifer? My Jenny-bean?" Ginny said, before leaning her head on Jan's shoulder. "It's Mom...."

\*\*\*\*

## Ginny's Homemade Granola Bars

### Ingredients

4½ cups rolled oats
1   cup whole wheat flour
1   teaspoon baking soda
⅓   cup butter, softened
⅓   cup peanut butter
½   cup honey
1   teaspoon vanilla
2   cups either chocolate chips, peanut butter chips, raisins, or a variety of all three.

### Directions

Preheat oven to 325 degrees F.

o   Grease a 9 x 13 inch baking pan.
o   Mix rolled oats, flour, baking soda in bowl.
o   In separate bowl, mix together butter, peanut butter, honey and vanilla.
o   Add wet ingredients and chocolate chips and/or raisins and/or peanut butter chips into dry ingredients, mix until well blended.
o   Press mixture into greased pan, smoothing until level.
o   Bake for 18 to 22 minutes, until golden brown.
o   Cool 10 minutes after removing from oven, cut into bars and let cool completely.

# Chapter Eight

Eric yawned so widely his jaw cracked. God, he was beat. Morning had arrived too quickly and he was having trouble keeping his eyes open as he fed Layla, seated in her highchair, her breakfast.

"Mmmm," she enthused, as she took the banana he held out and began mushing it into her mouth.

"Glad you approve," he said, grinning, despite his tiredness. She made the early morning rising worth the effort.

Kimberly shuffled into the kitchen in her rose pink slippers and headed straight for the coffee pot on the counter. She picked up a bright orange mug with a yellow daisy painted on its side from the steel dish drainer and asked, "Coffee?"

Layla, seeing the familiar cup, parroted, "Coffee!"

Eric shook his head and pointed to his cup, emblazoned with *Best Daddy* in neon green, on the table. "Got some, already."

Kimberly put the cup on the counter then paused to peer at her husband. "Did you get any sleep at all after your Mom called, because you look seriously bagged."

"Not much," he replied, before running his fingers through his hair. "And thanks, by the way."

She chuckled and shook her head, trying to explain. "Sorry, I didn't mean it as an insult. It's just that you look like you could already use a nap."

"Please," he said, wryly. "So much flattery so early, I can't take it."

Kimberly bit her lip to keep from smirking and picked up the carafe.

"Coffee!" Layla exclaimed, again.

Kimberly grinned at her affectionately then opened the refrigerator for the almond milk. "Yes, coffee for Mommy."

"Milk!" Layla cheered.

Eric yawned and leaned back into his chair. "If I didn't know better," he offered, "I'd think you were getting some sort of perverse pleasure over my tiredness."

She shot him a puzzled look as she shut the fridge door with her hip. "What? What would make you say that?"

"Oh, I don't know," he said, grinning at her obvious attempt to look bewildered. She wasn't fooling him. "Call it a hunch."

Kimberly added milk to her coffee then retrieved a spill-proof mug from the cupboard. "I refuse to dignify that with a response," she said, while pouring milk into the cup.

Eric chuckled and picked up his coffee.

"So, do you think she got home okay?" Kimberly asked, returning to the subject of his mother as she twisted the lid closed on the cup and handed it to Layla.

Eric watched his daughter take the cup eagerly and said, "Pretty sure. She was with Jan and Dixie and possibly one other person."

"Safety in numbers, I suppose," Kimberly offered, dryly.

She found the whole thing off-putting. Grown women out to all hours, drinking and possibly carousing. It was repugnant.

"She just sounded so tanked, though," Eric said, still a bit shell-shocked by it all. "Seriously, I don't think I've ever heard her like that."

"Tanked!" Layla's face lit up in delight before she tilted her head back to guzzle her milk.

Kimberly left the carton on the granite countertop and rolled her eyes. "A new word. Lovely."

"I mean, sure," he went on, undaunted, "she's been known to have a glass or two of wine at Christmas and get a bit giggly, but *this*. This was a whole other arena of slurring and rambling."

"Also, lovely." Kimberly tightened the sash on her silk, fuchsia-pink robe, picked up her coffee and carried it to the table. "Did she happen to mention, during the rambling, where she was?"

Eric shook his head while she put down her cup then backtracked to pull a cloth from a drawer and wet it under the tap.

"She didn't tell you anything at all? Not even before she and *the girls* left for their night out?"

"No. She said Jan was surprising her and she wasn't sure where they were going."

Kimberly frowned as she walked over to Layla and began wiping her face with the cloth. Layla started to squirm, so she sped up her efforts before she began to outright resist and protest.

"What?" Eric asked, pretty sure the frown was about his Mom, not Layla's fidgeting.

"Well, all I can say is, it's very upsetting! I've been trying to hold my tongue, but I just can't. Here we thought she and her friends were going out to dinner or some such thing and, instead, they were out god-knows-where, drinking god-knows-how-much and getting up to who-knows-what."

Eric couldn't help himself and grinned at his wife's choice of words. She sounded like *she* was the sixty two year old, instead of his mother.

"Okay, you're done," Kimberly said, to Layla, before tossing the cloth into the sink.

She removed the white tray on the highchair, handed it to Eric, then released the safety belt around Layla's waist and lifted her from its confines.

"I'll give her a call later, to make sure she's okay," he said, placing the tray on the table.

"I should say so," she said, before setting Layla on the floor.

"Say so," she mimicked, toddling over to her toys strewn across her play mat on the other side of the room.

"It's time you got to the bottom of things," Kimberly clarified.

The phone rang and Layla sang, "Ring, ring!" as she sat her pajama clad bottom on her mat.

Kimberly looked at the clock on the microwave then reached for the receiver on the countertop. "Hello? Oh, hi. Yeah, he's here, hang on." She extended the phone to Eric. "It's your sister."

Eric raised his eyebrows in surprise. Jennifer was not one to call first thing on a Sunday morning. He placed the phone to his ear.

"Hey, Jen. What's up?" He grimaced and added, "Yeah, she called me too."

Kimberly sighed and went back to her coffee.

****

"So?" Chris asked, as he set plates, a bowl of cornmeal biscuits and strawberry jam onto the kitchen table.

Jennifer hung up the phone and nodded. "Yup. She got him, too."

"Hey, guys," Chris called out, to Grace and Mason. "Food."

Jennifer refilled her red, stoneware mug with coffee and waited. A moment later her children came scuttling around the corner from the family room, both in their pajamas and robes.

"Yellow for you," Chris said to Grace, pointing to her plate on the table.

"And red for me!" Mason enthused, pulling himself swiftly into the chair adjacent to his sister's.

Grace reached for the biscuits, jam jar and a butter knife. On the verge of completing third grade, she'd recently decided she could do *all* things for herself and took offence when tasks were done for her; claiming that having Mommy or Daddy do it was for Kindergarten kids.

"Mine, too?" Mason asked, wide-eyed and hopeful in his Spiderman PJs.

Grace grinned. She loved being the big sister. "Yes," she said, sliding his plate over. "Yours, too."

Jennifer exchanged a look with Chris, the two of them smiling behind their coffee cups.

"That's very nice of you," Chris praised. "You're a good big sister."

Mason nodded his agreement. "Thank you," he said, without being prompted.

Jennifer raised her eyebrows. Who were these polite children and what had they done with her real daughter and son?

"Are you having a biscuit, or would you like toast instead?" Chris held up a loaf of bread.

Jennifer pulled out a chair at the table and smiled at him. In his plaid pajama bottoms and grey t-shirt, his blonde hair ruffled from sleep, he looked like a teenager.

"No toast for me, Daddy," Mason said, as Grace finished putting jam on his biscuit and slid his plate back toward him.

"Me, either," Grace confirmed, as she pushed her long tangle of dark hair from her face and tucked into her breakfast.

"Jen?" Chris asked.

"I'll just have a biscuit," she said, before taking a sip from her mug.

Chris nodded and pulled two slices of bread from the bag for himself.

"Did Gramma make these?" Mason asked, his lips smeared red by the strawberry jam.

"I did, but it was her recipe," Jennifer said, then turned to Grace. "We'll have to get your hair brushed out soon, Ms. Bed-head."

Grace looked up from her plate and nodded. "Maybe a ponytail today?"

"Sure." Jennifer covered her mouth as she yawned.

"You look tired, Mommy," Mason offered, before reaching for a glass of orange juice Chris had poured for him earlier.

Jennifer laughed. "Thanks, bud."

"What did Eric say about your Mom?" Chris leaned against a cabinet as he waited for the toaster.

Jennifer got up from her seat and joined him at the island. "She was pretty much the same with him, telling him she loved both him and Kimberly and the kids as well. How it's important to make sure the people you love know how much they mean to you, that sort of thing."

The toaster popped and Chris retrieved the freshly crisped bread. "How about the part about entering a line-dancing competition? Did she share that, too?"

He tried and failed to restrain a smirk from decorating his face as he slathered butter onto his toast. Ginny's drunken rambling cracked him up.

"He didn't mention, so I'd guess not," Jennifer said, smiling in response to his expression. "But he did say she called him back a second time and told him about wanting to travel the globe."

Chris laughed and reached for the jam on the table. "Fantastic."

"Who's going to start dancing?" Grace's face with bright with curiosity.

"No one," Jennifer told her.

"But you said—"

"I *said*," Jennifer cut in, hoping to stop the train before it left the station. "Some people like to dance."

"Line dance?" Mason cocked his head, his tumble of fair hair falling into his eyes. "What's that?"

Jennifer shot Chris a pleading look.

"When people dance the same way," he said, simply.

Mason nodded. Good enough for him.

Jennifer caught the look in her daughter's eye, more questions were mulling. "Do you want another biscuit? How about dressing another one for Mason?"

Grace's eye's lit up at the offer and Jennifer sighed, relieved she'd managed to shift gears without much effort. She was too tired for effort.

****

Ginny sighed at the gentle, rhythmic patting on her cheeks, as though someone was tapping her with small pillows. That is, until the patting began to feel like smacking and the pillows were revealed as Martini's paws.

Ginny attempted to open her eyes to the sunlit bedroom then audibly groaned at the glare while snapping her lids shut. It was blinding. Why, oh why, had she not had the presence of mind to close the heavy draperies on her windows when she'd finally arrived home in the early hours of the morning?

Oh, right.

One word.

Tequila.

"Please, stop it," Ginny said, her voice sounding like gravel as she gently pushed Martini aside.

God, her mouth felt as dry as parchment and tasted worse - had she been smoking, or was that Dixie? Maybe both?

At Ginny's touch, Martini let his body go limp and more or less oozed away from her face onto the neighboring pillow.

Ginny forced herself to face the daylight, opened her protesting, gritty eyelids and mentally took stock of her bodily condition. Judging from the way she was feeling, it was entirely possible she'd fallen at one point the previous evening and been trampled. If she ever felt human again, she'd have to ask Jan.

"Oh, Martini," she exhaled. "If only you were human and could bring me some tea and toast and pain pills."

Martini yawned widely, displaying his sharp white teeth.

"Fine," she said, before yawning in return. "I'll do it. But don't think I won't remember this."

Martini closed his left eye and watched her with his right as she gingerly pulled herself upright.

"Oh, brother," Ginny complained, rubbing her face with her fingertips then pushing back the covers and easing her weary legs from beneath the blanket.

Martini switched eyes and continued his observation.

Ginny slide herself forward until her feet met the hardwood floor. One hurdle down. She groaned as she pulled herself upright and had to assume the task of supporting her own weight. Finally, she began to shuffle across the room, making a graceless beeline for the ensuite bathroom.

"I suggest you stay put," she said, to Martini, when she got to the bathroom. "It's not a countertop lounging sort of morning."

By way of reply, Martini closed both eyes and nestled his head comfortably on the pillow.

Ginny sighed and closed the door.

****

"Yes, Sweetheart," Ginny said, into the phone, in the family room. "I'm sure. I'll be just fine."

She waited a beat while her son, Brian, continued his inquisition. She'd, apparently, called him in the early hours of the morning as well (her memory of the call was sketchy at best) and he was checking in to make sure she'd made it home safely.

"Honestly. I've had some toast and I'm going to have a cup of tea and take it easy."

Martini momentarily appeared from around the corner, then swiftly crossed the room to disappear through the adjacent door that lead into the kitchen. Ginny watched him go then squeezed her eyes closed. Her head was beginning to throb in time to the sound of Brian's voice.

"No, I haven't seen the photos," she said, rubbing her temple. "Dixie said she'd text them, or email them to me. How on Earth do you know we took photos?"

Ginny listened to him explaining he'd been on Facebook and seen the photos on Dixie's wall. Oh, boy. Maybe she should think about caving in to the kid's insistence she get a page.

"Okay, dear. Thank you, again, so much for checking up on me. I'll call you later, okay? Love you. 'Bye."

Ginny hung up the phone and exhaled heavily. Clearly she wasn't twenty, or even thirty for that matter, anymore. Granted, she'd never gone on benders when she was either of those ages, what with work and then kids to consider. It was entirely possible she was feeling appropriately torn up and just didn't know it.

"Tea," she muttered, under her breath, while easing herself up and out of the softly padded, beige armchair to begin her shuffle to the kitchen.

The front doorbell sounded, stopping her in her tracks on the rose colored carpet. Who could that be? The thought of someone seeing her in her current state was mortifying. When she'd managed to get herself into the bathroom earlier, she'd gasped at her reflection in the mirror. She'd looked as badly as she felt; as though she'd aged years overnight. Her makeup had smudged and flaked down her face, her hair had looked as though she'd been through a wind tunnel and her wrinkles had appeared etched, as opposed to lightly sprinkled, onto her face.

The doorbell sounded a second time. Whoever it was, wasn't going away.

"Oh, hell," she said, smoothing a hand across her hair and turning on her heel to make her way back through the family room into the front hall.

She took a deep breath, pulled open the door and squinted when the sunlight hit her smack dab in the face.

Eric, waiting on the step, took one look at his mother and burst out laughing.

\*\*\*\*

## *Ginny's Cornmeal Breakfast Biscuits*

### Ingredients
1¾ cups of whole wheat flour
⅔  cup of cornmeal
2   tablespoons brown sugar
1   tablespoon baking powder
½  teaspoon salt
½  cup cold butter
1   cup buttermilk

### Directions
Preheat oven to 450 degrees F.

o   Grease baking sheets, or use baking sheets covered with parchment paper.

o   Combine whole wheat flour, cornmeal, brown sugar, baking powder and salt in a large bowl.

o   Cut in the cold butter with a pastry blender or fork (or, as Ginny does it, with clean hands, crumbling until the mixture resembles coarse crumbs.)

o   Add in buttermilk and stir until mixture is combined.

o   Drop batter by ¼ cupfuls approximately an inch apart onto the baking sheets.

o   Bake for 12 to 14 minutes, or until golden brown.

o   Remove from oven and transfer biscuits to wire racks to cool.

# Chapter Nine

"Oh, very nice," Ginny reprimanded, while cringing at the volume of Eric's laughter. It sounded a lot like gongs going off in her aching head. "Laugh at your Mother in her time of need. You're a terrible, terrible son."

Eric stepped inside, still snickering, and closed the door. "You weren't telling me that last night."

Ginny ignored his comment and exhaled in relief when the sunshine disappeared behind the closed door.

"It's shaping up into a beautiful day out there, by the way," he said, gesturing to his black shorts and green t-shirt. "Maybe you want to get out and enjoy it?"

She raised an eyebrow at him, making him smirk. "I'll pass, thanks."

He slipped off his sneakers. "Nice robe, is it new?"

Ginny tightened the terrycloth belt on her yellow bathrobe, attempted a second time to smooth her nest of hair and, finally, lead the way to the kitchen.

"It's still early enough for my robe, smarty pants," she commented, over her shoulder. "It's not even fully noon. *And* I haven't had a chance to do anything with my hair. Besides, it's Sunday—"

"The *morning after,*" Eric teased, as he trailed behind her and lifted a small, green cloth grocery bag he was carrying onto the wood tabletop. "Have you seen the photos?"

Ginny gritted her teeth. "*No,* I have not. I take you've been talking to Brian?"

"Oh, yeah," he said, chuckling. "Dixie posted a whole bunch. You should get on Facebook and see for yourself. Looks like you ladies had quite the night."

Ginny groaned and shuffled over to the kettle on the countertop.

"Speaking of which, Kimberly sends her best, and *this.*"

Ginny looked warily at the bag he'd set on the table. "Which is?"

Eric shrugged and walked over to Martini, lounging on the peninsula that separated the kitchen from the dining room. "She called it a *rescue kit.*"

"Rescue kit? From what?" She filled the kettle from the tap.

He picked up the cat and snuggled him in his arms. "If I had to guess, I'd say your night of *debauchery.*"

Ginny laughed then winced when her skull protested. "I'm almost afraid to look inside."

Eric grinned and put Martini back on the countertop. "I'm brave, let's have a look."

Ginny plugged in the kettle while he sat down and began to pull items from the depths of the bag.

"The first item we have, ladies and gentleman, is a detox cleansing and revitalizing tea." He held up the box for her to see. "Oooh, sounds interesting."

Ginny rubbed her eyes as he placed it on the table. "Or intense," she offered.

He reached back inside the sack. "The next items, ladies and gentlemen, are…" he read the labels on two plastic bottles, "Magnesium and vitamin B tablets."

"I have those," Ginny stated, as she reached into the cupboard above her head for mugs.

He placed the supplements beside the box of tea. "There's more, do we venture?"

Ginny shrugged. "Why not?"

"Excellent," he said, before once more adopting his studio announcer voice. "Into the breach one more time and we have... ginger!"

Ginny blinked. "Seriously? Ginger?"

"You bet," he confirmed, placing the jar of spice next to the other items on the table. "And tomatoes, cayenne pepper...." He paused when he saw her face twist with revulsion.

"Good lord," she said, reaching into another cupboard for her container of tea bags. "What must she be thinking? What on Earth did you tell her?"

Eric held up his hands as though in surrender. "Don't shoot the messenger, or bag boy in this case. I just told her what you said to me on the phone."

"Did *she* see the photos?"

He shook his head. Kimberly wasn't friends with Dixie on Facebook and he wasn't about to show her and give her more reasons to rant about his mother.

"Thank goodness for that small blessing." Ginny held up the metal tin of tea. "Earl Grey okay?"

He nodded. "She means well."

"Oh, I know that," she said, placing a teabag in each of their cups. "Is there anything else in there?"

"Yup. But *these* are from me." He pulled two bottles - one painkillers and the other sodium bicarbonate - from the bag. "I snuck them in under the radar when she wasn't looking."

Ginny laughed. Then she winced.

"I gotta be honest, though," he added, while Martini stretched his body like a long spring being uncoiled then padded across the countertop toward their mugs.

"About?" Ginny looked at him curiously as the kettle finished boiling and clicked off. When she saw the cat out of the corner of her eye peering into the large cups, she tapped her finger against his backside and said, "Watch it, you."

"About the fact that you are truly the LAST person I ever would have thought I'd be bringing *hangover* supplies to. Brings me back to my college days."

"Ahh, there's the words every mother longs to hear." Ginny advanced with the hot kettle and Martini backed away from the cups. "Clearly, money well spent."

"In fact," Eric went on, smirking, "I was going to bring you some hair of the dog until I realized I wasn't sure what your drink of choice was."

Ginny poured the boiled water and swallowed against the involuntary churning in her stomach at the mere mention of *hair of the dog*.

"Rum?" He prompted. "Gin?"

Ginny put her focus on breathing steadily through her nose, instead of recalling the memory of the many shots poured the previous evening.

"Vodka? Wine, perhaps?"

"I wouldn't say it was my drink of choice, but the culprit last night was Tequila."

Eric raised his eyebrows. "Wow. Impressive. I had no idea you were drunk-dialing on the hard stuff."

Ginny tried not to laugh and failed. He was such a smart ass. "Stop. It hurts my head to laugh."

He stood up and crossed the kitchen just as her cellphone trilled.

"That's yours," he said, opening the fridge door and pulling out the milk.

Ginny walked over to the sideboard for her phone, checked the message and sighed.

"You take honey in yours, right?"

"Yes, thank you." She held up the phone. "It's from Brian. He called me just before you came over, but clearly that wasn't enough."

Eric smiled, while he nudged Martini aside, and reached into the cabinet for the honey pot. "Yeah, he texted me this morning to tell me about the photos. He was pretty amused about the drunk-dialing. What'd he say?"

Ginny grimaced at *drunk-dialing*. It sounded so... unseemly.

She cleared her throat and read aloud, *"Hey, Mom! Forgot to mention, I'm looking forward to hittin' it with you when I come for my next visit. Break out the party clothes, Ginny's gonna raise the roof?"*

Eric burst out laughing and, even though it still sounded a lot like marbles clattering on the tile floor, Ginny joined him.

"You know, you never actually told me where you called from." Eric slid the rescue kit items aside and placed the milk and honey on the table. "Was it from that vehicle in the photos?"

Ginny tucked her phone into the pocket of her robe and went back to the tea. "We were in a limo Jan rented."

"That's good news."

"Meaning?" She tossed the teabags in the sink and picked up the cups.

"Kim was all in a lather when she heard Jen and I talking about you being in a vehicle when you called," he said, as she placed one of the mugs in front of him on the table.

Indignation flared in Ginny's chest as she sat down in the chair opposite him. "Surely she knows I'd never drink and drive."

"That's what I said, too, but—"

"Wait. You've already talked to Jennifer today?" Ginny interrupted. "Don't tell me she's seen photos, too?"

"'Fraid so."

"Good lord, the bloody grapevine."

Eric poured milk into his tea and remarked, "Oh, come on. It's not every day our mother calls all three of us in the middle of the night, three sheets to the wind. Cut us some slack."

Ginny raised an eyebrow, but said nothing. Instead, she took a spoonful of honey from the pot and stirred it into her cup.

"So, a limo," he commented, changing the subject. "Nice. Was it as posh as it looked in the photos?"

Ginny smiled. Men and cars. "As a matter of fact, yes. It was absolutely gorgeous. All soft leather, blue and red mood lighting and even a mini bar stocked to the hilt."

He nodded, approvingly. "Cool."

"Your Dad would have loved it. And our driver, Stefan, was the nicest young man. He was professional, yet personable. He deserved the tip we gave him."

"So was it you and Jan and Dixie and who was the other woman?"

She nodded then massaged her temple. "Gwen. She's a friend of Dixie's and she was a delight."

"Nice legs." Eric picked up the bottle of ibuprofen, twisted off the lid and shook out two tablets. He handed them to her.

"Excuse me?" Ginny asked, while tossing the tablets into her mouth and swallowing them with a mouthful of tea.

"Gwen," he explained. "She had nice legs in the picture Dixie took of her."

The doorbell rang and Ginny lifted her eyebrows in surprise. "Goodness, now who could *that* be?"

\*\*\*\*

Ginny took a breath and braced herself for the glare before opening the front door, but it didn't help. The brilliantly sunshine-filled morning nearly pushed her backward all over again.

"Glad to see you're still alive," Jan said, standing on the other side of the door, dark glasses shielding her eyes.

"Barely." Ginny stepped aside and opened the door further to let her in. "Come in before my head explodes."

"I wish I was still in my bathrobe," Jan said, crossing the threshold. "It's only because I have a morbid fear of being in some sort of car trouble and caught at my worst that I changed into these sweats and sweatshirt. Can you imagine how embarrassing that would be? Your car dies and there you are, caught out in your *pajamas*. Yuck."

Ginny closed the door. "I have a spare robe in the bedroom, if you want to change."

Jan laughed, then winced.

Ginny sympathized. It looked all too familiar. "Your head?" she asked, as Jan slowly shucked her trainers from her feet.

"I was afraid to brush my hair, my scalp is so tender." She reached up to massage her skull through her untidy brown locks. "I feel like I've been run over."

"Seriously, right? I was starting to wonder if something had happened that I wasn't remembering, like being trampled on the dance floor," Ginny said, gravely, while leading the way to the kitchen.

"And Darryl was completely unsympathetic," Jan complained, too tired to lift her sock-covered feet off the floor, so instead shuffling a step behind.

Ginny nodded as they rounded the corner. "Mmm, sounds familiar."

"Oh, hey, Eric," Jan said, lifting her hand in a small wave as they entered the room. She eased herself into a vacant chair at the table with a heavy exhale.

"Ah, yes. One of the partners in crime and *debauchery*," he teased, a smirk on his face.

Ginny bit her lip and refrained from comment. She set the kettle to boil one more time and turned to Jan. "Tea?"

"Yes, please." Jan yawned then raised an eyebrow at Eric from behind her dark glasses. "So, crime and debauchery is the charge, huh? I take it she told you about our night out?"

"*Told* me?" he replied, rubbing the dark stubble on his chin. "Not in so many words. But the drunk dialing at three in the morning, combined with the pictures on Facebook, pretty much got me up to speed."

"Oh!" Jan's face was a picture of shock, before she began to laugh. "I totally forgot about that!"

"Oh, yeah. She got all three of us."

Jan leaned forward to rest her forehead on the cool tabletop, her giggles still bubbling over.

"In fact," he told her, "Brian's even said he's looking forward to *raising the roof* with her when he next comes to visit."

Jan's chortling was infectious and Ginny started laughing. She was relieved to feel her head wasn't quite so touchy. The painkillers were kicking in.

"Raising the roof," Jan repeated, as she lifted her head from the table. "God, what does that even mean?"

"I think Dixie could tell you," Ginny remarked, while tossing a teabag into the mug she'd chosen and drowning it in hot water.

Martini jumped down from the counter and sauntered across the tiles toward Jan. She lifted him into her lap. "God, that Dixie. And there are photos on Facebook? Are you being serious, or just winding me up?"

Eric placed a hand over his heart. "I tell no lies."

"Hell," Jan said, stroking the cat's fur.

Eric pulled his phone from his pocket. "Here," he said, quickly tapping at the screen. "Have a look."

Jan winced and held up a hand. "Oh, god, no. Not until I've had my tea."

He laughed and turned his off phone.

"I know," Ginny agreed, shaking her head. "I'm afraid to look, too."

"There were some pretty young guys in those photos," Eric remarked, leaning back in his chair and picking up his mug of tea.

"Hey, it was all *Dixie's* idea to go line-dancing at that country bar," Jan stated, while eyeing up the items Eric had set out on the table. She pulled off her sunglasses, set them down and reached out to pick up the box of detox tea. "Not that it wasn't fun, but still."

Eric raised his eyebrows. The photos had revealed a lot of laughing and socializing, not that they'd actually been line-dancing. The very idea of his Mom doing so was... Odd.

"I'm a little afraid of when she sends the photos," Jan went on, while putting down the detox tea then transferring Martini back to the floor. "The stuff on Facebook I can hide, but on my phone might be more tricky. What if she got shots of me and that one guy...?"

Ginny grimaced and set Jan's tea in front of her on the table.

Eric didn't think his eyes could open any wider. He blinked at Jan and his mother, feeling as though he'd stepped into the twilight zone.

"For the record, *I'd* planned for us to go to a few wine bars, maybe a jazz club, do it in style; hence, the limousine." Jan reached for the honey. "But, she kept on *insisting* we should kick it up a notch and before we knew it—"

"She was a woman on a mission," Ginny confirmed, pulling out a chair and sitting down.

"And the karaoke," Jan chortled, while she mixed honey into her mug. "I had no idea she could sing like that, did you?"

Ginny shook her head. "None. A complete surprise to me, too. Maybe that's how she gets her plants to grow, she sings to them."

"How about all of that cash she kept on pulling out of her bra?" Jan snorted. "I think I got a photo of that!"

Eric, sipping from his cup, nearly choked. "Her *bra?*" he said, between coughs to clear the liquid from his throat.

Ginny swiftly reached out to pat his back. "Okay?"

He nodded and took a breath.

"It was really something," Jan said. "It was like she had a third cup hidden under her top, just for money. *Victoria Secret*, the banking collection."

Ginny watched Martini slink out of the room. "The bartender looked mightily impressed, too."

"Oh, God." Eric said, grimacing. "There was a bartender?"

"Oh, yeah," Jan replied. "And he was young. He was probably in one of the photos—"

"*Too* young," Ginny interjected. "He had to be under thirty."

"Very fit," Jan remarked.

"Arms the size of my thighs," Ginny agreed.

"And he certainly seemed willing and up for whatever Dixie was offering."

Eric felt slightly nauseated.

"That's true. But, do you blame him? Truth be told, I'm honestly surprised she didn't end up bringing him home with her." Ginny lifted her cup from the table. "I was ready to make room in the car."

Jan eyed her mug, warily. "This is regular tea, right? Not that detox stuff?"

Ginny grinned. "Yes, it's regular. That stuff is a gift from Kim."

Jan looked at the box, skeptically.

"You know, I'm starting to think it's a good thing Kim's not here," Eric commented. "She'd be falling all over herself, hearing you two."

Jan smirked and picked up her tea.

Eric shook his head, while she drank deeply from her cup, and added, "I seriously can't even imagine what she'd have to say about Dixie."

Ginny shrugged. "Dixie's a firecracker. She's been divorced for a couple of years now, not to mention she's only forty-eight."

"Yeah," Jan agreed, putting her mug back on the table. "And ever since her divorce, she's been working out like a demon and living the single life to the hilt."

"She looks fantastic," Ginny said, matter of fact.

Jan nodded. "I'll say. She has an ass you could bounce a quarter off and get change back."

Eric nearly choked a second time, it was like he was hearing an echo of Brian's voice in the comment.

Ginny chuckled. Her poor son, he'd never been privy to their conversations.

"I tried to explain it all to Darryl," Jan went on, referring one more time to her husband. "But, as I said, he had no sympathy and kept on saying I should have gone home with you, instead of bringing my drunkenness back to our house to share with him."

They both laughed at that.

"Awe, he loves you," Ginny said, reaching out to pat her arm.

"Well, you'll be happy to know, Mom, it was *Kim* who insisted I come over and check on you," Eric said. "She was sincerely worried."

Jan swallowed the last of her tea and said, "Awe, isn't that nice. A concerned daughter-in-law."

Ginny looked at the contents of the grocery bag still displayed on her table and raised an eyebrow. *Concerned* was not the word she might have come up with. She smirked, not being able to resist, and asked, "Can I offer either of you something to eat? I mean, besides a tomato?"

Jan caught her eye and grinned. "Do you have anything starchy? I need starchy."

Ginny got up from her chair. "As a matter of fact, I do. Soda bread muffins."

Jan's face lit up.

"She was going to come, too," Eric further informed them, while Ginny retrieved a container from her countertop.

"What's that, dear?" Ginny asked, as she carried the container to the table.

"Kim," he said. "She was going to come, but then she didn't want to bring Layla along."

Ginny exchanged a sidelong look with Jan. "Oh, dear. Is Kim upset with me? Am I in the bad Grandma books?"

"No," he said, shaking his head. "I just think, after Layla started imitating me and saying *tanked* at the top of her voice, that was about all she could handle."

Ginny bit her lip while Jan snickered softly.

"I'll have to make it up to her," Ginny said, handing each of them a muffin.

Eric shrugged. "She'll get over it."

"Just send her out with Dixie." Jan winked. "She'll be so busy nursing her hangover, she'll forget about everything else."

\*\*\*\*

## Ginny's Hangover Soda Bread Muffins

### Ingredients

2 cups whole wheat flour
3 tablespoons brown sugar
1½ teaspoons baking powder
½ teaspoon baking soda
½ teaspoon cinnamon
½ teaspoon salt
¼ cup butter, cold
1 egg, beaten
1 cup buttermilk
¾ cup raisins

### Directions

Preheat oven to 350 degrees F.

o Grease 12 cup muffin tin and set aside.
o Combine dry ingredients together in large bowl.
o Cut in butter using a pastry cutter or, as Ginny does, with clean hands - until the mixture resembles coarse crumbs.
o In a separate, small bowl, mix together the egg and buttermilk. Add this mixture to the dry ingredients/butter mixture with raisins and blend.
o Scoop batter into prepared muffin cups and bake for 15 minutes or until tester inserted in center of muffins comes out clean.
o Remove muffins from oven and transfer to wire rack to cool.

Enjoy!

# Chapter Ten

Ginny pulled her silver, Audi A6 into an empty parking spot next to the curb in front of *Possibilites*, Boxwood Hills' specialty bookstore.

"I still don't get why you're doing this," Jan, sitting in the passenger seat beside Ginny, remarked. "Other than the fact that it's a nice, Grandma type of thing to do, you don't owe Kimberly any sort of peacemaking gesture. It's ridiculous."

"Oh, I know," Ginny agreed, while leaning around her seat for her brown leather purse on the backseat. "But I like buying books for Layla and if it also helps temper things a bit, no harm done."

Jan snorted derisively as she released her seatbelt then smoothed the creases in her black capri pants and emerald green blouse. "What things? You had some fun outside of the Granny box and suddenly *things* are in a tizzy?"

Ginny released her seatbelt and tucked her keys into her purse. "She was really shaken up, apparently."

"Seriously? It's been two weeks!"

"I know, but Eric told me she seems unable to let it drop."

"Oh, for goodness sake," Jan said, shaking her head. "That girl needs to get a hobby."

"He also said, when he tried to explain about us trying to do new things and having some fun, she got all riled up and asked what was wrong with knitting, or scrapbooking."

"Get out!" Jan pulled her sunglasses from her face and stared at Ginny, incredulous. "Knitting? What, in your rocker with a blanket tucked snuggly around your legs?"

Ginny chuckled and pulled the sun visor down to check her soft pink lipstick in the lighted mirror.

"Hell, even Grandma Moses was known for going outside to paint."

"I think it might be connected to the fact that her parents are a decade older than me."

"So?"

"*So*, I think she sees me in the same light as them." Ginny snapped the visor closed.

"And what light is that? Nursing home? Being in your seventies doesn't immediately mean soft foods and Scrabble."

"I like Scrabble."

"You know what I mean." Jan opened her door and stepped out of the car. "Heck, there are people in their seventies running marathons."

Ginny opened her car door and slipped from her seat. "Yes, but not her parents," she said, closing the door behind her and pressing the lock button on the handle.

"Regardless, it's true," Jan countered, then draped her purse across her body, messenger bag style. "Seventy isn't what it used to be."

Ginny walked around the car and joined her at the curb.

"Anyway, after all is said and done, I stand by what I've said in the past."

Ginny smoothed the front of her grey, linen pants before hooking her purse over her shoulder. She met Jan's eye and waited.

"That is one uptight young woman."

\*\*\*\*

A slim brunette in her mid-forties waved from behind the front desk when Ginny and Jan entered the bookstore.

"That's Pat, the owner," Ginny told Jan, while waving back. "She's a lovely woman, right up your alley of age-is-nothing-but-a-number."

"I like her already," Jan said, while Pat finished helping a customer then came out from behind the front desk and crossed the gleaming hardwood floor.

"Ginny!" she said, reaching out to give Ginny a quick hug. "It's so good to see you. How've you been?"

"Really well, thanks. Keeping busy," Ginny said, before placing her hand on Jan's shoulder. "This is my best friend, Jan."

"Lovely to meet you," Pat said, warmly, while extending her hand.

"And, as I was telling you," Ginny continued, to Jan, "this is the infamous Pat I've told you about."

Pat raised her eyebrows, making Jan laugh. "Don't worry," she clarified, shaking the hand Pat offered. "Ginny has nothing but praise for you and your shop."

"That's good news," Pat said, feigning relief.

"How's *Ian*?" Ginny asked, a Cheshire grin spreading across her face.

Jan noted the teasing tone of Ginny's voice and looked at Pat, curious. Clearly Ginny hadn't revealed all.

"He's good," Pat said, simply, smoothing the front of her black trousers.

Ginny turned to Jan, her voice still amused as she said, "Ian is Pat's fiancé, or *young buck* as I like to call him."

"Oh?" Jan said, lifting her eyebrows.

Pat snickered and shook her head at Ginny. "Stop it, you brat. He's not that young."

Ginny giggled. "Hmmm, so says you."

Pat laughed out loud and deflected. "I love that scarf. The color is gorgeous on you."

Ginny fingered the dusky, purple scarf draped around her neck and let her change the subject. "Thank you. It was a present from Jennifer."

"That girl has exquisite taste. Every time she comes in with the kids, I'm admiring something or other that either she or Grace is wearing."

"I'll be sure to tell her you said so."

"And I love your hair," Pat told Jan, admiring her artfully messy pixie cut.

"Jan dimpled. "Thank you."

"I've been trying to grow mine out a little," she said, running her fingers through her chin-length layers. "But, seeing how cute yours looks is making me think I might have to book an appointment at the salon to get this mop back in order."

Ginny smiled affectionately at the pair of them. She *knew* they'd get along.

"You've really done an amazing job with this space, Pat," Jan praised, looking around. "I remember when it was the second-hand bookstore. I almost can't believe it's the same place."

The interior of *Possibilities* was painted a smooth buttercream. In dark contrast to the light walls, the floors and solid bookshelves were stained in a rich cherrywood. Hanging from the ceiling to illuminate the shop when the sunshine wasn't streaming through the large, plate glass windows, were funky bronze-toned light fixtures; each one slightly different from the other.

"And those light fixtures," Jan went on, staring up at them with open admiration. "They're fantastic. Where did you find them?"

Pat grinned, pleased they were noticed. "I love them, too. I had them made specifically for the shop. Each one is an original."

"Someone local?" Jan asked.

"Uh-huh. The daughter of the folks who own *The Bakery*—"

"Phil and Annie?" Ginny said, surprised.

"Yes." Pat nodded. "Their daughter, Jade, is a magnificent artist."

Ginny shook her head and said, "Amazing. I remember when she was just a little thing, creating water-color paintings at one of the tables while Phil and Annie worked. Who knew she'd turn out to be such a talent?"

"You know, now that you say it, I think I've admired her work in their shop," Jan commented.

"Probably," Pat said. "I've got her cards at the till, if you want one before you go. She does all sorts of neat stuff."

"Okay, sounds good," Jan agreed, before being distracted by the sight of a tangerine colored feline slinking down the staircase at the back of the shop.

Pat watched the cat as he padded silently across the floor, then said, "This is Whiskey."

Whiskey flopped over onto his back and waved his paws at them invitingly.

Jan chuckled and crouched down to gently stroke his chest, making him purr. "Aren't you a gorgeous thing," she said, quietly.

Ginny smiled appreciatively at the green-eyed charmer. "He's just as lovely in personality as he is in appearance. He makes Martini look positively aloof."

Pat laughed then told Jan, "My best friend, Melanie, gave him to me after I bought the store. One of the best gifts I've ever been given."

"Well," Ginny said, adjusted her purse across her shoulder. "I should get to it."

"Looking for something specific?" Pat asked, cocking her head.

"A book for Layla."

"We have some cute new titles in her age group," Pat told her, gesturing to a display of books on a table near the children's section of her store.

Jan straightened up and tucked her arm through Ginny's. "Shall we find a book that will put you back in Ms. Kimberly's good favor?"

Ginny snickered and let her lead her to the shelves.

****

Ginny walked along Jennifer and Chris' front path, admiring the blue star creeper that grew alongside the cobblestones. Their garden was shaded by two large oak trees that dappled the sunlight and gave the grass some much needed cover, adding an extra infusion of grace to their already lovely property. Such a change from when they'd purchased it, three years back. Then, it had been in a dismal state, left to deteriorate and crumble. Ginny remembered being skeptical when they'd shown it to her, but Chris had been completely confident in the bones of the place and their ability to restore it to its original beauty. Clearly, he'd been spot on to be so confident, as now, with the white picket-fenced yard, butter yellow clapboard-style siding and polished wood gabling accents, crisp apple-green painted porch and shutters gleaming in the sunshine, it was a picture of cottage charm.

Ginny climbed the two steps up to the expansive porch and enjoyed the shade provided while she rang the doorbell. Chris opened the door, a large welcoming smile across his face.

"Good afternoon," Ginny said, her tone matching his sunny grin. "Are those new?"

Chris looked across the porch to where she was indicating. Two pairs of white, solid wood rocking chairs and two complementary side tables complete with overflowing pots of orange mums graced the space.

"Yup," he said, opening the door - the same polished wood as the gabling - wider. "Just got them last weekend."

"Well, they're just lovely," Ginny said, stepping across the threshold. "Are they as comfy as they look?"

"More so," Chris informed her, closing the door then turning to call out, "Grace, Mason, Grandma's here."

Ginny grinned when she heard the dual cheers from her grandchildren as they charged from their upstairs bedrooms and thundered down the staircase.

"Whoa," Jennifer said, as she left the kitchen and walked through the dining room toward the foyer. "Slow down, guys."

Grace raced past her, Mason hot on her heels, and they both came to a breathtaking halt just before careening into Ginny's legs.

"Time!" Ginny announced, giggling at the pair of them. "Thirty three seconds. A new record!"

Grace and Mason gave each other a high-five.

"God, don't encourage them," Jennifer commented, amused by their game.

Ginny slipped off her blue sneakers and put down her brown purse. Then she grabbed both kids into a bear-hug. "I can't help it. They're so darn encourage-able!"

"We have ingredients for sugar cookies, Grandma," Mason said, when Ginny reluctantly let them go.

Grace nodded, her eyes bright. "And sprinkles and icing and everything."

"Could we at least let Grandma get past the door before we start bombarding her with information?" Chris asked, his voice teasing. "Maybe even be polite and offer her a cup of tea?"

They had the good grace to look contrite and Ginny winked at them. "We'll make lots of cookies when Mom and Dad leave," she assured them. "So many, we'll have to freeze some for later."

"Cool," Mason said.

Jennifer reached around them to give Ginny a hug. "Thanks for coming over," she said, enjoying the light, fresh citrus scent of her mother's perfume.

Ginny squeezed her back. "It's my pleasure. I'm glad I'm still allowed to babysit, quite frankly, and haven't been placed on the naughty Grandma list."

Chris chuckled and shook his head. "Not likely to happen around here. The *wild-child* Grandma list, maybe..."

Ginny looked at him affectionately. He was such a good sport about things.

Mason, following Grace toward the kitchen, spoke over his shoulder, "You could never be naughty, Grandma."

Ginny bit her lip to keep from giggling.

Jennifer caught her eye and grinned. "Little pitchers, as the expression goes."

"Isn't that the truth," Ginny agreed, before snapping her fingers. "Oh, wait a second. With that in mind, I had to resort to bribery to get back in Kimberly's good graces and I have something for the kids."

Jennifer raised her eyebrows at Chris as Ginny backtracked to the front hall.

He shrugged.

"Bribery?" Jennifer repeated, once Ginny had retrieved a bag from her purse and began walking toward the kitchen.

"I'll fill you in later," Ginny said, then held up the bag for Grace and Mason to see. "I have a gift for you two. I was at the bookstore and saw these and bought them for you."

Mason, an early reader, lit up when Ginny reached into the bag and pulled out a large book filled with one of his favorite cartoon strips.

"Cool," he said, taking the book. "Thanks, Grandma."

Grace looked equally pleased when Ginny held out a book with an enticing cover called *13 Gifts*. "I haven't read this one, yet," she said, delighted.

"Wonderful," Ginny replied. "I think you'll like it."

"Thanks, Grandma," she said, grinning from ear to ear.

Jennifer watched them with a warm heart. It was so like her Mom to do something for no reason other than it would bring joy. Foolish Kimberly, she thought. Can't see the forest for the trees.

"You're both very welcome," Ginny said, before looking pointedly at Chris and Jennifer. "Now, don't *you two* have somewhere else to be? Friends to be dining with?"

Jennifer nodded. "Yup. We're outta here."

Chris picked up his car keys from the countertop and led the way to the door to the garage. "Have fun and be good," he counselled.

Neither Mason nor Grace replied, already caught up in their respective reading.

Ginny figured it was up to her. "We will," she said, cheekily, giving a small wave as the door closed behind them.

\*\*\*\*

"I have a great idea."

Ginny raised a skeptical eyebrow at Dixie. They were sitting in her modern-styled kitchen, a vision of contrasts with espresso colored cabinets, gleaming white granite countertops, stainless steel appliances and a backsplash in an array of charcoal and moss green glass tiles. It was breathtaking.

Dixie laughed when she saw her face. "What's with the look?"

"Oh, I don't know," Ginny offered, leaning forward in her chair at the kitchen island to select a donut from a blue box with *The Bakery* emblazoned across the lid. "It's just that the last time you said you had a *great idea* I ended up nearly drowning myself in tequila."

Dixie cracked up.

Ginny took a bite of her donut and sighed. "So good."

"Double chocolate. Your favorite," Dixie said, matter of fact.

Ginny nodded and swallowed.

"So, come on, now that I've said it, aren't you the least bit curious about my idea?" Dixie served herself a cup of coffee from the stainless steel carafe sitting on the island-top and leaned over to choose a pastry for herself.

Ginny shrugged. "Maybe, a bit."

Dixie lifted a long john from the box then smiled so lasciviously Ginny snickered.

"You're terrible."

"Agreed," Dixie said, then took a large bite of the pastry.

"Alright, so let's say for the sake of argument, I am curious. What's the idea?"

Dixie grabbed a napkin from a holder in the middle of the island and wiped her mouth. "Gwen signed up for an art class in line drawings, charcoals, that sort of thing, and she invited me to come along."

"Okay, and?" Ginny said, taking another bite of donut.

"*And,*" Dixie elaborated, "it's not so much an art class as it is an art party for women only. It's called *Monet and Merlot*, or something close to that. Have you ever heard of it?"

Ginny shook her head and finished off the rest of her donut. She wiped her fingers on a napkin then said, "It does sound like it could be fun."

"There yah go," Dixie said, approvingly, while placing the remainder of her long john on a small, square plate next to her coffee cup. "We learn some art techniques, have some snacks and wine and laughs. I was thinking you and Jan might find it fun, too."

Ginny picked up her teacup and considered the information. It *did* sound intriguing.

"It's a two evening workshop, a week from Saturday, classes start at seven and it costs one hundred and forty bucks."

Ginny nodded. "Okay. Sounds fabulous. I'm in."

Dixie's face lit up. "Really? That's great! Do you think Jan would be interested?"

"She doesn't have any choice." Ginny beamed.

Dixie laughed and ate the rest of her pastry.

\*\*\*\*

## Grace's Favorite Sugar Cookies
### (Recipe borrowed from Grandma Ginny)

### Ingredients
¾ cup butter
1 cup brown sugar
½ teaspoon vanilla extract
2 eggs
2½ cups whole wheat flour
1 teaspoon baking powder
½ teaspoon salt

### Directions
Preheat oven to 400 degrees F.

o In a large bowl, cream together butter and sugar until smooth.

o In a separate bowl, beat together eggs and vanilla. Add to butter mixture.

o In another bowl, blend together flour, baking powder and salt. Add to butter mixture.

o Cover dough and chill for one hour.

o When dough is chilled, roll out on a floured surface to approximately ¼ to ½ inch thickness.

o Using cookie cutters, cut into shapes and place on ungreased cookie sheets - 1 inch apart to allow for spreading.

o Bake 6 to 8 minutes in preheated oven. Cool then transfer to wire rack to cool completely.

o Decorate as desired.

Makes approximately 30 cookies.

# Chapter Eleven

"I think today might be the day."

Ginny turned in her chair at the side desk and looked up at Tamara, looming over her. "For what?"

"First contact!"

Ginny's face twisted in confusion. "Isn't that a movie?"

Tamara began winding her hair up into a makeshift bun and shot her a wry look. "Yes. But don't act as though you have no idea what I'm talking about."

Ginny held up her hands, surrender style. "I honestly don't."

Tamara snapped an elastic around her hair then pointed at a container of cookies beside the computer. "What are those?"

Ginny picked up the container, pulled off the lid and extended it forward. "Jaffa cakes. They're delicious, have one."

Tamara chose one and bit into it. "Mmmm. Did you make them?"

"No." Ginny shook her head. "I haven't had as much time lately, for baking. I bought these at the farmer's market."

Tamara popped the last of the cake into her mouth and brushed her fingertips off on her navy blue skirt. "Anyway, as I was saying, I think today is the day."

"And, as *I* said, I have no idea what you're talking about." Ginny peered at her co-worker and added, "Have you been sneaking cocktails without my notice?"

Tamara laughed. "Hardly. Besides, if I had cocktails, I'd share. It would make the day a whole new adventure."

Ginny grinned and folded her arms across her chest. "Okay, so you'll have to be more specific."

"Well, it's almost two." She tapped the face of the watch on her wrist. "So that means mystery man should be arriving at any moment and I think today might be the day he finally gets up the guts to make contact with you."

Ginny rolled her eyes and went back to the bulletin she was preparing on the computer. "You have an active imagination, I'll give you that."

\*\*\*\*

Ginny hit *save* on the final draft of her monthly events bulletin for their website and Facebook page and sighed with satisfaction. It was a slow day in the library, which had given her a solid hour to get the thing completed and put to bed, as the old expression went.

"Right on time!" Tamara announced, as she came sailing around the front desk.

Ginny twisted around in her seat, slightly surprised. "You were timing me?"

Tamara stopped short. "What?"

"You were timing me writing the bulletin?"

Tamara gave her an odd look and said, "No. Why on Earth would I do that?"

"You just said, 'right on time'."

"Oh," Tamara said, before laughing. "No, I wasn't talking about that."

Ginny watched her, amused by her amusement. "So, what were you talking about, then?"

Tamara pointed a finger covertly toward the stacks across the room. "That. Told you so."

Ginny turned her seat in the opposite direction and followed the course of her finger point. It was the mystery man, standing once again in the cooking section.

"Didn't I say two o'clock?" Tamara said, smugly, folding her arms across her chest.

Ginny shrugged.

I wonder if he's a chef?" she went on. "Or, maybe going to open a restaurant. That would explain why he's in the food section so much."

"Or, maybe he can't cook worth beans and is trying to learn," Ginny offered, watching him pull a book from the shelf and begin flipping through the pages. Suddenly, as though he sensed her gaze, he looked up and met her eye across the room.

Ginny's eyebrows shot up at being caught, she gave a small smile and quickly ducked her head. Good lord, it was like being a teenager all over again.

"Here he comes," Tamara announced, excitedly. "I told you today was the day."

Ginny lifted her chin and peeked just as he got in line behind two women ready to check out their books.

"I'm going to help those women," Tamara hissed. "You be ready to step in when I'm done and help him."

"Doesn't that seem rather *obvious*," Ginny attempted to say, before giving up when Tamara turned her back and started helping the women at the counter.

She swallowed against her sudden nerves and got to her feet. No reason to be nervous, she silently counselled herself. Just another patron checking out a book.

Tamara handed the final book back to the woman she was helping and turned to smile encouragingly.

Ginny gave her a tiny grin in return and walked over to the counter.

Tamara stepped aside, her eyes sparkling with excitement and Ginny turned smoothly toward... another woman and her toddler, with an armful of books.

"He just couldn't choose, so we'll borrow them all," the woman said, cheerfully, as she set the books on the counter.

Ginny blinked, her face a picture of surprise. Where the hell had he gone? She looked at Tamara, her face equally startled as she shrugged her shoulders up and down.

"Oh, dear," the woman said, misinterpreting their faces. "Are there too many books?"

"No, no, not at all," Tamara said, swiftly, while plastering on her professional face. "Let's get these started right away."

Ginny stepped back, letting Tamara get on with it, and assumed an equally pleasant expression. She wasn't sure how, but it appeared that mystery man was able to vanish at will. What an extraordinary skill.

\*\*\*\*

## Ginny's Not-Homemade Jaffa Cakes

### Ingredients
None.

### Directions
- Go to a local farmer's market.
- Search for a vendor selling Jaffa Cakes.
- Purchase.

Enjoy!

# Chapter Twelve

Ginny stood in her kitchen and wrung her hands while looking back and forth between Eric and Kimberly. She hadn't considered the idea there would be so much... *tension* at her announcement of having plans. In fact, she'd foolishly thought they might be happy she was getting back into the world again. Apparently not.

"It's *fine*, Mom," Eric said. "Honestly."

"I really am so sorry, honey," she apologized, *again*.

Eric shook his head while Kimberly bounced Layla on her hip and gave her best effort to look as though she wasn't sucking a lemon.

"I do feel terrible—"

"No, seriously, don't apologize," he said, feeling completely wrong-footed. "We shouldn't have stopped in unannounced—"

"No, it's fine," Ginny protested.

"No, it's really not," he insisted.

Layla shook her head, grave-faced as she parroted, "Really not."

"*And*," Eric added, "not only that, but we definitely shouldn't have just assumed you'd be free to babysit on such short notice. It's entirely our own fault."

Kimberly exhaled heavily, flicked her hair back from her shoulder and continued to say nothing.

Ginny began to pace back and forth across her kitchen floor. "It's just that we made reservations for dinner beforehand and I've already paid for the classes and they're non-refundable."

"Really?" Kimberly said, finally breaking her silence. "What if a person has an emergency and can't make it? They keep the money? That seems rather shady."

"Well," Ginny said, stopping pacing. "I'm sure if it was something *that* serious they would do the right thing and refund, but since this isn't the case... well..."

"Mom," Eric interrupted. "Stop. There's no way we would ask you to dump your classes."

Ginny looked at Kimberly still standing in the kitchen doorway, not entirely convinced.

Eric shot a poignant look across the room at his wife.

"No. Of course not," she agreed, monotone.

"See?" He lifted his hands imploringly. "Kim agrees, too."

Layla brightened and imitated him, lifting her little hands in front of herself as though pleading her case. "See? Gamma, see?"

"And Layla agrees as well." Eric grinned at his daughter. "Anyway, you and Jan—"

"And Dixie and Gwen," Ginny threw in, then watched Kimberly's face twist into a frown.

Oh, dear. She'd had a hunch it was Dixie who was still the sore spot, but refrained from inquiry so as to avoid an all-out *discussion*.

"Right. And Dixie and Gwen," Eric repeated, clearing his throat. "The four musketeers. We want you all to have a good time at your art classes and don't give any of this a second thought. There will be lots of other times for Kim and I to go out. Lots. We can reschedule with our friends. It's no big deal."

Layla leaned her head on Kimberly's shoulder and said, "No deal."

Ginny glanced back and forth between them. She had a feeling Layla may have more accurately hit the nail on the head: no deal, no fun, no happy campers. Oh, boy.

****

"Say it," Eric said, drumming his fingers on the steering wheel of his vehicle as he waited for a red light to change.

Kimberly, sitting rigidly in the passenger seat beside him, glanced back to check on Layla sleeping in her car seat.

"Kim," he pressed.

She turned back round, facing forward. "What? What is it you want?"

Eric sighed and pressed the accelerator when the light turned green. "You know exactly what. You're pissed Mom's busy and, instead of us meeting up with Carrie and Dan on Saturday, we're going to be ordering take out."

"She was available for Jen and Chris to go out," Kimberly huffed, folding her arms across her chest. "That's all I'm saying."

And there it is, Eric thought, watching the traffic.

"Not that I think she shouldn't spend time with her girlfriends," she elaborated.

*And* there's more, Eric thought. *Quelle surprise.*

"But art classes? *Really?*" She pursed her lips. "She'd be better off working with *Play-Doh* with Layla. Creativity and quality time with her Granddaughter. Two birds with one stone."

Eric remained quiet.

"Granted," Kimberly said, her voice growing thoughtful. "It *could* all be about something deeper."

Eric glanced at her, then looked back at the road. "Meaning?"

Kimberly shrugged. "Meaning there could be something more going on. A bigger issue we're not seeing."

"Like?"

She peeked around her seat to make sure Layla was still asleep, before saying, "I don't know *exactly*. But it's very possible her acting out could be a sign of deeper things."

Eric clenched his teeth. "*Acting out*? You make her sound like a petulant two year old."

"Okay, mister smarty-pants. What do *you* think?"

Eric grimaced. He hated when she did that. It was a no-win question.

"Eric?" she pressed.

"*I* think I hope she has a good time," he said, choosing neutral ground. "She's had a rough couple of years, she deserves some fun."

Kimberly frowned, but reserved comment. What was she going to say?

"Chinese?" he asked.

"Fine," she replied.

He flicked on his signal light then reached to turn up the radio.

**** 

Ginny shared a grin with Jan then looked around at the room in which they'd be spending the next couple of days attempting to learn how to draw with charcoal.

Three of the walls were painted a fresh cream color and decorated with examples of previous works of art in pencil, paint and textiles. The fourth wall was made up of large windows, their accordion blinds pulled up and out of the way to allow full viewing of the sky.

Ginny sighed contentedly, picked up her glass of merlot and leaned back in her padded chair. She wasn't sure how successful she'd be, but she was pleased to try. After all, trying was what gave life to life, right?

"I'm so glad you asked me to come along," Jan said, reaching out to pat her hand. Her seat was next to Ginny's at a long table and they each had their own tabletop easel and a thick pad of blank paper at the ready.

"I'm glad you both came," Dixie said, overhearing the comment. She was seated on the other side of Ginny, to her left.

"*I'm* glad I didn't cave in and cancel out of guilt over Eric and Kim," Ginny stated.

"*Ohmygod*," Dixie said, vehemently. "I would have had to intervene there, if that had happened."

"And I would have backed you up," Jan agreed. "I mean, seriously, assuming she'd be available without even checking first? Rude."

Ginny patted her arm in thanks for her support then leaned forward, around Dixie, to address Gwen. They were four in a row. "And a special thanks to *you*, Gwen. If you hadn't come up with this wonderful idea and shared it with Dixie, neither I nor Jan would be here at all."

Gwen smiled. "It was my pleasure. And, after already spending a previous booze-infused evening carousing with the two of you—"

Jan burst out laughing, cutting her off.

Dixie raised her glass and said, "A toast. May we all have a great weekend of further carousing!"

Ginny, Jan and Gwen lifted their glasses to clink them together, all of them beaming like eager teens.

Ginny tipped her glass to her lips, savored the richness of the wine and looked to the head of the class. A plush, berry colored chaise longue was poignantly vacant, as though awaiting its next subject.

Ginny nudged Jan and gestured toward it. "Looks like they do human form art class here as well."

"I was thinking the exact same thing," she said. "Can you imagine stripping off for a group of strangers? I can barely put on a one-piece bathing suit with any confidence, I can't imagine how self-assured you'd have to be to do that."

Ginny regarded her and sighed. Her best friend had no idea how phenomenal her figure was. She was petite and curvy, her hourglass shape the stuff of men's dreams. She'd be able to rake in good money if she had the guts to disrobe for art.

"Oh, didn't I mention?" Dixie said, overhearing their conversation and leaning around Ginny to make sure she was heard by them both. "This class isn't just for learning how to draw in charcoal, it's also —"

The door to the room opened and Dixie stopped talking when a woman strode purposefully into the class. Adorned in a candy pink, silk kimono, her fiery-red curls tumbling across her shoulders, she was captivating.

"Hey, all!" she said, raising her hand in greeting, her face lit up in a friendly smile.

"Is that the instructor?" Ginny asked, in a hushed tone.

She was a bit surprised, truth be told. For some reason, she'd expected the person leading the class to be younger, not around her own age. And, of course, she hadn't expected she'd be so informal.

Another woman followed in behind the redhead, also smiling in welcome. "A full class," she said, looking around at the room where every chair held a female seat. "Wonderful! I'm Corrina and I'll be your instructor for the next two days as we learn a little about the beauty of impressionism."

"Ahhh," Ginny said, turning to smile at Jan.

Jan nodded back.

Corrina, in her mid-thirties, her long blonde hair pulled off her face in a loose ponytail and dressed in navy blue capri pants and multi-colored peasant blouse, was more along the line of what Ginny had been expecting.

"Do you think the other woman is her assistant," Jan whispered.

Ginny shrugged.

"And this lovely woman," Corrina extended a hand toward the redhead, "is your model. Please extend a warm welcome to Josephine."

Josephine gave another friendly wave and a small curtsy. "Please be kind," she teased. "Or, at the very least, have another glass of wine before you start."

Corrina and the class laughed appreciatively.

Ginny and Jan exchanged slack-jawed looks before turning confused eyes toward Dixie and Gwen.

Dixie chortled when she saw their faces. "As I was about to tell you, this class isn't just about learning to work with charcoal. It's also about learning to draw the human form."

Gwen nodded, a happy grin on her face.

Before either Ginny or Jan could find their voices to ask how on Earth this nugget of information had not been passed along ahead of time, Josephine walked over to a large, silver hook on the wall, pulled loose the sash on her kimono and let it fall from her shoulders.

They watched in stunned silence as she hung the silky material from the hook, turned around and strode without any sort of apparent self-consciousness toward the empty chaise.

"Wow," was all Ginny could utter as Josephine modestly and tastefully arranged herself on the lounger, draping her body languidly across the furniture as though it was the most natural thing in the world to recline, naked, in front of a room full of strangers.

"I'll say," Jan agreed, her voice brimming with the same reverence and respect.

"Okay, then," Corrina said, all business. "Josephine is ready. Let's get to work."

\*\*\*\*

"I gotta be honest," Jan said, wiping the last of the charcoal from her fingertips. "I didn't find that nearly as awkward as I first thought I would."

"I know!" Ginny agreed. "Me, either!"

"At first," she continued, "I was all where-do-I-look, but then I just sort-of got over it and pretty soon I wasn't seeing her as naked so much as seeing her as art."

"That's exactly how I felt, too," Ginny said, nodding her head up and down. "In fact, when she put her robe back on, it was almost a surprise to see her clothed."

Jan laughed and set her rag on the table.

Dixie and Gwen, wine glasses securely in hand, were across the room, chatting with Josephine. Dixie turned and waved exaggeratedly, extending her arm high for them to see.

"Dixie's beckoning," Jan said. "Should we?"

"Definitely." Ginny led the way, a big smile on her face.

\*\*\*\*

Dixie made room for them beside her and was quick with her introductions. "Josephine Wright, please meet Ginny and Jan. The other two that make up our fun-loving foursome."

Josephine fixed her bright, hazel eyes on them and her face broke into a wide grin. "So nice to meet you! Are you enjoying yourselves?"

Ginny extended her hand. "Very much, thanks."

"Have you tried the pain au chocolat?" Josephine asked, shaking the hand Ginny offered. "It's out of this world."

"It really is," Gwen agreed, sighing.

"How about the merlot?" Josephine raised her glass of wine. "Any favorites, yet?"

"*Dirty Laundry*'s is fabulous," Dixie said.

Josephine nodded, enthusiastically. "I agree! I love that one, too."

"Did I try that one?" Gwen asked, her face thoughtful.

"It was the second glass we had," Dixie reminded her. "The one that I said was perfect with the desserts."

Gwen's eyes lit up. "Ahh, right. I'm definitely going to be looking for that one again."

"I don't know if I tried that one," Ginny said.

"No time like the present," Dixie replied.

"The class was amazing," Jan threw in, changing the conversational course. "*You* were amazing."

Josephine widened her eyes at Jan's proclamation. "Me? What did I do, besides stay still and resist the urge to scratch an itch on my arm?"

Dixie chuckled appreciatively at her humor.

Gwen spoke up, backing Jan's statement. "Well, aside from your self-control, you're an absolute champ, being willing to strip down for strangers."

"Oh, well..." Josephine waved her hand dismissively and took a long swallow from the wine glass in her hand.

"It's true," Dixie agreed, matter-of-fact. "Seriously ballsy."

Josephine threw her head back and released a peal of laughter. "Girls, truth be told, tonight was a lovely, relaxing time. If I told you some of the things I've experienced on other occasions doing this, you wouldn't believe me."

"Okay, that sounds far too enticing to bypass," Ginny said, a glint in her eye. "Can we bribe you with lunch tomorrow, to share some of your tales?"

Josephine raised her glass. "Just tell me where and when and you have yourself a deal."

Dixie quickly pulled her phone from her pocket. "Can we get a picture of all of us? This is just too great to pass up."

They all clustered together around Josephine while Dixie enlisted another woman in the class to take a number of photos. By the end of it, there was so much laughter and so many pictures being snapped, they'd all become fast friends.

"To the magic of art class!" Dixie cheered, raising her glass.

She was immediately greeted with a roar of female voices, celebrating along with her.

\*\*\*\*

"So, Saturday night," Brian said.

"Yup," Eric replied, leaning back in his chair and propping his feet on his desk next to his laptop.

The brothers were catching up on Skype, Brian from his office at work and Eric from his home office.

"Any big plans on tap?"

"Nope."

"By the way, you know I can't see you when you do that, right?" Brian leaned closer to the webcam on his own computer and pretended to try and peer around Eric's feet.

Eric snickered and repositioned the laptop. He adjusted the angle of the screen and asked, "How's that?"

Brian nodded. "Better."

"So, how about you? What're you up to?"

"No, no," Brian said, shaking his head. "We weren't done with you, yet."

Eric yawned then asked, "What about me?"

"I asked you if you have plans and all I get is a 'nope'. What's that about?"

Eric shrugged. "Nothing. We did have plans, but they didn't pan out."

"Okay, then," Brian said, nodding. "So, you actually *had* plans, instead of the usual crashing on the couch?"

"Yes, smart-ass, we did. But we didn't think through the babysitting arrangements and got side-lined."

"Huh," Brian said, his face thoughtful. "Gotta be honest, bro, that doesn't sound like Kim at all. Sounds more like you."

Eric couldn't help himself and laughed. "Yeah, well this time it was both of us. We made plans with friends to go out for dinner, dancing, the whole deal, and figured Mom would be around to babysit—"

"And she wasn't."

"You don't sound all that surprised."

"And you sound pissed," Brian said.

Eric shook his head. "No, I'm not. Not really."

"*Okaaay,*" Brian said, unconvinced.

Eric paused, then pulled his feet off the desk and leaned in closer to the webcam.

"Whoa!" Brian leaned back in mock horror. "Warn a guy when you're going to do that."

"The thing is," Eric said, his voice hushed. "Kimberly won't let it go."

"Won't let what go?"

"That Mom had plans. She just keeps harping on it and harping on it as though it's some sort of god-damned crime she has other things to do besides be at our beck and call."

Brian watched him frown and exhale in frustration. Yikes.

"I mean, Jeez, it's like she expects Mom to stay in freaking mourning forever. As though, God forbid, after two years since Dad died she's out of line for daring to do something besides babysit our kids."

"How long does she usually hold a grudge?" Brian asked, trying to sidestep Eric's irritation and get to the crux of things.

Eric exhaled and rubbed a hand along the stubble on his chin. Brian was well clued-in about Kimberly's sometimes rigid nature. There was nothing to hide. "Depends on the situation," he said, finally. "I'd imagine this will blow over in a couple of days, probably after the weekend is over."

Brian said nothing. Sounded like his brother was going to be walking on egg shells for a while longer.

"On the positive, she's agreed to us going to Mom's next weekend with Jen and Chris, no kids, so…"

"Sounds like Mom's offering a peace making gesture for not being available."

Eric nodded. "Yeah, that's exactly what I thought, too, when she texted me about it."

Brian shook his head. "She doesn't have to do that."

"I know," Eric agreed. "But, try and tell her that and you're wasting your breath. You know our mother, she hates it if she thinks she's let one of us down."

Brian smiled affectionately. "Could be worse."

"I suppose," Eric agreed, before shaking his head. "Anyway, enough about my shit, what's on tap in your world?"

Brian got the hint and let him change the subject. "Just me and some friends—"

"And *Paige?*"

Brian stopped short, a wry grin spreading across his face.

Eric chuckled. "Are you bringing her out anytime soon?"

"Jennifer?" Brain asked, knowing it was really their sister behind the question.

Eric nodded. "She won't shut up about it."

"Yeah, she's at me, too," Brian admitted. "I'm sure she'll wear me down soon enough and I'll be bringing Paige out just to shut her up."

Eric nodded, again. That sounded about right. There were many things both he and Brian had done growing up, just to shut their sister up. Why would it change now?

"So, *anyway*, we're all heading out to check out a new restaurant that just opened up downtown. *Le Pain Croustillant.*"

"The crusty bread?" Eric said, trying to recall his high school French.

Brian laughed. "Yeah, something like that. Supposedly great food."

"Sounds like a good time," Eric said, doing his best to keep the wistfulness from his voice.

"Hey," Brian said, checking the time on his laptop. "Listen, bro, speaking of dinner, I gotta run. I promised Paige I'd pick up something for her before I go pick her up and I'm cutting it close."

Eric grinned. Suddenly, he felt slightly less married-guy-stuck-on-the-shore watching the single guy float off, carefree, in his rowboat.

"Yeah, yeah," Brian said, looking at his brother's face and knowing exactly why he was smirking. "Catch you later."

"Have fun," Eric managed to say, before Brian hung-up.

****

## *Ginny's Art Class Pain Au Chocolat*

### Ingredients
None.

### Directions
- Sign up for an art class that includes wine and food.
- Search for the pastries and hope they have pain au chocolat.
- If found, consume with gusto.

# Chapter Thirteen

Ginny washed red grapes in a stainless steel colander at the kitchen sink, doing her best to distract herself from what was to come. Or, more to the point, *who* was to come. It was silly, she knew, to be so jittery about the idea of her own children arriving, but they'd proven in the recent past to be unreliable about their reactions to things; more directly things about *her* and her choices.

"It's going to be fine, right?" Ginny said, to Martini, sprawled bonelessly across a chair at the kitchen table.

The cat blinked and looked back at her with grave eyes, as though pondering the question.

"Goodness, so serious," Ginny commented, before the doorbell sounded and cut her off. For good, bad or ugly, it was show time. She took a breath, wiped her hands on a dishtowel on the countertop and called out, "It's open."

"It's us," Jennifer called, back while opening the front door.

"Come on in." Ginny touched her hair, nerves bubbling to the surface.

"Chris saw Eric and Kim driving behind us, they should be here any minute," Jennifer continued, as she slipped off her shoes and walked through the family room into the kitchen.

"Okay," Ginny replied. "Did you bring wine?"

"Red and white," Chris said, following behind Jennifer, carrying a bottle in each hand.

"Hello!" Eric's voice rang out, as he pushed open the front door.

His voice was drowned out by Jennifer, hollering, "Holy shit, Mom!"

****

"Okay, okay." Ginny patted the air in front of her in a soothing manner. "Everyone just calm down."

Eric and Kimberly had come dashing into the room when they'd heard Jennifer's expletive and then nothing but chaos and voices tripping over each other had ensued.

"It's just *hair*, for goodness sake," Ginny said, matter of fact, as her children and their spouses finally began to find seats at the table.

"It's *darn fine* looking hair," Chris affectionately corrected, a grin on his face as he looked at her with appreciation. "You look glamorous, Gin."

Ginny reached out and patted his arm appreciatively. "Thank you, dear."

"What on heaven and Earth prompted you to go blonde, of all things?" Jennifer demanded, unable to stop staring at Ginny's newly golden locks.

"It was Dixie's idea."

"Dixie's?" Jennifer repeated, trying to wrap her brain around her mother's new look. From formerly faded brown with a heavy smattering of grey, to this rich, buttery color was startling, to say the very least. In a single moment, her mother had gone from background to foreground, her features receiving a boost of youth and vitality with every glossy strand of hair.

"Uh-huh," Ginny said, walking over to her china cabinet.

"And a mani-pedi!" Jennifer pointed at Ginny's fingernails, then her toes, all decked out in shell pink polish. "Get outta town!"

Kimberly, silent, her eyes roaming over Ginny's new hair, red blouse, tan palazzo pants and dressed up feet, turned to shoot a look at Eric.

He shrugged, not sure what the *look* was about.

"And maybe even a makeover?" Jennifer asked, as she peered closer at Ginny's face.

"Again, all Dixie. After our art class last weekend, she started nattering at me to freshen my look. Eventually I gave up resisting and she took me to her stylist. She's on a roll and, apparently, I'm her project."

"Another *fun* thing to do with the girls." Kimberly's voice was tight and laced with sarcasm.

Eric frowned and shot *her* a look while Ginny pulled wine glasses from the cabinet. He got up from his seat at the table and went over to open the first bottle of wine on the counter.

"As a matter of fact, yes," Ginny replied, lightly, carrying the glasses to the island then going back to close the glass-front doors on the cabinet. "And her stylist is just the loveliest young man. His name is Michael and works at *A Cut Above*. I know you and the girls have someone you trust, but if things change, I highly recommend him."

Jennifer rose from her seat and walked over to Ginny. She reached out and wrapped her in a hug. "I think it's fantastic, Mom. Seriously fantastic. A huge shock, of course, but you look gorgeous. It takes ten years off you, at least, and you deserve to look and feel fantastic."

Ginny's eyes teared up and she hugged her back. She swallowed against the rising tide of emotion and said, softly, "Thank you, sweetheart. I'm just trying to keep going forward. After your father.... Well, it just seems in poor taste to do otherwise, you know?"

Jennifer nodded and released her. "I totally get it. Totally. Time waits for no one."

"And," Ginny said, lightening the mood. "Dixie will be thrilled when I tell her you all finally saw the new do. She's been dying to post about it on her Facebook page, but didn't want to spoil the surprise."

"Hey," Chris piped up, while Eric began pouring and distributing glasses of wine. "Speaking of which, what about those art classes, anyway? I'm guessing from everything we're seeing, they were good? Should we be getting ready to cheer on the next up and coming artist in our midst?"

Ginny laughed and took the wineglass Eric offered. "Not quite. You can refrain from clearing a space on your walls anytime soon. But it was a lot of fun and I did learn a few things."

There was a bell-chime sound and everyone looked at everyone else.

"Not me," Eric said.

Kimberly reached into her purse for her phone. "Me, neither."

"I think it was you, Ginny," Chris said, while both he and Jennifer quickly checked their own phones and found nothing.

Ginny walked over to where her phone was lying on the counter, picked it up, read the text and started laughing. "See? I was right. It's Dixie, asking if you all have seen my hair yet." She put her wineglass down and continuing chuckling as she quickly typed a response.

"So, what sort of artwork did you end up doing in the class, Mom?" Jennifer asked, before taking a long sip from her wineglass.

Ginny put her phone back down and pointed at the refrigerator door. "Charcoal drawing. Have a look."

Eric walked over to the refrigerator.

"Those are two of my drawings," Ginny came up beside him, wineglass in hand, and pointed at the papers tacked to the door. "The others I left in the classroom for their wall of student art."

Eric peered at them and his eyebrows spiked on his forehead. "Whoa! Mom!"

"What?" Ginny said, taking a sip of wine and finding his reaction amusing. "That's Josephine, the model. She was fantastic."

He took a step back so fast, the wine sloshed in his glass.

Ginny smirked and continued, "And funny! God, she told us some stories; she actually had a guy faint in class when she took off her robe. Not that surprising, really, considering how gorgeous she is. And she's MY age! Can you imagine?"

Chris watched Eric's face, his mouth opening and closing as he tried to find some sort of words, and couldn't stand it any longer. He had to see for himself. He took a large, bracing swallow of wine and went over to the refrigerator, leaned in for a closer look then laughed out loud.

"Christopher!" Jennifer admonished.

He shook his head, quickly defending himself. "No, no, don't get me wrong, I'm not laughing at the work. It's actually really good. Very life-like. Very surprising, but very life-like."

Ginny grinned. "Thank you, dear."

Jennifer and Kimberly quickly scrambled from their seats and hustled over to the refrigerator door.

"Wow," Jennifer exhaled, blinking very fast. She had not expected to see a naked woman lying prostrate on a chaise lounge on her mother's refrigerator; or anywhere else in her house for that matter.

"Ewww!" Kimberly's face twisted in revulsion and she slapped Eric's shoulder.

"Hey!" he said, putting his glass on the island when the contents sloshed for a second time. "What was *that* for? What did *I* do?"

Ginny's eyes widened. Goodness. Such a reaction. Maybe she was an artist after all.

"You could have said that it was a drawing of a fully naked woman! Then I could have at least prepared myself!"

Chris laughed. "Prepared yourself? For what? It's not porn."

Jennifer exchanged a look with Ginny. Oooh, her husband was being braver than usual.

"As good as," Kimberly huffed.

"Oh, come on," Chris groaned. "It's a naked woman, sure, but she's tastefully *arranged*."

Kimberly folded her arms across her chest and countered, "Sounds like you know what you're talking about. Anything we should know?"

Oh, oh, Ginny thought. Time to stop this train in its tracks. "As I was saying, her name is Josephine. She was so friendly and outgoing, we nearly forgot she was...." She paused to choose a PG word. "Disrobed."

"And you said she was *your* age," Jennifer inquired.

Ginny patted her arm in appreciation for helping things along. "Uh-huh. Amazing, isn't it? She's in terrific shape. I only wish I looked that great."

"Did you get a good look, Eric?" Jennifer asked, her eyes sparkling with mischief as she picked up her wineglass from the table. "Did you get a good long look at Mom's drawing? And she's Mom's peer, too. It's like, I don't know, they're the same."

He cut his eyes at her and nodded. "Uh-huh. Great."

Ginny raised an eyebrow. Okay, maybe Jennifer wasn't helping as much as it first appeared.

"What are you getting at?" Kimberly asked, frowning first at Jennifer then turning her attention to Ginny. "What's she saying? You're not getting some crazy idea to toss off your clothes like *that woman* and let people draw you, are you? *Ohmygod*, is *that* the reason you changed your hair?"

"Me?" Ginny laughed at the very idea.

Eric groaned and pressed his hands to his eyes. Jennifer had to bite her lip to keep from laughing.

Chris, as bad as his wife, threw an arm around his brother-in-law's shoulders. "Can you *imagine it*? Mom on the refrigerator doors of the students in the art class?"

Ginny shook her head at them, knowing full well now what they were doing. Brats.

Kimberly clearly didn't get that they were teasing and blurted, "No way! That's not on!"

"Don't get yourself all wound up, now," Ginny placated, putting her wineglass on the island next to Eric's. "*I'm* not taking off my clothes for anyone."

"Well, thank heavens for that," Kimberly said, tightly.

"*Dixie* on the other hand, that's anyone's guess. She's so fit she could star in her own workout video. She has nothing she needs to hide."

"Okay!" Jennifer clapped her hands, cheerleader style. "I think it's time we got started on the appetizers and enjoying these delicious bottles of wine we brought.

Otherwise, we'll all have to get back to the babysitters before we've had a chance to have a proper catchup."

"Hear, hear, I'll help," Eric said, avoiding the glare Kimberly was desperately trying to send him from across the room.

\*\*\*\*

Eric drove along the quiet roads, the hum of the vehicle the only sound as the street lamps illuminated the interior of his car at regular intervals. He wanted to turn on music, but had a strong suspicion if he showed too much relaxation it might spur Kimberly, next to him in the passenger seat, to start talking.

Not that he didn't want her to talk, but the tension coming off of her in nearly visible waves was so thick he was concerned as to what exactly would come out of her mouth.

"So, are we going to discuss it *at all*? Or just sweep it under the rug as usual!"

Eric jerked at the suddenness of Kim's sharp voice and took a steadying breath. So much for keeping things silent.

"Well?" She turned her head to stare at him.

Eric could see her in his peripheral vision and chose to keep his eyes on the road. The expression, 'don't make direct eye contact' rang in his head.

He braced himself and asked, "Discuss *what*, exactly?"

Kimberly frowned. "Are you being serious?"

As a heart attack, he thought, but didn't vocalize.

"Because, if you're not," she went on, "tell me now, so I don't waste my breath."

Eric yearned to tell her not to waste her breath, *but....* Yeah, not going to happen. He wanted to be allowed to sleep *inside* the house, after all.

"Your mother is heading down a *path* here." Kimberly shook her head. "I know I've commented on it before, but it seems worth saying again."

"What? What are you talking about? What path?" he ventured, stopping at a traffic light. "Did you not hear her tell Jen she's trying to move forward?"

She folded her arms across her chest. "Yes, I heard her. But it's one thing to do something normal like... I don't know, plant new flowers! It's a whole other deal to change over your entire look that you've had for ages and ages."

The light turned green and he accelerated forward. "I don't follow."

She rolled her eyes at him and took a breath. "It's like a trend is starting."

"A trend?" He turned onto their street and drove slowly toward their house.

Kimberly flashed him a look of annoyance. "Yes, a *trend*. A trend where she isn't so much moving forward as running from her past."

"Oh, come on—"

"FIRST the drinking and gallivanting," she interrupted, emphatically driving home her point. "THEN she seems to have stopped baking. Did you notice that, by the way? Store bought cookies? When has she ever offered store bought baking?"

Eric bit his tongue. It was too much effort to argue.

"And *now* we've added not wanting to babysit in favor of attending erotic art classes to the list."

Eric laughed as he pulled up onto their driveway and clicked the remote control that opened their garage door.

"What's funny?"

He drove into the garage and cut the engine. "It wasn't an *erotic* art class, Hon."

She shrugged and opened her door. "Near enough. Anyway, it could be the start of some really reckless behavior. Actions she might regret."

Eric got out of the car. "Let's not get ahead of ourselves. She's trying to move forward, which is a good thing. It shows she's feeling better and embracing some change, that's all."

Kimberly unlocked the door to the house, her face skeptical. "We'll see."

****

## *Ginny's Store-Bought Macaroons*

**Ingredients**
None.

**Directions**
- Walk/drive/take a bus to your local grocery store, or favorite bakery.
- Chose macaroon cookies that strike your fancy.
- Purchase.
- Share with family and friends.

# Chapter Fourteen

"You look ah-ma-zing!" Tamara positively beamed as she shared her enthusiasm, her grin so wide Ginny could see all of her straight, white teeth. "You should have done this ages ago."

Ginny cocked her head of blonde waves and raised an eyebrow.

Tamara's eyes widened and a flush blossomed on her cheeks. God, she had to learn to think before she spoke. "Not that you weren't beautiful before," she amended, her voice pleading to be let off the hook yet another time. "Of course you were. It's just now you look so...."

Ginny watched her squirm and did her best to hide her amusement.

"Glamorous!"

Ginny burst out laughing. It was too much. She reached across the library front desk and grabbed Tamara's hand, squeezing it affectionately.

"Oh, thank god," Tamara exhaled, massaging the bridge of her nose. "I am the worst! I need a speech writer for every damned occasion."

Ginny released her hand. "I *know* what you mean, dear. And thank you. Truth be told, it's still all so new I'm finding myself a bit startled when I look in the mirror."

"Startled in a good way, I hope," Tamara said, smoothing her dark hair back from her face. "Because I mean it, you look gorgeous. Not just the new hair, but I love the new outfit as well. It's like you've been on one of those personal makeover shows."

"And it felt like it, too," Ginny admitted, glancing down at her black and purple, check print tunic, the cinched belt accentuating her small waist. "My girlfriend, Dixie, was all business. If she wanted to give up real estate, she could become a personal shopper and makeover expert in a flash."

"Do you know what the real shame is?"

Ginny shook her head.

"The real shame is that mystery man isn't here to see you." Tamara waggled her eyebrows. "Can you imagine his eyes? Ahh-oo-gaaa!"

Ginny laughed and put her hands up in surrender. "Stop. Or else my newly colored head will get too large to fit through the doorway."

"Fine, fine," she relented, with a giggle, before gesturing to a box of treats on the desktop. "Homemade?"

"No, sorry. It's been a bit hectic lately—"

"No need for apology." Tamara waved her words away as she lifted the lid on the box and peered inside. "It's not like you have a baking clause in your contract. Ooh, donut holes!"

Ginny watched her grab a chocolate one and pop it into her mouth.

"You know what you should do now?" Tamara said, around her chewing.

"Get to work?"

"No! We still have…" Tamara looked at the oversized, round wall clock hung above the entrance to the library. "Twenty minutes until we open the doors."

"So, what then?"

"Create a Facebook account!"

"Oh, for goodness sake," Ginny said, shaking her head. "You sound just like Dixie."

"The makeover guru?"

"That's the one."

"Well, why not?" Tamara insisted, before looking around at the quiet library. "We could get you set up in no time."

Ginny shrugged. "I don't know…"

Tamara quickly sat down at the staff computer and pulled up a chair for Ginny, too. "Come on. It's a piece of cake, I'll walk you through it." She saw Ginny's skeptical expression and added, "You can always delete it if you really don't like it."

Ginny shrugged, again. "I suppose."

"Oh, come on," Tamara cajoled, while choosing another donut hole from the box. "New hair, new attitude, new fun!"

Ginny couldn't help herself and grinned. "Alright, fine," she said, sitting down.

"Atta girl!" Tamara said, popping the pastry into her mouth as she'd done with the first one then starting to type.

****

Kimberly frowned as her fingers flew across the keys of her laptop, typing out her thoughts. She was chatting with her sister, Kris, on Facebook, and was having a hard time wrapping her head around what she was saying about their Dad.

*"I don't understand. What are you trying to say?"*

*Kris: "I think it goes deeper than new shirts and shoes and golf dates. God, I don't even want to say it out loud, but..."*

"But, what?" Kimberly pressed. She hated when Kris was vague.

*Kris: "I think he may be having an affair."*

Kimberly nearly fell off her seat. *"What?! Why? What's happened?"*

*Kris: "I saw him."*

Kimberly hesitated. She didn't want to ask, but knew she had to: *"Saw him? What does that mean?"*

*Kris: "Exactly how it sounds. I saw him with a woman at a cafe. They were holding hands across the table and not in a friendly way."*

"Holy shit," Kimberly exhaled, running her fingers through her hair as she stared at the computer screen. She didn't know how to respond.

*Kris: "I know it's a shock. I actually felt nauseous when I saw them. But, that aside, the real issue is, do we confront him? Or keep out of it?"*

Jesus, Kimberly thought. What the hell is happening to the old people? First Ginny getting weird and now her Dad spotted with another woman!

*Kris: "Hello? You still there?"*

She took a breath and started typing. *"Yeah, sorry. Just reeling a bit. I have no idea what we should do. This reminds me of what's going on with Eric's Mom, Ginny. It's different in that she's a widow, but still, she's doing strange stuff and acting way off her normal self. I think it's a sign of something deeper and he's just brushing me off."*

*Kris: "Tell him about Dad, that'll make him sit up and listen."*

Kimberly grinned. She had a point. *"First we have to be sure about Dad."*

Kris: *"I suppose, but it looked pretty obvious to me. When I told Grayson about it he said much the same as you, that we have to be sure first."*

Kimberly nodded, even though Kris couldn't see her, glad that her brother-in-law was of the same mind. *"We definitely don't want to falsely accuse. That would be a nightmare."*

Kris: *"Yeah, I know. I'll keep an eye out and let you know if I notice anything else suspicious."*

Kimberly bit her lip then asked the question she'd been dreading to pose. *"Do you think Mom suspects?"*

Kris: *"Grayson asked me the same thing and I said I don't think so. I could be wrong, of course, but she hasn't indicated anything so...."*

Kimberly sighed. It would have to do, for now. She was about to sign off, when a friend request popped up at the top of her screen. *"Hang on a sec,"* she typed, before clicking on the icon.

Kris: *"K."*

"OH, MY, GOD!" Kimberly blurted, when she read the name and saw the photo staring back at her.

"Kim?" Eric called out, before charging down the hallway into their bedroom.

"This is too much!" she said, pressing her fingertips to her temples.

He regarded her with concern. "What? What is it? What's wrong?"

Kris: *"Hello?"*

Kimberly took a cleansing breath and began typing furiously. *"Sorry! Didn't mean to leave you hanging. I've got a situation here, I'll fill you in tomorrow."*

Eric lifted his hands imploringly when Kimberly continued to look at the screen, instead of answering him. "Kim? Where's the fire?"

Kris: *"Oh, dear. Okay. I'll let you go. Hope everything's okay."*

Kimberly clenched her jaw then wrote: *"Love you,"* before turning to glare at Eric.

His eyes widened while, on Kimberly's screen, Kris' chat window disappeared.

"Unbelievable," Kimberly stated. "Un-bloody-believable."

Eric took a breath to stop himself from yelling, released it and said, "What. Is. It?"

"Your *mother*," she said, her hands balling into fists.

He frowned. "My mother?"

"She's sent me a friend request," she said, her words becoming shrill. "On Facebook!"

Eric blanched. "What?"

"Yeah," Kimberly spat, jabbing a finger at her screen. "Yeah, that's what I said! Your sixty-two year old mother has sent me a bloody friend request on Facebook!"

Eric walked over to where she was sitting on the bed and peered over her shoulder. Sure enough, there it was, a friend request from his mother; her smiling face glowing at him in her profile photo. Jesus.

"Are you serious right now?" Kimberly asked.

Eric dragged his eyes away from the screen. "What?"

"You find this *funny*?"

"What?" he said. "No! Why would you—"

"Then why the hell are you smirking?"

Was he? He paused to consider his face and, sure enough, there it was. His lips had unconsciously formed into amused smirk. Guilty as charged.

Kimberly glared at him then snapped her laptop shut. If he didn't see that this was even more reason to be concerned about his mother, she sure as hell was in no mood to educate him.

"Listen," Eric began, trying to smooth things over. "It's no big deal. It's just Facebook. Probably Dixie put her up to it. It's nothing."

"I'm going to take a bath," she said, pushing her laptop aside then getting up and breezing by him, out of the bedroom. "Layla is still napping, listen for her in case she wakes up."

Once he was alone, Eric relaxed his shoulders. Then, as soon as he heard the sound of water running in the bathroom, he gave in to his deeper impulse and the smirk deepened into a grin.

****

## Ginny's Not-Homemade Donut Holes

### Ingredients
None.

### Directions
- o Drive to your local donut house.
- o Order one box of assorted donut holes.
- o Purchase.
- o Share.

# Chapter Fifteen

G inny stood in front of her bathroom mirror and smoothed the cap sleeves on her new dress. Sapphire blue with a V-neck bodice and knee length, shutter pleated skirt, it brought out the color of her eyes. She smiled encouragingly at herself in the mirror, feeling a bit foolish but certain she'd read in some magazine that it was a good way to rev up good energy in the body.

Her phone sounded on the vanity beside her and she picked it up to read the text.

*Dixie: "All ready for your night out?"*

Ginny grinned for real and typed: *"As ready as I'm ever going to be. At least this time there are no fix-ups involved."*

*Dixie: "Send me a photo of how great you look!"*

Ginny laughed then grimaced.

Dixie, as though reading her thoughts, wrote: *"Come on, one selfie! You can do it!"*

"Oh, fine," Ginny said, then moved next to Martini, languishing comfortably across the bathroom countertop. "But, you're going to be in the photo with me."

The cat stared at the phone as though he'd been trained for selfies and Ginny snapped a photo of the two of them, using the bathroom mirrors' reflection to further showoff her dress.

*Dixie:* "*Woohoo! You look gorgeous! You should post that one on Facebook. And Martini looks very handsome as well, btw.*"

Ginny giggled and typed: "*xoxoxoxo*"

*Dixie:* "*I'll see you later tonight. xoxo*"

Ginny sent back a thumbs-up emoji then turned off her phone and told Martini, "I'll only be gone a couple of hours. You'll barely have time to notice I left before I'm back."

She took one last look in the mirror, rechecked the tortoiseshell clip holding up her creamy pale waves, clicked off the light and left the room.

****

Eric increased the volume on the TV as, behind him in the kitchen, Kimberly alternately sighed and made an obvious show of her mood with every slam of a cupboard door. They were staying in, *again*, as Ginny had plans and, go figure, it wasn't going down well.

"Kim," Eric pleaded, from his seat on the family room sofa. "Can we please just let it rest?"

Kimberly snapped her laptop shut on the kitchen counter. "What?"

"Your pissy mood because Mom isn't available tonight," he said, over his shoulder, throwing caution to the wind and just saying it.

"What if your Mom isn't just making changes and, in fact, is actually going through something and you're just too stubborn to see it?"

Eric turned down the volume on the TV. "What? What are you talking about?"

"I'm talking about her sudden behavior changes—"

"Oh, Jeez," he said, cutting her off. "Can we please just let that drop, already?"

"See?" she said, pointing at his back. "It's possible her changes are indicative of something more serious going on and you refuse to consider it. Did you see the selfie she posted on Facebook? A *selfie*, from your sixty two year old *Mom*. That's not unsettling to you?"

"What's your point?"

"Can you see my Mom doing that?"

No, Eric thought, considering that her mother was decade older than Ginny, and not on Facebook.

She exhaled, exasperated, and said, "What I'm getting at is, when I was talking to Kris - ironically *on* Facebook—"

"Kris?" He said, turning around on the couch. "Wait, you were talking about this to Kris?"

"*Yes*," she replied, annoyance distorting her features. "She's my sister and we discuss things. You and Jennifer discuss things and you don't hear me getting all up in arms about it."

"Yeah, but we're talking about *our* mother, not *your* parents."

"Oh, so now you're telling me I'm not supposed to care about *my* mother-in-law?"

He sighed. Talk about a no-win situation. "At least tell me you were talking via private messaging?"

"Of course." Kim looked at him as though he was stupid. "I'm not sharing this information publicly for everyone to offer their two cents worth."

"Fine." He turned around on the sofa, back toward the TV.

"Anyway, Kris agreed with me." She moved her laptop to the small desk adjacent to the kitchen cabinets.

"With *what*, exactly?" he said, flatly. "And, please, do not start talking about the fact that she's daring to have a life of her own, because that just makes you look like the crazy one."

"No, not that," she replied, with a huff. "She agreed we may not be reading the signs."

Eric breathed, in and out. Did he keep going, or not? He was so bloody tired of the subject.

"She's not wearing your Dad's wedding ring anymore."

Eric frowned. "What are you talking about?"

"She's not wearing it," Kimberly repeated, with an air of triumph, as she walked out of the kitchen and into the family room. "She's always had it on the chain around her neck and I noticed the last time we were there, it was gone. She had some sort of butterfly pendant on, instead. Look at her *selfie* on Facebook and you'll see what I mean."

He looked at her smug face as she sat down beside him. "Your point?"

"Really?" She folded her arms across her chest and cocked her head at him. "The wedding band she's been wearing on a chain around her neck for almost two years since your Dad passed away has disappeared and you don't think that could mean *anything*?"

Eric sighed. "She took off *her own* wedding band a few months back, it's only reasonable she'd eventually do the same with Dad's. For all we know, the grief therapist she was seeing told her to do it when she was ready."

Kimberly unfolded her arms and got up from the couch. She placed her hands on her hips and spoke down at him. "And now she is and nothing more? Is that what you're saying?"

"Maybe so." He shrugged his shoulders and went back to channel surfing.

She shook her head at him, her face grim. "You mark my words. I didn't want to say it before, but I've been thinking on it and doing some research—"

"Oh, Jeez," he said, running his fingers through his hair. Fucking Google made it way too easy for people like his wife to find *research* to support their theories.

"*And*," she continued, "it's highly possible your Mom's behavior isn't just about *moving forward*, but could be a sign she's losing the plot. She's *sixty two*, Eric, not sixteen."

Eric looked at her, bewildered. "What the hell is that supposed to mean?"

"It means people don't start making drastic, erratic changes unless something else is *going on*!" She gritted her teeth as she added, "It's like a house of cards, or in her case a stack of *teacups*, is falling and you people are refusing to see it."

His eyes widened at her vehemence. "So, what? You've moved on from being pissed off she's getting a life to thinking she's going loopy?"

"It's possible!" she shot back.

"Okay, *enough*," he said. "Seriously, enough. Just drop it. It's none of our business, anyway."

"*Fine*," she said, her teeth clenched. "I'll drop it. In fact, I won't say another word about it, again!"

Eric watched her flounce out of the room and down the hallway toward their bedroom, leaving nothing but cool silence in her wake.

"Can I get that in writing?" he commented, to himself, before returning to the TV.

\*\*\*\*

Jennifer, dressed in blue cotton PJs, padded into the family room, cellphone in hand. The house was quiet, both kids were on sleepovers at friend's houses, and she and Chris were enjoying a night of sushi takeout and loud, over-the-top action movies.

"Well, that was weird," she said, snuggling up beside Chris on the sofa.

He put his iPad down on the ottoman. "What's that?"

"I just texted Eric to ask if he and Kimberly and Layla wanted to come over on Sunday for brunch and he said it would depend on whether or not Kim was talking to him."

"Trouble in paradise?"

Jennifer shrugged. "Apparently they had a huge disagreement about Mom and now he's not sure what sort of mood she'll be in."

"Disagreement about what?" he said, picking up a glass of red wine from the wooden tray on the ottoman. "Did something happen with your Mom?"

"Not directly, I don't think. This is what he wrote." She tapped her phone and began reading the text out loud. *"Kim's still upset over Mom's recent behavior and thinks we're making light of it. Says she thinks there's something deeper going on that we aren't addressing. Personally, I think she's just pissed off she no longer has a sitter whenever she wants, but can't say that out loud for fear of being lynched."*

"Something deeper?" Chris repeated. "Jeez, talk about cryptic."

"I know, right?"

"God, that woman can be a real piece of work." He shook his head then took a sip of wine. "Don't get me wrong, most of the time I think she's fine, but whenever she gets an idea in her head, look out."

Jennifer looked thoughtful and sighed. "Apparently Mom changing things up has put a crimp in Kimberly's lifestyle and she thinks we need to challenge her to try and make her stop, *for her own good."*

He laughed. "*That* I'd believe. Making something out of nothing."

"I don't know how Eric stands it, sometimes. I mean it's not that Kim doesn't have her redeeming qualities, but doesn't it seem like she can be a lot of work at times?"

"Maybe her family is the same way and that's how she's learned to communicate."

Jennifer looked at him in admiration. He always tried to see the best in people and it was one of the qualities she'd found most attractive in him when they'd met. She still did.

He put down his glass and picked up the remote to start their movie. ""Why don't you give your Mom a call and get the other side of the story so we're prepared if they do come over for brunch."

"I like the way you think," she said, smiling.

****

Ginny took a deep breath and reached out to ring Jan's doorbell. The chimes announced her arrival and she smiled when the door opened and Darryl, Jan's husband, welcomed her.

"Gin!" He opened the door wider and gestured for her to enter the house. "Wow, look at you!"

Ginny flushed and tried to wave his words away.

He let out a low whistle then said, "Jan wasn't kidding. Blonde bombshell!"

Ginny laughed and stepped across the threshold. "Oh, you're a kind, kind man, Darryl Flynn," she said, as he closed the door behind her.

"Not often," he said, grinning. "Just stating a fact."

"Well, thank you," she said, before lifting a hand to indicate his charcoal grey slacks and crisp, sky blue dress shirt. "And you clean up pretty well, yourself."

He reached out to give her a warm hug, his six foot five frame enveloping her almost completely. "All thanks to Jan. Without her, I'm sure I'd be a fashion *don't*."

Ginny hugged him back. He was a bear of man with a thick head of dark wavy hair and a beard to match and his hugs made you feel safe from any possible harm.

"Well, it really does make you look fantastic. Hot stuff," he said, when they'd untangled themselves.

Ginny smiled into his kind face then shrugged. "Dixie insisted. You know what she can be like. I gave up and gave in."

He laughed as he took her pashmina, the color of cinnamon, and hung it in the closet.

"I brought wine," Ginny said, extending the bottle in her hand.

"Excellent," he said, before taking the bottle and reading the label. "*Dirty Laundry, Merlot.*"

Ginny nodded. "We had it at our art class. Jan liked it."

"Ahh, right." Amusement curved his lips upward. "I heard your work drew mixed reviews."

Ginny chuckled.

"So, anyway," he said, "about tonight. I'm really glad you could come. You're doing me a huge favor in helping to bring up the numbers."

Ginny doubted that was the truth, but appreciated him saying it. He was so personable, there was no way he'd ever have difficulty filling a room. It was more likely he would have to turn people away.

"Having local folks to meet my new business partners goes a long way to giving them a better sense of what Boxwood Hills is all about when we start working on the new developments."

"That makes sense," she said, before Jan interrupted with a loud "Hey! I thought I heard the bell!" and power-walked down the hallway toward them, her curvy hips swaying beneath her black pencil skirt.

"Gin's here," Darryl said, "and she brought wine."

"Hey, Sweetie," Ginny said, before kissing her best friend's cheek. "You look terrific. That blouse is stunning." She reached out and touched the rich, wine colored silk. "Makes your skin glow."

"And you're a vision. I'm still getting used to the makeover, I almost didn't recognize you. Love the dress. Blue is your color."

"*I* told her she looks like a blonde bombshell," Darryl put in.

Jan cocked her head. "Are you trying to tell me something?"

Ginny grinned at the doe-in-the-headlights expression that swept across his face.

"A not-so-subtle way of telling me you wish I was a blonde, perhaps?"

"Hell, no," he shot back, before grabbing her around her narrow waist and pulling her against the length of his thigh. "You're my dark and dangerous pixie and I like it that way."

Ginny watched them, their obvious adoration of each other, and felt a twinge of.... Envy. It surprised her. Hadn't she already had her *moment*, with George? Shouldn't she be grateful she had experienced a loving, nurturing relationship and be content to move on to living her life for other things, besides romance?

She glanced at them a second time, felt a flutter of mixed emotions and realized, maybe not. Maybe she hadn't had her fill of romance, after all. And, if she was to be honest with herself, her relationship with George hadn't actually been what one would call romantically *charged*. More like comfortably reliable. She frowned to herself as she shifted her clutch purse from her left to her right hand. No, that didn't sound right. Made them sound like roommates when they'd been good together. Happy.

Ginny peeked once more at Jan and Darryl and thought, happy or not, any sort of passion that may have existed between she and George before he'd died had long been replaced by contented familiarity. Was that so terrible? She wasn't sure.

"Okay, you," Jan said, pushing him away, her eyes dancing. "Ginny's going to need a barf bag soon if you don't watch it."

Ginny laughed at the comment and shook off her thoughts. There was plenty of time for musing and a party wasn't the best place to start.

"Alright, Blondey," Jan teased, linking her arm through Ginny's. "Let's get you a drink."

She nodded. "Lead the way."

\*\*\*\*

Despite her initial reservations about attending the party, Ginny was having a very good time. Darryl had been telling the truth about her knowing a lot of people there and she'd spent the greater part of the last hour relaxing, chatting and catching up with friends she hadn't seen in a while.

Jan smiled and waved from the adjoining dining room and Ginny made her way through the crowd to meet her at the table.

"Having fun?" Jan asked, as she picked up empty platters.

"More fun than I expected."

"Wonderful," Jan said, while Ginny grabbed the empty tray she couldn't carry.

"Uh-huh," Ginny went on. "I can't tell you how lovely it is to be able to socialize sans awkward blind-date setup."

Jan chuckled and led the way toward the kitchen. Ginny turned to follow and narrowly missed knocking into a man attempting to walk past her.

"Whoops!" she said, stopping short.

"Whoa, pardon me," the man said, reaching out a hand when the oval, glass platter rocked back and forth in her grasp.

"My fault," Ginny insisted, tightening her grip on the tray before looking up into his green eyes, then nearly dropping it all over again. "*Ohmygod*, it's you!"

The man's eyebrows shot up on his forehead and Ginny could tell he was trying to place her.

"I'm sorry, have we met?" he asked.

"Sort of," she said, a twinge of awkwardness starting to blossom in her chest. "Well, no, that's not entirely true. You go to the library, from time to time—"

"And we met there?" he offered, trying to help things along.

"Yes, well no," Ginny stammered, as awkwardness gave way to full-blown discomfort. "I work there, is all."

"Alright," he said, his eyes kind as he tried to follow her lead.

"And, the thing is, I'm usually behind the counter and…" She wracked her brain then snapped the fingers of her free hand. "I used to be a brunette! Well, sort of. More mousy brown with a generous dash of grey…."

She tapered off when the first sign of recognition finally registered on his face and a slow grin bloomed, capturing his mouth in a wide smile. Thank God.

"Of *course*," he said, sounding genuinely pleased. "I should have known. What are the odds?"

She shrugged her shoulders. "Pretty good, apparently."

He laughed and regarded her with such blatant admiration, a flush of color began to heat her cheeks. His green eyes were captivating and she hadn't failed to notice that, up close, his broad shouldered physique was even more evident beneath the cut of his expensive suit.

"Umm, I should probably get this in to Jan," she said, glancing at the platter in her hand. Any excuse to break the eye contact that was causing her stomach to fill with butterflies.

Jan returned from the kitchen, took one look at her friend's face and swiftly calculated the scene before her. *Well, well, well.* "Here," she said, spiriting the platter away from Ginny. "I'm all good now. Everything's under control. You go ahead and continue mingling."

The man pulled his gaze from Ginny's face and smiled politely, giving Jan the opportunity to ask, "I'm sorry, forgive me, I don't know if Darryl, my husband, had a chance to introduce us?"

He extended a hand. "Maxwell Rhodes, but please call me Max. You must be the lovely Jan we hear so much about?"

Ginny was impressed. He was smooth. A lot smoother than she would have imagined after watching him loitering between the bookshelves in the library.

Jan put the platter down on the table and shook his hand. "Very nice to meet you, Max. I've heard nothing but good things." He chuckled appreciatively while she gestured to Ginny and added, "And I see you've met Virginia Hughes, my best friend."

He immediately gave Ginny his full attention. "Virginia, lovely. It's so nice to finally have the opportunity to put a name to the beautiful face."

Wow. While Ginny did love the sound of her full name coming from between his lips, she had to get a grip.

Jan's face was a picture of surprise. *Finally?* What *finally?* She wanted to pull Ginny aside immediately and demand details but, instead, took a steadying breath and accepted she'd have to get that story later.

Ginny swallowed, trying to regain her composure and follow Jan's lead. "Please, call me Ginny," she clarified, extending her hand.

He grasped it warmly, almost intimately, with his own and when he let go Ginny felt slightly let down.

"Right," he said. "Wonderful. *Ginny.*"

Jan's eyes were bouncing back and forth as though she was watching a tennis match. "Well," she said, clearing her throat and grabbing the empty platter from the tabletop. "I'll just get this back into the kitchen for a refill."

Ginny watched her retreat with a mixture of gratitude and stark terror. Now what?

"May I get you a drink?"

She smiled shyly and nodded. "I brought a bottle of wine, a Merlot. I think it still needs to be opened, would you like to try it?"

"I'd love to," he agreed, before motioning for her to lead the way.

\*\*\*\*

Ginny couldn't remember the last time she'd laughed so much. Seated on Jan's raspberry colored sofa in her family room, she was delighted to discover Max wasn't just handsome, but terribly witty and personable to boot. They'd been exchanging all sorts of stories about their respective histories and she found the more they talked, the better she liked him.

"No word of a lie," he told her, more serious now, regarding his frequent trips to the library. "My original mission was about searching out research for the new development we're collaborating on with Darryl and was supposed to be a onetime thing. Then, once I saw you, I had to go back."

"And, yet," Ginny teased, "you didn't even remember me, tonight."

He cleared his throat, before leaning in closer. "Alright, moment of truth. Between you and me, I might have more easily recognized you tonight had I dared to overcome my vanity and put on my driving glasses so I could see you with greater clarity when I was looking at you across the library."

Ginny blushed and took a sip from her wineglass. My goodness, she loved the sound of his voice. Such a deep, velvety timber.

"Even blurry, you were captivating and I wanted to approach you," he went on, while picking up his wineglass from the coffee table. "But I kept losing my nerve."

"I find that very hard to believe."

He chuckled - the rich, warm sound making the hairs on Ginny's arms stand on end - and shook his head. "I don't blame you. It does sound odd—"

"No, no, that's not what I meant." She looked at him earnestly. "You just seem so... confident. I can't imagine you out of step."

He smiled at her with such admiration, her breath caught in her throat.

"It's amazing what a beautiful woman can do."

Ginny bit her lip and wracked her brain for something to slow her pulse down.

"And another confession, some of those books I looked at," he revealed as he pushed back the rolled sleeves of his apple green dress shirt to expose strong, muscled forearms, "I already own. I just needed something in my hands to look legit, you see."

Ginny chuckled, appreciating his candor, and placed her glass on the end table next to the sofa. She studied him covertly, noting his resemblance to James Brolin was even stronger up close, and felt her stomach flip over. What on Earth was happening to her?

"Hey, hey, hey, Gin blossom!" a female voice called out, jolting Ginny from her observations.

Max looked up to watch a tall, dark, vivacious woman in a very short teal skirt and shockingly high heels march purposefully across the room toward Ginny.

"*There* you are! I've been searching high and low."

Ginny grinned as Dixie swooped in to give her a strong, heavily scented hug. Trust her friend to make a grand entrance.

When they'd untangled themselves, Dixie cast an appraising eye at Max. A sly, knowing grin spread across her face as she looked from him, to Ginny, then back again.

"Max," Ginny said, immediately starting introductions. "This is my dear friend, Dixie."

He smiled, stood up and extended his hand. "Nice to meet you."

"Dixie," Ginny continued, "this is Max, he's working with Darryl—"

"Oh, no need to explain, I'm up to speed," Dixie interrupted, still grinning like the *Cheshire Cat* as she shook the hand Max offered. "Jan told me you were off somewhere, *enjoying the company* of Darryl's new partner. Just thought I'd check things out for myself."

Max chuckled, low and deep, appreciating Dixie's straight-forward manner, while Ginny tried her best not to die of humiliation at the implications in her tone. She gave a 'later for you' look to her cheeky friend, making her giggle and wink.

"Anyway," Dixie said, already scanning the rest of the room. "I won't interrupt, but before I go…"

Ginny watched as Dixie pulled her iPhone out of her cleavage. Oh, help, she thought.

"Just a quick photo together, since you look so gorgeous," Dixie said, winking at Max. "Isn't she a vision? Such a waste if we don't capture the memory."

Max grinned as he watched Dixie press herself up against Ginny while holding the phone out at arm's length and saying, "Smile like you mean it!", making Ginny laugh.

Dixie checked out the photo then nodded as she showed it to Ginny, then Max. "Perfect! Should I send you a copy?"

Ginny widened her eyes when she realized Dixie was not looking at her, but at Max.

"Oh, come *on*, Gin," Dixie said, giggling when she saw her friend's face. "I'm only teasing! Max knows that, right?"

Max chuckled and nodded. "Of course. However, if *Ginny* wants to share it with me after you've sent it to her, I wouldn't say no."

Dixie threw her head back and laughed appreciatively.

"Oh, well," Ginny began, unsure of how exactly to respond. Thankfully, Dixie rescued her.

"Alright, I've taken up enough of your time. I'll leave you two to *get back to it*, as it were."

Ginny resisted the urge to cover her face like a child.

"It was very nice to meet you, Dixie," Max said, meaning it.

"You, *too*," Dixie replied, looking him straight in the eye. "You be nice to our Ginny, now, and I'll hope to see more of you in future."

Max and Ginny watched her spin on her heel and stride away from them, her gait strong and sure as always.

"I don't know if I should be apologizing, or not," Ginny said, shrugging her shoulders. "Dixie really is a gem, honest. It's just that—"

"She's charming," Max immediately assured her.

Ginny took a breath, both relieved and pleased. Some people didn't get Dixie and found her confidence intimidating. Thankfully, Max didn't appear to be one of them.

"And there was one thing she said I'm hoping you'll agree to."

Ginny lifted her eyebrows, curious.

"Letting me see you again," he stated. "I think it's an amazing act of fate we managed to finally meet here, at your best friend's home. I don't think it's something we can ignore and, if you'd let me, nothing would make me happier than to take you to dinner."

Ginny swallowed. Wow. He was asking her on a date. Her first real date in nearly forty years. She didn't count the numerous fix-up attempts in the past year. This was the real deal. No one else chaperoning. Just the two of them.

Max watched her, hopeful.

"I'd like that very much," she said, finally, as a grin took over her face. She felt like a teenager.

His mouth split into a smile to match hers. "Brilliant. When are you free?"

\*\*\*\*

## *Ginny's New Favorite Wine*

**Ingredients**
Wine.

**Directions**
o Frequent your local liquor store (or the winemaker's vineyard, if circumstances allow.)
o Chose a bottle (or two) of *Dirty Laundry Merlot.*
o Purchase.
o Take home, or bring to a party.
o Share with friends and, if you're lucky, get a date.

# Chapter Sixteen

"Hey, Mom," Jennifer said, holding the phone to her ear with her shoulder as she checked the pot of stew cooking on her stove.

"Hi, sweetheart," Ginny replied, warmly. "How are you? How are Chris and the kids?"

"Good. Everyone's good." She placed the lid back on the pot then leaned against the countertop. "Saw the photos Dixie posted on Facebook."

Ginny chuckled. "Yes, I did as well."

"You looked beautiful," Jennifer complimented. "And it looked like you had a good time. Where were you, anyway?"

Ginny's pulse quickened and she cleared her throat. If only her daughter knew how good her evening had been, but there was no way she was sharing anything about anything, not until there was something of pertinence to actually say.

"Hello? Mom? You still there?"

"Yes, sorry dear," Ginny quickly replied. "My mind wandered for a moment, what were you saying?"

"Nothing," Jennifer said, shifting the phone from her left ear to her right. "So, listen, I'm calling to ask if I can borrow your waffle maker."

"Of course. But, I thought you already had one."

"We do, but we're going to have Eric and family over for brunch tomorrow and figured it would be faster if we had more than one. Double the output at once."

"Smart," Ginny said. "When do you want to get it?"

"Chris is going to be out this afternoon, running a few errands, he could pop in if that's okay with you."

"That's perfect. I've been doing some baking, red velvet cupcakes, I could send some along with him."

"Red velvet?" Jennifer said, surprised. "What's the occasion?"

Ginny felt her face flush and was glad Jennifer wasn't there to see it. Telling her daughter she'd been asked out on a bonafide date with a handsome stranger and was celebrating with red velvet wasn't a part of her plans for the day.

"Mom?"

"No occasion," Ginny said, then quickly deflected. "Oh, and make sure to tell Chris to check around back if I don't answer the door. I'm going to be doing some gardening this afternoon and might not be inside when he rings the bell."

"So you'll be home all day, today, then?" Jennifer was aware the question sounded leading, but figured it was the best way to start the ball rolling regarding her supposed *deeper issues*.

"Yes." Ginny paused, wondering what the tone was about. "You sound surprised. Anything I should know about?"

"No, not really," she said. "It's just that Eric mentioned you couldn't babysit for them because of wherever you were in those photos, so...."

"Oh, for goodness sake," Ginny sighed. "I was at Jan and Darryl's for a business gathering Darryl had put together."

"Oh."

"He needed a good turnout and I'd already made the commitment, so I wasn't going to back out at the last moment. I didn't realize it's now required I divulge every darned detail of my plans beforehand. Do I need to put it in writing, or will verbal be enough?"

Jennifer winced at her mother's irate tone and felt foolish for even starting the conversation. Chris had been right, Kimberly was making something out of nothing. Her mother was just fine and having her own activities didn't mean she was acting out of the ordinary, or harboring *issues*. She was planning to garden all afternoon, for goodness sake, not go parachuting.

"So, what now?" Ginny asked. "Am I in trouble again and supposed to be smoothing things over for not being available?"

"No!" Jennifer startled herself with her emphatic reaction and pressed her lips together. She cleared her throat and said, more calmly, "You don't need to explain yourself to anybody. I'm sorry I even brought it up."

"I have a strong feeling a certain daughter-in-law may be behind this," Ginny stated. "She didn't sound very pleased when I told her I was busy."

"Too bad," Jennifer said, bluntly. "You've always been willing and helpful, but you have the right to a social life outside of being a child-minder and that's that."

Ginny smiled. Her daughter. So strong. So fair.

"So, I'll tell Chris to check the backyard for you if you don't come to the door," Jennifer said, moving things along.

"And I'll search out the waffle maker and have it waiting."

"Perfect."

\*\*\*\*

"Jesus!" Kimberly blurted, frustration bubbling to the surface.

Eric, entering the house via the garage, stiffened. What *now*? He felt a pang of regret he'd decided to take the afternoon off.

"What the BLOODY HELL is happening?" Kimberly said, unaware she was being overheard.

Eric closed the door with a solid thump, to announce his arrival.

Kimberly jerked her head upright from her computer screen then quickly slammed it shut. The last thing she needed was Eric reading over her shoulder what Kris had written about their Dad.

She fumed silently. What in God's name was the man thinking? It was bad enough Kris had seen him with that woman once, but to see him *again*? It was too much to ignore.

She rubbed her face, massaging her jaw. They needed to come up with some sort of plan of action, that was clear. They couldn't just sit on the sidelines, while their poor mother was innocently going along believing her husband was out doing... what? Playing golf? Tennis? What sort of reasons for his absence he was giving her, was anyone's guess.

Eric ventured into the room, when Kimberly stopped talking out loud to herself.

She quickly smoothed her hair behind her ears and asked, "Lawn done?"

He nodded and reached into the fridge for the juice jug. "Yup. Everything okay in here?"

She cut her eyes at him. "Yes. Why?"

He kept his expression neutral while he poured himself a glass of orange juice. "I just thought I heard you talking to someone—"

"Well, clearly not," she snapped, folding her arms across her chest.

Eric pulled another glass from the cupboard. "Juice?" he asked, ignoring her sharp tone.

"What the hell is happening to the old people, anyway?"

He paused, glass in hand. "Meaning?"

"They're coming, they're going, they're *stepping out of their comfort zones*." Her face grew increasingly grim with each statement. "Is there something in the water? Because it's like they've lost the plot and ability to act their god-damned age!"

Eric busied himself pouring more juice. Was this another rant about his mother? Could she have done *yet another thing* considered inappropriate? Dare he even ask?

Kimberly reached out and picked up the glass Eric had set on the countertop. She shut up and drank the freshly squeezed orange juice, annoyed at herself for almost blurting out what was going on. She'd done too much speculating out loud about Ginny and they still didn't know for sure what was going on with her; if she added critique about her Dad before they knew all the facts, it could destroy her credibility instead of enhancing it.

Eric put the juice jug back in the refrigerator while Kimberly gathered up her laptop and left the room without another word. As politically incorrect and caveman-esque as it might have made him sound, he sincerely hoped it was just PMS.

****

## Ginny's Red Velvet, Celebration Cupcakes

### Ingredients
2 cups whole wheat flour
1 teaspoons baking soda
1 teaspoon salt
2 tablespoons cocoa powder (unsweetened)
2 cups brown sugar
1 cup vegetable oil
2 eggs
1 cup buttermilk
2 teaspoons vanilla extract
2-4 tablespoons red food coloring
1 teaspoon white distilled vinegar
½ cup prepared, hot coffee - cooled.

### Directions
Preheat oven to 325 degrees F.

o Grease muffin tins, or use paper cups, and set aside.
o Whisk together whole wheat flour, baking soda and baking powder, cocoa powder and salt in medium sized bowl.
o In a separate, large bowl, combine the sugar and vegetable oil.
o Blend in the eggs, buttermilk, vanilla and red food coloring.
o Add coffee and white vinegar and mix until combined.
o Add the wet ingredients to the dry, mix.
o Distribute batter evenly amongst muffin cups and bake on middle rack for 18 to 20 minutes, or until tester inserted in center of cupcakes comes out clean.
o Remove from oven and let cool completely before frosting.

# Chapter Seventeen

Tamara observed Ginny humming quietly to herself and a small smile bloomed on her face. Something was *up*, she was sure of it. What it was, was anyone's guess, but something was definitely *up*.

"What?" Ginny caught her staring and turned to face her. "Why are you looking at me like the cat that got the cream?"

"I'm not sure, maybe *you* should tell *me*," Tamara said, her eyes lighting up in expectation.

Ginny's insides clenched, but she kept her cool. She smoothed her green blouse and kept her features neutral. "I don't follow."

Tamara cocked her head, her hair a waterfall of dark waves spilling over her shoulders. "You're different."

"Different?" Ginny blinked.

"Uh-huh." She narrowed her eyes. "I'm not sure what it is, but there's *something* different. Ever since you went to that party at Jan's, there's been a whole new vibe going on."

Ginny's pulse quickened. She *was* hiding something, namely Max, but she wasn't about to come clean. Not when they hadn't even had their first official date yet. She had to divert the direction of Tamara's train of thought. Fast.

"You seem... lighter, somehow."

"Lighter?" Ginny cocked an eyebrow and offered, teasing, "Is this your kind way of trying to tell me I need to lose weight?"

Tamara laughed and began sorting the books in the returns bin. "Not like *that*! I mean you seem more relaxed, more breezy."

"I have been gardening more," Ginny said, still directing the conversation into safer waters. "I love being out there in the sunshine, the fresh air, nothing but me and my plants and the feeling of everything plodding along as it should."

Tamara paused, book in hand and pondered her words. Maybe that was it. Maybe not. But, whatever it was, she clearly wasn't going to find out. Not yet, anyway.

"And I even have a bit of a tan," Ginny pointed to her forearms in her short-sleeved, white cardigan. "Me!"

Tamara put down the book and held her hands up in mock surrender. "Fine, fine. You're gardening and getting some sun. We'll leave it at that. But, I have to say, if that's your recipe for this newfound breeziness, maybe I'll have to check out some books on growing plants in my own yard."

"You should."

Tamara watched Ginny as she went to check the computer, a gentle grin curving her lips. Gardening? Doubtful. But, for now, her lovely co-worker was - pardon the cheesy metaphor - a closed book.

****

"We're going out!"

Brian, grinning widely on Eric's computer screen, chuckled at his brother's exuberance. They were both on a lunch break and Eric had sent him a message on Skype, in hopes he had a moment to talk.

Eric laughed along with him.

"Working from home, today?" Brian asked.

"Yeah, Kim had some sort of pressing appointment, so I arranged my day so I could be here for the afternoon instead of at the firm."

Brian nodded and leaned back in his desk chair. "So, you sound like you've gotten ahold of a day pass."

"Sad, isn't it? It used to be going out on Friday was the norm. *Now...* not so much."

"So, Mom's finally able to watch Layla for you guys?"

Eric shook his head, leaned back in his office chair and propped his feet on the desktop.

"Feet," Brian stated.

"Oh, right, sorry." Eric shifted his legs to the left. "Mom's busy—"

"Seriously? Two Fridays in a row, our mother has plans?"

"Yeah, something with garden club I think."

"So how are you and Kim getting out of the cage, then?"

Eric smiled, wryly. His brother had no idea how close to the bone he was. "Jen and Chris offered when we went to their place for brunch last weekend."

"Nice." Brian yawned and ran his fingers through his brown hair.

"Yeah, I think it was Jen's way of trying to help smooth the waters here."

Brian raised an eyebrow. "Trouble in paradise?"

"Not really. Sort of." Eric shrugged, remembering their visit at Jennifer and Chris'. It had been, for the most part, very pleasant. However, when the topic of their mother had reared its head things threatened to get heated.

Brian waited, watching Eric grimace.

"Long story short, Kim's still bent out of shape because Mom's been busy with her own stuff. She's even pushing it and saying it's a sign of some deeper issue."

"Deeper issue about what?"

"Her mental state, or something like that."

"Wait, what?" Brian said, trying to follow. "Like she's losing it, or something?"

"Yeah, something like that. Or acting out on her hidden grief over Dad..." He rolled his eyes. "Kim changes it according to her mood."

"Hidden grief?" Brian repeated. "Mom has hidden grief?"

"No," Eric said, rolling his eyes. "She's fine."

Brian nodded. "Okay, so then what was up with Kim and Jen?"

"They nearly got into it," Eric finished, shaking his head.

"Into it?" Brian leaned forward, intrigued. He knew his sister and Kimberly didn't always see eye to eye, but this sounded different. "*Into it*, how?"

"Mom posted a photo on Facebook and—"

"Was that the one of her and Dixie?"

Eric stared for a half second at his brother then said, "You've seen it?"

"Sure," Brian said.

"How?"

"Mom friended me and Dixie had posted it on her wall, too, so I saw it."

"Mom friended you? Jesus." Eric rubbed his hand across his face.

"What?" Brian asked. "She probably friended you, too. If you checked Facebook more often, you'd be up to speed on things as well."

Eric brushed away the comment. "Yeah, yeah, heard it before. Anyway, that photo started a conversation where Kim more or less accused Jen of being too preoccupied with her own stuff and not giving a crap about Mom."

"Whoa." Brian sat back in his chair, his eyes wide. "Brave girl."

"Yeah, you're telling me." Eric shook his head. "Thank god Chris was on the ball and diffused everything, more or less playing mediator."

"Said the lawyer," Brian stated, his voice laced with irony.

Eric laughed then said, "I honestly think if it would have been me doing it, both of them would have turned on me. I'm way too close to the situation, being brother to one and husband to the other. Chris still holds the appearance of neutrality."

Brian nodded, acquiescing the point, then asked, incredulous, "And, even though that happened and despite them almost seriously falling out, Jen and Chris are going to watch Layla for you guys tonight?"

"Believe it or not," Eric acknowledged, lifting his hands in a 'who-knew' gesture. "Once everything was patted down, Jen extended the olive branch and said we deserved some time to ourselves and, next thing I knew, they were setting it up."

"Huh," Brian said. "Maybe Chris should consider a career change."

Eric waited.

"You guys could even try a job swap," Brian went on, smirking. "You step into his landscaping shoes and he can trade his spade for your briefcase."

And there it was.

Brian laughed at the expression on Eric's face. "Oh, come on, it was funny!"

"Hysterical. Asshole."

Brian laughed harder.

Eric chuckled along with him.

"Listen," Brian said, catching his breath. "I gotta fly. Paige and I have plans and I can't be late leaving the office tonight. Have fun with your wife and I'll talk to you next week."

Eric rang off, a smile still on his face.

****

Kimberly strode purposefully through the arts and crafts store, shopping basket slung across her forearm, making a beeline for the knitting supplies. She looked down at her phone to check her list, at the same time as a sales clerk stepped out from between two aisles, directly into her path.

"Oh!" Kimberly exclaimed, when she nearly ran straight into her.

The saleswoman's eyes widened and she stepped to the side to avoid a collision. "Whoops!" the smiling young woman said. "Nearly had a situation there!"

Kimberly stared at her.

"So, is there anything I can help you find, ma'am?"

Kimberly smoothed her orange tunic-style top over her black leggings and peered at the name tag on the girl's vest. "No, thank you, *Indigo*," she said, through clenched teeth, wondering how it could be anything but obvious she knew exactly where she was headed.

"Okay," Indigo said, cheerfully. "If you change your mind, just holler."

Kimberly gave her a tight smile and refrained from chewing her out for calling her ma'am. She was on a mission *and* a schedule, no time for unplanned stops.

Instead, she stepped around *Indigo* as though she was nothing more than a bothersome object in her way and strode away at her original pace without a backward glance.

\*\*\*\*

"So, let's hear it, what are you wearing?"

Ginny grinned at the excitement in Jan's voice on the other end of the telephone. Her best friend was as eager, if not more so, as she was about the date to come. Date night. Ginny couldn't help herself and giggled at the very idea. She hadn't thought about Friday night, date night, in so many years, it was comical.

"My purple dress," she said, standing in front of the full-length mirror in her bedroom and smoothing the fabric over her hips.

"Ooh, that's gorgeous on you," Jan said, approvingly. "Good choice."

"Better than what Dixie would have had me wearing."

"Which was?"

"Something much too short and much too revealing." Ginny shook her head, amused as she recalled Dixie's near apoplectic excitement after finding out about the date. "She forgets I'm well past being a forty eight year old woman; not that I would have had the bravery to wear such things then, either."

"She means well," Jan said, affectionately.

"Of course," Ginny agreed, tucking her feet into her new tan, open-toed mules and walking a few steps to adjust to their height. "And once I told her about the purple dress choice, she was full of encouragement."

"How are you doing your hair?"

"Partially up, with some soft wisps around my cheekbones."

"Sounds gorgeous, send me a photo."

Ginny shook her head. "Oh, for goodness sake, not you too."

"What?" Jan asked. "What are you talking about?"

Ginny sat down on her bed and reached out to pet Martini, sprawled across the center of the soft comforter. "Dixie is always telling me to send a photo and, now, you are as well."

Jan laughed then took an audible sip of something she was drinking. "Hey, it's the times were in, babe. Roll with it."

"I suppose so," Ginny agreed. "But, maybe I'll wait until I'm out with Max and ask him to take a photo to send to you."

"Smart plan," Jan offered, agreeably. "He'll love the chance to snap your photo and maybe want to have one of the two of you as well."

"What are you drinking?" Ginny asked, slipping her shoes off her feet then flexing her pink-polished toes.

"Wine."

Ginny laughed. "And?"

"It's a Shiraz from *Jackson Triggs Estate Winery*, fabulous."

"Sounds lovely," Ginny sighed. "Wish I could join you."

"Meaning you're nervous?"

Ginny took a deep breath when a shiver ran up her spine. "Yes. Although, it's absurd that I am, isn't it? It's just dinner."

"No, I get it. He's a very handsome man."

"Yes, but it's not like it's my first date since George passed, so...."

"It kind-of is," Jan said, gently. "All the others were set-ups."

"Okay, fine. I know that's true. I've been trying to tell myself otherwise to calm my nerves."

"If it helps, I think you're going to have a really good time," Jan soothed, sipping more wine. "And Darryl confirmed he's as nice as he seems, no act whatsoever. And, at least you've already had some time with him, some conversation, that sort of thing. You aren't going in cold."

Ginny grinned, then warned, "Not a word to anyone, remember."

God forbid her kids found out. The last thing she needed was their hysterics over her going on one lousy dinner date. They'd already made a production over something as trivial as her changing the color of her hair. A date with a stranger, as opposed to a fix-up, would send them into orbit.

"Mum's the word," Jan assured her. "Darryl has been warned, on penalty of me making his life a living hell, his lips remain sealed."

Ginny chuckled. Poor Darryl. Max had started asking all sorts of questions about her after she'd left the party and; thus, whether he liked it or not, he was involved. She was certain he wished he was in the dark about it all.

"So, I take it you haven't said anything yet to Tamara at work?"

"God, no." Ginny shuddered at the idea of her coworker knowing anything about her potential relationship with Max.

It had been a real challenge, too. He'd gone into full-on courting mode after they'd agreed to their date and that had translated into daily texts, flower deliveries and baskets of specialty tea showing up at the library. She'd been successful in intercepting the gifts without notice, but who knew how long that would last?

Ginny felt her stomach flip and caught her breath. Though it had been seven days since she'd last seen him in person, Jan was right and she already felt she knew Max to a certain degree. It was both strange and thrilling.

"When will you tell her?"

"Not until when, or *if*, there's something to tell," she stated, firmly, getting up from the bed and walking out of the bedroom.

Jan chuckled. She knew all about the messages and gifts and adoration going on. She highly doubted it was an *if* sort of situation. "But, *if* there is something to tell?"

"She'll go crazy and probably put a bulletin on the board and our website and Facebook page for everyone to read about finding love amidst the book stacks."

Jan laughed. "I'm surprised you two haven't already been discovered. She's pretty on the ball."

"Tell me!" Ginny shook her head as she entered the kitchen. "She nearly did find out on Wednesday. Max sent me a text that made me laugh and she wanted to read what it said and I had to frantically *accidentally* delete it...." She exhaled. "I can't tell you how foolish I felt trying to come up with a plausible reason for laughing."

"Which was?"

"I said the text was a joke, sent by Dixie, and that I'd be rubbish at telling it without being able to read it."

Jan laughed, again. She knew how terrible her best friend was at lying, especially off the cuff.

The doorbell sounded and Ginny looked at the clock on her kitchen wall. She still had another hour until Max was due, who could that be?

"There's the door, do you want to hang on, or will I call you back?"

"I have dinner going. Call me back when you can."

"Okay, love you," Ginny said.

"You, too," she replied, before hanging up.

"Coming," Ginny called out, while placing the phone on the counter.

She walked through the family room to the foyer, remembering to use the peep-hole before opening the door. She looked through the hole and was startled to see the fish-eye distorted image of Kimberly, waiting on the other side.

"Hey, there," Kimberly said, when Ginny opened the door. "Surprise!"

"I'll say," she replied, opening the door wider to let her in. "What brings you here?"

Kimberly crossed the threshold and closed the door, a grin on her face. "What, can't a daughter-in-law surprise her favorite mother-in-law once in a while?"

Ginny raised an eyebrow.

"Okay, okay, fine." She laughed, knowing full well she was not one to do the whole surprise visit thing. She was a call and schedule girl, through and through.

Ginny smiled and reached out to give her a brief hug. "Well, regardless, it's lovely to see you. To what do I owe this impromptu visit?"

Kimberly slipped her black ballet flats from her feet and held up a bag she was holding. "I have a small gift."

Ginny placed a hand over her heart. "Well, that *is* a surprise," she said, leading them into the family room.

"It's nothing too grand," Kimberly explained, as she settled herself on the couch and handed over the bag. "Just something I saw and thought of you."

Ginny accepted the gift, curious. What on Earth could she have seen that made her think of her?

"Well, go on. Open it."

Ginny smiled and reached into the bag. "Oh, my," she said, pulling a hank of lavender colored yarn and a set of knitting needles from its depths.

"Isn't the color gorgeous," Kimberly gushed.

Ginny blinked, taken off guard. What the hell?

"As soon as I saw it, I knew it would flatter your skin tone. You could make a scarf, or a wrap of some sort."

"Oh. Well, umm, that's very sweet, dear. But, I don't actually know how to knit, so…"

"I thought maybe you could invite the girls over," Kimberly went on, as though Ginny hadn't spoken, "put on your comfy clothes, have some tea and a nice evening *in*."

Ginny fingered the yarn, puzzled. Was there a hint in all of this she was supposed to be picking up on, or was she just being sensitive?

"Truth be told, it was the photo Dixie posted on your Facebook wall of the two of you at Jan's party that was the catalyst," Kimberly said. "I was struck by the inspiration of how fun it would be for you gals to learn together. A new activity that would allow you some time to relax on the couch and still feel productive."

Okay, Ginny thought, *that* comment was making it more challenging to ignore the unspoken undertones.

"Or, maybe Dixie already knows how to knit and can teach you and I'm the silly goose for thinking you'd learn together!"

Ginny pressed her lips together to keep a straight face. The idea of Dixie doing anything remotely close to knitting bordered on the ridiculous. The woman barely managed to keep her garden alive enough to stay in the gardening club - and she only did so because it was a social opportunity she didn't want to give up - so if she was presented with the idea of knitting, Ginny was pretty certain her friend would laugh her straight out of the room. However, all that aside, the clock was ticking so… "Well, aren't you a dear thing, thinking of me when I don't even realize it."

Kimberly dimpled and sat back into the cushions, satisfied.

"But, here's the thing," Ginny went on, placing the yarn, needles and bag on one of the side tables adjacent to the couch. "I'd normally offer you a cup of tea, but as you may remember I have plans *to go out* tonight, so...."

Kimberly's eyebrows pulled together as she noticed, for the first time, her mother-in-law's outfit.

Clothed in a dark purple, knee length shift-dress, Ginny scratched her cheek and tried not to squirm under Kimberly's blatant scrutiny.

"Right. Yes, I *do* remember," she said, finally, blinking rapidly as she took everything in. "And you look lovely."

"Thank you."

"And it's a *garden club* night, yes?"

"It is," Ginny agreed, fingering the cloth of her dress self-consciously, feeling put on the spot.

"And *that's* what you wear?"

Ginny winced at her incredulous tone. "We're having a guest speaker, *so*...." She hated fudging the truth and hoped by keeping her answers simple she would save herself from having to put her atrocious lying skills on full display.

Kimberly stared, waiting for more. When nothing came, she cocked her head and shifted gears, asking, "Do you have a radio on, or something?"

Ginny brightened and nodded, glad for a change of topic. "Yes, in the kitchen. Sounds like that *Jason Derulo* fellow, doesn't it? Have you heard his new song? It's really quite good."

Kimberly's face went blank and her jaw slack.

Ginny swallowed uncomfortably at her glazed expression. "Not a fan?"

"*What?*" Kimberly squinted and rubbed her temple. It was too much random information at all once.

"Of *Jason Derulo?*" Ginny began to clarify, before being abruptly cut off.

"No! Or, yes. Maybe." Kimberly shook her head then stood up, all business. "Anyway, I should go. You have your *garden club* and I have to get dinner for Layla before we drop her off with Jen and Chris."

"Right. Of course," Ginny agreed, startled by her sudden, no-nonsense demeanor.

Kimberly turned and strode briskly from the living room; so unexpectedly Ginny had to leap up then more or less scurry behind her to keep up with her long-legged stride.

"The gift really was a nice surprise. Thank you, again, for thinking of me," she offered, hoping to slow down her rapid retreat.

"It was my pleasure," Kimberly said, over her shoulder, before stopping abruptly in her tracks.

"Oh!" Ginny blurted, nearly slamming into her.

Kimberly, completely unaware of how closely Ginny had come to colliding with her, stuffed her feet into her shoes then whirled around to give her a perfunctory hug before pulling open the front door and dashing down the steps.

Ginny's eyes widened at the chaos of her exit.

"Have fun at your garden club," she called out, before slipping into her car and slamming the door closed behind her.

"Drive safe," Ginny said, reflexively, her words carried away by the breeze while Kimberly revved the engine and sped off into the evening.

****

Eric rubbed a hand across the dark stubble on his chin. He and Kimberly were cleaning up from dinner while Layla sat in her highchair, occupied with a plate of soft fruit. The information that she'd stopped at his mother's, with a gift of knitting needles and yarn no less, had taken him by surprise. He'd never known her to be a crafty sort of woman and why Kimberly would think she was, was beyond him.

"*Well?*" Kimberly said, her face expectant.

He shrugged his shoulders. "I have no idea what you want from me. What are we talking about, anyway? The knitting, her having plans, the way she styled her hair?"

Kimberly cut her eyes at him, unsure of whether or not he was being smart. He looked back at her, wide-eyed, and she decided not.

"You're going to have to give me more to go on, 'cause I'm not following," he stated.

"Not follow," Layla echoed, then picked up a piece of melon and put it into her mouth.

Kimberly sighed, in that manner than made it clear she thought he was being thick, and hung the tea towel she'd been using to dry dishes on the handle of the stove. "I'm talking about your mother being dressed to the nines for a garden club meeting, Eric. *Garden club.*"

"Garden," Layla said, grinning, her fruit laced little teeth on full display.

Eric chuckled.

"You know, the club where they talk about flowers and dirt and bugs and stuff," Kimberly said, wryly. "And you don't think it warrants at least a smidgen of surprise, perhaps even a bit of concern, that she looked ready for a night out on the town?"

"The town," Layla repeated, while poking her finger into a slice of banana.

"I don't know." Eric sat down at the table and grinned at his daughter.

"What don't you know?" Kimberly challenged. "Which part? The simple oddity of her appearing to be overdressed? Or, that it might actually be cause for some concern that she seems to have lost the ability to gauge the appropriate attire to wear for such a gathering?"

Eric refused to bite and took the middle ground. "How do I know? She did say they had a guest speaker and maybe it's their norm to dress up. Or maybe - here's a thought - she had *other* plans as well."

Layla gave him another fruit-laced smile and shrugged her shoulders at him. "Don't know."

Eric laughed appreciatively.

"Why wouldn't she just say she had other plans as well? Why be so vague and fail to mention it?" She reached into a jar on the counter and pulled out a cookie. "It seems shifty or, as I said, maybe the real issue is she didn't even realize her outfit was too much, even for a guest speaker, until I noticed it. How about that?"

Eric sighed and rubbed his face with his hands. "And yet, after all this speculation, we're still going round in circles and still don't know if it's the norm or not that they dress up, do we?"

She handed the cookie to Layla. "Coconut chewy?"

"Chewy!" Layla said, eagerly taking the treat. "Gamma!"

Kimberly nodded. "Yes, Grandma's recipe."

"Do we?" Eric pressed, refusing to relinquish his point.

"No," she conceded, reluctantly. "I guess we don't."

He nodded, satisfied she admitted it. It was a lot more than he usually got.

"*However,*" she said, refusing to be bested. "We do know for sure we've never heard her listening to *Jason freaking Derulo.*"

Eric took a cookie for himself and raised it in the air at Layla. "Cheers!"

She grinned, lifted her own and said, "Cheese!"

Eric laughed and bit into his cookie.

"Hello?" Kimberly said, insistently. "*Jason Derulo?* What the H-E double hockey sticks was that about?"

Eric chewed and smirked. Admittedly, that tidbit was out of left field.

"Oh, for goodness sake," Kimberly said, throwing her hands in the air when she saw his face. "Just forget it."

Eric swallowed and thought, gladly.

\*\*\*\*

"Ohmygod, ohmygod, OHMYGOD!"

"Starting again, without me?" Max teased, turning his long, muscular frame toward Ginny on the king-sized bed.

Ginny reached out and slapped him across his bare bicep then pulled the tangled covers over her naked torso. "No! I'm just having a difficult time believing I did this!"

Max chuckled and reached out to stroke her cheek. God, she was beautiful. Just looking at her made him want her all over again. He glanced at the state of his hotel room and the sight made him grin. Their clothes were strewn from door to bed; shoes scattered from being kicked off in a fury, her dress in a purple pool on the carpet, his suit pants and shirt tossed across the armchair and her delicates lost somewhere in the disheveled sheets.

Ginny sighed at the touch of his hand against her skin and closed her eyes. She'd forgotten. In the two barren years she'd been alone, she'd forgotten the intimacy, the complete and utter rapture that was created when a person shared themselves with another. It took her breath, again, just thinking about it.

Max, watching her, asked, "Are you okay, Sweetheart?"

Ginny opened her eyes then was startled to realize they were wet with tears.

Max's brow furrowed and his stomach clutched. He'd asked all sorts of questions of both Darryl and Jan after Ginny had left the party where they'd met. He understood the full story about George, his car accident and her journey through a year of grief counselling to help her get back on her feet. He admired her for her strength and was already feeling a strong desire to protect her from further unhappiness. The thought that he'd pushed too fast was too much to bare.

"Ginny? Honey? What is it?" He sat up and swiped gently at the moisture on her cheeks. "Oh, god. I'm sorry. So sorry. Was it too soon?"

Ginny reached for his hand. "No! Stop," she said, squeezing his palm. "I'm fine. I'm more than fine, honest. I just didn't expect..."

He waited, letting her gather her thoughts.

"Well, basically, I'd forgotten," she said, dropping his hand to gesture back and forth between them. "About the depth of this."

He nodded, listening.

Ginny thought about the way their bodies had joined together, remembering how swiftly she'd lost track of where each of them had begun and ended. The feel of his lips and fingers as they blazed a trail of heat across her skin. The silence when her thoughts had just stopped, suspended, as each breath and sigh moved them closer and closer together. A shiver ran through her as she met his blue eyes. "And, to be completely honest, I guess I'd closed this chapter in my mind and now here is it, surprising me—"

"Closed this chapter?" Max repeated, shaking his head. "What do you mean? Forever?"

Ginny chuckled at the disbelief in his voice. "Well, yes, if you must know. I'm not exactly a spring chicken. Never mind that I've never in my life skipped dinner to race to a man's hotel room to engage in... *this* sort of thing."

Max ran his fingers through his hair, taking it all in. "And you're not six feet under, either," he countered, before casting a lascivious eye at her sheet covered body. "Far from it."

He reached out, wrapped an arm around her waist and pulled her deftly across the bed. She murmured appreciatively when he tucked her up against his body and he relished the warm touch of her back against his torso. He pushed her hair away from her neck, revealing the soft smooth skin for him to kiss.

"Can I say something, now?" he asked, while she closed her eyes and let his touch wash over her.

"Of course," she said, simply, opening her eyes to give him her full attention.

Max gently released her then shifted so he could lean up against the headboard as he spoke. "This isn't a one night fling for me, Ginny." When he saw the skepticism on her face, he continued, "I understand why you'd probably question that statement, after all you barely know me and I've already proven I'm willing to hop into bed pretty fast."

"There's an understatement," she said, a wry grin decorating her face. "I didn't even get dinner, only a couple of appetizers."

His grin matched her's as he carried on. "*Anyway*, I want you to understand that while I'll admit I've had a sometimes *active* past, I made the choice quite some time ago to close that chapter of my life."

It was Ginny's turn to reposition herself. She pulled the sheets along with her as she resettled herself into the pillows still left on the bed.

"You may think you're no spring chicken, but I'm definitely not a young man anymore—"

"Not old, either."

He leaned forward to kiss her shoulder for that kindness then settled back against the headboard. "The facts are, I'm sixty four years old, I've had a few long term relationships that ran their courses, and now the only desire I have is to be near you."

Ginny blinked. She hadn't expected *that*.

"I know it sounds rather quick, but if there's one thing I've learned about myself it's to trust my instincts. There's a reason I do so well in business."

"How romantic," she said, dryly, making him laugh and pull her up against his side.

"I'm not finished," he said, kissing the top of her head.

Ginny giggled. "Go ahead."

He took a breath and said, "I was smitten from the moment I laid eyes on you in the library—"

"Blurry eyes," she couldn't resist teasing.

He grinned and said, "Yes, blurry eyes. But, either way, with each moment that passes that I know you, the more I want to be with you."

*That* stopped the giggles in their tracks. Ginny was so shocked, she didn't quite know where to find the words. She'd been married for nearly forty years, had put all things man and woman related behind her and now, *this*.

Max saw the emotions flitting across her face and nodded. "I understand your confusion. It makes sense to me. I just ask that you give me a chance."

Ginny's face softened as she looked into his eyes. She saw kindness, consideration, affection, humor, intelligence, passion; a heady combination.

"Can you do that?"

"Of course," she said, simply. It was such an easy request, she couldn't turn it down.

He grinned and leaned in to kiss her. When they came up for air, he asked, "How about some room service? I can finally deliver that meal I promised."

Ginny shivered when a wave of pure, unadulterated joy shot through her. Who knew she'd feel passion for another man so late in the game.

"That sounds perfect," she said, as he reached for the hotel restaurant menu on the bedside table.

****

Jennifer pressed the 'OFF' button on the phone then stared at it. "That's odd."

Chris, putting the last clean plate from the dishwasher into the cupboard, looked over at her and asked, "No signal?"

"No," she said, placing the phone back on its base. "It's Mom. She's not answering her house phone or her cellphone."

Chris glanced at the clock on the stove. 9:45 pm. "Maybe she's in the bath?"

Jennifer shrugged. "Maybe."

"You don't sound convinced."

Jennifer filled the tea kettle with water from the tap and plugged it into a socket on the wall. "No, no, you're probably right and I'm making something out of nothing."

Chris began to root around in the freezer.

"What are you looking for?" she asked.

"Cookies," he said, turning around.

She grinned. "In the freezer?"

"Well, there aren't any around, so I thought maybe we had some frozen that I could thaw."

"Optimist," she said. "Sorry, none to be found at the moment. Mom hasn't been baking and I haven't had the time. You'll have to resort to store bought."

Chris closed the freezer and headed to the pantry.

The kettle clicked off and Jennifer poured the water in a waiting teapot on the counter. "You have to admit, though, it's odd she's not available at this time of night."

"Do you think we need to drive by?"

She shook her head. "No. As I said, I'm probably making something out of nothing. She probably just decided to have an early night and us going over will just disturb her. I left her a message, so I'm sure I'll hear back when she gets it."

"Ah-ha," Chris said, finding a box of cookies on the pantry shelf.

Jennifer chuckled. "Come on, cookie monster. Let's go watch our movie."

\*\*\*\*

## *Ginny's Coconut Chewy Cookies*
*(recipe borrowed by Kimberly, since Ginny seems to have stopped baking.)*

### Ingredients
1¼ cups whole wheat flour
½ teaspoon baking soda
¼ teaspoon salt
¼ cup butter
¼ cup coconut oil in solid state
1 cup brown sugar
1 egg
½ teaspoon vanilla extract
1⅓ cups flaked coconut

### Directions
Preheat oven to 350 degrees F.

o In mid-sized bowl, combine the flour, baking soda and salt.
o In separate, larger bowl, cream together butter, coconut oil and brown sugar.
o Beat egg and vanilla in butter mixture until fluffy.
o Blend flour mixture into butter mixture then add in coconut, mixing until all blended together.
o Drop dough by teaspoonful onto ungreased cookie sheets, approximately 3 inches apart to allow for spreading.
o Bake for 8 to 10 minutes, or until cookies look lightly toasted.
o Remove from oven and cool on wire racks.

Recipe yields approximately 3 dozen cookies.

# Chapter Eighteen

Max put away his electric shaver and gave one last feel to his face to make sure he hadn't missed any spots. Nothing but smooth skin met his palms and he grinned at his reflection in the mirror. God, he was happy. So happy it was a bit unnerving. An image of Ginny, her smile and beautiful, blue eyes looking at him crossed his thoughts and his stomach flipped over. Jeez, it was like being a teenager all over again.

Max laughed at himself and walked out of the bathroom into the bedroom of his hotel suite. The clock on the bedside table told him he still had close to an hour before he needed to leave to pick up the woman who's memory was playing havoc with his emotions and he figured getting a bit of work in beforehand would be a wise option. Otherwise, Darryl would start to wonder if he'd made the right choice in joining forces. Couldn't have that.

Max's cellphone rang and he walked through the bedroom into the sitting room to retrieve it from the desk beneath the window. Darryl's number lit up the screen and he thought, speak of the devil, before swiping his finger across the screen.

"Hello?"

"Max," Darryl said. "Good morning. I know it's Sunday, hope I'm not waking you."

Max chuckled. "No, no worries about that. I'm an early riser."

"Excellent," Darryl said. "Jan was giving me grief about calling so early, in case you were… you know, *busy*."

Max coughed then cleared his throat, those teenage feelings charging back to the forefront.

"Sorry," Darryl said, feeling wrong-footed. "It's none of my business, of course."

"No, no," Max quickly assured him. "You're fine. I'm just feeling a bit, umm…"

Darryl remained quiet and wished he hadn't let Jan push him into trying to get more information.

"For lack of a better word," Max said, "I'm feeling young. Like when I was fresh out of the gate and had a crush on a gorgeous girl, that sort of feeling."

Darryl grinned. Now that was something his wife would be happy to hear.

"I hope I'm not making a total fool of myself here," Max said, uncomfortable at the silence on the other end of the line.

"No!" Darryl blurted. "Of course not, man. I was just thinking about how Jan is going to grill me for information about this conversation."

Max burst out laughing.

Darryl joined him.

"So, she's seeking information, is she," Max said, still chuckling.

Darryl took a breath and said, "Any and all she can get."

Max nodded. Made sense. "Okay, so do tell her what I just said and that I'm acting like an idiot over her best friend and can barely concentrate upon anything but her. Will that suffice?"

"Perfectly," Darryl said. "I'll even write it down and show her."

Max chuckled some more then asked, "So, other than a reconnaissance mission, I'm assuming you're calling about something work related?"

"Yes. Just had a quick question for you regarding the last changes we drew up."

"Hang on a sec," Max said, all thoughts of anything else swiftly taking a backseat as he pulled up the desk chair and opened his laptop. "I still have about an hour before I need to take off, let me bring up my notes and we'll go through it."

\*\*\*\*

Ginny watched Max effortlessly haul his black golf bag from the back of his rented SUV, set it on the ground, then do the same with hers. She was still tickled he'd bought her her own set of clubs; especially as she'd never played a game in her life. She'd tried to insist she rent a set of clubs - who knew if she'd even take a liking to the game - but he wouldn't hear of it. Instead, the next thing she knew, they were purchasing a shiny set of clubs and, while she'd gaped at the price tag, Max had paid for them as though they were only costing him pocket change.

"Okay," he said, closing the tailgate on the vehicle. "You feeling up to carrying these to the clubhouse?"

Ginny grinned. Novice or not, she did love the look of the pretty grey, white and pink bag holding her shiny, new clubs. She'd even bought a white sun visor with a pretty pink flower on it to match, much to Max's amusement. She followed his example and swung the bag strap over her shoulder then nodded. "Lead on, McDuff."

Max grinned and set out across the parking lot toward the clubhouse. He had a feeling it was going to be an entertaining morning.

****

Ginny tried to stand exactly as Max had taught her: legs apart, but not too far apart, slight flex to her knees, but not bent, blah, blah, blah. She took a deep breath, exhaled, then swung her club, connecting with the ball and sending it sharply… nowhere. Or so it felt, when it only sailed about a hundred yards down the fairway.

"Arggg!" Ginny exhaled, suppressing the desire to stamp her foot in annoyance like one of her grandchildren.

Max chuckled and put a hand on her shoulder. "Relax, darling. You're doing just fine."

"Sure, for a newbie," she huffed, while looking with annoyance at her still too visible ball. "Yours takes off so damned far I need binoculars to spot it. Mine, on the other hand, is mocking me."

Max shook his head and asked, "Newbie?"

Ginny couldn't help herself and giggled. "Blame my granddaughter, Grace, for that one."

Max pulled a water bottle from his bag and offered it to her. "She sounds *interesting*."

Ginny, taking a swig from the bottle, nearly choked as she laughed at his magnanimous *observation*.

Max quickly reached out to pat her on the back.

"She actually is," Ginny said, managing to swallow without spitting everywhere. "Honest."

He regarded her affectionately. "I'm certain of it. How could she be anything but, with you as her Granny?"

"*Granny*?" She grimaced, handing the water back to him. "Good lord, that makes me sound like I have one foot in the grave."

Max chortled as he tucked the bottle back into his bag.

"I am 'Grandma' not 'Granny', thank you very much." She wrinkled her nose, again, at the very sound of it.

"Alright, then," he said, placing a hand across his heart. "You have my word that Granny will never cross my lips in your regard, again."

Ginny grinned at him. Goodness, he was adorable. And sexy. And charming. And.... She swallowed and reined in her thoughts. Golf was the thing at the moment.

"So, feeling any better?" He gazed down the fairway in the same direction she had moments ago. "Ready to press on, or do we call it a day?"

Ginny squared her shoulders. She was a lot of things, but a quitter wasn't one of them. "Let's do this," she said, firmly.

He looked at her in admiration. Fabulous woman. Sexy woman. Funny woman. Intelligent woman.... He took a breath and nodded. Golf.

\*\*\*\*

Ginny grimaced as she lowered herself into the deep soaker tub in her ensuite bathroom. She'd filled it with therapeutic bath salts and foaming bath oil and, as they combined with the hot water, it began soothing her muscles. She breathed a sigh of relief and silently praised the gods of bathtub creation.

Who knew a round of golf could make a person feel so... decrepit. Granted, she'd never played before, but still. She now knew not to be fooled into thinking that walking on her treadmill and doing some yoga classes here and there was all that was needed to prepare a person for the hours of walking and swinging a club that made up the game of golf. Noted.

"Mmmm, that's good," Ginny murmured, reveling in the heat of the water while her thoughts wandered to Max, making her feel all the warmer. She had a strong feeling, after watching him play with grace and ease, he wasn't in need of hydrotherapy.

Martini, taking up residence in his usual spot on the vanity, seemed to be in an equally serene mood, closing his eyes and looking much like a resting Egyptian sphinx.

"Good plan," she told him, following his lead and closing her eyes as well while she settled further down into the heavenly scented passionflower bubbles. It was her determination to stay put, only her head above water, until the tub began to cool; however, the insistent sound of her cellphone ringing shattered that plan pretty much immediately.

"Oh, hell," she muttered, sitting upright and reaching out for her phone resting on the tub's wide edge. "Hello?"

"Mom?"

"Hello, dear. Hang on a moment," Ginny said, while grabbing for a dry cloth to wipe the bubbles from her hands and the phone. "Okay, there, I'm back."

"You sound odd," Jennifer said, on the other end of the line. "Where are you?"

"In the tub. I was cleaning suds from my hands."

"Oh. Do you want me to call you back?"

"Is it urgent?"

"No," Jennifer said. "Nothing that can't wait."

"Okay," Ginny said. "I'm just trying to soak away some very sore muscles. Why don't I call you back when I get out?"

"Sure," Jennifer agreed. "Are you feeling okay?"

Ginny laughed and said, "Of course. Nothing a bit of tub therapy and a glass of wine won't cure."

"You're not drinking in the tub, are you?"

"Of course not," Ginny said, chuckling at the alarm in Jennifer's voice. "It was an attempt at a joke. Clearly I missed the mark."

"Okaaay…"

"Honest, sweetheart," Ginny assured her. "I'm just going to have a soak and I'll call you back when I'm done."

"Okay, okay," Jennifer said, relenting. "Talk to you in a bit. 'Bye."

Ginny hung up the phone and placed it back on the ledge. She lifted her glass of Shiraz from beside the phone and sighed. Her daughter hadn't sounded at all convinced she was fine which made her wonder when, exactly, had the tables begun to shift and she was being treated more as the child than the parent. Ginny took a long swallow of her wine and predicted she'd have to come up with a satisfying - non worrisome - reason for her soreness; one that didn't involve a certain tall, charming and handsome man. She couldn't help but grin at the humor of it all. Sixty two years old and hiding a boyfriend. Wasn't life a funny thing?

\*\*\*\*

Chris strolled into the bedroom, took one look at Jennifer and said, "Whoa, what's with the face? Has something happened?"

"What?" she said, shifting on the bed for him to sit beside her.

"You look upset. Has something happened?"

"No." She shook her head and put the phone on the nightstand. "At least I don't think so…"

He took off his glasses to rub his eyes while he waited for her to finish her thought. He knew his wife well enough to understand she sometimes had to gather her thoughts before she started to speak.

"So, that was Mom," she said, pulling her knees up to her chest and wrapping her arms around them.

"Oh, good," Chris said, placing his glasses next to the phone.

Jennifer gave him an inquiring look.

"Didn't you said you were worried, earlier today, because she wasn't answering her phone," he said, by way of reply. "Something about it was becoming a habit and you were starting to get a bit concerned?"

"Oh, right."

"So, what's with the face?"

Jennifer released her knees and stretched out on the bed. "Exactly what you said. I was trying to reach her all day, *again,* and when I finally do get her she doesn't even mention the messages I've left, just says she's in the bathtub for her sore muscles."

"Okay," he said, lying down beside her on the comforter and tucking his pillow beneath his head.

"Well, at the risk of sounding like Kimberly, what the hell?"

Chris laughed and said, "You could never sound like Kimberly."

"Well, maybe not exactly," she said, "but, as she's often prone to saying, doesn't that seem a bit odd?"

"Which part?"

"All of it. Suddenly, she's going days being off the grid and now she's claiming she has muscles so sore she has to soak in the tub? Sore from what? Where has she been? What's she been doing?"

"I don't know," Chris said, rubbing his eyes. "But, she *is* sixty two. I'd imagine, aside from the fact she's been incommunicado, she gets sore once in a while. Heck, I'm thirty five and, believe me, there are days I'd welcome a soak in a hot tub."

Jennifer grinned at him.

"What?" he said, a small smile playing at his lips. "I would."

"I suppose. It's just that she sounded so…" Jennifer searched for the word. "Tired."

Chris glanced at the bedside clock. 10:13 pm.

"I know, I know," Jennifer said, looking at the clock as well. "But this didn't sound like typical end of day tired, you know?"

"No," Chris said, yawning widely and scratching his scalp. "I honestly don't."

"Oh, forget it. If I don't stop, I'm going to start doing something scary like actually channeling Kimberly. Mom will call back and explain where she's been and that will be that."

Chris got up to head to the bathroom. "You are a wise and logical woman," he said, giving her a small bow before he left the bedroom.

Jennifer rolled over onto her side and stared at the phone on the bedside table.

\*\*\*\*

## Ginny's Bath Time Wine

### Ingredients

One bottle of wine, your choice (Ginny went with a Shiraz).

### Directions

- o   Pour wine into a generous glass.
- o   Recline.
- o   Sip.
- o   Relax.

# Chapter Nineteen

Jan moved around Ginny's kitchen as though it was her own. Not surprising, of course, as their friendship was so long-lived she felt just as much at home there as in her own. She put a jar of mayonnaise back in the fridge and smiled at the bowl of potato salad on the countertop. It looked good enough to eat.

"Oooh," Ginny said, while entering the kitchen from the door to the backyard. "Is it done?"

"You bet," Jan said, pulling a sheet of plastic wrap from the rectangular container on the countertop.

"Eeek!" Ginny said, kicking off her orange flip-flops then dashing inside to quickly grab a spoon from the cutlery drawer. "Let me taste first!"

Jan laughed and waited for her to scoop some of the salad from the bowl, before wrapping the top of it. "Well?"

Ginny mock-swooned as she chewed then swallowed. "You make the best potato salad I've ever tasted. If there was a competition, you'd win hands down."

"Thank you, kindly," Jan said, adding the dish to the rest of the food in the refrigerator, prepared for the barbecue they were hosting, then closing the door. "And you made mint brownies, yes?"

"Yup. Haven't baked in a good long while, so I whipped some up." Ginny dropped the spoon into the sink then brushed her hands together in satisfaction. "I think that's about everything for the moment. The lawn furniture outside is all clean, Eric and Kimberly are bringing the snacks and Jennifer and Chris are bringing the meat. We have nothing else to do but have a glass of wine until they get here."

"Sounds perfect," Jan said. "I love that top on you, by the way, is it new?"

Ginny looked down at her sleeveless, V-neck blouse; more marigold in color than daffodil. She was still surprised that she'd gone ahead and bought it, it was so outside her usual style of dressing. "Yes and no. I bought it a while ago, but just haven't yet felt the impetus to wear it. I guess today, with the barbecue and everything, it felt like the right fit."

"The color is perfect on you. You should wear it more often."

"Thanks, I think it must be the new hair," Ginny said, tucking a lock behind her ear. "I never would have worn this color before. I would have felt too washed out."

"Or," Jan said, grinning. "Maybe it has something to do with a *certain business partner* of Darryl's who shall remain nameless for the sake of privacy."

Ginny pointed at finger at her. "You promised, remember?"

Jan swatted the finger away then smoothed the front of her black tank top. "And I'm good for it. You know I am."

"And Darryl knows the score?" Ginny asked, walking over to her china cabinet.

"Of course." Jan snickered and pushed Ginny's flip flops aside so they wouldn't trip on them. "And even though he claims he wishes he was completely in the dark about everything, I think the truth is that he's a tiny bit thrilled."

Ginny raised her eyebrows. She hadn't expected that. "Thrilled? Seriously?"

"Absolutely. While there's no question Max is completely on-board now with the new development, him being so smitten with you has inadvertently made you Darryl's ace in the hole."

Ginny laughed as she retrieved wineglasses from the cabinet and brought them over to the table. "Ugg, that sounds sordid."

"Only if you're lucky," Jan teased, pulling a chair out and sitting down at the kitchen table. "Maybe you can put that yarn and needles Kimberly gave you to work and make a *snuggle* quilt."

"Oh, yuck." Ginny grimaced and shook her head, making Jan laugh.

"God, that still cracks me up. Knitting paraphernalia as a gift! Talk about sending a message. Next, she's going to ask if you'll teach the grandkids how to make a sweater."

"Don't you mean ask *us*? Hmmm? She did think of both you and Dixie as well, you'll remember," Ginny said, smirking as she reached across the table for a bottle of white wine.

"I think you should just cut her off at the pass and tell her your *lover* is keeping you too busy to arrange a girl's knitting night."

Ginny groaned then opened the bottle.

"Oh, come on, they're grown-ups. Sure they might be a bit shocked at first, but…"

"No way," Ginny said, cutting her off. "Not yet. Not until I'm sure it's anything really worth talking about."

Jan shot her a look.

"What?" Ginny said, pouring the wine into the glasses. "What's with the look?"

"You know he's pretty taken with you, is all I'm saying. Doesn't seem a whole lot of question there that he thinks there's something worth talking about. Heck, as you know, he's *been* talking; at least to Darryl, anyway."

Ginny put the bottle back onto the tabletop. "Still…"

"Ginny and Max, sitting in a tree," Jan teased, then sipped from her glass.

Ginny shook her head. "Seriously, all kidding aside, where the kids are concerned I really feel I have to proceed with caution."

Jan stopped her school yard chant to let her speak.

"Until I know for absolute sure there's something to say, I'm not opening it up to the masses. I don't need the chaos." Ginny shifted in her seat. "I mean, we've only just all managed to get to the point now where we can have these family gatherings without someone mentioning George."

Jan nodded.

"Not that I'm saying they shouldn't…"

"Of course not."

"But, we're finally at a place where all of us getting together is a good thing and it doesn't feel lacking." Ginny took a sip of wine. "And, of course, there's the other issue of them being practically in my back pocket."

"Mmm," Jan said, agreeing.

"I understand it, of course, it scared the hell out of them when George passed. But, now the pendulum has swung too far in the other direction and we've gone from normal, occasional communication, to the way Jennifer has been acting over the past while; harassing me if I don't stay continually available and in contact."

Jan gave her a sympathetic smile.

"And I love them for it, I do," Ginny clarified, sighing. "It's just that…"

"You need to find a balance with them before you consider bringing a new man into the mix, especially when you don't feel you know yet where the relationship is going to lead. It wouldn't do anything but be a possible catalyst for more upheaval. Once you've opened the can of worms, you can't close it, so better make sure it's worth opening."

"Exactly," Ginny breathed, relieved she understood.

"Knock, knock! Anybody home?" Jennifer's voice rang out, as she opened the front door.

Ginny lifted her glass toward Jan's and the two of them clinked in an unspoken toast of solidarity, as only best friends can do.

****

Ginny stood at the kitchen island tossing together the green salad and savoring the melodic sound of friendly conversation going on around her. These were the moments to treasure, she knew, the ones that weren't about anything except connection to the ones you love. She listened to Eric and Jan bantering back and forth, Darryl adding the occasion amused chuckle into the mix, and was so engrossed she complete missed Kimberly questioning her from her place at the kitchen table.

"I *said*, tell us how the guest speaker was!"

The conversation between Eric and Jan ground to a halt and in the ensuing silence Ginny paused in chopping celery and cucumbers to frown at her daughter-in-law. "I'm sorry, dear, were you talking to me?"

"*Yes*," Kimberly said, straightening her already perfect ponytail, "I *was*. I was asking how you enjoyed the guest speaker."

Ginny glanced at Jan, who shrugged her shoulders in return, then said, "I think you'll have to be more specific."

Eric, sitting at the table and offering Layla pieces of cut up strawberries one at a time, also sent an inquiring look to Jan. She gave him an identical shrug of her shoulders.

"The last time I popped in with my gift, you said your garden club was having a guest speaker."

Eric suppressed a groan. *Now* he had an idea of where she was going with her question.

Ginny put the salad tongs down and wiped her hands on a dishtowel while Kimberly cocked her head and added, speaking in slow, measured words, "Do, you, not, remember?"

Eric cringed at the tone in his wife's voice; implying his mother was hard of hearing, or comprehension, or both.

Jan, seated across the table from Eric and Layla, released an audible snort.

Ginny shot her a warning glance.

She feigned an expression of innocence then tried to exchange a look with Darryl, leaning up against the island. He put his hands up in surrender before picking up his wineglass and exiting the house via the back door.

"Oh, right, *that*!" Ginny lifted her hands in an 'awe-shucks' manner. "I've been so busy since then with work and such, it completely slipped my mind."

"Slipped *something*," Jan remarked, under her breath, snickering.

"JAN!" Ginny blurted, then felt a flash of satisfaction when her friend visibly startled. "Do you mind going *away* outside and asking Chris how long it will be before the burgers and hotdogs are done?"

Jan knew she was being banished and had the good graces to look properly contrite. She stood up, smoothed the front of her tan, cotton capri pants and left the house without another word.

"So, the speaker?" Kimberly repeated, her stare never wavering.

Good lord, Ginny thought, rubbing the back of her neck, she was like a dog with a bone.

"Are you planning on taking up gardening, or something, Kim?" Eric commented, while handing Layla the last strawberry from the yellow bowl on the table.

That caught her off guard and broke her concentration. She looked at him in confusion. "Pardon?"

He grabbed a wet paper towel he had waiting on the table and began wiping Layla's hands and face. "It's just you seem awfully interested in Mom's garden club, all of a sudden. I figured you'll be asking me to start digging you a plot at any moment."

"Plot!" Layla blurted, grinning at the sound.

Kimberly, meanwhile, flushed at the accusation and straightened her spin as she replied, "*No*. I'm just showing an interest in her life. A lot more than *you do*, I might add."

Eric stared at her gravely and Ginny got that uncomfortable feeling of being inadvertently caught in the middle of an awkward conversation. "It's fine," she jumped in, patting things down. "And yes, Kimberly, the guest speaker was just fine. Perfectly acceptable."

Kimberly arched an eyebrow at her husband and smoothed the creases from her vintage, floral print shift-dress before trailing Ginny out of the house into the yard. "So what did he, or *she*, talk about? Did you learn anything interesting?"

Jan, reclining on a wicker lounge chair on the patio, caught Ginny's eye. Ginny could practically hear her thinking *drop it, already*, and rolled her eyes in return.

Jennifer, sitting cross-legged on the lawn and watching Grace push Mason on the swings, turned toward them and asked, "About what?"

Ginny busied herself counting plates and napkins on the picnic table. Maybe they'd forget she was even there.

"Your Mom went to a garden club meeting and they had a guest speaker," Kimberly stated. "I was just curious as to what they talked about."

"In case she suddenly gets hit by the overwhelming desire to start crawling in the dirt," Eric commented, unable to resist one more dig as he joined them on the patio, Layla in his arms.

Ginny sighed. So much for blending into the background. If she stayed there, it might end up an all-out war.

"Was that the night I called and called and you didn't answer the phone?" Jennifer asked, standing up and brushing grass clippings from her denim shorts. "Well, the *first* time it happened, anyway."

Oh, for the *love of god*, Ginny thought, slamming the remaining plates in her hands down on the tabletop. "Yes. We had a speaker, I turned my phone off out of respect for those around me, *as I already told you*, and failed to remember to turn it back on until later. Alright?"

Jennifer swallowed uncomfortably and nodded.

Ginny gave Jan a 'see what I mean' look before turning to Kimberly and hammering out, "Yes, the speaker was *fine*. Very insightful. He shared information about gardening on a larger scale, for developments."

"That seems odd," Kimberly remarked, completely missing the exasperation in Ginny's tone.

"*Really?*" Eric cut in, his dark eyes glittering dangerously as he pointed back and forth between her and Ginny. "*That's* the thing going on here that strikes you as odd?"

Jennifer exchanged a wide-eyed look with Chris, standing at the barbecue cooking the meat. Her mother's tone had come out of the blue and she'd never heard her brother sound so brittle with his wife. Yikes.

Kimberly ignored him and pushed on, saying, "Isn't your club made up of people like you?"

"Like *me?*" Ginny repeated. "Meaning?"

"You know, hobbyists."

"Oh," she said, understanding. "Well then, yes, sure. Many of us are. But there are a number of members who work part-time at it as well, so they were happy to hear about larger scale planning."

"There you go, questions answered," Eric said, shooting Kimberly a 'drop it now' look as he put Layla down and she made off to join her cousins on the play-set.

"Huh," she offered, ignoring his silent communication and, instead, brushing away imaginary dust from her dress. "See. I wasn't aware of that."

Ginny released a breath of air, relieved it seemed the subject was put to bed. Sure, she'd fudged the truth about going to listen to a guest speaker, but only the timeline of *when* she'd gone, not the actual content. It was the only reason she'd been able to convey information about the topic without hedging and giving herself away.

"Hey, Mom," Jennifer said, cocking her head.

Ginny turned toward her, hopeful somebody was going to change the subject.

"You look lovely, did you buy a new bronzer or something?"

Ginny's eyebrows lifted and she shook her head. "No. Why?"

Jennifer walked across the patio to get a closer look. "You look like you've got some pretty color in your cheeks, so I thought it might be something new and wanted to know what type."

"Oh. No, sorry, I didn't. It's probably from when I went golfing."

Everyone went still. Except for the children. They kept right on playing, taking no notice of the halt in adult conversation.

"Wait now, what? Did you say *golfing?*"

Ginny's insides clenched at the incredulous tone in Eric's voice. Damn it. She hadn't thought before she opened her big mouth and look what it got her. More bloody inquisition. She sighed and nodded.

"You went golfing?" Jennifer said, equally gob smacked. "*You?* Since when do *you* golf?"

"Well, umm," Ginny hedged, wracking her brains for a reply.

Jennifer pulled a purple scrunchie, the same shade as her tank top, from around her wrist and lifted her hair up into a slap-dash bun. "Are you hearing this?" she asked Chris.

He shrugged his shoulders, hoping to stay out of things.

Jan shot Darryl a pleading look.

He met her eye then loudly said, "She went with us."

All eyes turned toward him; Ginny's overflowing with gratitude.

"Earlier in the week," Jan added, helping her husband along. "It was a work thing, last minute. Darryl needed to even up a...." She frowned, searching to remember the right word.

"Foursome," he finished, for her.

She smiled at him. "Right. So, your Mom kindly agreed to help out."

"Wow, okay," Eric said, then turned toward Darryl. "If it ever happens again, you know you can call me, right?"

Darryl nodded. "Sure. Of course."

"Wait," Jennifer said, snapping her fingers. "Was *that* the reason you were off grid again and soaking in the tub when I called you?"

Ginny rubbed her temple, feeling a headache threatening. She walked over to a lounger in the shade beside Jan and sat down.

"You remember, right?" Jennifer insisted, almost accusing. "When I called you? You never gave me a reason why you were so sore."

"I suppose," Ginny said, vaguely, leaning back in her chair.

"Well, why didn't you say so?" Jennifer pressed. "You could have just said—"

"Well, I guess I didn't realize I had to give an explanation for everything I do!" Ginny said, sharply.

Jennifer shot her an affronted look, but got the message and shut up.

Jan patted her arm and Ginny gave her a tiny, appreciative smile.

"Didn't George hate golf?" Kimberly asked, a brittle edge to her voice.

Ginny stiffened. Would it never end?

Jan frowned at the accusation in Kimberly's tone and spoke on Ginny's behalf. "What the hell does that have to do with anything?"

"From a psychological standpoint, I'd say a *lot*," Kimberly countered.

"I agree," Eric put in, much to his wife's surprise. "While I understand you were helping Darryl out, I still find it strange you'd suddenly go and play a game you knew Dad hated."

Ginny exchanged a look with Jan. She gave a subtle nod. It had to be done. It was time to start pushing that damned pendulum in the other direction.

"Believe it or not," Ginny said, her jaw rigid as she swiveled in her seat to meet both Eric's and Kimberly's gaze straight on. "When I agreed to go, the very last thing I thought of was your *father's* views on the game. From a psychological standpoint, *that* seems to me like a strange thing to do!"

Kimberly placed a hand on her chest, as though she'd been slugged. "No need to get so confrontational—"

"Hey, Chris!" Jennifer blurted, jumping into the middle of things and smartly cutting Kimberly off. "How about those burgers and dogs? Are they almost ready, because I think the troops are getting hungry."

Darryl quickly grabbed the thread and helped, too. "Mason, Grace! Layla! You guys getting hungry?"

"Yes!" Mason cheered, while Grace reached for Layla's hand to lead her across the grass.

Ginny cast an appreciative smile at Darryl then patted Jan's shoulder. She had good friends.

\*\*\*\*

## Ginny's Mint Chocolate Brownies

### Ingredients

2½ cups whole wheat flour
1   teaspoon baking soda
½   teaspoon salt
1½ cups brown sugar
1   cup butter
4   tablespoons milk
3   cups chocolate chips
1   teaspoon peppermint extract
1   teaspoon vanilla extract
4   large eggs

### Directions

Preheat oven to 350 degrees F.

o  Combine dry ingredients, flour, baking soda and salt, in bowl and set aside.

o  Combine butter, sugar and milk in a medium saucepan, over medium heat. Heat the mixture just to a boil, stirring constantly to avoid burning.

o  Remove from heat and add half of the chocolate chips and both the peppermint and vanilla extracts to the mixture, stirring until smooth.

o  Add the eggs, one at a time, stirring well after each addition, making sure they are well blended into the mixture.

o  Add in the flour mixture and the other half of the chocolate chips, mix well.

o  Spread into a greased 9 x 13-inch baking pan and bake for 20 to 30 minutes until set.

o  Cool completely before cutting.

# Chapter Twenty

Darryl and Max walked side by side, takeaway coffee cups in hand, their work boots leaving imprints in the freshly packed earth of the area recently cleared for their new multi-family complex. It was early, crack-of-dawn-early, the sun was still below the backside of the mountain tops, bathing their rocky heights in a warm glow while leaving their fronts in shadow.

Max took a deep lungful of the fresh, slightly damp morning air and sighed contently on his exhale. It already felt like a good day ahead. "It's good to get out here before things really get going," he said, while they weaved their way through the numerous construction vehicles waiting to be brought to life for another day by their human operators. "I'm glad you suggested it."

Darryl nodded. He, too, always appreciated the opportunity to walk the site while it was still and quiet. It allowed him to 'see' the finished project in his mind's eye and, if necessary, make changes before the foundations were being laid and it was too late to do so. He stopped them at about the halfway point and took a drink from his takeaway cup. The coffee was hot and rich, brewed from Ethiopian beans that held floral and berry notes. Delicious.

"Can I buy you breakfast when we're done?" Max offered, squinting into the steadily brightening morning sunlight. "We'll probably have no trouble getting a table."

Darryl chuckled. "Sure, thanks. Jan won't be up for a while anyway, so no need to get back anytime soon. Not to mention, she'll probably head over to Ginny's for their usual Sunday catch-up and I'm guessing it will involve a lot of back and forth about the barbecue yesterday."

"Oh, right," Max said, taking a sip of coffee and pretending it had slipped his mind. "That was *yesterday*."

Darryl took another swallow from his cup while looking at him levelly.

Max had the good grace to laugh at being caught out. "Okay, so obviously I didn't forget. But now you have me completely curious as to what happened that Ginny and Jan need to discuss it after the fact."

Darryl started walking again, leading them around an oversized dump truck and pointing off to the left. "See there? That's the park area we talked about. Looks about the right size, wouldn't you say, now that we're seeing it in person?"

Max followed the direction of his point and nodded. "You're measurements are spot-on. I don't think there's anything left to change, now we just have to give the final go-ahead for the project to move forward."

Darryl grinned. He was excited. Max and his team had brought a much appreciated injection of fresh ideas and insights into this project and he knew the final outcome was going to be sensational.

"Do you want to go further?" Max asked, stopping to fish his sunglasses from the pocket on his black golf shirt.

Darryl shook his head, also searching out his sunglasses from the pocket of his navy chinos as the sun finally crested the top of the mountains.

"Wow," Max said, as the evergreens growing on the craggy mountain side seemed to shimmer and the entire site was suddenly lit up like a movie set. "The people who purchase these are going to get one hell of a morning view."

Darryl patted him on the back then turned to start the walk back to the car. "That's exactly why I was so keen on this spot."

"Good call," Max said.

"You know," Darryl said, his footfalls steady and rhythmic as he retraced the path they'd made in the soil with their boots on the way out. "Ginny's kids are great, just great."

Max matched his pace and said, "Doesn't surprise me one bit. But, I suspect a *but* is coming."

Darryl gave him a wry grin and said, "You suspect correctly. They've gotten really overprotective of Ginny since… you know, *George*."

Max nodded, his face grave, then drank his coffee.

"Anyway, the result of them trying so hard to watch over her, is that she can barely make a move without one of them wanting to know where she is and what she's doing. It's like she's an eight year old all over again."

"And that was an issue at the barbecue?"

"It definitely came up," Darryl said, tipping his cup to his lips and drinking the last of his coffee.

"How?"

"They started in about the time she was out with you and she ended up having to do some serious deflection."

Max's eyebrows lifted. "She told them?"

Darryl shook his head. "No way."

Max's eyebrows dropped into a furrow. "So, how did they know she was out with me?"

"They didn't. It wasn't about who she was or wasn't with, it was about her seeming to be out of their radar range. So, she had to reiterate her story about the guest speaker at her garden club and some other bullshit..." Darryl exhaled and shook his head at the memory. "Anyway, I don't know all the ins and out of it and I don't want to. I just tried to stay out of it, other than to help keep her cover."

Max cleared his throat and said, "I'm glad you told me. She's mentioned a bit about how they've been and that's why I told her we'll take things at whatever pace she sees fit. It's good to get a different perspective on it, thought, to better understand it."

They reached the car and Darryl unlocked the doors. "She'll get it handled," he said, while they both got into the vehicle. "It might take some time, but she'll get things straightened around."

Max settled into the passenger seat, put his cup in the center holder and clipped his seatbelt into place. "I'm a patient man and she's worth the wait."

"Got that right," Darryl said, putting his cup beside Max's. "She's a survivor, our Gin."

Max gazed again at the site and mountains beyond. "I can understand how easy it is to feel at home here," he said, his voice thoughtful.

Darryl started the car and put it into reverse to turn around. "Boxwood Hills is that kind of place. Once it gets under your skin there's nowhere else you'd want to call home."

Max thought of Ginny and the amazing joy she'd already brought into his life in such a short time. It wasn't something that came around very often in a person's life, if at all.

"Breakfast?" Darryl asked, watching his new friend's face and the emotions flitting across it.

Max took a breath. "You bet."

Darryl reached out to pat his shoulder before putting the car into gear. "I know the perfect place."

\*\*\*\*

Kimberly tapped at her keyboard. She'd cleaned the house and put Layla down for her nap and was now grabbing a moment to connect with her sister, while their homes were free of husbands and kid's demands, to discuss the latest development with their father. She glanced at the glass of water on the table beside her laptop, starting to feel she would have to have a much stiffer drink at hand just to survive the updates.

She typed: *"I'm having a hard time believing this."*

Kris: *"I hear you and I'm the one who saw them, again."*

Kimberly wrung her hands then typed: *"And he honestly got angry when you confronted him?"*

Kris: *"Very."*

Kimberly raised her eyebrows. The very idea was outlandish. Sure, growing up, they'd received their share of reprimands and the like. When they broke the rules there were consequences. All the usual stuff. But, their Dad actually becoming truly angry was a rarity and even more so once they'd become adults.

Kris: *"I don't remember ever seeing him sooo.... Indignant."*

Wow, Kimberly thought.

Kris: *"He more or less told me his life was none of my business."*

Kimberly frowned. *"Yeah, but what about Mom and her life?"*

*Kris:* "*That's exactly what I said to him! And he proceeded to tell me he and Mom's relationship was between them and only them and that was that. Butt out.*"

Kimberly flushed as though he'd said it directly to her and wrote, "*God. Sounds guilty as hell.*"

*Kris:* "*Tell me about it. Grayson said the same thing, so did Renee and Penelope.*"

"*You told them?*" Kimberly asked, taken aback. While she really liked both of Kris' sisters-in-law, it seemed a pretty intimate thing to share.

*Kris:* "*Yeah, of course.*"

Kimberly bit her lip. She often felt like Renee and Penelope were more like Kris' real sisters and *she* was the in-law. It was childish, she knew, but she felt it anyway.

*Kris:* "*Why, have you not told anyone besides Eric?*"

Kimberly squirmed in her seat. For Kris to believe she'd shared what was going on in her family with Eric was a logical assumption. However, it was anything but the truth. She'd not told him or, for that matter, anyone else. She'd thought about talking to Jennifer and getting her feedback, but they'd been off-track for a couple of months since Ginny had gone strange. Things felt stilted. Formal. She hoped they'd get back to normal but, so far, they hadn't. She wrote: "*Not in so many words.*"

*Kris:* "*Why not? Is something going on with you two?*"

Kimberly quickly replied: "*No. Just been a bit crazy around here and there hasn't been a chance.*"

*Kris:* "*What about Jennifer? You guys are pretty close, right? Or your other friend you've told me about, Becca?*"

"*I just haven't had the chance,*" Kimberly reiterated, feeling very uncomfortable she was fudging the truth.

*Kris:* "*Well, you should make the chance 'cause this isn't something you want to sit and stew on by yourself. Having Renee and Penelope to talk to about all of this is the only thing that's keeping me from flying off the handle.*"

Kimberly could hear her sister's advisory tone in her head as though she was sitting across the table, instead of typing on a computer. *"I know, I know, and I will. But, listen, I hear Layla waking from her nap, so I should sign off."*

Kris: *"Okay. I'll keep you posted when I have more news. I have a feeling this isn't over. Love you, little sister."*

Kimberly sighed. *"You, too. xxx."*

She signed off and closed her laptop. Layla was actually still sound asleep, so nothing but silence from the empty house met Kimberly's ears. However, in that moment, it was blissfully welcome in the face of the information being presented by her sister.

\*\*\*\*

Ginny tucked away the last of the throw pillows she'd placed on the floor in the children's section of the library for story time. She stood up and smoothed her grey palazzo pants then quickly checked the large clock on the wall above the front desk. Only a half hour to go until she had to leave for her *appointment* at the dentist; or so she'd claimed was the reason for her taking the remainder of the afternoon off.

The real truth was she was meeting Max.

Ginny grinned to herself, despite the wave of guilt that washed over her at keeping the truth from Tamara. Following in the wave's wake; however, the adage *'needs must'* came to mind and she had to press her lips together to keep from snickering out loud. Maybe Max was the devil in disguise.

"Mrs. Ginny?"

Ginny smiled as she turned toward the sweet sounding voice calling out to her. All the kids called her Mrs. Ginny and it still amused and delighted her. She looked down and her gaze was met by a pair of sparkly eyes looking back at her.

"I really liked the story today!"

"Jayda," Ginny said, enchanted by the young girl's enthusiasm. "How nice of you to let me know. Is Mommy here, too?"

Jayda nodded then cocked her head to look Ginny up and down. "You look different, today."

"Do I?" Ginny asked, further amused by her candor.

"Uh-huh," Jayda began, before her mother came charging around the bookshelf that created the separation between the children's section and the rest of the library.

"THERE you are!" she blurted, her tone so sharp Jayda swiveled on the heel of her lemon yellow sneaker to stare with wide eyes at her stern face.

"Charlotte," Ginny said, hoping to diffuse the situation. "How nice to see you! Jayda was just telling me she enjoyed our story, today."

Charlotte smoothed her blonde curls from her face and caught her breath.

Ginny sympathized with, what was clearly, her distress at losing track of her daughter.

"You HAVE TO tell me where you're going," Charlotte said, to Jayda, before turning to Ginny. "Sorry, I don't mean to be so intense, but—"

"No, no," Ginny said, patting her elbow. "I raised three children. I understand, completely."

"Sorry, Mommy," Jayda said, contrite.

Ginny was impressed the little girl hadn't burst out crying in the face of her mother's upset. At that age, in the same situation, Jennifer would have had crocodile tears leaking from her eyes.

"I just wanted to tell Mrs. Ginny I liked the story."

Charlotte nodded, regaining her composure. "Okay. Just remember the rules. Always tell Mommy where you are."

Let off the hook, Jayda brightened then pointed at Ginny. "She looks different."

Charlotte's face twisted into an expression of mortification, while Ginny pressed a hand to her mouth to suppress her giggles. "We don't point at people," she said. "Remember? It's not nice."

"Know why?" Jayda asked.

"You don't need to tell us," Charlotte said, wringing her hands.

Ginny grinned. Clearly Jayda was willing to share her opinions, much to her mother's dismay. She decided to play devil's advocate and said, "Why?"

"You look pretty," Jayda said, simply.

Charlotte looked so relieved, Ginny wanted to give her a hug.

"And you smell nice," Jayda added.

It was all Ginny could do to refrain from asking the question, compared to what?

"And not as tired as before," Jayda further clarified. "More shiny. Like my Grandma."

Okay, that was too much, Ginny couldn't hold back and laughed out loud.

Charlotte groaned then gave in and giggled a bit, too.

"Well, that's certainly good news, Jayda," Ginny said. "Shiny and smells good sounds a lot better than tired, don't you think?"

Jayda nodded, her elfin face full of cheer at being understood, then pointed toward a bookshelf. "Can I go find a book to borrow, Mommy?"

"Yes, of course, please go," Charlotte agreed.

Ginny watched her skip across the carpet as she made her way toward the shelf; her waterfall of dark hair reminding Ginny of Grace.

"I am *so* sorry," Charlotte said, the moment Jayda was out of earshot. "We've been working on the pointing thing and learning about how people's feeling can be hurt if you aren't careful how you say things. It's a work in progress, believe me."

Ginny lifted a hand and waved it dismissively. "No need to apologize. Honestly. I've experienced my share of uncensored comments in my lifetime. And many of them have come from children."

Charlotte grinned at the teasing tone in Ginny's voice. "Well, thank goodness for that."

"Is there anything I can help either of you find," Ginny asked, moving things along.

"Oh, no thanks. I'll let her browse," Charlotte said, before adding, "and for the record, you're nothing like Jayda's Grandmother."

Ginny cocked her head as a memory of Charlotte lamenting her mother-in-law's antics came to mind.

"Seriously," Charlotte went on. "*You* look lovely!"

"Thank you," Ginny said. "That's very kind—"

"Your hair color and your clothes are classy, not…" Charlotte's face twisted with disdain. "*Obvious.*"

"Oh, well," Ginny muttered, vaguely, unsure of how to respond.

The woman is a piece of work!" Charlotte added, tugging sharply at the hem of her already smooth white t-shirt. "And, naturally, because she doesn't do *normal*, Jayda thinks she's the best thing she's encountered, but—"

"Normal?" Ginny echoed.

"Oh, well, *you know,*" She released her t-shirt, dropped the brown bag she was carrying over her shoulder onto the floor at her feet then began counting on her fingers for emphasis as she spoke. "She dresses *inappropriately*, too young for her age. Her hair is so red it's almost garish. She's the first one to start pouring the wine—"

"You know," Ginny interrupted, acutely aware Charlotte was only beginning her tirade and hoping to stop the flow before it really got going. "I've never met her, but I'd hazard to guess I'd like her."

Charlotte stopped short, her hands dropping to her sides as she stared blankly at Ginny. It was the last thing she'd expected to hear.

"Please understand, I'm not trying to pry into your business, really," Ginny swiftly made clear. "But since you brought it up, I do have a rather advantageous point of view as I, too, am a woman of a *certain age*."

"But, you're NOTHING LIKE HER!" Charlotte blurted, then looked embarrassed she'd raised her voice.

"As you've said, yes," Ginny agreed, reaching out to pat her arm. "However, I do know what it's like to grow older and leave stages of life behind and how that can be an *adjustment*."

Charlotte said nothing, just shrugged her shoulders in acknowledgement.

Ginny took advantage of her silence figuring, in for a penny, in for a pound. "All I am trying to say, Charlotte, is often it's wise to remember not to judge a book by its cover."

"Well, of course," she agreed. "But this book and cover seem to match exactly."

Ginny nodded then asked, "Do you remember when you were a younger woman than you are now, completely free and on the brink of all the adventures of life?"

Charlotte's face grew puzzled. She didn't follow.

"What I'm getting at," Ginny further explained, "is that you must remember what it feels like to be at a certain stage and then move into another. Like, for instance, young and without a care in the world then finding yourself no longer such a fresh-faced youth but, instead, a young mother."

Charlotte smiled as she glancing over at Jayda. "Yes, of course. It was an adjustment for sure."

"Right. But, when you think about it, did you really *feel* any differently?" Ginny queried. "I mean, after the first bit of adjustment was done, did you suddenly feel that that youthful part of you was utterly gone from your personality and you were suddenly an entirely different person?"

Charlotte considered then shook her head. "No. I suppose not."

"Right," Ginny agreed. "Of course you didn't. Sure, you were different in that you'd learned more things, but *that* girl, that younger version of Charlotte, was still a part of you. *Is* still a part of you. And, if you're to be honest with yourself, did you not - *do* you not - sometimes wish it was more *appropriate* to let go of the responsible adult for a bit and let her out to play?"

Charlotte's face softened and she nodded. "I have my moments."

"Don't we all," Ginny said. "But we get so caught up we often forget that all people feel that way at one time or another."

Charlotte blinked her blue eyes a few times as the point hit home. "I've never considered it that way before."

"No," Ginny said, patting her shoulder. "And you're no different than most. We get sidetracked by the exterior of the person and believe the image we see in front of us is all that they are."

"Which it's not," Charlotte said, as she full impact of what Ginny was saying sunk in. She tugged again at her t-shirt and added, "I used to be fifteen pounds lighter, but since having Jayda I've been having trouble shaking it."

Ginny smiled at her.

"God," Charlotte said, suddenly connecting all of the dots. "Do you think my mother-in-law is feeling the same way, only with years instead of pounds, and that's why she acts like she does?"

Bingo, Ginny thought.

Charlotte's face twisted and she looked into Ginny's eyes. "I've been such a..." She paused to make sure Jayda was still out of earshot then said, "Bitch."

Ginny shook her head. "No. That's not true. You've been normal. The simple fact is, we're all in this together and the one common denominator we have is that every stage of life will be lived by each and every one of us. That is, if we're lucky enough to live that long. Often the kindest thing a person can offer another is the freedom to be who they are."

Jayda chose that moment to come barreling back toward them. "Mommy! Mrs. Ginny! Look!"

Charlotte squared her shoulders and smiled at her daughter. "Find a book?"

"This one," Jayda said, holding up a book with a vibrant, multi-colored cover.

"Looks perfect to me," Ginny said, before turning to Charlotte. "Mommy?"

Charlotte regarded Ginny with friendly eyes. "Perfect."

"Can we pick something for Grandma?" Jayda asked.

Ginny smiled. Out of the mouths of babes.

"I think that's a great idea," Charlotte said, then turned to Ginny. "Any recommendations?"

She chuckled and indicated toward the opposite side of the library. "This way."

****

"You're absolutely sure you'll be okay if I take the afternoon off?"

Tamara pushed her long, brown locks away from her face and rolled her eyes. "Oh my goodness, you have to stop fretting, of course I will. It's always slow mid-week and if it turns out I need back-up I can call Maddie."

Ginny nodded and fiddled with the sleeve of her pink peasant blouse.

Tamara laughed when she saw the doubt on her face. "Seriously, stop fretting. The world won't screech to a halt because you're having your teeth cleaned."

Ginny inwardly winced. Hiding the truth was so tough on her.

"You should get going," Tamara reminded, looking up at the clock. "Or you'll be late."

"Right." Ginny picked up her purple leather handbag and squeezed Tamara's shoulder affectionately. "Thanks for holding down the fort."

She waved her off. "Don't give it a second thought."

****

Max regarded the collar on his blue and white striped dress shirt in the refection of the bathroom mirror, in his hotel room. Did it need further pressing, or was he just looking for something - *anything* - else to focus upon besides the excited butterflies battering around his insides? Probably the latter.

"Steady on," he counselled himself, taking a deep, calming breath. "Just pretend it's nothing more than a run-of-the-mill business meeting."

The reason for his internal tremors was simple; he was nearly due to pick up Ginny for their date and, instead of feeling cool, calm and mature, he was being revisited by the emotions of his gangly teenage years. It had been so long since he'd felt anything of the sort, he was alternately loving and abhorring the roller-coaster. It was simultaneously absurd and exhilarating.

"Right," he told his reflection, with a curt nod. "No need for such theatrics. She's a lovely woman...."

His thoughts stopped there as he remembered her lying next to him in his hotel bed, her flushed cheeks, the sparkle in her blue eyes, the curve of her hips and the sweetness of her laugh.

He stared into his own eyes and exhaled. "Maxwell, my friend. You're in trouble."

****

Ginny leaned into Max, enjoying the feel of his strong arms around her and sighed. They'd spent the sunny, summer afternoon taking a wine tour and she'd be the first to admit, she was feeling more than a little tipsy. It was the only explanation as to why she was being so brazen and snuggling up to the man on her front porch, in plain view of all of her neighbors.

"Thank you for a perfect afternoon."

He gently lifted her chin, kissed her deeply and when they came up for air, said, "The pleasure was all mine."

"Apparently, I'm a cheap date," she said, giggling hard enough to make herself snort.

Max chuckled while he held her shoulder to steady her on the step. She was a delight.

"Goodness," Ginny said, shaking her head at herself. "Good thing I took the entire afternoon off of work, or I'd have to fib again and say they gave me laughing gas for my cleaning."

"Are you absolutely sure you don't want me to come inside and make you something to eat?" he asked.

"No, no." She waved away his offer with a lazy flick of her hand. "I'll be just fine. You have a meeting and that's more important than heating up cheese toast. Don't let me get in the way of work."

"You know, I could come back later tonight and make you something, if that's alright."

Ginny blinked and reached for the door frame. "Really?"

"I'm afraid it would be slightly more than cheese toast," he teased, an amused grin on his face.

Her stomach flipped at the idea of seeing him again so soon and she caught her breath. "I like the sound of that."

"Ginny!"

Max startled at the sound of Ginny's name ringing out in the crescent and he spun around on the steps.

A woman, late 50's with red kinky hair, wearing an orange tank top and flowing multi-colored, ankle-length skirt was speed-walking from her house to Ginny's, waving energetically.

Ginny leaned around Max and grinned. "That's Donna," she managed to say, before her neighbor charged up the front walk.

"I'm so glad I caught you," Donna effused, before smiling coyly at Max and adding, "Or at least that *someone* did."

Ginny laughed and stepped slightly away from Max. "How are you Donna? This is my friend, Max."

Donna raised an eyebrow at the word *friend*, but left it alone and, instead, reached out a hand in greeting. "Nice to meet you, Max."

Max shook her hand and smiled politely while noticing she wasn't wearing shoes. "You, too."

"So, what's up?" Ginny asked, cocking her head.

Donna's hands began moving as she talked, waving here and there for emphasis. "Douglas and I are having a Black-eyed Susan party and we want to make sure you know you're invited and, of course, any *friends* you'd like to bring along."

An amused grin decorated Max's face when Donna winked at him while she said *friends*.

Ginny shook her head. "I'm sorry, did you say Black-eyed Susan?"

"Yes!" Donna laughed at the puzzlement on both Ginny's and Max's faces. "They're blooming and we're celebrating it!"

"Blooming?" Max echoed. "They're a plant, of some sort?"

Donna nodded enthusiastically then pointed at her yard, the beds overflowing with the bright yellow flowers. "There they are, in all their glory!"

"Well, thanks for the invitation," Ginny said, reaching out to hold onto Max's arm to steady her on her feet. "Let me know when and the time and I'll check my schedule."

"Of course, of course," Donna said, doing a small tap dance as she began her retreat back down the path. She stopped in her tracks and called out to Ginny, "Oh! I just remembered, I have apricots for you. Come by whenever you want to get them."

"Perfect, thanks, Donna," Ginny said, waving her off as she set off again toward her house, humming all the way.

"Wow," Max said, when Donna was out of sight.

Ginny laughed. "Yup, she's something alright. But, aside from her quirkiness, she has a heart of gold."

"And apricots, apparently."

"Didn't you have to get to work so that you could get back here?" Ginny asked, leaning into him.

His eyes lit up. "Correct. Then I'm cooking for you, as I remember, amongst other things."

Ginny blushed.

"I'll text you when I'm on my way, if that works?"

"Perfectly," she said, pulling him closer for one more kiss.

\*\*\*\*

Ginny giggled to herself as she padded around her kitchen and munched on microwave popcorn straight from the bag. What an afternoon! Sunshine, wine and great company; a perfectly heady combination. And, of course, there was Donna's brief visit. What was she saying, something about a party?

"You know, I think I should probably have some tea," she said, to Martini, sprawled sleepily across the tile floor. "Otherwise, I might be in danger of doing something silly like...."

She paused to think of something fun.

"Dancing!" She snapped her fingers loudly, making Martini widen his eyes. "Time to strut our stuff!"

She pranced over to the boom box on her dining room console and turned it on, grimacing when the voices from a talk show filled the room. "That won't do," she said, twisting the dial. Moments later, music from a top forty station reverberated through the speakers and she grinned.

"That's more like it," she said, turning up the sound and enjoying the four-four beat. She ate more popcorn, danced a few steps and picked up her kettle for tea.

Martini flattened his ears and narrowed his eyes into slits, making her snicker.

"Not a fan?" she asked, just before a sharp knock sounded at her front door.

She put the kettle down on the stovetop and looked questioningly at the cat. "Did you hear something?"

He blinked lazily in return.

A second rap at the door made Ginny realize she hadn't imagined the sound. "Maybe Max forgot something," she offered, before stepping over the cat and making her way through the family room into the foyer.

"Just can't get enough of me, huh?" she said, flirtatiously, as she swung open the door.

Eric, standing on the other side, raised his eyebrows. "What?"

"Oh!" Ginny slapped a hand against her chest. She'd assumed it was Max as he'd only just left. The possibility of he and her son nearly crossing paths was startling.

"Sorry to turn up without warning, Mom," Eric said, before peering at her. "You okay?"

Ginny laughed and waved him into the house. "Of course! Come in!"

"You sure? You looked pretty shocked." He stepped across the threshold and paused when he heard the music thumping. "Uhh, am I interrupting something?"

"No!" she blurted, closing the door behind him.

He looked toward the kitchen, then back at her, his face skeptical.

"I was just making some tea and felt like music to break up the silence. That's your old boom box, remember? We kept it after you moved out, seemed a waste to throw it away."

"Still plays well," Eric offered, slipping off his black oxfords.

"It does!" Ginny enthused. "Anyway, it's just me and the cat. Nobody else. Nobody whatsoever. Did you want some?"

"Some what?"

"Tea, of course. I'm making some."

Eric shook his head. "No, thanks."

"Ahh, well, too bad for you."

He raised an eyebrow at her unexpected, flippant reply.

Ginny ignored the eyebrow and turned on her heel, wobbling slightly as she made her way toward the family room. "So, what brings you by, dear? Aren't you supposed to be at work?"

Eric held out a bag he was holding. "I finished early with my client—"

"Well, that's not something you hear every day from a lawyer! Aren't you usually charging things to the minute?"

Eric watched her giggle at her own joke then said, "*Anyway*, Kimberly asked that I drop this off to you while I was doing some errands."

Ginny stopped chortling and took the bag. "Oh, good god. What is it now?"

"What?" Eric stared.

Oops, Ginny thought. Too obvious, perhaps.

"I *mean*," she said, shaking the bag, "she just gave me a surprise gift. What on Earth could *this* be?"

"Right," he said, leaving it alone. "More yarn, I think. She said something about how happy you were about the other stuff she gave you, so she wanted to add to your collection."

Oh, help, she thought, snorting through her nose then tossing the bag onto the side table without opening it. Jan would pee herself laughing when she shared this with her.

Eric's eyebrows furrowed on his forehead and he peered at her a second time. "Mom, are you sure you're okay?"

Ginny blinked at him. "Of course I am. Why wouldn't I be?"

"Well, you seem a bit..." He rubbed a hand along the back of his neck. "I don't know... Tipsy."

Ginny's eyes became very wide. Hell's bells. "*Tipsy?*" she volleyed, taking a step back in case she still had wine on her breath. "You think I've been drinking?"

He shrugged, suddenly uncomfortable.

"What a question," she deflected, walking into the kitchen and talking loudly over her shoulder. "That's hysterical."

Eric followed her and watched as she tempered the volume on the boom box and began opening and closing cabinets and drawers.

"Are you sure I couldn't talk you into having a cup of tea? Last chance."

"No, thanks. I can't stay."

"Apricots? Donna said she has some for me. I could pop over and get them."

Eric shook his head. "Umm, no, I'm good."

"Well, maybe next time then," she said, picking up her kettle from where she'd left it then giving it a shake to see if she'd already filled it with water.

"Yeah," he agreed, taken aback at the indifference in her tone. "I still have a few more errands to do before I head back."

"Okey-dokey, then," she said, her voice taking on a sing-song quality as she shimmied in time to the music while she brought the kettle over to the tap and turned on the water. "Drive carefully and thank Kimberly for me, please. Apparently a girl can't have too much yarn."

Eric didn't know what to say. Was that a sarcastic remark?

"Bye-bye," she said, dancing the kettle back to its base to boil. "Love youuu."

Eric took a few steps out of the kitchen, nonplussed that he'd basically been dismissed. What the *hell*? And was that an actual slur he'd heard in her voice? No, he silently chastised himself as he exited the house, closing the door solidly behind him. No way. It had to have been his imagination.

\*\*\*\*

Dixie laughed and laughed at Ginny's story.

Ginny smirked and shifted to stretch her legs along the length of the sofa in her sunroom. Dixie had called just after Eric had left and she'd been so full of adrenaline from their encounter she'd blurted out everything.

"I wish I could have been a fly on the wall to see his face," Dixie said.

"Just imagine him frowning," Ginny said, while cradling the phone between her shoulder and ear.

"And more yarn!" Dixie whooped. "Have you told Jan about that yet?"

Ginny chortled. "No."

"Oooh, can I do it," Dixie begged. "Please?"

Ginny chuckled some more. "Yes, go ahead."

"Take a picture of it and send it to me."

"What?"

"Get the new yarn and take a photo and send it to me," she repeated. "I'll sent it to Jan and get her up to speed."

Ginny grinned, imagining her best friend's face. "Okay."

"Do it now."

"Oh, for goodness sake," Ginny said, good-naturedly. "Hang on a moment."

She put the house phone down and went to retrieve her cellphone and the bag of yarn from where she'd tossed it aside. Once she had both in hand she brought them back with her to the sunroom and picked up the phone lying on the sofa.

"Okay," she said. "I'm taking the photo."

"Goodie," Dixie replied, eagerly.

Ginny laid the yarn out on the sofa then snapped the shot, just as her doorbell rang. "That's my door," she said, getting up. "Hopefully, it's not Eric returning. Otherwise, he and Max will definitely cross paths this time and the idea of that is too much to contemplate."

"Want me to let you go?"

"Sure. I'll send the photo off in a moment. Wish me luck."

They hung up and Ginny went to her front door for the second time that day. She peeked through the peephole and saw Max's face on the other side. Thank god. She threw the door open wide as she'd done with Eric, a large grin on her face.

He smiled back, but looked slightly frazzled.

"Max?" she said, while he crossed the threshold into the foyer. "Everything okay."

"I have apricots," he said, by way of reply.

Ginny burst out laughing. He didn't need to explain further, clearly he'd been accosted by Donna and made to go over to her place to receive the bag of apricots he was carrying. "Did you meet Douglas?" she asked, taking the bag from his hands.

"I did."

Ginny led the way into the kitchen and put the apricots on the countertop. "Give me a sec, I have to send a photo to Dixie."

He ran a hand over his face then through his hair. "Sure. After that encounter, nothing's going to phase me."

Ginny went to the sunroom to retrieve her phone, still chuckling to herself. She was used to Donna, but remembered the first time she'd gone into the so-called belly of the beast; her house. It was a lot to process, no question.

"It was like taking a step back in time in there," Max commented, as she carried her phone back into the kitchen and hit 'send', delivering the photo of the yarn to Dixie.

"Yup," Ginny agreed. "Back to nineteen eighty-something."

"Okay, well," Max said, pretending to shake it off then grabbing her around the waist and pulling her in close. "It's not nineteen eighty-something in here and I have food and other things to cook up for you, young lady."

"Hurray for the present day," Ginny cheered.

\*\*\*\*

"It was really strange," Eric explained, to Jennifer, as he drove along Main Street, heading toward the hardware store. "She was totally scatty."

"Scatty?" Jennifer replied, skeptically, her voice coming out of the speakers and filling the vehicle interior. "Is that even a word?"

Eric shrugged and came to a stop at a red light. "Possibly."

"Maybe she'd just gotten up from a nap and was still a bit logy. That could make a person seem half in the bag," she suggested.

Eric watched a young woman crossing the street with her white, standard poodle. "No, I don't think so. She had music blaring from the boom box in the kitchen. Sounded like she was getting ready for a party."

Jennifer laughed and said, "God, I can't believe she still has that thing. It was yours, right?"

He grinned. "Yeah. They got it for me for my birthday and then I'm pretty sure they regretted it because I never turned the damned thing down when they asked. Ironic that that's the thing setting off the alarm bells."

"No, no," Jennifer placated. "There's no need for alarm bells. So she was playing music loudly, so what? Maybe, at worst, her hearing isn't what it used to be. Besides, did you actually see any evidence of booze anywhere?"

"No," he admitted, as the light changed and he continued driving.

"See, there you go. No need to make anything more out of what you saw."

He turned on his left signal light. "Yeah, you're probably right."

"Are you going to say anything to Kim?"

He grimaced. "Definitely not."

"Think she'll read something into it?" she asked, knowingly.

"What do *you* think?" he countered, turning into the strip-mall when there was a break in the traffic.

Her laughed filled the vehicle.

Eric chuckled along with her.

"I'll keep an eye on things," she offered, "if it'll make you feel better."

"Just don't make it obvious, or she'll—"

"Hang on," she interrupted, before shouting, "Mason! Do *not* do that! Grace is three years older, you have to wait your turn."

Eric grinned. It reminded him of when the three of them were kids. Shades of days gone by.

"Sorry about that," she said, returning to the phone.

"That's fine, I was just having flashbacks." He snickered, looking for a parking spot near the hardware store.

"Speaking of which, have you spoken to Brian lately?"

"A little while ago."

"Is he planning on coming to visit anytime soon?"

Eric found a parking spot and pulled the SUV into it. "Not sure, why?"

"I just think it would be a good idea. Mom would appreciate it."

"Yeah, she could probably use a distraction from her routine," he agreed, putting the vehicle into park.

"Exactly."

"I'll talk to him about it the next time we talk. He's been pretty wrapped up in Paige lately, so sometimes it's hard to catch him."

"Okay," she said. "But, listen, I'd better go before there's all out mutiny here."

Eric laughed. "Talk to you later. Good luck."

\*\*\*\*

"Oh, my," Ginny gasped, catching her breath.

Max grinned into the darkened bedroom as he settled back into the soft pillows on her bed. "I'll second that."

"When you said you were bringing dessert with you, I have to admit, I thought something else entirely."

He laughed and reached out to run his fingers along the length of her naked torso.

"You seemed like you were still tense about the unexpected arrival of your son earlier, so I thought we could use a bit of *distraction* before we indulged in the real thing."

"If *that's* what we're calling it, I'm all for it, distract away," she sighed, enjoying the pleasure of his touch. "However, you do realize you'll have to hide in the closet if he returns unannounced. Right?"

"Of course," he said, swift on the uptake. "You can sneak the Tiramisu in to me and I'll be just fine to wait it out."

"Oh, no." She quickly shook her head. "As highly as I think of you, I'm afraid that wouldn't be possible."

"You'd keep it all for yourself?" he asked, feigning shock.

"What can I say?" She shrugged and turned toward him, letting her hands find his warm flesh. "When I like something, I'm not very good at sharing."

His breath left his lungs in a whoosh when her searching fingers made contact. "You know," he offered, his voice low in his throat. "I think I'm okay with that."

Ginny chuckled.

\*\*\*\*

## *Max's Tiramisu*

### Ingredients
Bakery-made Tiramisu

### Directions
- Stop at your local Italian bakery.
- Purchase delicious Tiramisu.
- Bring confection with you to your date's house.
- Consume with hedonistic pleasure.

# Chapter Twenty-One

"She's *baaack*."

"What?" Ginny looked up from her computer, alarmed, and began scanning the library for signs of Max; his strong jawline, his broad shoulders. Had he turned up without her notice and was going to force her to feign ignorance and pretend not to know him?

Tamara grinned and pointed toward the children's section. "Yup, second week in a row now. Hoping it's the start of a trend."

"Oh, you said *she*," Ginny said, her shoulders relaxing as relief coursed through her. Tamara's point had nothing to do with Max and, instead, was directed at the young woman - around her age in her late thirties - standing next to one of the child-sized tables.

Tamara raised an eyebrow. "What did you think I said?"

"Nothing," Ginny replied, waving her hand dismissively. "It doesn't matter."

Tamara let it drop, only because she wanted to focus on the woman they were speaking about. "I'm calling her mystery *woman*, since mystery man no longer seems to grace us with his presence."

Ginny nodded at the little girl, aged four or five, with her. "You *have* noticed she doesn't come alone, right?"

"You bet. But, that doesn't mean anything. She could just as easily be her niece as her daughter."

Ginny looked at her skeptically.

"Besides," she went on, leaning up against the desk, "either way, she's not wearing a wedding ring. So, if she is her daughter then she's probably single anyway, which means instant family. Don't even need to add water!"

Ginny couldn't help herself and laughed. "I'll give you credit, you always find that silver lining."

Tamara winked while Ginny's phone began to trill from inside her purse. "We don't do ourselves any favors, looking for the negative. For example, who knows, if we think positively maybe another tall, roguishly handsome mystery man will turn up and even be brave enough to ask you out!"

Ginny turned her head and reached into her bag for her phone, glad for the excuse to avoid a reply. As Tamara made a bee-line for the children's section, she read on the screen: *Still on for lunch at 2?*

She rapidly typed back: *Yes! See you there.*

\*\*\*\*

Darryl lifted his pint of beer to his lips and took a large swallow. Across the table from him, Max finished off the remainder of his fries. They were taking a long lunch as they'd started their workday an hour before the rest of their crew and the pub was starting to fill up around them.

"I'm always a bit amazed at how many people seem to have time to hang in a pub in the middle of the afternoon," Max remarked, looking at some of the tables near them.

Darryl put his pint back on the table. "They could be like us, started work early and are taking a longer lunch break."

"Yeah, maybe," Max said, leaning back in his seat. "But there are people here who were here when we arrived and something tells me they're going to be here after we leave."

Darryl chuckled. "Yup, takes all kinds as the saying goes."

Max grinned and picked up the check to have a look at the total.

"Remember, today is on me," Darryl said, before his voice changed and he said, "Oh, boy."

Max glanced at him. "Something wrong?"

Darryl cleared his throat as he watched Ginny's son, Eric, come through the entrance to the pub on the other side of the room. "Ummm," was all he could think to say.

Max followed his gaze then said, "Ahhh," when he recognized Eric from the photos at Ginny's house.

"Right," Darryl said. "Chances are he's going to see me, how do you want to play this?"

"He has no idea who I am," Max stated. "Just introduce me as who I am to *you*. Your business partner and nothing more."

Darryl nodded in agreement just as Eric locked eyes on him, lifted a hand in greeting and started to thread his way through the tables toward them.

"Show time," Darryl said, under his breath.

"Steady on," Max replied, keeping his face neutral. "Just your business partner."

\*\*\*\*

Ginny lifted her hand to wave at Dixie when she walked through the entrance of *Polly's* restaurant. "There she is," she said, to Jan, seated across the table.

Dixie waved back, indicated to the hostess she was going to join them and made her way through the restaurant toward their table in the corner.

Ginny stood up to give her a hug when she arrived.

"Sorry I'm late," she said, squeezing Ginny then releasing her to hug Jan as well.

"You're a vision," Jan said, admiring their friend's emerald green silk blouse. "That color is exquisite on you."

"Thank you." Dixie smiled her appreciation as she smoothed her black pencil skirt then sat down at the table. "I was getting the paperwork ready for a couple changing their wills and it took longer than I'd expected."

Ginny nodded, understandingly. When she wasn't selling houses, Dixie worked part-time as a paralegal. She'd been hugely helpful and insightful during the legal processing of George's will.

"How do you find enough time in the day to get everything done?" Jan asked, as she lifted a bottle of mineral water from the middle of the table.

Dixie picked up her glass and extended it. "You'd be amazed at what you can accomplish when you don't have a husband in the way."

Jan laughed and poured the water. "Well, I'm not sure I'm willing to cash Darryl in quite yet, so I'll just quietly envy you."

Dixie grinned and reached out to pat her hand.

"Tamara nearly gave me a small heart attack this morning," Ginny said, changing the subject.

Dixie raised her eyebrows.

"I thought she saw Max come in and—"

"You still haven't told her?" Dixie cut in, before taking a long drink from her glass.

"I'm waiting for the right time."

"When will that be, at your engagement party?" Jan stated, topping off both hers and Ginny's water glasses.

"Oh, stop," Ginny countered.

Jan cocked her head then put the bottle back on the table. "What? Am I so far off?"

"We're not that serious yet, it's only been a month and a half we've been dating. It's not like we're in each other's back pockets."

Dixie set her glass on the table and shot her a skeptical look.

"Seriously," she defended, leaning back in her chair. "Take last week, for example. He was gone for most of it on business, so it really doesn't count as time together."

"He texted you and called you every day, multiple times I might add." Jan chose a breadstick from a basket on the table. "You guys are in closer communication than a lot of people who live in the same house."

Dixie laughed and picked out a breadstick from the basket as well. "Gotta agree with Jan on that. My marriage to Don, the rat-bastard, was a communication waste land compared to you two."

Ginny grinned. She couldn't help the pleasure that washed across her face. They was right. Max was wonderful.

"Oh, hey!" Dixie pointed the breadstick at them. "There's something I wanted to ask you guys. I have a great idea. You're going to love it."

Ginny and Jan exchanged looks.

Dixie laughed then took a bite of her breadstick. She chewed and spoke at the same time. "I promise it won't involve drinking to excess or nudity...." She paused to swallow then added, "Well, that's not entirely true. People have done this naked, but usually it's part of a fund raiser."

"Oh, boy," Jan said, starting on her own breadstick.

"No, no." Dixie took another bite then patted the air in front of her. "Hear me out, before you refuse."

Ginny laughed. It was a reasonable request. "Okay, fine. Spill."

"Zip-lining."

Ginny and Jan stared at her while she continued eating and drinking her water, waiting for more.

"What?" she said, when she saw the blank looks on their faces. "Have you not heard of it?"

"Yes." Ginny said.

"But, you can't be serious," Jan added, finishing her bread and wiping the crumbs from her fingers onto a small, white side plate.

"I thought this might happen, so...." Dixie reached into her purse for her iPhone and began tapping on the screen. "I found some videos to get you excited about the idea."

She handed the phone over and Ginny and Jan sat together, shoulder to shoulder, watching the screen. Dixie finished off her breadstick and watched their faces as the sounds of cheers and laughter flowed from the phone's speaker, hopeful for enthusiasm.

"Well?" she finally asked, when they finished watching the video.

"You know I'm scared of heights, right?" Jan said.

Dixie took back the phone and tucked it into her purse. "It only *seems* high," she stated, waving away her concerns. "But once you're all strapped in, you'll feel totally safe."

Jan laughed. "Yeah, right."

Dixie turned to Ginny, hoping for a better response. "Gin blossom? Thoughts?"

"*Well*...." She shrugged. "I will admit, they did make it look fun."

"Yes!" Dixie jumped on her words and sweetened the pot. "And, even better, you could invite Max."

Ginny's face opened up at the mention of his name.

"Uh-huh," Dixie went on. "And Jan could bring Darryl and they could bring any of their colleagues and we'd make it a group thing. Sort of a corporate event thing. They offer those. And that would mean you'd get to spend the day doing something fun and new and be able to share it with Max completely out in the open."

Jan groaned when she looked at Ginny and the smile blooming on her face. "Oh, hell. I can't believe I'm going to be flying down a god-damned zip-line."

"Yay!" Dixie said, right before both Jan and Ginny's phone's started sounding, signaling the arrival of text messages. They all shared a look of surprise.

"Simultaneous messages," Ginny said, reaching into her purse for her phone. "That's a first."

Jan picked up her phone from where she'd set it on the tabletop. "It's from Darryl," she said, reading.

Ginny, also reading her text, said, "Oh, dear."

"What? What?" Dixie insisted, leaning forward in her seat.

Jan looked at Ginny and asked, "Is it about Eric?"

Ginny nodded and Dixie thumped the table to get their attention. "Me, me! Tell me!" she said, making Ginny giggle.

"Darryl and Max were just out for lunch," Jan informed her. "And they ran in Eric, of all people."

"Oh," Dixie said, taking a breath and sitting back. "And?"

"It's fine," Ginny said, rereading Max's message. "They just said Max was Darryl's business partner and left it at that."

Dixie grimaced and Jan nodded, knowing exactly what she was thinking; things were definitely going to be a lot more awkward when the time came that Ginny introduced Max to the family.

****

*"My God, my mother-in-law is becoming one elusive woman."* Kimberly huffed to herself, as she alternately typed her message to Kris on her laptop and cut up fruit for Layla.

*Kris: "You mean like Dad?"*

Kimberly put down the knife in her hand and replied: *"No, not that bad. But, nearly. It seems like every time I try to get in touch with her she's playing a game of hide and seek."*

*Kris: "Yeah, well I wish Dad was playing a little harder."*

Kimberly ate a piece of the fruit on the cutting board then typed: *"What now?"*

*Kris: "He's making no effort to hide his indiscretions and I think he's doing it on purpose."*

*"What? Why would he do that?"* Kimberly rubbed her forehead, flummoxed.

*Kris: "Because he wants to get caught."*

*"Oh, for god's sake!"* Kimberly stopped typing to pace back and forth in front of the kitchen island.

*Kris: "I know, I know. I think he wants Mom to catch him and deal with the fallout."*

Kimberly read her words and had to grab the countertop to steady herself when a surge of vertigo made the room tilt.

*Kris: "You still there?"*

Kimberly nodded, only to remember Kris couldn't see her. She took a breath and typed: *"Yes. I just can't wrap my head around this. Do you need me to come home?"*

*Kris: "No. Not yet. I'll let you know if it comes to that. Hopefully it won't."*

Tears began to form in Kimberly's eyes. Too much was happening too fast.

"Hello!"

Kimberly jolted at the sound of Eric's voice. She quickly typed: *"Gotta run. Eric just arrived."*

*Kris: "Okay, talk soon."*

Kimberly closed her laptop as he walked into the kitchen.

"Hey, you!" he said, grinning.

"You're home early," she said, by way of reply.

The grin on his face sagged. "Only an hour."

"And that's all it takes, doesn't it?"

The grin disappeared completely and Eric looked at her, puzzled. "What?"

"An hour," Kimberly repeated, her voice rising. "That's all it takes for everything to change!"

Eric looked around the kitchen, truly confused. What was happening?

"First your *mother*," she practically hissed. "And now my bloody *father*!"

"What?" Eric said, feeling out of the loop. "Your Dad? Is something wrong?"

"Dammed rights!" she spat. "He's having a god-damned affair!"

Eric's eyes widened as he registered what she'd said. "What? Seriously? Your *Dad*?"

Layla began to call out from her bedroom as she woke up from her nap.

Kimberly threw her hands in the air in exasperation. "We'll discuss it later," she said, before storming from the room.

Eric put down his briefcase and loosened his tie, digesting the information. There had to be more to it, but be damned if he was going to press her to divulge before she was ready. That wasn't her style, he'd learned the hard way. No, she wasn't a woman to be coaxed. He just had to be patient and she'd eventually share everything.

He sighed and removed his tie. She'd been right on one thing, he silently acknowledged while looking at the clock on the microwave: All it took was an hour - in this case an hour early - for everything to change.

\*\*\*\*

Max squirmed uncomfortably in his seat on Ginny's couch. Her request was the last thing he'd ever thought she would ask of him and he'd had a lot of odd requests in his day.

Ginny moved around the room, plumping already plumped pillows and dusting perfectly clean tabletops, while watching him from the corner of her eye as he digested what she'd asked. Finally, when he continued to say nothing and just sat there pondering, she dropped her dusting cloth on the coffee table and said, "Goodness, it's not like I'm suggesting we walk over hot coals."

"But, if you had, I'd immediately say 'no thanks'," he stated, running his fingers through his thick hair. "Been there, done that."

Ginny's eyes widened and she threw her hands in the air. "Well, see! *That* you've done, but *this* makes you go all contemplative and hesitant?"

Max couldn't help but grin at her vehemence. "Two very different things, my dear."

She shot him a dubious look and sat down next to him on the sofa.

"It's true," he insisted, leaning back into the cushions. "With the hot coals I was in charge of things like timing, speed and the like. This zip-lining thing on the other hand, I'm just at the mercy of it. Very different, indeed."

Ginny nodded and smoothed her hair back from her face. Got it. So the real question was, how was she going to convince a controller to let go of the reins?

"Dixie is quite the firecracker," he offered, attempting to change the subject. "I think she and my partner, Hamish, would get on like a house on fire."

"Ah-ha! There you go!" Ginny blurted, pointing at him as she swiftly rerouted the conversation back toward her original target. "I forgot to mention that when Dixie suggested the zip-lining idea, she also said we could make it a corporate event type of thing."

Max's brow furrowed as he tried to put two and two together.

"And," Ginny further explained, "that would mean Darryl and his crew and you and Hamish could all do it together with us as a sort of bonding activity."

Max let out a bark of laughter. "Bonding? Really? That's your sales pitch?" Ginny folded her arms across her chest and stared at him and he quickly quelled his laughter and said, "I'm sorry, darling, you took me off guard. But the truth of it is, if I said that to Hamish, he'd never let me hear the end of it."

"Okay, then how about this," she added, unfolding her arms and placing a warm hand on his knee. "It would also mean we'd be together in public without me fretting about being seen and having to explain our relationship."

"Which, if we're sticking to the facts, you don't actually *have to* do," he added, affectionately, while picking up her hand to kiss it.

Ginny thought about how Eric had run into he and Darryl at the pub and how she'd had to practically hang up on him to avoid talking about it, when he'd mentioned it the next day while calling to ask if he could borrow her leaf blower. All she could think about was Darryl introducing him to Max as his wife's best friend's son and Max having to pretend he didn't know her. God, the potential complications it added to things was the stuff of a bad sitcom. Her knee-jerk reaction had been to use the flimsy excuse of cleaning Martini's litter box as the reason she couldn't talk, in order to halt the conversation in its tracks. She shuddered at the memory.

Max gently squeezed her hand, having a pretty good idea as to what she was thinking by the expression on her face.

Ginny shook it off then pulled her hand away to snap her fingers. "I know, what about my bucket list!"

"Pardon me?"

"You *know*, a bucket list," she explained. "The things you want to do before you die."

"I *know* what a bucket list is," he said, meeting her eye. "I'm just having a hard time believing *zip-lining* is one of the items on your so-called list."

Ginny slumped back into the sofa and threw her hands in the air. Time to play hard ball. "Okay, *fine*. Forget it. To tell you the truth, I'm not all that surprised by your attitude."

He raised an eyebrow, curious as to where she was going.

Ginny picked at a none-existent thread on the hem of her pink blouse and said, "There's no way George would have agreed to do it, either. Perhaps it's best to accept it's a younger man's thing."

Max narrowed his eyes while he rubbed a hand across the silver-grey stubble on his chin. Okay, now he knew *exactly* what she was doing. It was hardly subtle. He volleyed back. "Really? You're actually playing the deceased spouse card?"

Ginny dropped the hem edge of her blouse and raised her chin sharply in the air. "Don't sound so shocked. I happen to know George would support me one hundred percent. Heck, if I didn't play the card, I'm sure he'd be disappointed."

"Right," Max chuckled. "Good to know. Sounds like he and I would have gotten along."

"Oh, I don't doubt it for a moment," she said, with deep affection.

He regarded her, impressed. She hadn't let George's death destroy her sparkle and while she was moving forward with her life, it was clear she still held him in her heart. She was one hell of a woman.

"Alright then," Ginny sighed. She waited a beat then cleared her throat and stood up from the couch. "I was thinking of making tea, would you like some? I can make chamomile if you like? Or if you wanted something a bit stronger, I think I have peppermint."

Max burst out laughing at her obviousness. She wasn't going down without a fight. "Alright, damn-it, I'll go. You can cross it off your bloody bucket list."

Her face lit up. "You will?"

"Yes." He grinned. "I'll go with you and do George proud."

She pressed a hand to her chest, over her heart.

"*And* I'll have an espresso, thank you very much." He shot her a sidelong glance. "Not some weak, flower water."

It was Ginny's turn to laugh, before saying, "Oh, dear, then you're out of luck. I don't have an espresso maker."

He stood up and pulled her toward him, enveloping her in his embrace. "Then I guess I'll have to go and get some. But, before I do...." He looked her in the eye, his grin lascivious.

"Oh, boy," she said, before he leaned down to kiss her and all other thoughts were obliterated by his mouth on hers.

\*\*\*\*

## *Ginny's Chamomile Tea*
### *(or Peppermint, if you want something stronger)*

### Ingredients
Tea bags (whatever flavor you desire).
Water, boiled.

### Directions
- Boil water.
- Add teabag.
- Steep.
- Enjoy.

# Chapter Twenty-Two

Kimberly gave a last swipe of the cleaning cloth in her hand across the kid's table in Layla's playroom and nodded with satisfaction. Everything was ready. In just forty-five minutes, her new friend, Cara, would be arriving with her daughter, Summer, for a playdate with Layla. They'd all met at a toddler's tumbling class and since the two little girls had shown a liking for one another, she and Cara had exchanged phone numbers to arrange a get together at a later date. Today was that date.

Kimberly walked through the adjacent kitchen into the laundry room to put the cloth into the wash pile and only then did she stop short with a gasp. "*Ohmygod!*" she blurted, grabbing the counter beside her washer and dryer for support when she suddenly realized what she'd done; or, in this case, not done. The baking, she'd forgotten to do the baking.

"How could I be so thoughtless?" she asked herself, pulse beginning to race as she darted out of the laundry room to check her fridge in case she'd somehow - maybe while sleeping - created the muffins she'd intended upon baking for the playdate.

She pulled the fridge door wide open and… nothing. There was the cut up fruit, the cubes of cheese and the assortment of juice boxes all ready and waiting to be consumed, but no muffins to be found. Kimberly hung her head for the briefest of moments, giving herself a chance to catch her breath and shake off the panic. Then, she squared her shoulders, straightened the hem of her purple tank top and snapped to attention. This could be remedied, she knew it could, all she had to do was think. It shouldn't be that difficult to come up with a solution, she'd had problems that were leaps and bounds more pressing than this when she was managing the art gallery and she always formed a game plan that made everything turn out fine. This was, excuse the pun, child's play by comparison.

"Ah-ha!" she exclaimed, pointing her finger at the ceiling, when the obvious answer came to mind. She closed the fridge door and pulled her cellphone from the pocket on her chocolate colored shorts then rapidly tapped on Ginny's phone number, in her contacts.

"Hello?" Ginny's said, through the phone's speaker, a moment later.

"Ginny!" Kimberly said, relief that her mother-in-law was home causing her to flush.

"Hello, dear," Ginny said. "How are you?"

"Good thanks," she replied. "But I need to ask a quick favor."

"Oh, dear," Ginny said, her voice uncomfortable. "I hope it's not babysitting tonight, because I'm so sorry, I already have plans."

"No, no," Kimberly assured her, while she began pacing back and forth in front of her kitchen island and watching the time on her microwave. Fifteen minutes until Layla would wake up from her nap.

"Oh, good," Ginny said, clearly relieved. "So, what can I do for you?"

"I need baking, muffins if you have them."

"Pardon?" Ginny said, taken aback by the unusual request.

"You see," Kimberly rapidly explained, "usually we have some sort of baking around the house from you, but it's been a while since you've dropped any by. So, I've been picking up the slack and, wouldn't you know it, the one day I truly need a set of muffins, as I'm having company over, is the day I seemed to have forgotten to get them done."

"Okay," Ginny said, slightly unnerved at the hint of mania in Kimberly's voice. "And you want me to do what, exactly?"

"Bring me muffins, of course," Kimberly stated, before quickly softening her tone when she realized how sharp she sounded. "I mean, if you wouldn't mind. It would be such a lifesaver, I would be so, so grateful."

"When do you need these for?"

Kimberly glanced at the microwave clock again. "Twenty minutes."

"Twenty minutes!" Ginny repeated.

"Okay, that's a bit short notice, I admit. How about we say an hour?"

"You want me to bring you a dozen muffins in an *hour*?" Ginny clarified.

"Yes, please," Kimberly said, completely missing the incredulous tone in Ginny's voice.

"Well, Kimberly," Ginny said, still striving to keep up with the unexpected request. "I have plans as I said, so—"

"Oh, that's okay!" Kimberly assured her. "As I said, I'm having company, so there's no need for you to feel obliged to stay. You can just drop them off and go, no worries."

"But—"

"I can't tell you how much I appreciate it, Ginny, really. But, listen, I have to go now as I hear Layla waking up from her nap. Thanks again, you've saved my bacon. See you in a little while!"

She pressed 'END' on her phone, gave herself a mental high-five at successfully solving her crisis and went to get Layla up and ready for her playdate.

****

The sound of the doorbell rang through Kimberly and Eric's house and Layla went "Oh!" her blue eyes wide and expectant as she added, "Doorbell!" Kimberly and Cara laughed at her reaction then Kimberly looked at the microwave clock for the time.

"That must be my mother-in-law," she said, getting up from her seat at the table where they were having coffee and watching the girls play. "A little later than she said, but trust me her baking is well worth the wait."

Cara smiled and said, "I'll watch the girls," while Kimberly strode out of the room and down the hallway to the front door.

Kimberly opened the door and relief washed over her when she saw Ginny waiting on the other side. "Thank goodness you're finally here," she said, stepping aside to let Ginny in. "My friend, Cara, is in the kitchen," she explained, lowering her voice to a whisper. "I didn't tell her I forgot to bake, instead I said that you insisted you wanted to do it and I couldn't say no because you're such a fabulous baker." She winked at Ginny then finished with, "It will be our little secret."

Ginny said nothing and Kimberly didn't seem to notice. Instead, she turned to lead the way back to the kitchen, so Ginny slipped off her black sandals and followed in her wake.

"Cara," Kimberly said, extending her hand toward Ginny with a flourish. "This is my mother-in-law, Ginny."

Ginny placed the pink box she was carrying onto the island and extended a hand to shake Cara's. "Lovely to meet you, dear."

Cara, a petite woman with a blonde pixie cut and big brown eyes in her heart-shaped face, smiled and said, "You, too. I've heard nothing but lovely things about you."

Layla, hearing Ginny's voice, leaped up from where she was playing beside Summer and came charging over as fast as her chubby little legs would carry her. "Gramma!"

Ginny smiled in delight at her granddaughter and reached down to pick her up into a warm hug. "Hey there, sweet-pea. Having fun?"

Layla wrapped her arms around Ginny's neck and plastered a kiss on her cheek.

"My goodness, Layla," Kimberly said, clearly playing to her audience. "You sure love your Gramma, don't you?"

"Love," Layla repeated, leaning back to smile into Ginny's face.

"Awe," Cara said, while Summer toddled over to be picked up. "You must spend a lot of time with her, that's such a blessing."

Kimberly dimpled and nodded. "We're a very close family."

Close enough, apparently, to think it's fine to issue baking demands, Ginny thought, churlishly.

"Gamma play?" Layla asked, starting to squirm in Ginny's embrace.

"Oh, no, no," Kimberly said, while Ginny placed Layla back down on the floor.

Layla's face crumpled and Ginny quickly amended, "Gramma is going to come back another time, though, okay? Soon, we'll play, okay? Today, you get to play with…" She glanced at Cara, holding her daughter; her glossy strawberry blonde ringlets and rich brown eyes making her look like a doll sitting in her mother's lap.

"Summer!" Kimberly quickly stated.

"Right," Ginny nodded. "Layla gets to play with Summer today. Lucky Layla."

It struck the right cord as Layla's face perked up and she smiled sweetly at her new friend.

"Okay, well, I do have to run," Ginny said, smoothing her red blouse over her tan trousers. "It was lovely to meet you, Cara, and you too, Summer."

Cara put Summer back down on the floor and the little girls made an immediate beeline back toward the toys. She stood up and extended her hand again to shake Ginny's. "Very nice to meet you as well."

Kimberly took a step forward to see Ginny out, but she waved her hand to stop her. "No, no, I'm fine. You girls continue your visit. I'll see myself out." Kimberly barely managed to utter "okay", before Ginny beat a rapid retreat and was gone from the house.

"Well, she sure seemed nice," Cara said, sitting back down at the table and picking up her cup of cooling coffee.

Kimberly nodded. "Oh, definitely. She's one in a million." She rubbed her hands together and added, "Now, let's get to that baking I've been talking about."

Cara watched as she turned toward the island then paused abruptly, as though frozen in her tracks. She took a sip of her coffee then asked, "Is something wrong?"

Kimberly stared at the bright pink box on the countertop, wondering how she'd missed it when Ginny had carried it inside. Emblazoned across the top of the box were the words "*The Bakery*" and like a smack to the face she realized she'd been given store-bought baking, not freshly baked muffins, delivered straight from her mother-in-law's kitchen as she'd so effusively bragged was arriving.

"Kimberly?"

"No!" Kimberly said, jauntily, her thoughts on overdrive as she scrambled to come up with yet another rapid-fire solution. She craned her neck over her shoulder and asked, "How's your coffee, need a warm up?"

"Sure," Cara said, getting up. "I can get it. How's yours?"

Kimberly kept her back turned and swept up the box in front of her so that Cara couldn't see it as she moved around the expanse of the island. "I'm sure I need some, too, thanks."

Cara walked over to the coffee pot on the countertop next to the stove and Kimberly made use of her distraction to swiftly dump the pink box into the sink, pull open its lid and start yanking muffins from its interior in a frenzy. She dropped them onto a blue plate she'd had waiting on the countertop, still keeping her back square to block her actions, and hoped they would crumble a bit in the process to give them a more authentic, home-baked quality.

"Okay then," she said, brightly, tossing a hand towel across the pink box to conceal it then picking up the plate and turning around, silently praying Cara didn't frequent *The Bakery*. "Here we go, something for the grownups."

Cara grinned as she sat back down in her chair at the table. "Aren't we the spoiled ones, getting fresh baking. You'll have to thank your mother-in-law for me."

Kimberly smiled tightly and brought the muffins to the table. Oh, she'd be saying something alright, but she doubted it would resemble the words *thank you*.

\*\*\*\*

Max pulled off his reading glasses and wiped the moisture from his eyes as he continued to chuckle. He and Ginny were out to dinner and sitting across from one another at a lovely candle lit table and her story had him in stitches. She did such a great job of telling it, giving inflections to her voice and descriptions that made him feel he'd been there, he had to take a breath to regain his composure.

Ginny sipped her wine and smirked behind her glass, amused by his amusement. She felt a little disloyal to Eric, giggling at what she'd done to his wife, but not so much she felt remorse for her actions. As far as she was concerned, Kimberly should have been grateful she'd gone to the trouble to bring anything to her house at all. The cheek of believing she could just treat her as her personal baker was insulting, to say the very least.

"So, now the burning question," Max said, grinning. "Have you heard anything from Eric yet?"

Ginny put her wineglass on the table and shook her head. "No. Not a peep. I'm not sure if that's a good thing, or not."

He placed his glasses next to his menu and reached across the tabletop for her hand.

She flushed and squeezed his fingers when she met his eyes. His gaze made her feel like a school girl.

"You're something else, Ginny Hughes," he said, lifting her hand to his lips for a gentle kiss.

"Mister Rhodes," she said, the admiration in his voice making her stomach flip. "You're making me blush."

He chuckled and released her hand. "Somebody has to. It looks good on you."

"So, tell me," she said, fiddling with the cutlery on the table. "Do you think you're going to be gone long?"

Max picked up his wineglass and sat back in his seat. "No. It should only be a couple of days. Just a quick check in at the main office and I'll be back. Darryl really needs me here on site, so I'll be calling Boxwood Hills home for a while longer."

Ginny felt her heart catch. *A while.* Those were the operative words, weren't they? He was still a visitor, didn't actually reside there, so that meant he still had another life waiting for him. Another life in which she held no part.

"This is a nice restaurant," he commented, taking a sip of wine and looking around in appreciation.

The lighting was low, with just a subtle wash from the candle light on the tables and lanterns hanging from the numerous leafy trees growing in large, square, brick-clad planter boxes throughout the room. The floor was a pale beige porcelain tile and the walls a rich terracotta, while the doorways were framed in chunky travertine stone. Add in the rich walnut tables and chairs with their sparkling white dishes, gleaming cutlery and pristine cloth napkins and it all blended together in a relaxing harmony.

"I had no idea Italian was available downtown."

*In this town*, Ginny wanted to add, then felt awful for thinking it. What was wrong with her? She gave herself a mental shake. She had to stop it. She was going to ruin their evening.

"Have you eaten here a lot?"

Ginny stopped fiddling and gave him her full attention. "No. But, enough times to know the food is as fabulous as the ambience."

"Excellent," Max began, but was then interrupted by a woman walking toward them calling out, "Ginny?"

Ginny felt a light tap on her right shoulder and turned in her seat. When she saw who was standing beside her, her stomach lurched in an entirely different, much less pleasant manner. "Pat!"

"I thought that was you," Pat said, her eyes flitting over Ginny, taking in her royal blue shift dress, her soft blonde waves and evening makeup - oh, let's just say it: *date* makeup - then shifting over to checkout Max seated on the other side of the table.

Ginny watched her taking him in, handsome, confident, dressed in charcoal grey slacks and an open collared, tailored dress shirt that matched his green eyes, and panic began to well up in her chest.

Max sipped his wine and watched the interaction.

"What are *you* doing here?" Ginny asked, then laughed - slightly hysterically - at her own question. "I mean, *obviously*, you're here for dinner. But are you with Ian? Or just grabbing some takeout?"

"Melanie and I are having a girl's night out," Pat said, kindly grabbing hold of the conversational thread Ginny seemed to be unraveling.

"Oh, right. Girl's night," she offered, nodding her head up and down sharply then scanning the restaurant for Pat's best friend. "You look lovely. That shade of red really suites you."

"Thank you," she said, before pointing across the room. "She's over there."

Melanie waved from her table.

Ginny lifted her hand in return.

"Anyway, I just thought I'd say a quick hello," Pat said, before smiling again at Max.

He put down his wine, stood up from his chair and offered her his hand. "Maxwell Rhodes."

"Yes!" Ginny blurted, as Pat shook the hand he extended. "My goodness, where are my manners? This is Max! He's, uhh, Darryl's business partner. You know Darryl, right? Jan's husband?"

Pat nodded. "Lovely to meet you. Pat Keegan."

"Anyway," Ginny blathered, slightly wild-eyed as Max sat back down in his seat. "We're meeting them for dinner and they're running late, *obviously....*"

Pat's eyebrows lifted.

"And by *we*, I mean we are *each* meeting them," Ginny blazed on. "Separately. Not together. We both just happened to arrive at the same time. Max is from the east coast!"

Pat's eyes widened in surprise at Ginny's sudden, verbose change of topic.

"Well, my *family* is," Max said, picking up the conversation ball Ginny lobed his way. "I've always been a bit more here and there, work keeps me moving about. And, I must add, Boxwood Hills has turned out to be even more impressive than Darryl was able to convey."

Pat grinned. "That's wonderful to hear. I own the bookstore, *Possibilities*, on Main Street. If you're ever in the area, feel free to drop in."

Ginny picked up her wineglass and drank deeply from its depths, grateful for a reason to shut her mouth.

"Thank you, I just might do that," Max replied, before Pat gave a small wave and retreated from their table.

Ginny waved her off and put her glass down beside the bread basket on the tabletop.

"Well, that was certainly interesting," Max offered, a barely veiled smirk twisting his lips.

"*Ohmygod*," Ginny moaned, wishing she could press rewind and reverse everything that had just happened. "Was it as bad as I think it was?"

Max regarded her with affection and replied, kindly, "No, no. It was fine."

"You're a terrible liar," Ginny said, making him laugh.

"Alright, fine," he amended, still chuckling. "It might have been a bit... *odd*, but—"

"But now they have some great dinner conversation ahead of them," Ginny interrupted, grimacing. "And then even more to talk about when Jan and Darryl don't show up at all!"

Max released a bark of laughter.

"It's not funny," Ginny insisted, biting her lip to keep from smirking in the face of his blatant amusement.

Max cleared his throat and reached into the bread basket. "So, why on Earth did you say they were meeting us?"

"I panicked. Nobody knows about us—"

"Except for Jan and Darryl," he threw in, taking a bite of the fresh bread. "And Dixie."

"Okay, *fine*, except for them," she agreed. "And I know how rumors can get started in this town, so I just wanted to throw her off the scent…"

"She seemed perfectly lovely," Max interjected, putting his piece of bread on the small side plate provided.

"And she is," Ginny stated. "In fact, Pat is one of the few people I know who I'd feel confident would keep her mouth shut. She went through enough stuff of her own, she doesn't get involved in local gossip."

Max leaned an elbow on the table. "Right. *So?*"

"*So*, as I said, I panicked." Ginny sighed and glanced toward the restaurant entrance. When she saw who was standing there, she went as white as a ghost.

Max saw her face and his eyebrows shot up. "What's wrong?"

"I cannot believe this." She swiftly turned her head and grabbed for her menu to hold up beside her face. "It's my daughter and her husband. At the door."

Max glanced casually to his left.

"She has brown hair and he's blonde. Jesus, what are the odds?"

Max observed the young couple standing at the entrance door. Yup, just as he remembered from the photos at Ginny's house. Her daughter was even more lovely in person. Not that he was surprised.

"What are they doing?" Ginny attempted to peer around the edge of her menu.

Max smirked at how comical she looked and replied, "Looks like they're waiting for a table."

"Oh, hell. I can't let *them* see us, too. I don't have it in me to fudge the truth with my own kids." Her voice was shrill in her panic and she lowered it to a harsh whisper. "I have to leave."

"Leave?" Max looked at her in surprise. "Certainly that's a bit extreme?"

"What other option do I have? If they see me, they'll come over." She winced. "What would I say?"

"Oh, I don't know," he replied. "How about something like, 'I'd like you to meet my friend, Max,' or something similar."

Ginny shook her head. The word *friend* echoed in her ears and bothered her more than she cared to admit. Was that how he saw them, as intimate *friends*?

"No," she said. "You say what happened with Pat. I'll make an ass of myself. Not to mention, the last man they saw me with was George. How awkward will that be, if they start asking how we met and we have to keep on tap dancing around things."

He nodded, noting the discomfort in her tone. "Yes, that makes sense. But, how do you propose we leave without their notice?"

Ginny thought quickly, as she scanned the restaurant from behind the wall of her menu. "I don't know, but I'll figure it out. I'm going to go into the bathroom and I'll text you from there. Maybe we can leave separately, or something."

Before he could reply, Ginny put down her menu, grabbed her bag and got up from her seat. She strode swiftly toward the bathrooms at the back of the restaurant without a backward glance.

Max watched her go and picked up his wineglass. Whatever happened next, he had to acknowledge, she wasn't dull.

\*\*\*\*

"Mom?"

Ginny spun around, her face a picture of surprise. "Jennifer!"

"What are you doing here?"

"Using the facilities, same as you," she replied, with a small laugh.

Jennifer shook her head. "Obviously. No, I meant what are you doing *here*?" She gestured to the restroom door to indicate the restaurant.

"I'm here for dinner, *obviously*," Ginny lobed back.

Jennifer raised her eyebrows, taken aback by the sharp tone. "*Here?*"

Ginny knew what she was implying. The restaurant did tend to lend itself to the couple's crowd. Sure, there were friends like Pat and Melanie who frequented it once in a while, or a larger party for an anniversary or birthday, but in general it was seen as a date spot.

"With who?'

"Jan and Darryl!" Ginny blurted, slightly shrill.

"Oh." She looked at the stalls. "Is Jan inside...?"

"No!" Ginny bit her lip when Jennifer frowned at her twitchiness.

"Are you feeling okay?"

Ginny reined it in. Her tone sounded exactly like Eric's had the day he'd stopped in unannounced after she'd just returned from the wine tour; nervous yet suspicious. She took a breath and said, pleasantly, "I'm fine. Jan and Darryl haven't arrived yet, so I thought I'd get freshened up while I waited. You look just lovely, by the way. Purple is definitely your color."

"Thanks," she said, smoothing the edge of her blouse over her tan skirt.

"And I love your hair up like that," Ginny further complimented. "Very chic."

Jennifer tucked a stray strand behind her ear, trying to remember what they'd been talking about.

"Are you here with Chris?"

"Uh-huh. You guys should come by our table when—"

"Oh!" Ginny interrupted. "There goes my phone!"

"I didn't hear anything," Jennifer said, frowning.

"I have it on vibrate," Ginny confided. "Don't want to disturb anyone." She gestured toward her small purse and added, "I'll just get that," before stepping sideways and into a vacant stall.

Jennifer blinked as the door closed and her mother disappeared from sight.

\*\*\*\*

Max's cellphone vibrated on the table and he picked it up. It was a text from Ginny.

*"Am in bathroom stall, don't ask. Jennifer found me, so going to make a break for it, if I can."*

He chuckled and wrote back: *"Alright, Nancy Drew."*

Her reply came swiftly: *"Ha ha."*

\*\*\*\*

"It's just too bad, is what it is," Ginny said, as she and Jennifer exited the restroom.

She'd tried to get out alone, but no dice. Consequently, she had no choice but to claim Jan and Darryl had to cancel and she was going to leave.

"Are you sure you won't join us? It seems a shame, especially when you're all dressed up."

"I'm sure," Ginny said, when they arrived at the table Chris was holding for the two of them. "Hello, dear. Good to see you."

"So, you were right," Chris offered to Jennifer, before telling Ginny, "Jen said she was sure she saw you going into the ladies room, but I didn't believe her. Shows you I should never doubt my beautiful wife."

Ginny smiled and leaned in to give him a quick kiss on the cheek. She could feel Max's eyes watching her across the restaurant and it was nearly killing her to restrain herself from looking his way.

"Mom's plans with Jan and Darryl fell through, so I told her she could join us."

"Of course," he agreed, always on his best manners. "You look beautiful and it shouldn't go to waste."

He started to rise and pull out another chair for Ginny, but she waved her hands at him and said, "No, no. You kids enjoy your child-free evening. You're paying for a sitter, for goodness sake. I'm not going to play gooseberry to your date. Have a wonderful evening."

Before either of them could argue further, she stepped away from the table and forced herself to walk steadily through the restaurant and out the front door. She could feel Max's eyes on her back with each step, saw their waiter's confused expression from the corner of her eye and felt her heart sink a little further with every click of her heels on the floor. What a nightmare.

\*\*\*\*

Jennifer was lying on her bed, the telephone pressed to her right ear as she spoke to Eric. Once she and Chris had arrived home from their night out and checked on the kids, she'd quickly changed into her PJs, washed the makeup from her face then put a call in to tell him about the run in with their mother.

"It was just a bit surreal is all," she said, summing up, while scrunching her pillow under her head.

Chris, lying beside her, flipped the page in his magazine and commented, "She was definitely off her game."

"Did you hear that?" Jennifer asked, holding the phone away from her head toward Chris then putting it back to her ear.

"Maybe she was a bit self-conscious at being stood up; putting on a brave face and all that," Eric said, trying to find a reasonable explanation.

"Maybe." Jennifer shrugged and pulled the covers up around her torso as she sank further into her pillow. "But, if I didn't know better, I'd have bet money she'd been drinking. *Alone.*"

"God, don't say that." Eric ran his fingers through his hair.

"Don't say what?" Kimberly walked into the den, where Eric was having his phone conversation.

"Is that Kim?" Jennifer asked.

"Yup."

"Are you going to tell her about this when we hang up?"

"Is that Jennifer?" Kimberly demanded. "Did you tell her about your mother this afternoon?"

Eric stretched his neck then looked at the expectant expression on his wife's face. Between the tension she was clearly carrying about her Dad - which they *still* hadn't discussed - and his mother's antics, he was feeling stretched to his limit. The parental conversations were turning into minefields.

"Hello?" Jennifer said.

"Well?" Kimberly asked.

"I don't know, maybe," Eric replied to Jennifer's prompt, while simultaneously shrugging his shoulders at Kimberly.

She frowned at him and said, "You'd better tell her," then left the room.

"Make sure you tell him about that guy we saw," Eric heard Chris saying to Jennifer.

"Oh, right." She chuckled.

"What guy?" Eric asked, glad to change the subject.

"Oh, it was nothing, really. After Mom left, we saw a man about her age - well put together, a class act - at another table on his own. We were saying we should have stopped Mom from leaving and introduced them. After all, everyone else seems to want to set her up, we should get a crack at it as well."

"God," Eric said, shuddering at the idea. "Keep me outta that."

Jennifer laughed. "Seriously, right? No thanks."

"So, is that it?"

"I think so," she said. "Hopefully her behavior isn't a sign of a trend."

"Agreed," he said, flatly.

\*\*\*\*

Ginny typed speedily on her cellphone while, beside her, Max drove them home. She'd waited in the parking lot for him to come out of the restaurant, skulking near his car and feeling foolish as hell. But, what was she supposed to do? Introduce him with a flip of her hand as her new lover? And then what was she going to say after that, when the wash of questions started flowing about their relationship; the relationship where, by *his* suggestion, she introduce him as her *friend* who will still be around, apparently, for the solid noncommittal period of a *while*. God, it was turning into a minefield and she wasn't sure how to navigate the terrain.

Jan's reply came through, finally, and Ginny read: *"Just take a breath. It will be fine."*

Ginny: *"But, am I being out of line here? He says he cares and such, but then he talks about how he's sticking around because Darryl needs him. I can't start parading him around my kids with so little substance."*

Jan: *"No, you're not out of line. And I think you're perfectly fine to keep things to yourself until you think it's appropriate to share."*

Ginny peeked at Max, his eyes were on the road ahead, and wrote: *"If it ever gets to that point."*

Jan: *"Just take it one day at a time."*

Ginny: *"Okay, thanks. I'm going to go because we'll be at my place soon."*

Jan: *"Then he's gone for a couple of days, right?"*

Ginny sighed and wrote: *"Yes."*

Jan: *"Love you, talk later."*

Ginny: *"You, too."*

"Was that Jan?" Max asked, eyes still forward.

Ginny jumped slightly, startled to realize he'd been monitoring her the whole time. She put her phone back into her purse and said, "Yes."

"You told her what happened?"

Ginny grimaced and looked out the passenger window. "Yup."

Max flicked on the signal light to turn right and said, "And did she say the same thing I did, that it's fine and not to worry about it?"

Ginny shrugged her shoulders then realized he might not be able to see her in the darkened interior, so replied, "More or less, yes."

"Good," he said, turning the corner onto her street. "Because I don't want it to be on your mind while I'm away. I say we just forget about it and when I get back we'll carry on as usual and celebrate my return."

A lump formed in her throat and all she could do for a moment was nod. He was such a decent man.

Max pulled into the driveway of her house and put the car into park. "Okay. So, you're going to be alright for the next couple of days while I'm away?"

Ginny turned toward him and leaned across the car interior to plant a solid kiss on his lips. When they came up for air, she said, "And there will be more of that waiting for you when you get back."

Max grinned and said, "Excellent. I won't even go back to the hotel when I get back, I'll come straight here."

\*\*\*\*

## Ginny's Last Minute Bakery-Made Muffins

### Ingredients
Bakery-made muffins.

### Directions
o   Rush to your local bakery.
o   Purchase an assortment of muffins.
o   Deliver.

# Chapter Twenty-Three

Ginny grinned as she watched Tamara practically dancing around the library as she returned books to the shelves. She'd been in good spirits all day and it was all connected to one person, Kate; the woman that Tamara was pining over until she finally mustered up the guts to approach her. They'd been an item ever since.

Suddenly, a thought occurred to her: Was that how she'd been acting since Max came into her life? Was she just as obvious but didn't realize it? Because, if that was true, then it was a guarantee Tamara knew *something* was going on and was just waiting for it to be revealed.

Tamara returned to the main desk pushing the empty library cart, a spring in her step and a smile on her face.

"Aren't you just a ray of sunshine," Ginny commented, thoroughly enjoying her joy.

Tamara's smile blossomed into a full-blown toothy grin. "Life is good," she said, simply.

And, just like that, Ginny was hit by the desire to share.

"What's with you?" Tamara asked, cocking her head. "Something on your mind?"

Ginny blinked; was she really that transparent?

Tamara walked around the desk to stand beside Ginny. She gestured to the almost empty library and said, "It's quiet, we have a moment, spill."

"Okay," Ginny said, her heart beating faster as she made the choice to tell all. "First of all, I haven't been keeping this a secret for any other reason than I didn't want to share until I felt it was something worth sharing."

Tamara's eyebrows lifted. "Wow, okay. So, something heavy." Her face twisted and she reached out to grab Ginny's arm. "Oh, god, is it something bad?"

"No, no," Ginny quickly reassured her. "No, it's something good."

"Oh, thank god," Tamara exhaled, releasing her arm and sitting down. "You had me worried for a moment there."

"Sorry, I didn't think."

"Anyway," Tamara pressed. "Tell me, what's the news?"

"I've been seeing someone," Ginny blurted, then braced herself.

Tamara's brow furrowed and she said, "Seeing someone? As in what? A therapist?"

"What? No!" Ginny laughed at the misunderstanding.

"So what then?" Tamara said, before her eyes suddenly widened as she put two and two together. "Wait, do you mean a *man*? You've been seeing a *man*?"

Ginny, still giggling, nodded.

"*Ohmygod!*" Tamara screeched, jumping up from the chair and throwing her arms around Ginny. "Who? Where? When?"

Ginny hugged her back, aware that they'd drawn the attention of the few patrons who were in the library.

Tamara released her, but then clasped her hands in her own and bounced up and down on her toes. "Tell me! Tell me!"

"We've got an audience," Ginny said, jerking her head toward the library shelves.

Tamara released her hands then turned to frown at the six people staring. "Show's over. Go back to your browsing."

Ginny snickered when eyes widened and they all quickly averted their gaze.

"Okay," Tamara said, leaning up against the desk. "Spill."

Ginny took a breath then released it. "It's been a couple of months now—"

"A couple of months!"

Ginny clamped her lips together and shot her a look.

"Sorry, sorry," she said, lowering her voice to just above a whisper.

"Okay," Ginny said, as calmly as she could in hopes of keeping things peaceful. "Yes, a couple of months. But, you must know I've still only told a couple of people. You're in a very tiny, exclusive group."

Tamara dimpled. She liked that.

"Right," Ginny said, nodding at her reaction. "So, once I tell you, you have to keep it to yourself until I say otherwise."

"Okay," Tamara agreed. "But, one question, who are we keeping it *from*?"

"My kids."

"Okay," she said, again, running her fingers through her hair and pulling it back from her face. "Which begs the question, why?"

"I'm just not ready yet to introduce the idea to them that I'm dating."

"But they've known about the set-ups, right?"

Ginny nodded and sat down in the heavily padded, wooden desk chair in front of the computer. "Sure. But those weren't much of anything and they knew it."

"And this man you're seeing?"

"Is quite the opposite," Ginny clarified.

Tamara grinned. "So, tell me, where did you meet?"

Ginny cleared her throat and said, "Here."

"Here?" Tamara gestured to the library. "How? When…. Wait a minute!"

Ginny braced herself as she put things together.

"Mystery man?" she said, pointing a finger. "It's him, right?"

Ginny nodded.

"I knew it!" Tamara said, smugly, folding her arms over her chest.

Ginny chuckled.

"But, how?" she asked, unfolding her arms and reaching for a *Hershey's Kiss* from the glass bowl on the desk. "Every time he was here, he never spoke to you. Or did he and I missed it?"

"No," Ginny told her. "He's actually working with Jan's husband and I met him that way."

"Wow," Tamara said, unwrapping the chocolate and popping it into her mouth. "Meant to be."

A person approached the desk, her arms laden with books, and Ginny said, "Now, remember, mums the word until I say otherwise."

Tamara nodded and said, "got it," then moved forward to help the woman at the checkout.

Ginny turned around to face the computer, happy she'd shared her news. It made it feel more real with each person that knew about it. She logged onto the server then suddenly had a thought that turned her happiness on end: What about Max? Was her need for secrecy making it feel less real for him? Was she, in fact, unintentionally diminishing what they had and; thus, making him believe it wasn't that big of a deal? After all, upon reflection, when they'd first started seeing each other he'd told her his depth of feelings and desires, but now - just the other night at dinner in fact - he was talking about Darryl being the reason he was staying in town. Ginny's heart lurched. Was she inadvertently stomping on things before they even had a chance to get started?

****

Eric bounced Layla on his knee in front of his computer, while he talked with Brian on Skype. He was keeping her entertained so Kimberly could get ready for their night out without interruption.

Brian, on the screen, smiled at his cherubic niece while asking Eric, "Is the cold war over then?"

Eric gave Layla the pink sippy-cup she was reaching for on the desk top and replied, "I think so, or at least I hope so. She hasn't actually spoken to Mom since she brought the muffins over, but she has talked to Jennifer and it seems she managed to smooth things over."

They were speaking, of course, about Kimberly's outrage over Ginny delivering bakery-bought muffins to her door, instead of homemade. God forbid. As Eric said, Jennifer had managed to inject some common sense about the incident and, it appeared, Kimberly had pondered what she'd said and had decided to lay down her indignation.

"Excellent," Brian said, waving at Layla. "The last thing you need is a war between your wife and Mom."

Layla waved back, grinning behind her cup.

Eric looked over his shoulder then leaned into the computer. "Tell me about it. I can't talk now because we're leaving in a few minutes, but there's more than just Mom she's upset about."

Brian leaned in as well, his face closer to the screen.

"I'll fill you in more, later, but it looks like her Dad is having an affair!"

"Get outta town!" Brian blurted.

"Outta town!" Layla cheered, making Eric jerk in surprise.

Brian started laughing. "Man, you should've seen your face."

"You should have felt my heart rate," Eric volleyed back, making Brian laugh more.

Layla started squirming and Eric lifted her off of his lap and down onto the floor. She made a beeline for the open office door. "I'll fill you in later," he repeated. "But I gotta go and grab her before she starts getting into stuff and Kim gets all bent out of shape."

Brian nodded. "Have a good dinner."

"Thanks," Eric replied, then signed off and charged out of the room in pursuit of his daughter.

****

Ginny leaned up against the island and watched Max move around her kitchen with both an easy confidence and finesse. It was impressive and sexy all at the same time. His time away had extended from two days to a full week, but he'd made good on his promise to come straight from the airport to her house, instead of the hotel. She felt a jolt of pleasure, then a shot of nerves, when she thought of his bags sitting in her bedroom. It all made her weak in the knees. If she kept this up, she'd need to sit down.

Max, his back to her, lifted the lid on the casserole dish sitting on the stovetop and inhaled the full-bodied scents of bacon, onions, red wine and baking chicken with an audible "ahhh" of pleasure. Ginny had the fleeting thought she wished she was that dish.

"It smells fabulous in here," she said, raising her wineglass in a toast to his efforts.

He turned around, grinning. "It should be about another hour and we can eat."

"You are a man of many talents, Mister Rhodes," she further complimented, tipping her glass to her mouth.

"Well, I did tell you I'd cook for you," he said, reaching for Martini, sitting regally at his feet. "And, at least this way, we don't have to worry about you running out before the salads arrive."

Ginny put her goblet down on the table and pulled out a chair to sit down. Even though it had been seven days since she'd abandoned him at the restaurant, the memory was still uncomfortably fresh. "I'm still mortified," she said, wincing.

Max laughed while he pet the cat. The cat, in return, began to purr.

"I can't imagine what you must be thinking of me by now."

"I think you're wonderful. And quirky. And kind. And considerate."

She grinned at him. "And I think you're exceptionally kind."

Max gently set the cat back on the floor then walked over and sat down opposite her at the table. He reached for her hand and said, "I understand your feelings. You'll tell your kids about us when you're ready."

A swell of gratitude washed over Ginny as she met his steady gaze, only to be replaced by a cold shiver as she revisited the worries she'd had earlier that day at the library. Was she diminishing things?

"I mean it," he said, wanting her to believe his conviction. "There's no rush. I'm not going anywhere."

Ginny nodded and gripped his hand with her own while the thought *for now* dared to mutter quietly in her mind.

****

Eric watched the road and taillights of the cars ahead while Kimberly sat beside him in the passenger seat, her back straight and her face determined. They were on-route to his mother's house, with the intention of surprising her with a piece of chocolate cake from the restaurant they'd just been to for dinner.

"Are you sure about this?" he asked, as thunder rumbled overhead and a few raindrops began smattering against the vehicle's windshield.

"Absolutely," she said, immediately.

"But, shouldn't we call first?"

"That would ruin the surprise," she replied, shooting him a look of exasperation. "I want her to know I'm holding no ill will about the muffins and that it was a misunderstanding."

"Does she know you were holding ill will? Did you speak to her?"

"No," she said, smoothing her bangs. "But, that's exactly *how* she would know. I usually keep in touch and I haven't been, so now she'll know it's all in the past."

"And you think cake is going to do all of that," he stated, flicking on his windshield wipers when the rain began to fall with a steady patter on the glass.

"Trust me, she's a woman and she'll get it. *And,* by the way, she'll also be touched we thought of her. I know if it was Layla doing it for me when I'm all alone, I'd be happy about such a thoughtful gesture."

Eric grinned into the dusky interior of the car. "So, what are you saying? You think you're going to outlive me?"

Kimberly heard his teasing tone and snickered. "I won't dignify that with a response."

He chuckled as they stopped at a red light. "What if she's busy?"

"Doing what?"

"I don't know," he shrugged. "Washing her hair. Taking a bath."

"I'm sure it will be fine." She waved his worries away with her hand. "She's probably just having a quiet night in with the cat. Maybe *finally* starting on some knitting. She'll probably welcome the company."

The light turned green and Eric accelerated toward his mother's house.

\*\*\*\*

"How much longer did you say we had until that chicken is done," Ginny asked, breathless from the intensity of Max's kisses.

Following her train of thought, he swiftly reached beneath her and swept her off of the floor into his arms, a suggestive grin on his face. "Long enough."

Ginny burst out laughing as he stepped around the cat and began carrying her toward the bedroom. He was a man of action, that was certain.

"Onward," she began, only to be interrupted by the sound of the doorbell ringing through the house.

Max stopped in the hallway. "Expecting someone?"

"No." She shook her head, her face puzzled.

He placed her back on her feet. "Want me to get it?"

She shook her head again and smoothed her red skirt. "I'll see who it is. Hang on a moment."

He hung back as she disappeared around the corner, just in case it was someone she didn't want knowing he was there.

****

Ginny quickly ran her fingers through her mussed hair then peeked through the spy hole. "Oh, hell's bells," she muttered, under her breath, before opening the door.

"Holy cow!" Kimberly said, stepping forward into the house with such force she nearly knocked Ginny sideways. "It's coming down in buckets out there!"

Eric, following behind her, paused to give a sharp shake to the umbrella he was carrying.

"Hurry up!" Kimberly badgered, while thunder rumbled and shook the house.

"I'm coming," he replied, tightly, folding up the umbrella then stepping inside.

Kimberly slipped off her shoes and said, "Whew, it's nice to be out of that."

"I didn't realize it was raining," Ginny commented.

"Seriously?" Eric said, closing the door and propping the dripping umbrella up against it. "Didn't you hear the thunder?"

A hot flash washed over Ginny as she remembered what she and Max had just been on their way to do and the reason she hadn't noticed. "I must have missed it. But, besides that, what on Earth brings you two here at this hour?"

Eric slipped his shoes from his feet and shot Kimberly an 'I told you so' look before he said, "We were out to dinner and Kim suggested we stop in and surprise you —"

"With chocolate cake! Tadaaa!" Kimberly thrust a white, takeaway container she was holding, toward Ginny.

Ginny, trying to keep her bearings while scanning for signs of Max, jumped at the unexpected movement. "Oh, my!"

"We heard about your cancelled dinner plans with Jan and Darryl last week," Kimberly said, still holding out the box. "So, I said to Eric we should surprise you with restaurant cake. A little something to take the sting out of having to miss out the last time."

Ginny took the box then smiled, genuinely touched. "Well, isn't that kind of you. Really. Such a nice thing to do. Thank you."

Kimberly shot an 'I told *you* so' look back at Eric. "So, did you want to have some now? We're happy to stay and keep you company."

Ginny's brow creased as she began to cross the room, making her way to the kitchen with Kimberly firmly in tow.

"Something smells delicious in here, by the way," Kimberly went on, before stopping short in the doorway.

Ginny waited a beat and, sure enough, her daughter-in-law turned around; her face a picture of confusion. Ginny's insides clenched. Could it get any worse?

"What is it?" Eric asked, also noting Kimberly's expression.

"Maybe we should ask your Mom."

Eric looked questioningly at Ginny. "About what?"

She shrugged, noncommittally.

He walked across the family room and swept past Ginny to see for himself.

Ginny beetled behind him. "It's not how it looks," she said, when he, too, stopped short beside Kimberly in the doorway.

Eric turned around and looked at her, his eyebrows high on his forehead. "It's not? Then what *does* it look like?"

Ginny saw what he saw and could only imagine how it appeared from their perspective. Dim lights, food cooking, a wine bottle on the table, candles lit, place settings for two, a vase of fresh flowers; incriminating was the word that came to mind.

"What's going on?" Eric scratched his head as he tried, and failed, to come up with some logical reason for what they were seeing. Especially as it was clear his mother was alone.

"You're all dressed up," Kimberly stated, suddenly aware of what she was wearing.

"No, I'm not." Ginny shook her head, refuting her words.

Kimberly looked her over, noted the red cocktail dress, gold chandelier earrings, quaffed hair and expertly applied makeup and insisted, "Yes, you are."

Panic began to rise in Eric's chest. He needed some sort of reasonable explanation and he needed it now. "Mom?"

Ginny sighed and walked around them to place the container of cake on the countertop. "Don't look at me like that. Can't a woman create a nice meal for herself without feeling like some sort of oddity?"

Eric looked at the room, again, then back at her. "What?"

"I'm just saying, do I have to be doomed to a life of eating meals standing over sinks, or sitting at boring tables, just because I'm on my own?"

Kimberly shrugged her shoulders while Eric gestured at the table and said, "No, of course not, but *this*—"

"I mean, really," Ginny said, warming to her theme. "I'd like to think, out of anybody I know, *you two* would be the ones who would understand and cut me some slack."

Kimberly and Eric exchanged a sheepish look.

"Well?" Ginny asked, daring to press even further.

Eric nodded and ran his fingers though his hair. "Okay, sure, I get what you're saying. "

"And?" Ginny encouraged.

"*And*, I guess it's not fair to expect you to suddenly give up everything, like nice meals, just because you're on your own."

Ginny exhaled. It looked like she may have done it and thrown them off the scent.

"And, by the way, looking at this, I do remember how you used to make things really nice for you and Dad."

Ginny smiled. "Yes, I did."

"Okay, well don't let us interrupt any further than we already have," Kimberly said, before quickly adding, "unless you want company?"

Ginny thought of Max, hidden somewhere down the dark hallway, and shook her head. "No, no. You two already did a kindness by bringing the cake, you probably need to get home to the sitter."

Kimberly checked her watch and nodded. "We do."

"Right, so…" Ginny said, hoping to usher them toward the front door.

Eric, looking over Ginny's head, peered at the countertop, his face incredulous.

Blast, Ginny thought, knowing full well what had caught his eye. She braced herself for more questions.

"Eric?" Kimberly said, tugging on his arm. "Your Moms' right, we really need to get going."

"Uh, Mom," he said, instead of responding to Kimberly. "Is that what I think it is?"

Kimberly stopped pulling at his sleeve and began scanning the kitchen for whatever had taken his attention. "What? What are you talking about?"

Eric stepped out of the doorway and crossed the kitchen floor toward the object of his focus.

"What it is?" Kimberly asked. "An ice cream maker?"

"Umm," Ginny said, searching her brain for something, *anything*, to explain the appliance on her countertop.

"And it's a Bosch, too," Eric breathed, shaking his head while standing in front of the silver and black machine. "Hard core. This thing must have set you back a few bucks."

"So, it's not an ice cream maker?" Kimberly pressed. "Is that what you're saying?"

"No, it's not an ice cream maker," Eric agreed, as he tore his eyes away from the machine and fixed them on Ginny. "Seriously, Mom. Since when do you drink espresso?"

"Espresso? That can't be right. She can't stand coffee," Kimberly said, as though Ginny was invisible.

Ginny's flesh broke out in goosebumps when the two of them turned to stare at her. It was true, she'd made a long, loud case for her love of tea over coffee. How in the world was she going to explain the sudden arrival of an espresso maker without giving away the plot?

Eric looked at her with wide, questioning eyes. "You drink *tea*. You've always drank *tea*."

"Drunk," Ginny reflexively corrected.

Eric shot her a look of exasperation, before saying, "My *point* is, I don't get *this*," he gestured at the espresso maker, "At all."

"It was Jan!" Ginny said, in a flash of inspiration.

"Jan?" Eric repeated.

"Yes," Ginny said, nearly triumphant.

"Jan?" Kimberly echoed. "It's Jan's machine?"

"No, no, no," Ginny began explaining, her words coming fast. "We went for lunch and she suggested I try an espresso and guess what? I loved it!" She laughed merrily, as though it was the darndest thing and pressed on. "I have to tell you, I was just as surprised as you and, wouldn't you know it, the next thing I knew I was purchasing my own machine. Carpe diem, that sort of thing."

"Carpe diem?" Eric parroted, while Kimberly's lips curled into a small, stiff smile.

"Exactly," Ginny agreed, rubbing her temple where the beginning of a headache was brewing. She not only was a terrible liar, but not telling the truth to her kids was giving her more pain than she could have ever imagined. First Jennifer, now Eric, where would it end? Perhaps she would have to just bite the bullet and tell all, to clear her conscience.

"Just like that?" Eric said, peering at her. "Out of the blue? Never mind that you've been a tea drinker for as long as we can remember."

"A person can discover they like new things. Or want to try new things. Not be set in stone until they die."

"Wait, what? What does *that* mean?"

Okay, maybe telling all wasn't quite the thing to do as of yet. If they were this perturbed by an espresso maker, what would they make of a boyfriend? She had to get them out of the house. Not only were they asking way too many questions, but the oven timer was going to go off soon and then what? Max had hidden himself away and she had no bloody idea of what to do next with the coq au vin.

"Listen," she offered, finally successful in her effort to usher them out of the kitchen toward the front door. "Let's not make this such a big deal. The next time we all get together, I'll have the whole thing figured out and we can have some fun, indulging on espresso."

"Right, sure," Eric replied, as she frog-marched them through the family room into the foyer.

"We can pretend we're in Italy!" Ginny added, snatching up the waiting umbrella and opening the front door.

"Umm," Eric murmured, as she thrust it into his hands and practically shoved them out onto the porch.

"Stay dry!" Ginny said, then shut the door firmly in their faces.

Eric turned to look at Kimberly with wide, confused eyes.

She said nothing, just grabbed the umbrella from his grasp, opened it and led the way down the steps toward their car parked in the driveway.

"Okay, seriously," he called out, following in her footsteps and getting pelted by the rain. "What the hell just happened?"

She held her hand out, traffic-cop style, and said, "Don't", before opening the passenger door and slipping into the car.

"Yeah, but," Eric began, while she wrestled with closing the umbrella and he dashed through the puddles to the driver's side of the car.

"Eric, so help me god," she warned, finally collapsing the umbrella and hurling it into the backseat. She had nothing to say. Too much was going on with both Ginny and her father and she needed time to sort out her thoughts before coming up with any answers. Any bloody answers *at all*.

He had the good sense to shut up, close his door and start driving.

\*\*\*\*

Ginny snorted with mirth into the bedsheets as the hilarity of what had transpired with Eric and Kimberly overtook her again. She and Max had already discussed it over their dinner, but it was worth a second rehash.

Max, lying beside her, added his own laughter into the mix.

"I shouldn't be laughing," she said, wiping tears of amusement from her eyes. "I'm a terrible, bald-face, lying mother."

"You were quick on your feet, that's for sure," Max said, admiringly. "Especially about the espresso maker."

Ginny giggled some more. "Hardly. I'm an atrocious liar and I'm sure my face was a blatant testament to that fact."

"Well, they seemed to buy it, so maybe you're better than you think."

Ginny readjusted the bedclothes around herself and sighed. "I have a strong feeling they *didn't* buy it, but just wanted to get out of here to discuss it without me present. Whatever the case, I'm in for it now. They're going to think I'm totally off my Granny rocker."

Max laughed and reached beneath the sheets to stroke a hand down the length of her thigh. "Some Granny," he said, raising an eyebrow.

Ginny turned toward him, sighing for an entirely different reason.

****

## *Eric and Kimberly's Chocolate Restaurant Cake*

### Ingredients
Chocolate restaurant cake.

### Directions
- Go to dinner at restaurant.
- Order extra chocolate cake to go.
- Share.

# Chapter Twenty-Four

Max breathed steadily in and out, in and out, trying to keep his thoughts on the thick green forest around him and not on what lay ahead. It was a beautiful day, the late-morning air crisp and the sky so blue it looked photoshopped. All that was needed, in his opinion, was a picnic basket, a shady spot, a bottle of good wine.... But, instead, he was facing a tall tower where an eighteen hundred foot zip-line waited to dangle him three hundred and fifty feet in the air as he sailed on a hope and prayer over the canyon below. Oh, boy, he thought, when his stomach lurched, better try harder to focus on breathing.

"Max?" Darryl patted Max on the shoulder. "You okay, buddy? You look a little pale and, let's be honest, that's really saying something for a golfer."

Max laughed, appreciatively, grateful for any distraction.

"You know you can change your mind, right?" Darryl said. "It's no big deal if you're not feeling up to it."

Max looked around them, his gaze falling on Ginny just a few feet away and sighed.

Darryl watched the mixed emotions flitting back and forth across his face and reiterated, "Seriously. You don't have to go through with it."

"Oh, but I do," he said, his voice heavy with resignation, still looking at Ginny.

She was chatting animatedly with Jan and Dixie, the excitement on her face like that of a child waiting in line at a theme park. He couldn't disappoint her, no way. The conversation they'd had about her ex-husband crossed his mind and he sent a silent message to the man he'd never met, asking if he'd mind sending along some nerve tonic to help him through the experience.

Darryl followed the direction of his stare and a wry grin twisted his mouth. "Gotchya," was all he had to say.

****

Ginny meandered away from Jan and Dixie, doing her best to look casual as she closed the gap between she and Max.

He grinned when she arrived at his side. "Having fun?"

"I'm so excited!" she enthused. "Our group is next."

He nodded, swallowing against the nerves that threatened to resurface.

Ginny peered at him, her face concerned, and surreptitiously reached for his hand; touching his fingers with her own. "Are you okay?"

"Fine."

She cocked her head. "Are you sure? You look a little green."

Max shook his head and repeated, "Fine."

Ginny's eyebrows laced together as she said, "Look, I know you said you're nervous of heights, so if it looks like it's going to be too much, that's okay. You don't have to do it. I'll do it for both of us."

He regarded her with eyes filled with blatant adoration. "Ahh, Gin, my darling. For you, I'll do *anything. Anything.*"

She blinked, speechless. There was so much raw emotion behind his words, she didn't know how to respond.

He gave her fingers a gentle squeeze and released her hand. "Best get on. We'll be lining up soon."

"Right. Okay." She nodded, still slightly dumbstruck by his statement.

He turned and walked over to join Darryl and the others, infused with renewed resolve. He said he was going to do it and be damned if he was going to let anything stand in his way.

"All set?" Darryl asked, welcoming him with a hearty pat on the back.

"Onward and upward," he replied, with a brisk nod.

\*\*\*\*

"*Ohmygod!* Look! Look!"

Ginny's eyes widened as Dixie first shouted then began pointing wildly.

"It's the guys that own the gym where I work out," she enthused, while waving her hand over her head. "Carl! Craig! Hey! Over here!"

Ginny exchanged a look with Jan when the two men Dixie was beckoning to, turned and looked their way. They were identical twins and built like proverbial brick shit houses. Pardon the expression.

"Holy Moses," Jan said, under her breath, as they began walking toward Dixie; their calves so large they looked as though they were smuggling oranges beneath their skins.

"Ditto," Ginny whispered back, watching their faces adopt matching smiles.

"They look like old-school bodybuilders," Jan commented, before Dixie reached out to wrap a hand around both her's and Ginny's forearms and yank them forward.

"Oh!" Ginny exclaimed, as they were plunked firmly into the threesome of Dixie and the two men.

"Guys," Dixie said, grinning from ear to ear. "Meet my friends, Jan and Ginny."

"Pleased to meet you," the one on the left said. "I'm Carl."

"Craig," said the other, his smile disarmingly friendly.

"Very nice to meet you, too," Ginny began, before being sharply cut off by the sound of two women shrieking.

Jan jolted in her harness and whipped her head around. "What the hell was that?"

Carl and Craig exchanged a look then started chuckling.

"Our fiancées," Craig explained, as the shrieking woman came running in their direction.

Carl raised his eyebrows and added, "They *are* the party."

****

Ginny clutched her sides. She couldn't remember the last time she'd laughed so hard. Carl and Craig's fiancées, Heidi and Denise, were like having their own personal stand-up show.

"Okay, we're up right away," Carl said, attempting to settle things down.

"Why are you looking at me like that?" Heidi asked, tightening the ponytail holder keeping her long, strawberry blonde hair off her face.

Carl shot her a wry grin and pointed at her shirt. "Just keep your top on this time or they're seriously going to tell us we can't come back."

Ginny chortled.

Heidi shot her a glance filled with mischief. "He says that like he means it, but...."

"I *do* mean it," Carl insisted, good-naturedly. "We had to sign a form last time, remember?"

Denise, overhearing, burst out laughing and clutched at Jan's arm. "He's not joking! She had to sign an actual form!"

"We're just lucky they didn't ban her outright," Carl said.

Jan giggled and pointed at Dixie. "We might have to look into one of those for you."

"Me?" Dixie tried to look indignant.

Heidi looked her up and down appraisingly and nodded. "You'd totally be a show. The guys would appreciate it."

Craig groaned and pulled Denise off of Jan's arm. "God, you two. Don't spread your madness."

Denise reached up and wrapped her arms around his neck. "It's not *me*," she said, before planting a kiss solidly on his lips.

Ginny watched them then stole a glance at Max, standing with Darryl and his co-workers.

"Thinking of going public?" Jan whispered in her ear, when she saw the wistfulness on Ginny's face.

Ginny thought about Max's statement and revisited the thrill it gave her. She wasn't sure exactly what to say, but thankfully was saved from having to think too hard when

Dixie pulled out her phone and began gathering them all together for photos.

"Come on, girls and guys," she said, waving at their group and the twins and their fiancées. "We have to have some pics to document our experience."

Ginny and Jan grinned at each other and went to join the group.

*****

Okay, Max admitted to himself, maybe he'd been a bit self-deluding when he'd strapped on his harness and adjusted his safety helmet. And maybe, just maybe, it was time to admit to himself that regardless of every positive thought and mantra he could pull from his mental arsenal, his heart was still beating a tad too quickly as he followed, sheep-like, behind Darryl's partner, Rick, toward the 'zip zone'.

"How're you doing?" Darryl asked, stepping in behind Max as they approached the tower that would take them skyward.

"Hanging in," he replied. "No pun intended."

Darryl chuckled. When Jan had pulled him aside to confide that Max was as fearful of heights as she was, he'd decided it was a good idea to keep a close watch in case he had a sudden turn. "Are those pills Jan gave you working at all?"

Max took a step forward, placed his foot on the stair that would start his ascent toward the platform at the top of the tower and hesitated. Were they? Jan had insisted they would, but...

"Max?" Darryl said, placing a steadying hand on his friend's shoulder.

"You know," he said, taking another step - a firmer one this time - on the stairs. "I think they just might be."

Darryl released the breath he'd been holding. "Excellent. She said they should kick in about now."

"I'll have to thank her properly at the other end," Max went on, enjoying the sudden shift in his emotions as he worked his way steadily upward. Instead of raw panic, he was feeling mildly giddy. Much better.

Darryl, following a step behind, grinned. "I'm sure she's in pretty good spirits by now, too."

"You know, I didn't even ask her what was in them," Max commented, over his shoulder.

"Nothing to worry about," Darryl assured him. "They're some sort of herbal concoction she gets from her Naturopath."

Max took another step upward and, just like that, he was high enough to see the wooden platform and the valley below. It was epic. And a really, really long way down. He breathed deeply, filling his lungs with fresh mountain air, hoping to keep the giddiness alive and the nervousness as bay.

"Look!" Darryl pointed ahead of them. "Ginny's next!"

"Over here, Gin blossom!" Dixie yelled, jumping up and down on the platform to get Ginny's attention while she snapped photos on her phone.

Max grinned while he watched her getting hooked up by one of the zip-line guides and his heart was near fit to bursting when she turned back, a huge smile on her face, and gave him a thumbs-up, then proceeded to clutch the bar over her head and cheer loudly as she slipped off the platform and flew away down the line.

"Look at her go!" Darryl whooped.

Max blinked back the sudden wetness in his eyes, startled by his depth of emotion. He didn't just adore her, he had a strong feeling he might....

"We're next, mate," Rick turned around to pat Max on the shoulder, before he moved toward a guide beckoning him forward.

Max took a breath and cleared his throat, centering himself as he took the last step up and arrived on the platform, alternately thrilled with himself he'd made it that far and slightly freaked out he was actually going to go through with it. The thing that kept him moving forward - besides the helpful sedatives - was knowing Ginny would be waiting for him at the other end.

"Okay, man," one of the young men managing the line beckoned Max forward. "You ready?"

Max watched Rick, seated in his harness with his hands above his head clutching the bar, sail away then said, "As I'm ever going to be."

"Cool." The dark-haired youth, the tag on his shirt labeling him at 'Thad', nodded. "Where are you from? Australia?"

Max chuckled as he got into position. "Not quite. The east coast."

"Cool," Thad said, grinning. "Tell all your buddies to come and see us for the best zip around."

Max smiled, feeling less and less apprehensive. Now that he was finally doing it, instead of just thinking about it, he was feeling charged. Besides, Thad seemed so relaxed about it, clearly it wasn't as terrifying as he was building it up to be in his head.

"Okay, you're set, man," Thad told him. "Have a good zip."

"Woohoo, Max!" Dixie yelled, taking photos of him in the same manner she had Ginny, while Thad gave him a push and he went sliding off the platform.

"Go, Max!" Darryl's voice cheered him on as he rushed away from the tower.

"Bloody hell!" he bellowed back, his heart beating wildly in his chest as his legs dropped out beneath him and there was nothing between him and the canyon below except air and trees.

Moving at speed, Max clutched the bar above him with moist palms, focusing on breathing steadily and reminding himself to enjoy the ride. The high-pitched sound of the metal as it raced down the line was startling, even though he'd been hearing it throughout the morning. Perhaps it was because it was right above him, reminding him it was the only thing keeping him in the air and not plummeting like a rock to the earthy floor below.

Max dared to look side to side, felt the cool wind in his face and began to grin. He was just thinking he could get used to it when the tower at the other end of the line was in sight. And there was Ginny!

"Woohoo!" she cheered, loudly, jumping up and down as he approached.

He laughed and put out his feet, ready to connect with the solid wooden platform.

"You did it!" She was beaming, and so was Jan, seated on the bench at the far end of the wooden dock. I'm so proud of you!"

The young man on the platform reached out to steady Max on his feet, unclipped his harness and patted him on the back. "Good zip, dude."

"It really was!" Max agreed, feeling euphoric. "Surprisingly so."

\*\*\*\*

Brian laughed as Eric reenacted the experience of Layla jumping into the community league swimming pool, in front of his computer camera in his home office. There was nothing quite like watching your older brother trying to mime an adorable two year old leaping with abandon. Hysterical.

"Thank God I was quick on the draw and kept her from going right under," he elaborated, pausing to catch his breath. "Or I never would have heard the end of it from Kim."

"Sounds like she's taking a page from Mom's book," Brian commented, running his fingers through his hair. "She's got the go-for-it gene from her Grandma."

Eric frowned and shrugged his shoulders. "I don't follow."

"Layla's willingness to fearlessly jump into the pool is like Mom doing the same sort of thing when she went zip-lining."

"Excuse me?" Eric began blinking rapidly while he sunk into his desk chair. "Did you say zip-lining?"

Brian raised his eyebrows. "Yeah. Didn't you see the pictures?"

"There are pictures? Where?"

"On Dixie's Facebook page," Brian told him. "And she tagged Mom, so on her page as well."

"I don't check Facebook," Eric said, sitting back in his chair.

"Yeah, I know, obviously, but didn't Kim show you?"

Eric shook his head and said, "No," then was cut off by a shriek from the other room and the sound of feet pounding along the hallway toward his office.

"What the hell was that?" Brian asked, wide-eyed.

"I'd hazard to guess it was my wife," Eric replied, just as the door flew open and Kimberly charged, wild-eyed, into the room.

"*Ohmygod!*" she said, throwing her hands up in the air.

"Let me guess," Eric said, keeping his voice calm. "Facebook?"

"Yes!" Kimberly's face was aghast and she put her hands on her hips as she stared at Brian on the screen. "Do *you* know about this?"

He reflexively leaned back from his computer, even though they weren't in the same room. "As much as you."

"Why on Earth would she do something so dangerous?" she demanded.

"It's no big deal," Brian said, rolling his eyes.

"It is too!" she insisted, scraping her fingers through her hair. "Don't they make you sign a waiver and declare your state of health, or something?"

"You're making a big deal out of nothing," Brian said, yawning.

"You saw the photos, correct?"

"Yup, looks like they had fun."

Kimberly turned on Eric. "Are you *hearing* this?"

"Uh, yeah. I'm *right here*," he replied, his words clipped. The last thing he wanted, or needed, was her treating him like a moron in front of his younger brother.

"Seriously, Kim," Brian tried again. "It's perfectly safe. Dixie wrote that they went as a group, as a sort of corporate event thing—"

"Corporate?" she repeated. "You mean the library took them zip-lining? Now I've heard everything."

Brian burst out laughing. "No," he said, between chuckles. "It was Darryl's company."

Eric snickered, too, at the idea of the library ladies and volunteers all going zip-lining. Many of them made his mother look young.

Kimberly turned on him, again. "I don't know why you're laughing. This isn't something to laugh about."

"So, what it is then?" Brian asked, playing devil's advocate from the safety of the computer screen.

Eric grimaced and braced himself.

"Something to *worry* about." She folded her arms tightly across her chest and volleyed her eyes back and forth between them. "First the sudden changes to her looks, then her apparent drinking and dining alone and now this? I think it's a sign of something else going on. Uh-huh, that's what I think."

Brian sighed and decided to attempt to pat her down. If anything, just to spare his brother the ordeal of having to do so once they hung up.

"Okay, so some of that stuff looks odd, but she did have perfectly reasonable explanations. And, in the case of her zip-lining, it was Darryl's company who initiated it and they wanted some more people along to beef up their numbers. Not to mention, it was probably a whole lot more fun for Jan having Mom there."

Eric nodded. Worked for him. "That makes perfect sense. Doesn't it, Kim?"

She frowned. "Maybe to you, but not to me." She cleared her throat and added, "It all reminds me a bit too much of my Dad at the moment, doing all his crazy things, trying new things and *people*, stepping outside his god-damned comfort zone bullshit."

Brian raised his eyebrows. "What are you talking about?"

Eric waited to see what she'd say. She'd been very tight lipped since she'd first revealed the news about her father's indiscretion and he was almost as clueless as Brian.

Kimberly pressed her lips together. "It's nothing," she said, finally. "Just something my sister and I are trying to work out. Family stuff."

Eric and Brian exchanged a look via their cameras.

"Anyway, it's nothing," she repeated, smoothing her hair back from her face.

"Like our Mom," Brian threw in, hoping to keep things going in a reasonable direction. "No big deal."

Eric held his breath. Would she argue?

"So, Eric was just telling me about Layla jumping into the pool," Brian said, switching gears. "What other antics did that little monkey do?"

Kimberly lit up at the mention of her daughter's name.

Eric exhaled and shot him a grateful look. His brother was a star.

\*\*\*\*

Tamara leaped up from her chair behind the reception desk at the library, when Ginny walked through the door to start her shift. She'd been waiting, not patiently, for her to arrive and she was finally here.

"Good morning," Ginny said, all smiles as she carried a pink box over to the desk and put it down next to the computer. She unwound her purple scarf from around her neck and added, "You're here early."

Tamara darted out from behind the desk and grabbed Ginny by the shoulders, her grin larger and more eager.

"Oh, my," Ginny said, speaking into Tamara's dark hair when she hugged her. "What's this in aid of?"

Tamara laughed then released her and said, "I saw the photos on your Facebook page, totally cool!"

Ginny couldn't help but delight in her enthusiasm, especially as it had been such a brilliant experience. Afterward, they'd all gone as a group to lunch - even Dixie's twin gym owners and their hysterical fiancées had come along - and it had been such a pleasure to be completely at ease with Max in a social setting. It had been a perfect end to a wonderful day.

"I also saw mystery man in the photos!" she said, releasing Ginny's shoulders and raising her eyebrows up and down. "You two looked so cute and it was cool to see him somewhere other than here, hiding between the bookshelves."

At that, Ginny winced. While there was no question Dixie had taken great photos of she and Max and the rest of the group, she knew her kids would see them as well. Eric had already met Max once, he was sure to recognize him. If he queried her about him after seeing them both at the zip-lining gathering, she wasn't sure what she was going to say. More fibs, or just throw things out there and see what happens? It sounded both exhilarating and potentially chaotic at the same time.

"What?" Tamara asked, cocking her head. "What's with the face?"

"Oh, it's nothing," Ginny said, not believing it herself.

"Your face tells another story," Tamara stated, while checking out the contents of the pink box. "Oooh, donut holes! You spoil us."

"Clearly not homemade but from *The Bakery*, so equally, if not more, tasty."

Tamara picked a chocolate one from the box. "I'll get my sugar and caffeine fix all in one shot. Score."

Ginny grinned and asked, "Still want a coffee?"

Tamara nodded. "Yes, please. And when you want to talk, let me know. 'Cause I'm telling you, there's no way that face was *nothing*."

Ginny watched her pop the donut hole into her mouth then head off in the direction of the history section. She sighed and thought, there was the real issue: her history was interfering with her present. No offence to George, but it had been two years since he'd left their lives and it was time she found a way to make it clear to her kids that she still honored her past, but needed to live in her present and look forward to her future. Timing really was everything.

****

## *Ginny's Bakery-made Donut Holes*

**Ingredients**
Already baked donut holes.

**Directions**
o   Purchase donut holes from bakery.
o   Bring them to work.
o   Share and enjoy.

# Chapter Twenty-Five

Jennifer finally finished separating and organizing the many different types of beads she'd bought for the girls to make jewelry at Grace's birthday party. Her eyes were starting to strain from staring at the multitude of shapes and colors and she stretched her neck to relieve some of the tension built up during the sorting.

Ginny, working at the island in Jennifer's kitchen, continued to ice the birthday cupcakes she'd brought over for the party. "I have to say, it's shocking to think Grace is now nine years old."

Jennifer smiled, ruefully, and said, "I know. I now understand what's meant by the expression bitter-sweet."

"Wow, Jennifer, you've really out-done yourself," Jan commented, as she walked into the kitchen from the adjacent dining room.

Jennifer dimpled and waved her hand dismissively. "No, not really."

"Oh, please. A jewelry making and treasure hunt party? It's brilliant! You and Stacey would have loved it at that age," she added, referring to her daughter, the same age as Jennifer.

Ginny nodded, never taking her eyes from her task. "That's the truth. And I love that you're giving them each their own wooden jewelry box to decorate. Whose idea was that?"

"Believe it or not," Jennifer said, giggling. "It was Chris' idea."

Jan whooped. "No! Really? He impresses me."

"Done," Ginny said, putting down the piping bag she was using to frost the cupcakes in purple icing.

"Did he suggest anything else?" Jan asked, picking up the piping bag to check for leftover frosting while Ginny washed her hands under the tap at the kitchen sink.

"He was amazing!" Jennifer expounded. "It was his idea to add the candy necklaces and rings to the take-home bags to go along with the theme. *And* he was the one who suggested the treasure hunt. He even came up with the idea of each treasure item being something princess themed."

"Wow." Jan's eyes were wide as she squeezed icing from the bag then ate it off of her fingers. "I think I'll hire him for my next party."

Jennifer laughed and said, "Good plan, I'll let him know."

"I must say, though," Ginny said, drying her hands on a dish towel. "There wasn't anywhere near this much effort for you kids when you were Grace's age. We did things like movies or sleepovers, remember?"

"Yeah, well, this generation might do more," Jennifer said, matter-of-fact. "But, sometimes it gets a bit much. Simplicity seems to be an archaic notion."

Ginny gave her daughter a sympathetic smile and hung the towel on a bar on the wall beside the sink. "That's why we're here early, Sweetheart."

"Absolutely," Jan affirmed, putting the piping bag in the sink. "God, that icing is addictive and sick-making all at the same time."

Ginny snickered. "I don't know if that's a compliment or I should be worried."

Jan grinned and said, "Definitely a compliment. The kids are going to love it."

Jennifer looked around them then clapped her hands together. "I think we're finally finished. The decorations are all done, the take-home bags are filled, the jewelry making station is set up, the extra cupcakes are baked and ready for the girls to decorate—"

"The red wine is breathing and the white is chilling," Jan threw in, cheekily.

Jennifer nodded her approval. "We're all set to go."

****

Ginny watched as Grace and her nine friends worked with the pre-cut jewelry wire, expertly threading beads and chatting animatedly the whole time. It was mesmerizing to witness the multitude of bracelets and anklets and necklaces coming to life before her eyes.

Eric came over to stand beside her, Layla sitting on his hip with wide, eager eyes. "I'm getting a glimpse into my future, I think," he said, wryly.

"Pretty!" Layla cheered, her eyes roaming over the shiny bobbles.

Ginny laughed and reached out to stroke her cheek. "Yup. Soon enough she'll be wanting these types of parties, too."

"From the sounds of it, I'm going to have to ask Chris for his party planning notes."

"They'll cost you," Chris said, coming up behind them. "And they're not cheap."

Eric laughed, making Layla laugh as well.

"Hey, Ms. Giggle-pants," Chris said, as he held out his arms. "Do you want to come with Uncle Chris and see if we can find a cupcake for you to decorate?"

Layla's face lit up and she extended her arms toward him. "Cupcake!"

"I'd say that's a yes." Eric handed her over. "You're a brave man. It's going to get very messy."

"Nothing I can't handle," he assured him. "Have you met my son? He makes getting messy an art form."

Ginny smiled affectionately at her son-in-law. He was a good man.

Eric waved to Layla as she was carried away, but she didn't even notice. "The lure of the cupcake is a strong force," he said, amused.

"Hopefully Kimberly will be as easy-going about it," she commented, raising an eyebrow.

He shrugged and refused speculation. Instead, he asked, "Isn't Darryl supposed to be coming today?"

Ginny nodded. "He should be showing up right away. Jan said he had a golf game then he'd be coming right afterward."

The doorbell sounded and Eric gave her an impressed look. "You must be psychic," he teased, while Jennifer opened the door, letting Darryl into the house.

Ginny grinned and followed his gaze. The smile slipped from her face and her knees went weak when, right behind Darryl, Max strode through the front door and into the family room.

****

"Come on in." Jennifer kissed Darryl on the cheek. "Jan's just refilling the snack bowls for me in the kitchen——"

"Darryl!" Jan blurted, interrupting her. She'd walked into the room, snack bowls held aloft, and nearly dropped them onto the carpet when she saw Max standing beside her husband.

Darryl's face went white when the full force of what he'd done hit him.

Max took a deep breath, locked eyes with Ginny across the room, and then let his gaze slide away as he took stock of the situation. "Maxwell Rhodes," he said, extending a hand to Jennifer. "Please call me Max. I'm Darryl's colleague, we're working on a new development project here in town."

Jennifer shook his hand and smiled, charmed by his politeness. "How nice, please come in and join the party."

Max patted Darryl's shoulder, jarring him from his frozen stance, and replied, "Only if I'm not intruding. When Darryl mentioned your gathering, he failed to mention it would be a *family* affair."

"Right," Darryl agreed. "Sorry about that, Max. I don't know where my head was. I can take you back to your hotel if you want—"

"Don't be ridiculous," Chris interrupted, as he came into the room behind Jan, Layla in his arms. "The more the merrier. Any friend of Darryl's is a friend of ours."

Eric, still with Ginny beside the jewelry making station, watched Chris and Jennifer welcome Max further into the house. "Oh, hey, I recognize him. He's the guy I met at lunch with Darryl."

Ginny said nothing. She was tongue-tied.

"And wasn't he at the zip-lining thing, too? Kim showed me the pictures Dixie took of you guys."

Ginny repressed a groan and stayed silent. Thankfully, he didn't seem to realize he was more or less talking to himself.

"Where's Kim?" he said, looking around. "I should be there to referee when she meets him so she doesn't start lecturing the poor guy on the dangers of over-exertion in men of a *certain age*."

"In the kitchen, I think," Ginny managed to utter.

Eric nodded and stepped away from the craft area then paused to ask, "Can I get you something when I'm in there?"

Ginny nodded and patted his arm. "A cup of tea would be wonderful, if you don't mind."

He turned on his heel and headed off to the kitchen. "No problem," he said, over his shoulder.

Ginny watched him go and silently wished he was bringing back a bottle of something stronger. Like tequila. She had a feeling she might need it.

\*\*\*\*

"Follow me, *now*," Jan hissed at Darryl, when no one looking.

His eyebrows shot up. "What?"

Jan huffed, incensed. Had he not noticed the icy glares she'd been sending him since he arrived with Max in tow? Surely her wanting to speak to him, without an audience, couldn't be all that surprising.

Darryl saw her face contort in irritation at his question and didn't ask again. He'd seen the way she'd been looking at him since he and Max had arrived and had a strong hunch he was about to hear what she thought about it.

They slipped out the patio door to the backyard and Jan motioned for him to follow her to the side of the house where they wouldn't be seen.

Darryl trailed behind, slightly nervous they wouldn't have witnesses.

The moment they were behind the tall cedar hedge that ran the length of the house, Jan turned and glared at him. "What the hell?!"

Darryl flinched. Oh, boy. "Listen, Hon—"

"No, *you* listen," she interrupted. "I know you didn't do it on purpose, but my god! How on earth could you have brought him here?"

He nodded. "I know, I know. And I'm really sorry. I guess, since I've been spending so much time with Max, both in and out of work, I just blanked."

Jan shrugged. It made sense... sort of.

"Besides," he went on. "They've been seeing each other for a while now. Don't you think it's time Ginny spoke up about it?"

Jan's jaw dropped.

Uh-oh, he thought. Wrong thing to say.

"Seriously?" she said, blinking fast. "*That's* what you're going to use to make light of this huge blunder?"

"Huge? Really?" he wheedled.

"Yes, huge!" She threw her arms up in exasperation. "What do you propose Ginny do? Pipe up and tell her kids that, surprise, Max isn't just your colleague, but her lover?"

He winced. Not an image he wanted in his head.

"She plans to tell them in her own time, but don't you think that this just *might* make it all a bit more awkward when she does?"

He swallowed uncomfortably.

"Can you imagine it?" She folded her arms across her chest and glared at him, not finished. "*Oh, hey kids, a bit of news. Not only have I moved on from your father's death, but I'm dating someone now and you've already met him and didn't even know it. Surprise.*"

He sighed. "Yeah, okay, definitely might be more awkward."

Jan sighed, too. She hated when they had heated words and she really hated that they were powerless to correct the problem he'd created for Ginny.

"I'll apologize to both of them," Darryl began, then stopped talking when they heard the sound of the patio door sliding open.

Chris stuck his head out and called, "Jan? Darryl? You guys out here?"

They exchanged a look and Jan cleared her throat.

"Yes, we're here," she said, walking around the side of the house, Darryl following behind. "I was just showing Darryl your gorgeous hedges, we're thinking of planting some and I wanted him to see how nice they look when they grow in. Do you remember what kind they are?"

"A Hybrid Yew," he said. "I can tell you more about it after the birthday cake is done. Jennifer's getting ready to do it now, so come on inside."

"Sounds good. I think we're done here anyway," Jan said, looking over her shoulder at Darryl.

He met her eye and nodded. "Yup."

＊＊＊＊

The party had wound down, the children were all cleared out and the adults were convened around Jennifer and Chris' sturdy, oak, ten-seater dining room table. Ginny, seated next to Jan, watched the tableau in front of them with something akin to awe.

It was surreal. Never in her wildest imagination would she have thought she'd be at her daughter's house, witnessing her secret lover sitting right smack in the middle of her entire family and regaling them with tales of his youth.

"Am I dreaming?" Jan leaned in and whispered into Ginny's ear. "Because, otherwise, this is...."

"I *know*," she agreed, leaving the sentence unfinished. It was too much for words.

The only one still seemingly cool and reserved was Kimberly. Not that that was any surprise. Her first reaction to most things was a mixture of caution and suspicion, so this was really no different.

"We really should all go golfing," Eric said, nodding his head encouragingly at Darryl and Max.

Ginny's jaw nearly dropped open and she pressed her lips together.

"I haven't been in a while," he elaborated, before winking at Kimberly. "And it's the one thing I'm allowed to do without asking for a day-pass."

She rolled her eyes good-naturedly, while everyone else chuckled.

Darryl's face became thoughtful as he tried to think of a reason why they couldn't. He'd already faced Jan's wrath once, if a golfing party was planned.... Good god.

"We'd need a fourth," Max said, simply, leaning back in his chair and doing his best to avoid eye contact with Ginny at the other end of the table.

"Yes!" Darryl enthused, then quickly squelched his robust reaction by coughing and clearing his throat. "Too bad."

"No, no," Eric said, raising his hand and pointing at Chris seated next to Jennifer. "Chris can make up the fourth."

Chris brightened and leaned forward, resting his elbows on the table. "I'm not very good, but I'm game if you guys agree to cut me some slack."

Max and Darryl exchanged a look.

Eric, completely unaware of what was going on silently between the two men, grinned. "Excellent. Let's set it up."

Ginny and Jan exchanged much the same look as had Max and Darryl. *This* was an unexpected development.

\*\*\*\*

## *Ginny's Birthday Party Cupcakes*

### Ingredients
2    Boxes of white cupcake mix. (Don't reveal your secret.)
1    Can of frosting.
Blue and red food coloring.

### Directions
o    Bake cupcakes according to directions on the boxes.
o    Mix frosting and food coloring until the frosting turns purple.
o    Ice baked cupcakes once they are fully cooled.

# Chapter Twenty-Six

Kimberly stared at her computer screen, shock making her numb. She was seated on the living room sofa and even though everything was familiar and in its usual place, suddenly it all felt foreign and jumbled.

"How could this have happened?" she asked the empty room.

Kris, her voice being seen as text instead of being heard as words, wrote: "*Are you okay?*"

Kimberly wanted to laugh at the ridiculousness of the question. Her sister had just written the words, "Dad has openly confessed to having an affair and has moved out of his and Mom's house" and now she was asking if she was okay.

*Kris: "Kim? Are you still there?"*

Kimberly slammed the laptop shut. No. No, it was too much to deal with. Her Dad was more than her father, he'd always been her rock. When she'd gone to school and then pursued a career as a curator, he'd been the one to cheer the loudest. Then, when she'd been given the job at the art museum back home, he'd been over the moon with pride. Heck, even when she'd made the tough choice of giving up her adored career to move to Boxwood Hills to raise her soon-to-be-born child, he'd been behind her choice one hundred percent. And now, finding out he was willing to throw their family aside for some... *affair*, it was too much to comprehend. It was like, in that one sentence written by Kris, he'd become a stranger.

Her phone rang, startling her from her thoughts and she reached across the coffee table to pick it up. Kris' number filled the screen and Kimberly pressed 'ignore'. She wasn't ready to face it and, until she was, her sister would just have to bloody wait.

****

"Great shot!" Eric whooped.

Darryl grinned at his effusive praise and watched as his golf ball sailed down the fairway, directly on target. It really was a fantastic shot.

Max, standing next to their golf cart, looked around them and drank it all in. It was mid-morning, the sunshine overhead was warm, the rich green lawn on the course was lush and a gentle breeze was keeping them cool and comfortable. A perfect way for four men to spend the better part of a day.

"You're killing it," Chris said, shaking his head. "I'm going to apologize now for slowing the game down."

Max chuckled and patted him on the shoulder. "Don't give it a thought. It's a beautiful day, we're out in the fresh air with nothing to do but play the round, I think we'll be just fine if we're not rushing it."

"I agree," Darryl said. "Nothing like the sun and the smell of freshly mowed grass to lift your spirits."

"Not to mention," Eric added. "It's a completely legit reason to be out without constantly having to check in."

Chris regarded him and kept silent. He knew Kimberly had been especially demanding as of late, but be-damned if he was going to bring it up.

"Right," Max said, nodding at the tee box. "Eric, I believe you're up."

Eric reached into his bag for a club and Chris turned his focus to Max. He was an interesting guy. And he could tell he didn't miss much. He figured it was probably the reason Darryl had worked so hard to bring him into a partnership.

Max, from the corner of his eye, could see Chris studying him. Seemed a distraction was in order. "Tell me, Chris," he said, casually. "How long have you and Jennifer been married?"

Chris brightened. "Coming up on ten years."

Eric took his shot and then turned around, his face a picture of surprise. "Holy cow. Has it really been a decade already since you guys got married?"

"I know," Chris agreed. "Hard to believe."

Max quickly did the math; married ten years and a daughter who just turned nine. Clearly, Grace had been in attendance beneath her mother's gown.

Darryl laughed as he remembered. "You guys were so green, just starting out."

"Well, I'd say Jen was the greenest," Eric teased, stepping aside.

Chris grinned and said, to Max, "In case he's not being blatant enough, she was a couple of months pregnant with our daughter at the time."

"I gathered," he said, nodding in understanding, before stepping up to take his turn.

"God, do you remember how my Dad was when he found out?" Eric whistled. "Ready to tear you a new one, if I remember correctly."

Darryl chuckled at the memory. "George was furious! He and your Mom came to our place for dinner shortly after they'd found out and he was beside himself, pissed off that you guys had been dating for too many years and then you went and ruined his daughter's prospects. *His* words, I might add."

"That's hysterical! Classic Dad," Eric said, chuckling.

Max stayed quiet and concentrated on his shot.

"Ruined her *prospects*?" Chris repeated, adjusting the cap on his head and feigning indignation. "What did he think I was? A temporary place-holder until something better came along?"

Both Eric and Darryl burst out laughing.

He shook his fist jokingly at the sky. "Darn you, George! I *am* good enough for your daughter!"

Eric nearly fell over from mirth.

Max cleared his throat and Darryl jumped. Jeez, he thought, suddenly realizing how it must be from his perspective. But neither Eric nor Chris had any idea of the truth of things, so what could he do?

"Chris," Max said, before stepping out of the tee box. "Your shot."

Chris cringed and grabbed his club. "This is on you, you know," he said, to Eric, pointing his club at him before setting himself up to take his shot.

"Sorry about that," Darryl said, under his breath, while Eric and Chris bantered about whose fault it was that Chris was in the game.

Max adjusted his sunglasses and patted Darryl on the shoulder, much as he had Chris earlier. "No need to apologize. Conversations take on lives of their own. Nothing to be concerned about."

Darryl nodded. He still felt badly, but he knew Max meant what he said. He was made of tougher stuff.

"Okay," Chris called. "Now that I've made a mess of that, we're off."

Darryl gave one last inquiring look to Max.

He chuckled and pointed at the golf cart. "Let's get going and show these boys how it's really done."

Darryl laughed, grabbed his clubs and loaded them into the cart. Fingers crossed, they'd get through the rest of the game without a hitch.

****

"I can't believe this," Ginny said, lifting her cellphone off the patio table in her backyard. "He's sent another one."

Jan and Dixie, seated in the neighboring chairs, laughed and shook their heads.

"He's got a sizeable pair, that one," Dixie said, lifting her eyebrow up and down suggestively.

Jan grimaced. The last thing she wanted in her head was a thought about the size of Max's *pair*.

"What's he saying?" Dixie picked up her glass of lemonade and took a long swallow.

Ginny read the text then shook her head. "Apparently, the conversation has taken a turn and become a sort of a memory lane, love-fest about George."

"What?" Jan's eyebrows shot up.

"Yeah," she said, nodding. "Eric and Chris have been telling tales about George; recalling some of his funnier moments."

Jan exhaled, exasperatedly. "My god, poor Max."

Dixie nodded in agreement.

"Where the heck is my husband, anyway?" she demanded. "Why isn't he trying to change the subject?"

Ginny's phone trilled again and she read the next message. "Seems Max read your mind. He's just said Darryl has been a champ, trying to move things along, but it's no use. The boys seem to want to reminisce."

"What sort of stories, does he say?" Dixie asked, placing her cup back on the patio table and leaning back into the plump cushion on her chair.

Ginny snickered. "He did mention one."

"Go on," Jan encouraged, leaning forward in her seat.

"The time when he tried to impress me with his cooking," she said, shaking her head and giggling. "For some reason, he got it in his head to cook—"

"Not his forte, I gather?" Dixie queried.

She chortled. "Hardly. While he appreciated good food, George was definitely a man to stay *at* the table, not work in front of the oven."

"Oh, I remember this," Jan said, smiling appreciatively.

"Well, come on then," Dixie prompted, before stretching her toned, shorts-clad legs and lifting them to rest on the empty chair neighboring her own. "Don't leave me hanging."

Ginny grinned and pushed her fair hair back from her face. "He made a complete mess of it, burned the lasagna beyond recognition and there was so much smoke from the grease he had in a pan on the stovetop that our neighbor actually called the fire department!"

"No!" Dixie blurted, her eyes wide.

Jan laughed out loud at the memory. Ginny had told her the entire tale. George had been horrified, but thankfully was a good natured guy and swiftly saw the humor in it all. He'd even offered to buy the fire crew pizza for their troubles.

"He took it well, once the smoke cleared," Ginny said, a soft smile on her face as she recalled George laughing along with them. "He was a man who could laugh at himself, thank goodness."

"And he even bought pizza for the fire crew," Jan reminded her.

"That's right," Ginny said, reaching over to pat her hand. "Thanks for remembering."

Dixie pressed her palm to her chest. "What a sweetheart."

Ginny nodded. "He had his moments, for sure."

Dixie whistled and shook her head.

"What?" Ginny looked at her expectantly.

She shrugged. "Oh, nothing. Except that it sounds like Max has some sizeable shoes to fill and by the end of that golf game, he's really going to know it."

Ginny blinked. She'd never thought of it that way. Her phone trilled yet again and she used it as an excuse not to respond to her comment.

"Max, again?" Jan asked.

"Uh-huh." She read the text and grinned.

Dixie watched her face and noted something there besides amusement. "What?"

Ginny read it out loud, "*Seems you were married to one hell of a guy. Not surprised, really. You're amazing, so it only stands to reason George was as well. BTW, your son is like his Dad. xoxo.*"

Dixie and Jan both went, "awe" and Ginny grinned foolishly, blinking back unexpected tears. *He* was one hell of a man, too.

\*\*\*\*

Ginny finished updating the library website, hit 'save' and pulled her reading glasses off her face. She blinked a few times then peered at the clock on the wall. One hour to go. One hour until she was done her shift and could be off to meet Max at home. Oooh, she liked the sound of that, even if it was just in her thoughts. Home.

"So, listen," Tamara said, as she strode behind the library desk, interrupting Ginny's mental musings.

She turned around in her chair, her face expectant. "What's up?"

"I have a favor to ask and I hope you'll say yes."

"Okay," she said, leaning back and folding her arms across her chest. "I'm all ears. Hit me."

Tamara slid a pile of books on the edge of the desktop out of toppling range and leaned up against the vacated space. "Okay, so, Kate has a friend who's a dance teacher and she's going to be having an open house at her studio and she asked Kate if she could spread the word and bring in new people."

"Okay, and?"

"*And* I was wondering if you and Max might be interested in coming along to learn a few new steps, that sort of thing."

"Oh," Ginny said, nodding and processing the information. "What sort of dancing?"

"Ballroom." She turned around and began sorting the pile of books she'd pushed aside. "She's a fantastic teacher and her classes are an absolute blast. That's why she has open house nights here and there; to give people a chance to check out her studio and try her out without any obligation."

Ginny grinned. She liked the idea. It sounded like fun.

Tamara stopped sorting and turned back to face Ginny. "Do you think Max would be game?"

"I have no idea, but I think it sounds like fun," Ginny commented, airing her thoughts. "I'll pass it by him and see what he thinks. Can I ask a couple of other friends to come along, too?"

Tamara's face lit up and she clapped her hands. "Absolutely! The more the merrier. Once you know how many you might bring, I'll tell Kate. She'll be ecstatic."

Ginny unlocked the cabinet beneath the desk and pulled out her purple, leather purse. She fished around inside it for her cellphone. "I'll send a few texts right now," she said, pulling it out and setting her purse back inside the cabinet. "What day?"

"Next weekend, actually." Tamara tugged a blue scrunchie from around her wrist and used it to secure her hair up off her face in a haphazard bun. "Saturday night, doors open at six."

Ginny nodded and began typing on the phone. "I'm going to ask Max when I see him after work, and I'll ask Jan and her husband, as well as Dixie and the guy she's just started dating."

"She's the one who tags you in all her Facebook photos, right?"

Ginny chuckled. "Yes, that's her."

"Excellent," Tamara gushed. "Tell her to bring her phone and take as many photos as she wants."

Ginny sent her text off to Jan then started on another to Dixie. This would definitely qualify as something new in their quest to continue trying things they hadn't done before. She was sure, if she was able to see his face, George would be smiling encouragingly; thrilled she was embracing the life she had while she still had it.

\*\*\*\*

Kimberly stood on Ginny's front porch, pressed the doorbell and waited.

She glanced around, noting the wooden railing that fenced the porch and the shutters on the windows could use a new coat of paint. She'd have to mention it to Eric. Maybe he and Chris could schedule time to get it done before autumn fully took hold and it was too cold.

She looked back at the door, frowning when it remained closed. Ginny's car was in the driveway - which astounded her, considering it was an Audi A6 and belonged safely stowed in the garage - so she had to be home.

She clutched her small, black purse under her arm and pressed the bell a second time, hearing it resonate inside the house. Nothing followed. No sounds of activity or footsteps nearing the door.

"Oh, come on," she muttered, then gave up and decided to try around back. Maybe her mother-in-law was working in her garden. It was a lovely afternoon and it was highly likely she was enjoying the sunshine while she puttered around the yard.

She walked down the porch steps and followed the path to the side gate, but was stopped in her tracks by a high-pitched, "Yoohoo!" coming from down the street.

"Oh, crap," Kimberly muttered, recognizing the voice. She took a breath then turned around and, sure enough, there was the neighbor, Dana, Dannie, Donnie... something like that, bearing down on her like a heat-seeking missile.

"Kimmy!" Donna called, waving her hand over her head as though flagging down aircraft.

Kimberly clenched her teeth; she hated being called *Kimmy*.

"Are you stopping in to see Ginny?" Donna asked, pressing her hand to her side, slightly out of breath from her power walk.

"Yes," Kimberly said, holding back from asking why the hell else would she be at Ginny's house, if not to see her? Instead she said, "You have no shoes."

Donna looked down at her naked feet beneath the length of her multi-colored, ankle length skirt and chortled. "Nope. Just me and Mother Earth communing."

Kimberly cleared her throat in an effort to keep her thoughts to herself.

"I'm sure she's home," Donna said, gesturing to Ginny's car, parked in the driveway. "I saw her arrive not too long ago."

"Right," Kimberly said, taking a step closer to the gate. "Thanks."

"Do you like crab apples?"

Kimberly paused, her hand outstretched for the gate. "Pardon?"

"Crab apples," Donna repeated. "Are you or your husband fans?"

"I've never thought about it," Kimberly said, placing her hand on the gate and giving it a push.

"'Cause our three trees out back are going to be dropping them soon," Donna explained, her hands flitting about like wildfire as she spoke. "We'll happily give some to Ginny to pass along to you and your family."

"Oh," Kimberly said, stepping through the opening and onto the other side of the gate and letting it swing shut. "That's very kind, thanks."

Donna turned on her naked heel and waved as she started walking back to her house. "Not a problem," she called, over her shoulder. "Tell Ginny I'll check in later."

Kimberly watched her charge away and disappear from sight, almost as though she'd never been there. A seriously odd duck, she thought, then resumed her original course of action, following the cobblestone path around the exterior of Ginny's house to the backyard.

\*\*\*\*

"Ginny? You out here?" Kimberly called, as she passed by the tall hedges lining the path to the backyard.

She walked further into the yard with the expectation of finding her mother-in-law at work in her flowerbeds and, instead, found... nothing. She scratched her head, flummoxed. Ginny's car was in the driveway and Dana-

Dannie-Donnie - although a questionable witness - said she'd seen her arrive not that long ago, and yet it seemed she was nowhere to be found.

Now what, Kimberly thought, tucking her hair behind her ears and tapping her foot on the path. Did she just leave or... wait a minute, maybe Ginny had gone back inside while Dana-Dannie-Donnie had been prattling on about crab apples. She snapped her fingers, that made sense, and decided to take one more stab at knocking at the door. She turned around, set on retracing her footsteps, when a movement from the kitchen window caught her eye. Ah-ha, she thought, it looked like she'd been correct and she'd just missed Ginny as she relocated from the garden back to the house.

Another shadow passed behind the sheer yellow curtains that covered the window and Kimberly reflexively dropped down into a crouch. Suddenly, the idea of being caught standing on the path in the garden felt embarrassing. As though she'd have to explain why she was there, instead of at the front door. She shuffled closer to the wall, no easy feat in black ballet flats and pink and blue patterned knee length skirt, feeling completely foolish and wracking her brain for a way to get out of the house's shadow and subsequent yard without being seen.

She'd have to peek inside, she thought. That was the answer. She could peek through the window, make sure Ginny wasn't in the kitchen and *then* dash away from the house and around to the front without being seen. She gave herself a mental pat on the back for her quick thinking then edged up to the windowpane and cautiously craned her neck forward to look into the room.

"What the hell?" Kimberly blurted, shocked to see that Ginny wasn't just home, but dressed only in a short black slip and flitting around the room. If she didn't know better, she would have said her mother-in-law was dancing. She had her hands out before her as though draped on an invisible man and was twirling and dipping, stepping and shuffling; all the while grinning and talking to an imaginary partner.

Kimberly was gob smacked and didn't know what on Earth to make of it.

"What the hell," she muttered, again, under her breath, peering a second time through the curtains to make sure she wasn't imagining what she was seeing.

Ginny, meanwhile, completely unaware she had an audience, continued to put on a show. The music changed to something that sounded a lot like pop-country and she reached out to the boom box on her console, turned up the volume and started to do a two-step with the same imaginary partner.

"*That's* why she didn't hear the doorbell," Kimberly said, nodding. Now it made sense. Or, at least *that* part made sense.

"Okay," she said, to herself, squaring her shoulders. Now that she'd confirmed for herself she'd seen what she'd thought she'd seen, she had to take some sort of action, get some sort of proof or Eric would never, ever believe her when she told him.

Kimberly hated herself for her next thought, but she knew she had no choice. It was this, or just sit back and do nothing until it was too late. She reached into her purse and pulled out her phone. Taking a breath, she aimed it at the window and pressed record.

****

Eric watched Kimberly bustle around their kitchen, making sure everyone had their coffee and cake. He knew her inability to sit still was caused by a case of nerves, which had surfaced in direct correlation to the fact that they were all together solely because she'd insisted they call a family meeting and, even more poignant, it was *her* actions that had inspired the need for their gathering in the first place. She'd dubbed their meeting *Operation Intervention* in an effort to lighten the mood, but it still remained that Jennifer and Chris were in their kitchen, and Brian was attending via webcam, for one reason: to figure out what sort of action they should take with Ginny.

"Hey, Bri," Eric said, smiling at his younger brother on the webcam of his laptop.

Brian grinned back and waved. "Hey, bro. Jen, you're all looking good."

"And Chris is here, too," Jennifer added.

"Hey, Bri," Chris called out from the armchair in the adjacent family room. He'd chosen to keep out of the immediate fray and just be there for backup should Jennifer need it.

"Chris!" Brian called back. "How's work?"

"Still digging in the dirt and getting paid for it," he quipped, making Brian chuckle.

"Okay," Kimberly said, clearing her throat and sitting down in the chair next to Eric.

"Oh, hey Kim," Brian said. "Didn't see you there."

"I was getting cake for everyone."

"What kind is this?" Jennifer asked, picking up her fork from the table.

"Chocolate miracle whip," Kimberly replied, lifting an eyebrow as she referred to Ginny's recipe. "Seemed *fitting*, considering why we're all here."

"Right, about that," Brian said, shrugging his shoulders. "I still don't get what the big deal is, about Mom."

"Did you watch the video I sent?" she asked, tightly.

He frowned. "Yeah. And I still think what you did was seriously odd. She'd be fucking furious if she knew."

Eric winced and exchanged a look with Jennifer. Brian always shot straight from the hip and didn't give a flip if it caused upset.

"What else was I supposed to do?" Kimberly insisted, leaning slightly to her right, her shoulder pressed up against Eric's to better see Brian on the screen. "You all wouldn't have believed me, otherwise."

"Yeah, see, that's the part I'm not getting," he said, sitting back in his chair. "What am I supposed to be *believing*, exactly?"

"I think Kim's concerned—" Jennifer started to say then Kimberly jumped in to talk across her.

"She might be slipping," she said, briskly.

Jennifer put her fork down and stayed silent. When the woman got an idea in her head, you just had to let her get it all out or you'd never get a word in edgewise.

"Slipping?" Brian's face took on a look of amusement.

"Yes," Kimberly stated. "And it's our job to make sure she's taken care of."

"Slipping how? Into some sort of dementia?"

"It's possible," she retorted, her foot starting to twitch underneath the table. "She was having a dinner for two at her house not that long ago and it was painfully obvious there was just her, on her own. Didn't Eric tell you about that?"

"Maybe she was dining with Martini?" Brian offered, wryly. "He counts, doesn't he?"

She rolled her eyes and picked up her fork.

"Did you happen to notice if there were extra cans of salmon on the countertop?" he continued, smirking as he warmed to his theme. "'Cause she may have been expecting a whole cat crew and they were going to eat family style and then do a few dance numbers—"

"Enough!"

Brian shut up and his eyebrows shot up when Kimberly shouted and slammed her fork back onto the table. It was the first time he'd ever heard her raise her voice.

"Kim," Eric said, soothingly. "Bri was just—"

"My father is having an affair!" she blurted, wild-eyed, jumping up from her seat.

Jennifer looked across the room at Chris, their expressions twisted into mirror images of shock.

Eric's jaw dropped. Now? She was finally going to talk about it now?

"Umm," Brian said, trying to act as though it was the first he'd heard of it. "Are you sure?"

She shot daggers at him. "Of course I am! And it's so god-damned out of character, we're starting to think he may have had a mini stroke!"

"Okay, let's just all take a moment," Eric coached, trying to reel things back in. "Everybody breathe."

She whirled around and leaned over him. "I haven't said anything further to you until now because I didn't want to put the cart before the horse, but Kris messaged me and confirmed it's true. He came clean."

"Jeez," he said, sympathetically. "Hon—"

"Save it," she cut him off, straightening her spine and brushing her hair back from her face. "*Now* will you finally take what I've been saying seriously? How do you people know that's not what happened to your Mom."

"What? A stroke?" Jennifer said, a hand pressed to her chest as though she'd been slugged.

Kimberly softened her tone. "Well, not necessarily that, but *something* she's not sharing. She's been doing such odd things for the past few months, she's been cagey, she's made comments about living life while you still have it…"

"Still," Jennifer rallied and waved her hand dismissively, "no way. She'd say something if there was actually something wrong."

"Yeah," Brian agreed, backing her up. "No way."

Kimberly's jaw tightened and she narrowed her eyes at him.

"I'm not saying it's not worth checking up on her," he clarified, holding his hands up in an offering of peaceful relations. "I just think it's probably not something that severe, you know? She seemed fine when I spoke to her, just under the weather."

"You actually *spoke* to her?" Kimberly lurched forward and nearly shoved Eric off of his seat as she jockeyed to get directly in front of the camera.

"Jeez," he said, sticking his foot out to regain his balance.

Kimberly ignored him and said, "When?"

Brian shrugged. "I don't know, a few days ago?"

Eric exchanged a look with Jennifer and she spoke up. "And she was under the weather when you talked to her? How? Like a bit of the sniffles, or something more?"

"I don't know, I guess I'd say a bit more than just sniffles. She was coughing quite a bit and blowing her nose." He frowned and asked, "Why? Why does that matter?"

"Because she's been keeping all of us at arm's length, is why," she told him. "Ever since Grace's party, we've barely seen or heard from her."

"Other than dancing around her kitchen with her imaginary friend," Chris offered, then clamped his mouth shut when Kimberly snapped her head around to glare at him.

"Be honest, do you think she was hiding something, Bri?" Jennifer asked, bluntly, a shot of nerves crawling up her spine and making her shiver.

Brian's face screwed up and he leaned forward toward the camera. "Hiding something? What does *that* mean? What the hell would she be hiding?"

"This is not good, not good at all," Kimberly said, standing up again to pace the kitchen floor. "First the strange behavior stuff, then the secretiveness, then the comments about carpe diem and now she's so sick she's staying under quarantine? Not good at all."

"Okay," Eric said, holding his hands up like a crossing guard. "Let's not get ahead of ourselves and make things even bigger than they might be."

"Yeah," Brian agreed, then said directly to Kimberly, "while I'm sorry about your Dad, Kim, we don't need to lump our Mom in with that shit."

Kimberly offered no reply, just sat back down and picked up her fork to attack her cake. No one else had touched theirs, except for Chris lounging in the family room, and while it probably wasn't as good as something Ginny would have made before she'd gone off the rails, she wasn't going to let it all go to waste.

"Okay," Eric said, again, wanting to keep them on track. "So, with everything we've said, it sounds like we need to talk to Mom as a group and get things out in the open."

"Agreed," Jennifer said.

Brian nodded and leaned back into his chair. "Fine. I'll book a flight out. See you in a couple of days."

****

Ginny pulled on her thick, yellow fleece dressing gown, tucked her feet into her fuzzy, pink slippers and padded slowly down the hallway toward the family room. When the doorbell first sounded, she'd debated upon whether to leave it or get up to answer it. When it rang a second time, getting up to answer it won.

"Coming," she called out, hoarsely, before sneezing so effusively she made herself light-headed.

She paused to pull a tissue from the box on the coffee table in the family room and blew her nose with gusto as the bell sounded a third time.

"Okay, alright, I'm here," she said, finally reaching the door and pulling it open. "What happened, I thought…" she continued, before tapering off and shutting her mouth when she saw all three of her children, and their spouses, standing on the porch.

"*Ohmygod*," Jennifer said, her brow creasing when she laid eyes on Ginny.

Granted, she wasn't exactly model perfect, her hair was ratty and unwashed, she wasn't wearing a scrap of makeup on her pale face and her nose was pink and chapped from all of the blowing she'd been doing since she'd developed her head cold. But, still, '*ohmygod*' was a bit over the top and not exactly flattering.

"What's happened? Why are you all here?" Ginny asked, ignoring Jennifer's comment.

Instead of answering her, Eric led the charge into the house followed by Kimberly, Jennifer, Chris and Brian.

"Brian?" Ginny said, when they'd all brushed past her and she'd closed the door against the damp night air. "What are you doing here? You never told me you were coming for a visit."

"That's because I didn't know I needed to come, until a couple of days ago," he replied, his voice aggravated and accusing while he took off his shoes.

Ginny coughed then sneezed loudly and they all looked at her in alarm. "Oh, for goodness sake," she said, reaching into her dressing gown pocket for another tissue. "What on Earth is going on with you all? You look like you've seen a ghost. Or you're at a funeral."

"Oh, gawd," Kimberly moaned, slipping her ballet flats from her feet and averting her eyes.

"What?" Ginny said, her pulse quickening. "What aren't you telling me? Is it Jan?"

"No, no, everyone's fine." Kimberly shook her head then gasped, pointing, "But, *you…*"

Ginny tightened the sash on her robe and tried to look indignant as she wiped her nose. "There's no need to be cruel, I *know* I look a sight. If you all would have called first, I could have told you not to come over."

"Clearly, we *had* to come," Jennifer said, sternly, her mouth set in a line while she dropped her purse with a thud on to the foyer floor. "You can't be all alone at a time like *this*."

Ginny's eyebrows scrunched together as she looked into their intense faces. "*This*, what? What are you talking about?"

Eric sighed and ran his fingers through his hair. "Stop it, Mom. Just stop it."

Another wave of light headedness drifted over Ginny and she walked gingerly into the family room, the five of them in tow.

"Jeez, Mom," Jennifer said, speeding to her side as she shuffled over to the sofa and sat down with a groan. "Are you okay?"

Ginny shrugged her shoulders "I've been better. But what I want to know is, what is this thing I'm supposed to stop doing. Eric, explain."

"You've been putting us off for weeks and now *look* at you," he said, while the other four nodded in agreement.

Jennifer sat down in the adjacent arm chair, ready, in case her mother suddenly toppled over. Martini sauntered around the corner of the doorway into the family room then stopped in his tracks when he saw them all there.

"I have not been *putting you off*. I *told* you," Ginny began, before Eric cut her off.

"No, stop it. It's *obvious* to all of us something is going on. Just tell us, so we can deal with it."

Martini resumed his course toward Ginny while she blinked in confusion. She looked at the five of them, all tense as though readying themselves for a blow, and then it hit her. "Oh my goodness. Have you all got it into your heads I'm hiding something serious? Like a terminal illness, or some such thing?"

"Aren't you?" Kimberly said, confrontation lacing her words while she crossed her arms tightly across her chest.

"No, I'm not." She blew her nose into a tissue at the same time the cat jumped up onto the sofa beside her and the sound of the back door opening came from her kitchen.

Eric turned his head, his eyebrows raised. "What was that? Was that your back door?"

"Oh, hell," she sighed, slumping back into the cushions. "I'm too tired for all of this. Enough hiding and worrying. You may as well know the truth. It was going to happen at one point, so now is as good a time as any."

"I *KNEW* it. All this time and you all didn't believe me," Kimberly said, righteously, pointing her finger at them.

"Okay, okay," Jennifer said, waving her hand dismissively at her sister-in-law, while keeping a keen eye on Ginny in case she passed out. "No need to be such a bloody know-it-all before we even know what's what."

Brian looked at her, impressed, and reached out to pat her on the shoulder. "You tell her, sis," he said, grinning.

Eric, meanwhile, looked past all of them and said, "What the hell?" interrupting the childish battle of words being thrown back and forth.

Both women, along with Chris and Brian, turned around to see what had earned his statement and found Max standing tall in the family room doorway, a bag of groceries in his arms. Martini leaped from the couch and dashed across the floor to greet him while he grinned at the group and winked at Ginny. "I'm home."

\*\*\*\*

Ginny dragged her voluminous sage green comforter over her body and tucked it around her shoulders then heaved a heavy sigh as she relaxed, finally, back in bed. She reached one hand out from under the covers to pull a tissue from the box beside her and blew her nose, pausing to hear the sound of the front door closing with a solid thump. Silence. Thank goodness. Compared to the last hour of chaotic, raised voices that had filled her sitting room, it was blessed peace.

She laid her head on her pillow and closed her eyes, only to feel a twinge of guilt she'd pretty much left Max to deal with everything. She could have done more, said more, but her head cold had wiped her out and besides, she silently consoled herself, he was a businessman. He made his living handling people.

The door to the bedroom opened and Max walked in, Martini at his heels, smile curving his lips. "Hey, beautiful, you're awake. How're you feeling?"

Ginny blew her nose again, by way of reply, while Martini sprang up onto the bed and curled up at her feet.

Max chuckled and reached out to gently smooth her hair from her forehead. "That good, huh?"

"I'm so sorry I left you to deal with the histrionics," she began, before he held up his hand to stop her.

"Don't give it a thought," he said, sitting down beside her and propping a pillow up against the headboard to lean back on. "It was probably better that way, anyway. They were bound to be more civil with a near stranger."

Ginny raised an eyebrow. Civil was the last word she'd have used when she thought of the chatter she'd heard coming through the bedroom door. More like a ranting group of monkeys.

After he'd announced he was 'home' there had been a brief moment of silence then the floodgates had opened; all three of her children had started firing questions and accusations left, right and center. Eric, being the oldest, had led the charge with, "What the hell is going on here, Max? I golf with you, you go to my sister's house for my niece's birthday and it never once seems appropriate to mention you call my mother's house *home*?"

Jennifer, quick on his heels, had folded her arms tightly across her chest and glared as she said, "Mom? Explanation, please."

Even Brian, the youngest of her brood and the most easygoing, had looked gob smacked at the appearance of Max and had sputtered, "Home? Who the hell *is* this guy? What the fuck does *that* mean?"

Ginny had wanted to slap his mouth at that. Such profanity in her house. He knew better.

Finally, Kimberly, never one to keep her trap shut for long, had fired off, "So tell us, Ginny, is this another one of your new *fun* things you've been doing?"

Ginny closed her eyes and sniffled noisily. She wasn't proud of herself, but when she'd seen their righteous faces she'd been disgusted. So much so that she'd turned to Max and said, "I can't deal with this now, I'm way too tired."

And bless his soul, he'd smiled adoringly at her and said, "You head back to bed, sweetheart. I've got this."

And he did.

Ginny had listened to him take the front line and answer their questions without the slightest bit of hesitation, nervousness or apology. He'd told the truth, that they'd been dating for quite some time and while, yes, it had been kept quiet, it was because their mother wasn't yet ready to go public and he'd fully supported her feelings. He was a calm spot in a sea of turmoil.

And when Jennifer had piped up and demanded to know his *intentions*, which had struck Ginny as humorous, she'd held her breath when she needn't have; he was calm under pressure and had told Jennifer he cared very deeply for her mother and intended to be in her life as long as she'd have him.

Ginny had sighed at that and snuggled further under the duvet. A perfect reply.

Brian, meanwhile, still caught up on Max's revelation of being 'home', had asked hesitantly if he was residing there. Ginny had braced herself yet again, but Max had kept things smooth and easy there, too. He'd simple explained he was in Boxwood Hills on business and while he was boarding at a hotel, he'd spent so much time at the house over the past few weeks he'd started affectionately calling it home.

Kimberly, right in character, had thrown out the final attempt to rattle his calm, but had failed as well. She'd more or less accused him of gold digging and Max, after he'd stopped laughing, had assured her he was interested in her mother-in-law for reasons that had nothing to do with her financial status. He'd said it so intimately that, in the silence that followed, Ginny had a strong feeling Kimberly had blushed to her roots.

Chris, while in attendance, had stayed mute. It appeared her lovely son-in-law was the only one in the room who felt they were overstepping their bounds with their inquisition and she adored him for it. Jennifer had snagged a good one there.

Finally, when the proverbial dust had settled, Max had firmly informed her children that she would be available to talk with them further once she was over her head cold. He'd also informed them they need not worry for a moment about her, as he was taking full-time care of her until she was back to her healthy self. After that, he'd sent them all on their way and Ginny had experienced a wave of appreciation wash over her like a soothing warm bath. She'd never before had any support when it came to her kids and their emotional issues. George, while strong in many ways, had always been absent when it came to affairs of the heart. It was thrilling beyond measure to experience just the opposite from Max.

"You were a rock star," Ginny said, simply, turning her head on her pillow to smile at him.

He grinned and reached over to gently tuck the covers around her. "As long as you think so, that's all that matters."

"I do," she said, closing her eyes.

"Right. Then the thing for you to do is listen to this rock star."

"Which means?"

"Three things," he told her, holding up his hand to count off on his fingers. "One, you must get some rest. Two, eat the delicious and health-packed soup I'm going to make for you. And, three, know that I love you."

Ginny's mind went still. It was the first time he'd said it. She opened her eyes to look at him and said, "Even after my kids were so much trouble?"

He laughed and sat forward. "Even more so. They're great people, Gin. And their concern for you is just further evidence of what an amazing mother you've been. Kids don't come together like that unless they've been shown how to do so. That's all you."

Tears prickled at the back of Ginny's eyes. She never would have thought she'd hear a man tell her he loved her again. Who knew life had more in store for her? She reached out to grasp his hand and smiled up at him. "I love you, too."

# Chapter Twenty-Seven

"I have to admit, I'm nervous," Jennifer said, pausing in folding the piles of freshly washed laundry strewn across the bed.

It had been a week since their last visit, or *invasion*, to her mother's house and they were planning to go over again; this time invited. Eric and Kimberly had also been invited and while she was happy they could, hopefully, use the gathering to smooth the proverbial waters of their last overstep, she was still wracked with butterflies as to how it was all going to go down once they were actually there in person.

Chris, beside her pairing up socks, reached out to stroke her dark hair and said, "I'm sure it's all going to be fine."

She shrugged and picked up a pair of Grace's jeans. "We were all pretty pushy and aggressive the last time we were there. Well, all of us except for *you*, mister stay-out-of-it."

Chris smirked and continued pairing socks.

Jennifer saw his face and smiled in return, before adding, "What if he thinks we're all terrible people and Mom ends up wanting nothing to do with us for being so rude?"

Chris laughed as he moved onto sorting their undergarments into individual piles. "Not a chance. Your Mom loves you guys more than anything else. Even if she was miffed, she's level-headed and will take it in stride."

"Do you think he'll be there?"

"Who, Max?"

Jennifer wrinkled her nose. She was still having trouble referring to him by name. Especially when she had flashbacks to the way he'd informed Kimberly of his *reasons* for being interested in her Mom. The undertones had been unmistakably intimate and steamy and she squirmed in discomfort at what they clearly implied. The mere *idea* of her mother with her father had been bad enough. The reality of her getting physical with that healthy, virile man in her family room was a whole other pill to swallow.

Chris snickered when he saw her face.

"What?" she said, putting down Grace's folded jeans and starting on her t-shirts.

Chris tossed the last pair of Mason's *Superman* underpants into his pile then replied, "I know what you're thinking and, trust me, you're going to have to not just get used to Max being around, but also to saying his name. From what I saw at your Mom's house, he's not going anywhere unless he's told point blank to hit the bricks." He shrugged and added, "Even then, I'd bet money he'd try to change your Mom's mind. He's in *deep*."

Jennifer shuddered at the double-entendre the word *deep* implied and Chris couldn't help himself and laughed at her reaction.

She smacked his shoulder and said, "Jerk."

He heard the amusement in her tone and laughed some more.

"Anyway," she said, taking a breath. "It comes down to one thing, if he's what she wants then I'll be supportive."

Chris stopped chuckling and looked at her with respect. "I know you will. This whole thing has come as a shock to all of us, but I know you'll do the right thing and support your Mom and I'll be right behind you every step of the way."

She looked him in the eye, now knowing what *he* was thinking. "Especially when it comes to Kimberly."

He raised an eyebrow and nodded. "Exactly."

****

Kimberly lathered soap into Layla's lunch dishes then started scrubbing as though her life depended upon it.

Eric, sitting in the family room with Layla snuggled on his lap while she watched *Bubble Guppies* on the TV, observed her working and asked, "Something wrong, Hon?"

Kimberly stopped her assault on the plastic bowl in her hand and took a calming breath. "No, just want to get this done. The sitter should be here in about twenty minutes and that will give her about a half hour before she can put Layla down for her nap."

"Right," he agreed. "Sounds good."

Kimberly put the bowl in the draining board and squeezed out the sponge. "I can't imagine what your mother has in mind with this gathering."

Eric heard the edge in her voice and chose his words carefully. "She's feeling better. Max said she'd be in touch when she was feeling better. I guess that means she wants to talk to us all face-to-face, now that she's feeling better."

She turned around, her face intense. "See, that's the thing. Talk to us about what?"

Eric ran his fingers through his hair. Clearly, repeating himself over and over throughout the course of the morning hadn't worked to diffuse things as he'd hoped. He wasn't sure what else to say.

"What I mean is," Kimberly clarified, while reaching into the cupboard for a glass. "What can she tell us that we can't already see for ourselves?"

"I don't know," he said, shrugging his shoulders as she poured herself some water from the tap then walked around the island and into the family room.

"Clearly, she's having some sort of latent reaction to your Dad's absence and taken *that man* in to...," she pursed her lips together in a grimace and sat down on the armchair adjacent to the sofa.

Eric's stomach rolled at the idea of what his mom was *doing* with Max, too. He wasn't going to admit it out loud, but the idea of them being anything other than movie watching buddies was seriously unsettling. And, judging from the way Max had spoken about her when confronted on his intentions, he was pretty sure they were doing a whole lot *more* than just watching movies.

"It's gross," Kimberly stated, matter of fact, then drank her water.

"Gross!" Layla parroted, taking her eyes from the TV screen to grin at her mother.

Kimberly snickered and nodded. "Yes, mademoiselle, it is. Gramma is being gross, gross, gross, trying to have some sort of romantic tryst. That's not proper Granny behavior at all."

"Gramma gross," Layla repeated.

"Hey, hey," Eric said, frowning at Kimberly. He didn't like the example she was setting, even if it was highly probably Layla didn't understand. "We're not starting to teach that sort of thing, are we? Setting her up to be some sort of mean-mouthed kid?"

Kimberly had the decency to look contrite.

"Gramma is good," he said, hoping she'd repeat him. "Good Gramma."

Nothing. Her attention was captured again by *Bubble Guppies* on the screen.

"Good one," he said, disgustedly, at his wife. "Nice thing to teach."

She squirmed in her seat. "Okay, sorry about that, I wasn't thinking. But, I'm still right. This whole situation is... *unpleasant*."

"Still," Eric said, shaking his head and gently setting Layla onto the empty cushion beside him. Her attention didn't waver from the TV.

Kimberly got up from her seat and followed him into the kitchen, refusing to be deterred. "We both know the whole idea of this... this... I don't know, *relationship*, is absurd. She's sixty two years old, for goodness sake! She should act her age. Act appropriately. Not like some hormonally charged teenager."

Eric listened and kept his opinions to himself. His feelings about his mom aside, he wouldn't have been upset if Kimberly had suddenly gotten back in touch with her teenage hormones. She'd been nothing but prickly for a good long while and he missed the way she used to be. He thought for a moment about how she'd been before Layla: playful, warm, welcoming, and felt a *stirring* in his groin.

"I mean, seriously," she said, placing her empty water glass into the dishwasher. "Did you *see* the way *he* looked when he spoke about your mom? It was so, you know... s-e-x-u-a-l. Ugg."

Eric exhaled as the *stirring* came to a jarring halt. Her blatant disgust was like a sharp, cold shower.

The doorbell rang and Kimberly smoothed the non-existent creases from the front of her caramel colored, knee length pencil skirt. "That'll be her," she said, referring to their babysitter.

Eric nodded and strode from the room. "I'll get it," he said, glad to have the excuse to claim some distance.

**** 

Jan looked up from where she was cutting up watermelon, when the doorbell sounded. She wiped her fingers on a towel and asked Ginny, "Want me to get that?"

Ginny smiled appreciatively. "Do you mind?"

"Not at all," Jan said, laying the knife in her hand on the kitchen island. "Dix, can you finish this?"

Dixie nodded and put her glass of wine down on the table. "Yup."

Jan strode out of the kitchen and Ginny looked at Dixie and said, "I'm actually a little bit nervous."

Dixie patted her arm before she got to work slicing up the remaining watermelon. "It will be fine. We're all here to run interference, if necessary, but I doubt we'll need to."

Ginny took a breath and nodded while the sound of Jan greeting her kids at the door drifted through the house. The backdoor opened as well and Max walked in with Darryl and Hamish in tow.

"How are things going in here?" he asked, wrapping his arms around Ginny's waist from behind and kissing her on the cheek. "Need our help for anything?"

Ginny grinned and blushed, still alternately thrilled they could be open about their relationship in public and a little shy about doing so.

"*You* can deal with these melons," Dixie said, pointing the knife she was using at Hamish and, consequently, making everyone laugh.

And that's how her kids found Ginny when they followed Jan into the kitchen; in Max's embrace and surrounded by the laughter of her friends. A good start to the afternoon? Only time would tell.

****

Ginny stood in the middle of the kitchen facing the table where Eric, Kimberly, Jennifer and Chris had settled with drinks at their fingertips. Jan, Dixie, Darryl, Hamish and Max were seated in the dining room as planned, close enough to be available for support, just not hanging over Ginny's shoulders.

"So," she said, fully aware she was going to be in charge of opening the conversation. "First I want to say, I'm sorry this all came as such a shock. I truly didn't intend for it to happen that way, but circumstances ran away with us and it has, so now we have to move forward."

"I have a question," Kimberly interrupted, holding up her hand.

Ginny paused and looked at her daughter-in-law.

"Let her finish, first," Jennifer said, frowning.

"It's okay," Ginny said, patting the air in front of herself calmingly. "What is it, Kimberly?"

She shot Jennifer a triumphant look then put down her hand and cleared her throat. "What do you mean by *it* happened? What is the *it* you're talking about, exactly?"

Jan exchanged a look with Dixie at the impertinence of the question. Was it really necessary Ginny spell things out so blatantly?

"Umm," Ginny said, searching for the words to politely answer the question.

"I can take this one," Max said, standing up and striding into the kitchen to stand beside her.

Ginny grinned at him, strong, sturdy, handsome and bright-eyed, while the four of them at the table immediately looked slightly wrong-footed. Well, that wasn't entirely true. Only three of them looked like that. Chris' face was as relaxed and open-minded as it had been when he'd first entered the house and given her a warm hug.

"Wait a sec," Max said, suddenly. "Aren't we missing someone? Where's Brian?"

"He's not coming." Eric said. "He had to get back for work, he only had last weekend."

"It's fine," Ginny said, still smiling at Max. "I spoke to him this morning, while you were out. We had a nice chat and he's up to speed on everything."

"He never told me," Eric commented, slightly put out.

"I asked him not to," she said, simply.

Jennifer raised her eyebrows at her brother, but said nothing.

"So, *anyway*," Ginny proceeded. "Your question, Kimberly, about what *it* is between Max and I?"

She offered no reply. The truth was, she'd asked the question to put her mother-in-law on the spot and, hopefully, make her realize they had rights to answers. Now, however, that Max was stepping into the conversation, she just felt uncomfortable and wished she'd kept her mouth shut.

"Right, that," Max said, rubbing his hands together and focusing directly on Eric and Jennifer. "Since Ginny is your mother, seems only right I address this to the two of you."

They nodded, neither of them wanting to speak for fear of getting all of the attention.

"It's simple. I'm in love with your mother."

They wore identical expressions of shock while, in the adjacent dining room, Jan and Dixie squealed at hearing the revelation.

"She knows how I feel about her," he continued, glancing at Ginny with open adoration before returning his attention to them. "As does anyone else who knows about the two of us. Turns out I'm a bit verbose when it comes to matters of the heart."

Darryl coughed and Hamish, seated between him and Dixie at the dining room table, laughed. Both he and Darryl had been Max's sounding board during the time everything was being kept hush-hush.

Kimberly opened and closed her mouth silently, like a fish. She was suddenly wishing she'd asked for something stronger than coffee.

Chris nodded, and lifted his wineglass in a silent toast to Max, his expression approving.

"I first laid eyes on her when I went into the library where she works. Then I kept on going back, but every time I was there I lost my nerve to approach her." He chuckled and ran his fingers through his thick hair. "It wasn't until the fortuitous gathering at Jan and Darryl's home a few months back that we were thrown together and I had a chance to pluck up the courage and ask her out for dinner."

"You've been dating *that* long?" Jennifer blinked, digesting the information.

Ginny shrugged. "I didn't want to say anything prematurely. You've all been through so much with your dear father passing, I wasn't about to bring Max into the picture unless what we had was something worth talking about."

"And you think it is?" Kimberly, tight-lipped, folded her arms across her chest.

Ginny looked at Max, her face softening. "Without a doubt."

Jan and Dixie shared a grin and clinked their wineglasses together.

"And, let me guess, the rest is history?" Eric said, while Kimberly rolled her eyes.

"Or the beginning of the future," Ginny offered.

"Amen," Jan said, raising her glass a second time for her best friend.

Jennifer nodded, thoughtfully, while Chris put his arm around her shoulders. She wanted her mother to be happy, it was just taking a moment to get up to speed.

"Well, while everyone is trying to make this out to be all warm and fuzzy, I'll say again what I said before to my daughter. I think this whole thing is gross."

Jennifer snapped her head around to gape at her sister-in-law. "Kimberly! My god, what a thing to say!"

Jan and Dixie joined in, muttering irritated comments under their breath and being patted down by Darryl and Hamish so as to avoid an all-out brawl.

"Whatever," Kimberly said, refusing to be made guilty. "It's how I feel and I, just like *them*, have a right to express it."

"Okay, okay, everyone just calm down," Ginny patted the air, again. She seemed to do a lot of that when her daughter-in-law spoke her mind.

Max, instead of being bothered by Kimberly's statement, cocked his head and asked, curious, "How so?"

Kimberly fixed him with a stern stare. "This is not just *some woman* you've supposedly fallen for. This is the mother of my husband and sister-in-law and the grandmother of our children. And if *you* think you can just roll up with your thick head of hair, tailored clothes and leering looks and turn everything upside-down while we sit idly by and say nothing, you're wrong. Ginny is a mature woman, she's lost a husband and she's into another stage of her life. She doesn't need you stirring the pot, filling her head with *ideas*, then going on your merry way when you're through having your fun."

Ginny's mouth went slack. Wow. She hadn't expected that. And, judging by the looks on everyone else's faces, neither had they.

Max cleared his throat and everyone in both the kitchen and dining room turned their heads to stare at him. What would he say in the face of all that?

"I appreciate your honesty, Kimberly, sincerely I do."

She sneered and said nothing.

"And you bring up some valid points." He turned to face Ginny. "Darling, there's something I have been meaning to share with you, and your lovely daughter-in-law's commentary has pretty much given me the perfect opportunity to do so."

Ginny's eyebrows lifted. It was the last thing she'd expected to hear.

"You remember I was off earlier this morning to get the final points settled in the contract with Darryl?"

All heads swiveled to look at Darryl and he went still in his seat under the scrutiny. Were they expecting something from him?

"Well, good news, the last *T* has been crossed and the last *I* has been dotted," Max went on, leaning up against the island.

"Congratulations," Eric piped up.

Jennifer frowned at him and he shrugged his shoulders.

Max smiled at him and nodded. "Thank you."

"Okay," Ginny said, reaching out for a chair at the table when he knees suddenly felt weak. "What are you saying?"

"Now that that's done," he told her, "I'm not needed around these parts for a while."

Jan and Darryl exchanged a look while Ginny said nothing and waited for whatever he was going to say next.

"*And*," he went on, "I haven't had a chance yet to mention it, but I have another deal in the works that needs me on site and will take me out of here for a good couple of months."

"Surprise, surprise," Kimberly muttered, with a sigh.

Jennifer, as engrossed as the rest of them in his conversation, ignored her to ask, "Where?"

"Italy."

Dixie looked at Hamish questioningly to confirm it was true and he nodded.

"Italy?" Ginny repeated, trying to digest the information.

He nodded. "I have a few developments there and now this new one, so they need my input in person before they move ahead with it."

"Ahh," Eric said, snapping his fingers then pointing to the espresso maker on the countertop. "Now that explains it."

Max looked at the machine and grinned. "Yup. Working off and on in Italy for so many years, I've developed a fondness for good coffee."

"So, that's it then, is it?" Kimberly said, contemptuously, her face hard. "You're letting our Ginny know you're done with your little *love affair* while we're all here to pick up the pieces?"

Ginny's stomach clutched.

Max shook his head. "No, that's where you're wrong, I'm afraid." He turned back to Ginny. "As I said, I had every intention of sharing this with you, but then you fell ill and I wanted to wait until you were well again."

"How long until you leave?" she asked, her shoulders tight as she held herself motionless in her chair.

"A fortnight."

"Fortnight?" Jennifer repeated.

He smiled. "Yes. Two weeks."

"Two weeks," Ginny exhaled, an ache of sadness starting to blossom in her chest.

Dixie looked at Jan and whispered, "Did you know about this?"

"Some of it, the part about a new project," she whispered back. "Not the part about Italy."

Max reached out and took Ginny's hand. "Anyway, the timeline is really besides the point at this moment."

She looked at him, trying to get her bearings. "Oh, I don't know, it seems it's everything at the moment."

He brought her hand to his mouth and kissed her knuckles tenderly. "Okay, let me clarify. While I do have to go, there's no way I want to go alone. I've spent nearly all of my adult life alone and now that I've found you, I don't want to spend a moment more than is necessary without you."

Ginny swallowed, her heart starting to beat faster in her chest.

"And so, with that said…" He paused, reached into his trouser pocket and pulled out a small, square box. "I would like, or rather *love* for you to join me on my adventures. At the very least as my fiancée and the very best as my wife."

"Oh!" Jan squealed, clutching at Darryl's arm.

Ginny gaped as he opened the box to reveal a stunning, vintage diamond ring. She'd never seen a piece of jewelry so lovely.

Jennifer and Kimberly gasped in unison when they saw it, while Dixie muttered, "holy Moses", under her breath.

Max got down on one knee in front of Ginny, still sitting motionless in her chair. "My darling, Ginny, I know you've already had a husband whom you loved dearly. And, if I might dare to speculate, I'd like to believe he'd be in support of my adoration for you. Obviously, I can't tell you I'll live forever, but I can assure you that as long as I *am* alive I will make it my joy to give you all of my heart and strive to bring as much happiness into your life as I am humanly able."

"*Ohmygod*," Jennifer said, so moved by the emotion he held for her mother tears began welling in her eyes.

He extended the box and said, "Virginia Grace Hughes, will you do me the honor of being my wife?"

Ginny glanced at her family, both in the kitchen and in the dining room, so grateful to them for caring so much and giving so much of themselves during the time since George's untimely passing. Without their support, she might not have been where she was; ready to move forward.

She looked at Max and smiled into his clear green eyes. "There is nothing that would delight me more than to be your wife."

\*\*\*\*

# Chapter Twenty-Eight

"I still can't believe we pulled it off," Jennifer said, grinning as she wrapped her arms around Ginny in a tight hug.

They were standing next to Ginny's luggage, one large yellow case and matching carry-on, in Boxwood Hills' airport terminal, and she was both excited and nervous at the same time.

Jan, beside Kimberly, nodded in agreement with Jennifer and added, "I'll give you credit, Kim. You can pull things together like nobody's business. In fact, if I need a party thrown together last minute, or with lots of notice for that matter, I'm calling you."

Kimberly grinned, genuinely pleased by the compliment. "I just wanted Ginny and Max to have a perfect day," she said, keeping a close eye on Layla hopping around the luggage. "And even though it was fast, that doesn't mean their wedding didn't deserve to be special."

And it had been fast. The expression, 'it was a whirlwind' was an apt description for how they'd gone from Max's proposal in the kitchen to a gorgeous, intimate wedding amongst the trees and flower gardens in her backyard in just twelve days.

From the moment she'd said 'yes' and the family had broken into cheers of congratulations, there was a shift in her children. Ginny had watched in amazement as they'd banded together, Kimberly of all people leading the show, to create an afternoon celebration for she and Max. Kimberly had put to work all of her organizational skills she'd been sitting on since leaving her job at the art gallery, and the result had been a day to remember.

"Hey, now there's an idea," Jennifer said, pointing at Jan, her arm still around Ginny's shoulders.

Ginny nodded, immediately following her train of thought. "A super idea."

Kimberly, *not* following the train, said, "What?"

"You should consider going into party planning," Jennifer told her.

"Party!" Layla cheered, doing a shimmy-shake sort of dance.

"Absolutely!" Jan agreed, smiling at Layla and reached down to tickle her little knees. Layla stopped dancing and said, "Daddy!" before dashing full-speed at Eric walking down the corridor toward them.

Layla!" Kimberly blurted, wincing as her daughter narrowly avoided being run over by a woman's trolley.

"Whoa, there, missy!" Eric said, scooping Layla up just before she barreled into his legs. "No running from Mommy, right?"

She nodded, shy in the face of her wrong-doing.

"That child will be my undoing," Kimberly said, taking a calming breath.

"You should really think about it, though," Jan said, to Kimberly, resuming their conversation. "You'd be sought after in a heartbeat for your ideas."

"Who has ideas?" Eric asked, propping Layla on his hip.

"Your amazingly talented wife," Ginny told him. "We were just saying she'd be a fantastic party planner."

Layla squirmed in Eric's arms and he put her back down on the floor. He met Kimberly's eye, lifted his eyebrows up and down, then reminded Layla, "No running, right?"

"Right," she agreed, resuming her hopping game around Ginny's luggage.

"What?" Ginny fished, watching them. "What's with the looks?"

Kimberly bit her lip while Eric's face split into a grin.

"Okay, seriously," Jennifer insisted, backing her mother up. "What's up?"

Kimberly cleared her throat. "Well, we weren't going to say anything until you were back because we didn't want to make today about us, but…"

"*Ohmygod,*" Jennifer said, her face lighting up.

Kimberly nodded, flushing with pleasure. "I'm pregnant."

Ginny and Jan cheered and hugged one another, inspiring Layla to clap her hands at their excitement. Ginny laughed and leaned over to kiss her granddaughter while Jennifer grabbed Kimberly into a hug.

Chris, standing next to Jennifer and having been told already by Eric, patted his brother-in-law on the shoulder.

"You knew?" Jennifer asked him, once she and Kimberly had untangled themselves.

He shrugged. "Your brother told me, but swore me to secrecy under penalty of having to play more golf."

Jennifer laughed and pointed a finger at Eric. "Smart."

Layla, in perfect imitation of her aunt, pointed her finger and said, "Smart."

"Oh, god, there's two of them," Eric groaned and pulled a horrified face.

Ginny turned to face Kimberly and wrap her up in a warm hug. She whispered into her ear, "You have given me the very best going-away present."

Kimberly's eyes filled with tears as she squeezed her back. "And I know I already said I'm sorry, during the wedding prep, for being so bloody difficult these past few months, but I want to say it again. It's the pregnancy hormones. I was the same way in the first trimester with Layla; a cat on a hot tin roof. I can't believe I missed it, but things have been pretty crazy, and I was so worried about you—"

"Don't give it another thought," Ginny assured her, leaning back to look her in the eye. "But you know I am in safe hands now, right?"

Kimberly nodded. "I do."

"How are things with your parents?"

Kimberly shrugged. "Okay, considering. Kris is helping them deal with anything that needs dealing with. And they've finally admitted things haven't been good between them for a while, so that changes the landscape. Dad's moved out and they'll take whatever steps they feel should be taken next."

Ginny nodded. She remembered Dixie's divorce and the reality that most of the time things are never one-sided.

"All I know for sure is, they're grownups and they'll have to work it all out however they feel best," Kimberly said, resting a hand on her abdomen. "I told them I'll help if they need it, but my first priority is *my* family."

Ginny smiled and patted her arm. "Good for you. It's time for you to take the best care of yourself."

"Okay, troops," Max called, out as he strode across the airport terminal, one hand holding Grace's and the other Mason's. They had fully taken him on as their new Granddad. "The flight's on time, we're almost good to go."

Ginny watched them approach and her stomach flipped over. He was fantastic, her new husband. Simply fantastic.

Layla stopped hopping and took a step forward, before Eric caught her eye and said, "Layla," in a firm, warning tone. She stopped and waited until the three of them were closer then closed the small gap by speed walking directly at Grace.

"We saw planes taking off!" Mason said, releasing Max's hand and running over to Chris.

"Maybe you'll be a pilot one day," Chris offered, ruffling his blonde hair.

"Or, me," Grace said, joining them, holding Layla's hand.

"Or, you," Chris agreed.

Jennifer's brow furrowed at the idea of either of her children thousands upon thousands of feet in the air and said, "Or maybe something else."

Chris chuckled and nodded.

"Hop, hop," Layla said, tugging Grace's hand toward the luggage.

Ever indulgent, she let her little cousin pull her forward and show her the game she wanted to play.

"We have news!" Ginny said, to Max, her face lit up.

He looked at her then at Kimberly, grinning beside her. "What's going on?"

"Can I?" Ginny asked, eagerly.

Kimberly and Eric nodded in unison.

"Kimberley's pregnant! We're going to have a new addition to the family!"

"Hey!" He said, his face lighting up to match Ginny's. "That's brilliant! Congratulations, you two."

Eric nodded and said, "Thanks," just before Max pulled him into a bear hug.

"And thank *you* for trusting me with your mother," Max said, quietly, keeping his words between the two of them. "I promise, I'll protect her with my life."

Eric pulled back and looked him in the eye. There was only one thing to say. "I know."

Max nodded and patted him on the shoulder, glad they understood one another.

"You're going to have a new baby, Auntie Kim?" Grace asked, while overhead, the announcement was made for Ginny and Max's flight.

"Uh-huh," Kimberly said, then turned her attention back to Ginny, just as her mother-in-law's eyes began to fill with tears.

Jennifer, seeing her mother's face and knowing it was time to say good-bye, immediately began to sniffle. Chris pulled her under the protection of his arm and whispered into her ear. She began to nod at what he was saying then took a deep breath and smiled up at him.

Ginny, wiping the moisture from her eyes, watched them and felt less upset about leaving. They were all going to be okay without her. They would look out for each other and take care of one another. And, besides, it wasn't like she and Max weren't coming back.

"You're going on a long flight, Grandma," Grace said, already showing how grownup she was getting by staying close to Layla, as she continued to play around the luggage. "Will you have a nap on the plane?"

Ginny grinned at her granddaughter and nodded. "Probably. Seems like a good idea."

Mason pushed his way through the adults to get to Ginny then hugged her around her legs. "Will you bring us presents when you come back?"

"Mason," Chris said, barely hiding his laughter at his son's cheek.

"Of course we will!" Ginny enthused, kissing the top of his head. "We'll be bringing something back for each and every one of you."

"And don't worry for a moment about Martini, Mom," Jennifer assured her, a slightly watery waver in her voice. "Grace and Mason are going to take very good care of him, right guys?"

The two children nodded in unison, their faces lit up in delight that Martini was going to be their houseguest for a couple of months.

Jan reached out and enveloped Ginny in a hug. "I'm going to miss you something fierce."

"I know," Ginny said, nodding into her shoulder while tears began to well again in her eyes. "Me, too. But you have Dixie—"

Jan laughed and pulled back, still holding her by the shoulders. "Dixie is so wrapped up in Hamish, I don't think any of us will be seeing her until you guys get back."

Ginny giggled. It was true. Those two had become inseparable since they'd hit it off at the dance studio open house they'd all been invited to via Tamara. Ginny, herself, had ended up being too sick to attend, but had received the full story the next day from both Jan and Dixie when each of them had called her to share. Their stories, while from different points of view, had both attested to the same thing: a new romance had bloomed in Boxwood Hills.

"There goes the final announcement for your guys' flight," Eric said, stepping forward.

Ginny gave Jan a quick kiss on the cheek. "I'll send lots of emails and post once in a while on Facebook to keep Dixie happy."

"Counting on it," Jan replied, taking a breath to keep her emotions from overflowing.

"Please tell Darryl I send my love, okay?" Ginny said, swallowing against the lump in her throat. "After all, if it wasn't for him…"

Jan's eyes glistened and she blinked and nodded when Ginny's voice broke. "I'll tell him when he gets home from work," she managed to say, sniffling along with her.

"Okay, good," Ginny burbled, then took a breath to steady herself.

Jan did the same and cleared her throat. "Okay, now do us proud and have the most fun you've ever had, got it?"

Ginny nodded. "Got it. Love you."

"Love you, too," Jan said, then moved away before they started all over again.

Eric immediately stepped in to wrap his arms snuggly around Ginny. "I love you, Mom. You two be safe, have fun and call, okay?"

Tears leaked from her eyes as Ginny nodded into his shoulder. When had her son become such a grown, strong and amazingly kind man? George would have been so proud. She loosened her grip around his torso and kissed him on the cheek. "I love you, too, my dear, dear son. More than you will ever know."

Eric looked at Layla, then stole a glance at Kimberly's newly rounding belly, then back at her. "I get it," he said, simply, before swiping at the tears in his eyes.

Ginny kissed him one more time then gave out hugs to Jennifer, Kimberly and Chris, telling them much the same as she had Eric. She was so proud of all of them and utterly grateful they were her family. Finally, she leaned in to squeeze each of her three wonderful grandchildren, told them all they weren't allowed to be all grown up when she and Grandpa Max returned, then took a deep breath and readied herself for what was ahead.

"Ready?" Max asked, looking into her eyes and extending a hand.

Ginny met he gaze steadily and nodded. She took the hand he offered in her own, knowing right then and there that wherever he was, was home.

# THE END

# ABOUT THE AUTHOR

Kathleen began storytelling in grade school and has many fond memories of passing summer afternoons, out on the swings in her backyard, creating tales that entertained her neighborhood friends.

Many years later, too many to talk about without seeming rude and nosey, Kathleen has channeled her imagination to the pages of her novels. She hopes you enjoy her tales and encourages you to feel free to read her stories on the swing set in your own backyard.

Kathleen now spends time in her backyard with her beloved husband, adored son and silly dog. They let her tell them stories and always laugh in all of the correct places. She's lucky, and she knows it.

**Connect with Kathleen Online**

Website:      kathleenkole.com

Facebook:   facebook.com/KathleenKoleAuthor

Twitter:       twitter.com/kathleenkole